T0279372

A
QUEEN'S
GAME

ALSO BY KATHARINE McGEE

A QUEEN'S GAME

KATHARINE McGEE

Random House New York

Text copyright © 2024 by Katharine McGee and Alloy Entertainment
Jacket art copyright © 2024 by Carolina Melis

Produced by Alloy Entertainment
alloyentertainment.com

Visit us on the Web! GetUnderlined.com

Educators and librarians, for a variety of teaching tools,
visit us at RHTeachersLibrarians.com

Library of Congress Cataloging-in-Publication Data
Name: McGee, Katharine, author.
Title: A queen's game / Katharine McGee.
Description: First edition. | New York: Random House, 2024. | Audience: Ages 14+ |
Summary: In Victorian Europe, the lives of three princesses are about to change forever
as they struggle to find love.
Identifiers: LCCN 2023050274 (print) | LCCN 2023050275 (ebook) |
ISBN 978-0-593-71070-8 (trade) | ISBN 978-0-593-71071-5 (lib. bdg.) |
ISBN 978-0-593-90258-5 (int'l) | ISBN 978-0-593-71072-2 (ebook)
Subjects: CYAC: Princesses—Fiction. | Love—Fiction. | Europe—History—1789–1900—
Fiction. | LCGFT: Romance fiction. | Historical fiction. | Novels.
Classification: LCC PZ7.1.M43513 Qu 2024 (print) | LCC PZ7.1.M43513 (ebook) |
DDC [Fic]—dc23

The text of this book is set in 11.25-point Goudy Old Style MT Pro.
Interior design by Michelle Crowe

Printed in the United States of America
10 9 8 7 6 5 4 3 2 1
First Edition

For Edward

CHAPTER ONE

May

MAY OF TECK HATED WEDDINGS.

It hadn't always been this way: she used to stare in girlish awe at the white-gowned brides, dreaming of when it might be her turn. And May had seen plenty of brides in her day. Say what you would about Queen Victoria, she'd certainly been prolific in the childbearing department; the family tree of the British royals was vast and tangled, and some family member or other was always getting married. Today it was May's cousin Princess Louise.

May had long ago stopped enjoying these occasions. Now every wedding she attended felt like a reproach, a reminder of her own dwindling possibilities. For six years she had been out in society: rotating around London's ballrooms and reception halls, always gowned and perfumed and stupidly hopeful. Yet no one ever took a bite, as if she were some appetizer that had grown stale on the platter.

May saw the future stretching mercilessly before her, a bleak existence filled with charity work and Sunday church and, worse, forever living under her father's roof.

She forced herself to smile and sit up straighter. The ballroom at Marlborough House, the home of the Prince of

Wales and his family, wasn't as grand in scale as the one at Buckingham Palace—no private ballroom was—but today it was the only place worth being. Women in dresses and men in tailored suits spun around the dance floor, the musicians struggling to be heard over the low hum of gossip and flirtation.

May wasn't a part of it. Like all the unmarried, unwanted women, she'd been relegated to these chairs tied with awful pink bows, tucked away along the ballroom's edge.

She noticed John Hope across the dance floor, and her smile softened, became more genuine. Perhaps her prospects weren't entirely bleak. Before she could question herself, May stood.

"John," she said warmly, when she'd come to stand near him. She and the earl's son had known each other for long enough to dispense with the formalities.

"May. It's always a pleasure." His smile revealed a turned canine tooth, though somehow the effect didn't diminish his attractiveness. "How are your parents?"

Bad, and getting worse. "They're doing well, thank you. And Dolly is still at Sandhurst," May added, naming her brother Adolphus—one of the few people in the world she actually trusted. She hurried to change the subject. "I wish Estella could have made it. I miss her."

May had grown up visiting the Hopes at their estate every summer; her parents were friends of the earl and countess. John's sister Estella was a few years older than May. She hadn't come to the wedding today, stuck at home with her newborn son.

"Estella sends her regards," John said absently, already

searching for someone else to talk to. Panic fluttered in her rib cage.

"Of course. I've been writing to her, and love hearing about little Alfred." May strove to bring the conversation back to their shared history. "Soon enough he'll be romping through the piles of hay in the barn just like we used to!"

"The hay is still there," John agreed. This struck May as a rather dumb thing to say.

Before she could think of an appropriate reply, John cleared his throat. "I have some news. You may have heard that I'm engaged to Camilla St. Clair."

No, May most certainly hadn't heard, though she knew all about Camilla: a seventeen-year-old debutante with no title to speak of, but an expansive bosom and even more expansive dowry.

"Congratulations." May forced out the word and fled before John could see her tears.

She was so weary of putting herself out there: begging men for their approval, then pretending it didn't hurt when they passed her over. The thought of starting again from scratch—facing all the house parties and dinners and shooting weekends of next year's Season, still as unmarried as ever—made her feel sick.

At times like this, May wished she weren't royal, or—more accurately—quasi-royal. A fringe, borderline member of the extended royal family.

As a great-granddaughter of King George III and Queen Charlotte, May should have grown up in a palace, or at the very least on an estate with countless servants at her beck and call. Yet May's mother had chosen to marry Francis of

Teck, a nobody prince from the backwater territory of Württemberg.

May knew that her mother's prospects had been slim. Even in her youth, Mary Adelaide had been a mountain of a girl, so large that she famously broke a chair at her own debut ball. Mary Adelaide had longed to get married, and it had been Francis or no one.

If those had been her choices, May would have stayed a spinster forever.

Her royal cousins, Princess Louise and her siblings, were always courteous to May while making their difference in status abundantly clear. They were Royal Highnesses, and May was just a Serene Highness. Two small syllables that changed everything. May and her parents existed on scraps of charity from the *real* royals: the grace-and-favor house bestowed on them by Queen Victoria, the trips to St. Moritz hosted by the Waleses.

When she was young and foolish, May used to think she might marry a prince. Her grandmother had broached the subject with several German princes—Friedrich of Anhalt, Günther of Schleswig-Holstein—but nothing came of it. There was even a brief discussion with the Russian Grand Duke Michael Michailovitch, yet that, too, fizzled out.

May had felt a flurry of excitement at age eighteen when the Prince of Naples came to London to "see the sights," though everyone knew it was a bridal interview for May. She sat next to Prince Vittorio at several dinners, and then two weeks later he left without a goodbye.

In some elusive, intangible way, May had failed.

Things might have gone differently if she had been wealthy

or beautiful. But her parents had long ago squandered what little fortune they had, and May couldn't marry on her looks alone. She wasn't ugly; she was just . . . ordinary-looking, with eyes too close together, and ash-blond hair that she struggled to tease into fashionable ringlet curls.

No, May would bring nothing to a marriage: no fortune, no lands, only a tenuous connection to the British throne. And her razor-sharp mind, which she was careful to keep hidden.

Society was very cruel to women who let on that they were smarter than men.

After her third Season ended with no prospects, May's parents had quietly given up on the foreign princes and started searching closer to home. As a Serene Highness, May couldn't marry just any aristocrat, but what about someone high-ranking enough for her—a widowed duke, or Lord Euston?

May hadn't told her parents about her secret plans for John Hope; they would have dismissed him as "not good enough." He was only an earl, and a Scottish one at that. But what other choice did she have?

She walked slowly around the reception hall, trying to gather her thoughts. The setting sun poured through the floor-to-ceiling windows, making the air inside feel stuffy. Before the fireplace stood the wedding cake: a multitiered confection over seven feet high, topped by a Greek temple done entirely of sugar, columns and all.

"May!"

At the sound of that voice, May sank into her deepest, most reverential curtsy. "Your Royal Highness."

She looked up and met the blue eyes of Prince Albert Victor Christian Edward, or as everyone called him, Prince Eddy. The heir to the British throne.

Standing there in his military uniform, medallions gleaming on his chest, Eddy looked like a prince from a child's storybook. His features were so fine and delicately carved that he would almost be pretty, if he didn't radiate such intense masculinity.

Eddy frowned, noticing the tears that still clung to May's lashes. "Are you okay?"

"Oh, yes. Just overwhelmed with joy for Louise," she demurred.

Eddy nodded, accepting this. He wasn't the most perceptive, but only because his blithe, carefree energy was always skipping along from one thing to the next.

A bold warmth was curling in May's chest, like when she snuck sips of her mother's sherry. Her eyes darted toward the couples in the center of the ballroom, and she decided to risk it.

"Have you danced much this evening?"

"Oh, of course!" Eddy grinned at her sheepishly. "I should have asked. May, would you like to dance?"

Dancing with Eddy would be like stepping into the glare of a spotlight, which was precisely what May needed right now. She had lost John, but there were other eligible men here, men who might take notice once they saw her with the prince.

Eddy's hand fell to her waist as they started forward. Other couples moved in a slow orbit around them, the wooden floor hidden beneath swishing skirts and shining dark shoes. Standing with Eddy, May felt that she reflected back some of his royal aura—that she looked brighter and prettier simply by being *near* him.

She tipped her head toward the groom. "Tell me more about Lord Fife. I'd never met him before today."

"Oh, you'd like Alexander," Eddy exclaimed, with a surprising amount of confidence given that he had no idea what sort of person May liked or disliked. "Louise really loves him, you know."

"That's wonderful," May murmured, though the match was actually preposterous. Alexander Fife was a nobody, a low-ranking nobleman whom Eddy's sister had decided she adored, and because she was a spoiled princess she had gotten permission to actually go through with it.

A princess, marrying for *love?* Only servants did that, or Americans.

May was far too much of a realist to believe in something like love. It was a plot device invented by novelists, as fantastic and nonsensical as pixie dust. Just look at what had happened to her mother. Mary Adelaide had married for love, or at least for lust, and once that lust had cooled, all she had was a husband who burned through her fortune and treated her with cool indifference. On a good day.

"And he's great company on the hunt," Eddy added, launching into some story about riding with Lord Fife at Balmoral.

When he'd finished, May smiled. "Are you headed to Balmoral soon?"

"Yes, though I have to come back to London in a month. The Shah of Persia will be visiting, and Sally says I have to entertain him."

"Sally?" she repeated, puzzled.

"Lord Salisbury. George and I call him Sally behind his back," Eddy said breezily.

It was shockingly impertinent to refer to the prime minister that way, even if you were a future king. May doubted that George, Eddy's younger brother, had had anything to do with the nickname.

"How fascinating that you'll get to meet the shah," she ventured. "He'll want to discuss the situation in the Black Sea, I imagine?"

Her words seemed to glance off Eddy. "I was thinking of taking him to Romano's. Surely he doesn't have any good whiskey in . . ." He trailed off with a disinterested shrug. May bit her tongue to keep from finishing his sentence. *In Tehran.* Didn't Eddy realize that Persia was of crucial importance, a key ally in Britain's growing tensions with Russia?

May looked up at the prince, but he was glancing over her shoulder yet again. There was something deliberate in his expression, unusual for Eddy, who was so rarely serious about anything. As the steps of the dance spun her around, May did her best to follow his gaze.

Of course. He was watching Alix of Hesse.

Stupid, perfect Alix, with her golden hair, her enormous blue-gray eyes, her soft, delicate features and narrow waist. Even in the bridesmaid dress Louise had chosen, a fussy thing of pink crêpe de chine with a watered-silk sash, she still turned heads.

May had always suspected that Eddy would propose to Alix. He was the future King of England, and everyone knew that Alix was the most beautiful princess of their generation—not to mention Queen Victoria's favorite granddaughter. Their pairing was simply inevitable.

If *she* had been born that beautiful, May thought bitterly, there would be no heights she couldn't reach.

Well, she would just have to make the best of what little she had. Finding a husband was a cruel, cutthroat business, but May would keep at it. She would find *someone* to marry, someone kinder and easier to manage than her father. The alternative was simply unbearable.

She could never admit it, because there was nothing attractive about a stubborn woman, but May refused to accept defeat. Even when it stared her in the face.

CHAPTER TWO

Hélène

PRINCESS HÉLÈNE LOUISE HENRIETTE D'ORLÉANS GLANCED across the ballroom of Marlborough House to where the footmen kept entering with champagne. The best thing she could say about this wedding was that the wine was good, and there was plenty of it.

She sighed, and her sister Amélie cast her a knowing look. "Shall we take a turn around the room?"

"Perhaps," muttered Hélène, though the one person she longed to see wasn't in this ballroom.

"Oh, you *must* take a turn about the room if you haven't yet." May of Teck, who was seated in a neighboring chair, clapped her hands in a silly show of enthusiasm. Oddly, her eyes were on Alix of Hesse, though she was speaking to Amélie. "Have you seen the flowers near the cake? They are *divine.*"

Alix blinked as if waking from a daydream. "Hmm?"

"We were just saying how lovely the wedding is," Amélie said gently.

"Oh yes!" Alix beamed at her. "How long are you in town, Your Royal Highness? You must come over for tea before you leave. All of you," she added, including Hélène and May in the invitation.

Hélène refrained from rolling her eyes, but only just. *You must come over for tea.* As if she had nothing better to do than nibble at scones and exchange gossip.

These noblewomen were all the same, not an original thought in any of their heads. When Hélène had learned that the Princess Louise was marrying for love—and not even a prince, but a mere aristocrat!—she'd actually thought this wedding might be interesting. But, as usual, her imagination had outpaced reality.

"That sounds lovely," Amélie agreed, when it was clear Hélène wouldn't say anything.

May smiled at Amélie. "This must bring back such joyous memories from your own wedding day."

Two years ago Amélie had married Carlos, the Crown Prince of Portugal. The two of them genuinely cared for each other, which was a rare gift in a royal marriage. Of course Hélène wanted her sister to be happy. Yet she missed the *old* version of Amélie, who used to follow along in Hélène's schemes and giggle at inappropriate jokes. She missed the closeness they had shared before marriage and motherhood came between them.

This trip was Amélie's first time away from her two-year-old son, Luis Filipe. Prince Carlos, clearly besotted with Amélie, had insisted she come home to see her family—or more accurately, come back to England, since *home* would forever be France for the Orléans family. They were still very much in exile.

It had happened long before Hélène was even born, when her father was just ten years old. His grandfather, King Louis Philippe, had been forced to abdicate as King of France. At least he'd had it better than the king in the *other* French Revolution, who'd died on the guillotine.

Hélène had grown up in Paris, in a townhouse that was beautiful, but certainly not a palace, her family treated like any other wealthy family—save the white roses that were occasionally strewn over their doorstep, a sign of illicit support from monarchists who wanted to see Hélène's father restored to his throne. Perhaps the monarchists had been growing in number, because when Hélène was fifteen, the tides of the Third Republic shifted, and her family was informed that they must leave France and never return.

They had lived here in England ever since.

Ridiculously, no one ever spoke of what had happened. The British aristocrats who ran in their social circles addressed Hélène's parents as the Count and Countess of Paris, a title that Queen Victoria had invented when she offered them asylum. Hélène's father had been forced to smile and thank her, no matter how galling it was to be a made-up count when he should have been king.

A murmur arose among the young women as Prince Eddy approached, his brother George trailing along in his wake. Hélène had known Eddy long enough to remember when he'd been a boisterous, enthusiastic child. He was a young man now, but there was still something boyish about him—in his floppy hair and carefree smile and the coltish way he moved, as if he'd grown in a sudden spurt and wasn't yet used to his long limbs.

The other girls smiled and tossed their heads coquettishly, but not Hélène. And, she realized, not Alix of Hesse. Alix was staring out the window again, lost in a world of her own making.

Eddy's eyes trailed over the line of women before him. When his gaze met Hélène's, she cut hers away in cool dismissal, as if the very sight of him bored her. He stiffened, then turned to Alix.

"May I have the honor of a dance?"

Of course Alix was who he wanted. That porcelain doll of a girl whom his grandmother had set him up with.

Hélène watched as Prince George asked May of Teck to dance. He was like a muted version of his older brother: his hair a deeper brown, his eyes a darker blue. George was stocky and solid where Eddy was lean and athletic, calm and even-tempered where Eddy was restless and loud.

A few of the other ladies, visibly disappointed that they hadn't been chosen, ventured off for glasses of lemonade, leaving Amélie and Hélène alone.

"Did you just *roll your eyes* at Prince Eddy?" Amélie whispered.

"So what if I did?"

"You can't keep frightening off eligible young men, especially not princes. How will you ever get married?"

"It doesn't matter; we both know that Eddy isn't an option." As future head of the Church of England, Eddy would need to marry a nice Protestant princess, and the Orléans family was exceedingly Catholic. "Besides," Hélène added flippantly, "I don't want to marry at all."

Amélie gasped. "Stop saying that! You're too pretty not to marry!"

Actually, Amélie was the prettier of the pair—or at least, she was softer and more delicate, which seemed to be what men preferred. There was something too bold and decisive about Hélène's beauty: her long dark hair and full lips and most of all her eyes, which were dangerously expressive, flashing a fierce golden-brown with her moods.

Hélène could only hope that since Amélie had married a crown prince, recruiting a powerful new ally to the Orléans cause, Hélène's parents wouldn't rush to find their other daughter a husband. She wasn't looking forward to being an *item for trade*.

It was all that princesses, and aristocratic women in general, lived for—all they ever seemed to talk about. They worried about marriage and having children and then, eventually, getting their children and grandchildren married. It was just an endless cycle that always came back to marriage.

When Hélène was younger, her governess had fought to make her one of those young ladies, the kind whose daydreams ended at the altar. But Hélène had lacked the patience for piano, singing, watercolor: all the things that made a woman ornamental and utterly useless. She'd escaped her lessons and fled to the stables so many times that her parents eventually told the governess not to bother.

Now she had other reasons for visiting the stables.

Feeling provocative, she turned back to Amélie. "If I ever do marry, it will be to someone adventurous, like a soldier."

"A *soldier*! Why?"

"I could travel with him, see the world."

Amélie's brow furrowed. "But you *can* see the world."

Hélène didn't share her sister's definition of *the world*, which was limited to fashionable society retreats and cloistered palaces. Back when they'd lived in France, she used to love their summer visits to their Normandy estate, the Château d'Eu. Hélène would plead with her father to take her to the quays—where she stood transfixed, inhaling the scents of tar and salt air, watching the sailors unload the various ships. Imagining the beautiful, distant places they had visited, full of magic and adventure.

Her brother Philippe got to lead that sort of life. He'd joined the British military and taken a position at an outpost in the Himalayas. According to his latest letter, he'd been mountain climbing in Tibet and hunting in Nepal and had met fortune tellers in Ceylon. *That* was the world Hélène longed to see.

"Of course, you're right about Prince Eddy. You could never convert to the Church of England." Undaunted, Amélie glanced back at the dance floor. "There are other princes here. What about Christian of Schleswig-Holstein or Frederick of Denmark? We should go say hello."

Hélène followed her sister's gaze to the couples moving in steps as narrow and choreographed as their narrow, choreographed lives. Jewels and champagne flutes gleamed in the afternoon light. Her blood felt suddenly hot, her skin prickly.

"I don't feel well," Hélène blurted out. Before Amélie could protest, she started toward the front door.

The driveway that led to Marlborough House was crowded with carriages, all of them emblazoned with their owners' coats of arms. Coachmen loitered near the steps, looking more disheveled than usual with their vests tossed aside, shirtsleeves rolled up in the heat. Most of them loosely clutched cigarettes, killing time until their employers were ready to head home.

It was so hot out; Hélène felt a bead of sweat sliding down her back. Still, it felt less stifling out here than in the crush of that ballroom.

Her eyes cut instinctively to the gold and blue of her

family's carriage, and there he was—the man she couldn't stop thinking about. Her family's coachman.

Laurent Guérard was certainly not the type of young man she should be alone with, though really, Hélène shouldn't be alone with *any* young man. He'd come with her family when they crossed over from France three years ago, along with their entire household: their ladies' maids and butler and chef, all the way down to their scullery maids. Royals, even those in exile, didn't travel without a full retinue.

Laurent reddened adorably at the sight of her. He was so handsome, with his sand-colored hair and shy smile, but it was his voice that had captivated Hélène. He'd been soothing the horses during a storm, his tone low and husky as he crooned songs she'd never heard: shockingly inappropriate songs that should have scandalized her, but only made her want more.

She remembered standing in the shadowed stables as thunder cracked overhead, the air heavy with the warm, familiar smells of hay and horses. Hélène had listened, entranced, as Laurent's voice wove around her like a spell. Even though she'd never done so much as kiss a man before that night, it had felt impossible *not* to go to him, to whisper his name in the enchanted darkness while rain pounded overhead.

That was over a year ago, when Hélène had just turned seventeen.

"Mademoiselle. Shouldn't you be at the reception?" Laurent spoke in French, as he always did when alone with Hélène.

She held out a hand so that he could help her into the carriage. "I don't feel well. I told Amélie that I'm heading home." It was only half a lie.

He hesitated. "Are you sure? This party will last for several more hours."

"Which means we have several hours to ourselves." Hélène smiled, a bit wickedly. "As I said, I don't feel well. I need to be taken straight to bed."

An unfamiliar emotion—confusion, or maybe regret—flickered over Laurent's face, but then he nodded and opened the carriage's gilded door.

When they reached Sheen House, Laurent steered the horses past the main front drive, heading directly to the stables. Hélène opened the door herself and went eagerly inside.

Laurent stared at her for a moment, eyes wide. "You look very . . . royal."

She realized that he rarely saw her like this, fully dressed as her princess self. Her bright blue gown was embroidered with shimmering silver thread. Diamonds blazed at her ears and throat, and her unruly dark hair had been coaxed into an intricate knot, atop which sat a tiara.

She reached for the pins that held her tiara in place and tugged it off, then set it on a hay bale. Sunshine sliced through the open window to catch on the diamonds, sending a spray of light over the walls.

"How about now?" Hélène tugged at her hair until it fell in a wild tumble over her shoulders.

Laurent swallowed. "There's something I need to tell you . . . that is, I . . ."

She started up the narrow staircase that led to the loft. "Tell me after you've helped me out of this gown."

He clattered up the stairs after her. They fell back onto the mattress he kept in the corner, beneath the swooping wooden rafters where small birds built their nests. Laurent's fingers fumbled with the intricate hooks and fastenings of her elaborate court dress, until Hélène impatiently yanked it, causing a delicate pearl button to fly into the hay. Oh well—Violette would have to sew it back on tomorrow.

She tugged Laurent's gold-braided jacket over his shoulders and flung it impatiently to the floor, then reached for his belt buckle. He was saying her name over and over, and the desire in his voice felt so thrilling; it felt right. Hélène tightened her arms around him as he fisted a hand in the curtain of her hair. She was aware of different sensations all at once: the brush of Laurent's stubble against her cheek, the strength of his torso as he settled over her. Warmth seemed to ignite everywhere he touched, spreading from her limbs and collarbone to spool deep in her core.

Up here in the loft, Hélène wished her life could always be this simple. That there were no obligations or restrictions, no gowns or tiaras—nothing but her and this man who held her, who loved her.

She felt certain that he loved her, even if neither of them dared speak the words aloud.

It wasn't until later, when Hélène lay nestled in the warmth of Laurent's arms, that she remembered.

She propped herself up on one elbow. "What was it you wanted to tell me?"

Laurent's lips twitched, as if he was about to speak, only to decide against it. "It's not important," he assured her, and leaned over to kiss her again. His hand crept beneath the blanket to skim over Hélène's body, and she stopped thinking about whatever confession he'd decided not to make. There was room in her mind for nothing in that moment but him.

CHAPTER THREE

Alix

THE NEXT MORNING, ALIX VICTORIA HELENA LOUISE BEATRICE, Princess of Hesse, forced herself to smile as she glanced around the patio of Marlborough House.

The reception last night had been hard enough, and now Princess Louise was having a send-off breakfast, too? Why did these weddings involve so many events?

Everyone else seemed to be in a jubilant mood. The sky was a brilliant blue overhead, the table bright with smiles and laughter as twenty-odd guests—only close family, not the extended cousins and foreign royals who'd been at yesterday's wedding—toasted the newlyweds.

"I can't believe you and Ernie are leaving so soon," said Prince George, who was seated across from her.

"I know. I'll miss you." Alix had always been especially fond of George, who was similar to her in so many ways. Perhaps he, too, was ready for the endless social rounds of this wedding to be over.

Though she doubted that his reasons for hating crowded events were anything like hers.

Her gaze drifted down the table to where her own brother, Ernie, sat with Prince Eddy and Alexander Fife, Louise's new husband. The three of them were laughing uproariously at something Eddy had said. Eddy shifted in his seat and stretched his long limbs, the movement lazily graceful, as if he were a panther settling itself in the sun.

"It's nice that Lord Fife gets along with the family," she observed.

There was a flash of hurt in George's smile. "Yes, he and Eddy are two of a kind, aren't they?"

Poor George, forever forced to come in second place. He and his brother had been inseparable as children: born hardly a year apart, they'd been effectively raised as twins, with the same tutor and same governess. During the (admittedly brief) interlude when they'd both served in the navy, they had even been staffed on the same ship. Alix had always thought that George would have made a perfect second son in medieval times, back when they sent the spare into church service. Now he was doomed to live in Eddy's shadow.

Alix used to be that inseparable from her older sister, Ella. But it was different for them, because she and Ella were both princesses—or at least they had been until Ella married Sergei, one of the Russian Grand Dukes. Whereas Eddy and George were forever set apart by the single, crucial thing that divided them: Eddy was the future King of England, and George was not.

A lanky figure approached her chair from behind, casting a shadow over the dining table. "Alix. Would you walk with me in the gardens?"

She blinked in surprise, as if there might be some other, different Alix here that Eddy was speaking to.

She and Eddy were cousins, yes, but Alix had a lot of

those: thirty-seven on her mother's side alone. When they'd been children at Balmoral, Eddy had gravitated toward her siblings and mostly ignored Alix. He and Ernie used to gang up together, playing at pirates or sneaking into the aviary, or pulling some prank on Ella, who responded with gratifying shrieks of outrage. Whenever they had tried to tease Alix, she'd just walked away.

"It's a lovely day to explore the gardens," Eddy repeated. As if he needed to explore a landmark that had been familiar to him since childhood.

Alix cast a puzzled glance around the table, but everyone else was deep in conversation or focused on their breakfast plates. A niggling suspicion arose in the corner of her mind; she resolutely ignored it.

"Of course." Alix stood, the peach-colored fabric of her day dress swishing around her legs.

Eddy's fingers twitched, almost as if he meant to reach up and tug one of her pigtails, the way he had when they were children, but then he held out a hand. Alix placed her palm in his, letting him lead her into the Marlborough House grounds.

"I'm so glad you and Ernie came for Louise's wedding," he began.

"She and Lord Fife seem happy."

"He's a lot of fun. We're going to Scotland soon to visit them. You and Ernie should join us," Eddy added.

For a moment Alix marveled at the cavalier way he'd invited her to be a guest in someone else's home. Perhaps when you were going to rule the entire country someday, you felt like the whole thing belonged to you.

"Thank you, but I need to get back to Darmstadt."

She might be a princess, but Alix's life was nothing like that of Eddy and George's sisters. Louise and Maud lived in grand style, while Alix was simply the daughter of the Grand Duke of Hesse, a minor German duchy. In Darmstadt she spent her days quietly, managing her father's household, sewing shirts for the poor.

Yet she was happier there. Alix wasn't equipped to navigate the hive of gossip and ambition that was the English court. Not to mention the attention that focused on her like a spotlight whenever she entered a ballroom.

Alix was self-aware enough to know that she was beautiful. People had been telling her that her entire life: seamstresses and dressmakers, other young women, and especially men. They had a disconcerting way of staring at her, their eyes unabashed and bold, as if she weren't a person at all but an object of scenery—a mountain, or a rosebush. As if she had no feelings about their stares, and they were entitled to look at her for as long as they liked.

"Tell me more about Balmoral. I haven't visited in several years," Alix said, realizing the silence had gone on for a moment too long.

To her relief, Eddy launched into a story about how he and Alexander Fife had tried to race their horses to Loch Nagar, only to end up at the wrong loch, where they'd befriended a band of local fishermen. He had a jocular, enthusiastic way of recounting things that always made them sound more thrilling than they'd probably been in real life.

Alix smiled and nodded, occasionally making little exclamations of surprise when appropriate. She and Eddy might not have anything in common, but at least he was an avid talker. Alix was always grateful when someone else bore the conversational load.

They turned deeper into the gardens, and Eddy fell silent. Roses and junipers bloomed around them, their fragrance thick in the summer air.

"Alicky," Eddy said, and she startled at the old childhood nickname. No one but her siblings called her that anymore. "I'm so glad you're here, because I want to talk to you about something important."

Anticipation knotted in Alix's chest. She walked a little faster, as if to outrun her growing suspicion.

"You know I've always admired you. You're so poised, and elegant, and beautiful. All the things I'm not," he added ruefully.

"Your Royal Highness," she said haltingly. Eddy waved away the title, but she'd used it on purpose.

Titles felt safer. Titles meant distance between them, and propriety, and rules.

"Everyone assumes we're already courting, so, you know . . ." He looked at her with a self-deprecating smile. "I suppose I should get the formalities aside. May I have permission to court you?"

Alix stared at him. For a wild moment she thought this was another of his outlandish pranks, like when he and Ernie once let two ponies loose in the halls of Sandringham.

"You want to court me?" she asked slowly, numbly.

"We've always known that we would get married someday. I think it's time we made things official, don't you?" Eddy spoke with indulgent patience, as if explaining something to a small child.

Had they known that? Maybe he was right, and everyone

in their family—everyone except Alix—had always taken their engagement as a given.

This was the sort of thing a mother would have helped explain to her, except that Alix had lost hers when she was six.

A suspicion crossed her mind, and she glanced over at Eddy. "By *everyone*, did you mean Grandmama?"

"Well . . ." Eddy seemed at a loss. Then he smiled as if suddenly understanding. "I do want to court you, Alix. What does it matter if it was Grandmother's idea first?"

She should have known. Queen Victoria was the puppet master silently arranging all their marriages, scattering her children and grandchildren across the thrones of Europe like pieces on a chessboard.

Before she could help it, the truth spilled out of her lips. "How can you want to court me when we aren't well matched?"

The moment she'd said it aloud, Alix winced, but Eddy seemed unbothered by her observation. He kept moving, leading her around a marble fountain where a goddess—Persephone, most likely—was forever strewing stone flowers.

"I know our temperaments don't align, but that's precisely why we *are* well matched." Eddy said this without an ounce of compunction; if anything, he seemed pleased. "We complement each other so well. The best marriages are when each partner has different interests, different strengths."

Alix thought of her parents, both quietly joyful, both soft-spoken, who'd been extremely happy together before her mother passed. She wasn't certain Eddy was right.

"You're so beautiful," he added warmly. "You'll be a spectacular queen."

Queen. Of *England*.

Somehow in all the shock of Eddy's words, Alix hadn't thought that far ahead, to the fact that he would someday be king.

Her breaths came faster, shallower. She clenched her hands into fists so tight that her nails dug into her palms, willing herself not to fall into one of her episodes. She had no desire to reveal that side of herself—her sickness, her brokenness—to Eddy. He would never understand.

"I'm sorry, but I—I don't know," she stammered.

For the first time, a wounded expression flickered over Eddy's features. "You don't know," he repeated. She heard the unspoken subtext: *You, the princess of a minor German duchy, aren't sure about becoming queen of the greatest empire on earth?*

The sun was beating down on her; Alix felt sweat gathering at her brow, along her armpits. She felt like she was falling backward, off a cliff into some chasm of shock. Oh god. She was going to descend into the familiar dark panic, right here in front of Eddy—

"I'm sorry. This has all taken me by surprise." Miraculously, Alix found the strength to sound calm.

"Of course. It's a big step," Eddy agreed. "Which is why we need to make our courtship more formal, to give you time to adjust to it. You'll sit with me at the opera tomorrow, won't you?"

She nodded, and he flashed her a blithe smile, tucking his hands into his pockets.

"Wonderful. Well, I'll give you a moment." Whistling cheerfully under his breath, Eddy started back toward the terrace.

Alix watched him go, a bee droning in the rose trellis behind her.

What happened today wasn't a proposal, she reminded herself. He hadn't gone down on one knee, didn't have a ring. All Eddy had done was ask to court her.

But they both knew where such a courtship would lead.

Could she go through with it—marry Eddy, become queen someday? Alix tried to imagine being like Aunt Alexandra, and then someday like Grandmama, living an excruciatingly public life. Everyone in the country, in the *world*, would know her name. She would ride in parades and wave from balconies, and each time she walked through a doorway, the entire room would fall silent.

And she would do it all as Eddy's wife. The reality hit her like a blow to the stomach: she would wake up with him, go to sleep with him, sit across from him at breakfasts and dinners. Eventually, though it was hard for Alix to imagine, she would have children that were half Eddy and half her.

He was handsome, of course. And good-natured, and entertaining. Yet it felt inexplicably *wrong*, as if she were shoving a puzzle piece where it didn't fit.

Alix slumped down to sit cross-legged on the ground, for once not caring that her dress would get grass stains. She braced her hands on the sun-warmed earth, wishing that she could cry, but no tears came.

She never cried anymore, not since the awful thing she had done all those years ago. Perhaps that was how grief worked. When you'd done something truly horrible, every other unhappiness paled in comparison. Even the prospect of marrying a prince you didn't love.

CHAPTER FOUR

May

MAY HELD HER BREATH AS SHE WALKED DOWN THE STAIRCASE, her hands tightening over the wooden railing. Maybe this time she could escape unnoticed—

"Mary Adelaide? Is that you?"

No such luck.

She drew in a steadying breath, then descended the last few steps.

May had never liked White Lodge, which had been designed as a hunting retreat years ago, its low-ceilinged rooms painted in muted colors. There was a stale, defeated air to the place, as befitted the Tecks' diminished status, but the living room was worst of all. When they'd returned to England after their years abroad and were granted use of White Lodge, the Tecks had stuffed it with old furniture from Kensington Palace—furniture that was drastically out of scale, making it look like the house had swallowed another house twice its size. Fringed ottomans sprang up from the floor like mushrooms, rugs overlapped each other in chaotic disorder, and oversized curtains dragged along the floor.

Her father, Francis of Teck, sat in one of the wingback chairs, staring listlessly into the empty fireplace. He did this a lot lately: just sat there, as immobile as the footmen who stood around Buckingham Palace. Except that they were young and dashing, while Francis was a shadow of his former self.

"Hello, Father," May said politely.

Francis had leaned forward at the sound of her footsteps, but when he saw that it was May, he sagged, as if he'd been craving the prospect of shouting at her mother. Now he was left with nothing but May, who never gave him the satisfaction of fighting back.

Sometimes, when he smiled, May caught a glimpse of the man he'd been before bitterness and abandoned dreams wore away at him. She remembered that version of Francis from her childhood, back when he used to make up silly games— like the one where they would each describe a made-up monster, and the other person attempted to sketch that monster while blindfolded. They used to dissolve into fits of laughter comparing their atrocious drawings.

Francis so rarely laughed anymore. Now he was almost always the other version of himself: apathetic, callous, cruel.

"What did you think of last night?" he asked, then answered his own question. "It was a little crowded for my taste, but I suppose when you're the Prince of Wales, you have to invite everyone to your daughter's wedding." The bitterness in his tone was caustic.

"There certainly were a lot of people." May had long ago stopped contradicting her father. At least to his face.

Francis grunted in agreement, then looked sidelong at his daughter. "You didn't dance very much."

"I danced with Prince Eddy," May hurried to say.

"No good barking up that tree!" Her father laughed as

if he'd said something uproariously funny. "He's as good as engaged to that Hesse girl. You know, the pretty one."

"Yes," May replied, because that was the safest word around her father.

An enormous beribboned form appeared in the doorway, and May's heart sank. She could just about manage her father when it was the two of them alone, because she knew how to placate him, to stay quiet and walk on eggshells. But her mother was too angry to behave. She deliberately provoked Francis, stomped on the eggshells.

"Well, look who the cat dragged in." Mary Adelaide's words were directed at her husband, who lifted one hand in a careless wave.

"Sorry to have been gone all night. I was otherwise occupied."

He may have spoken the word *sorry,* but there was no hint of apology in his tone. His words were sharpened like a weapon.

Mary Adelaide snorted. "I don't especially care who you spend your nights with, Francis. God only knows why I married you."

"You married me because no one else would have you," he spat.

"Please. I could have married a nice duke, and instead you came courting, poor as a church mouse, hat in hand."

"'A nice duke'?" her father repeated incredulously. "Not even the *baronets* wanted you. I should have known to back off when I saw the other princes running the opposite direction, the way they've all done to May—"

That would have stung, except that May had long since

grown numb to her father's cruelty. Of all the things he loved to criticize his wife about, May's failure to find a husband was one of his favorites.

She backed away, already forgotten by both parents.

May was sheltered, but she wasn't completely ignorant of other people's suffering. She had visited the poorhouse with other girls from church, had seen the women with bruises or broken limbs. *Things could be worse*, she'd told herself after that visit. At least her father never harmed her physically.

The bruises that Francis inflicted were invisible, emotional. He belittled May and her mother, laughed at their hopes, mocked things that mattered to them; and his mood swings were lightning quick. He'd always been erratic, but the cruelty had escalated after May's brother, Dolly, enrolled at the military academy at Sandhurst last year, leaving the two women with Francis alone.

Once, when May was a child, her father had bought her a shiny red balloon at a county fair. May remembered walking home with it tied to her wrist, heart swelling with pride.

The moment they got home, Francis slashed it with his knife.

May had started sobbing. She couldn't help it: the tattered remnants of her balloon drifting down through the air had such an awful finality to them.

"You see, May?" her father had asked, with that eerie, manic gleam in his eye. "Life can be unfair sometimes. You need to learn this at a young age. You care about things, and then you lose them, and there's nothing you can do about it."

May had valiantly tried to swallow back her sobs, which stung the inside of her throat. That was the last time she'd ever let her father see her cry.

She hurried toward the front of the house, a shattering sound echoing behind her. Francis must have thrown a vase, or perhaps even one of the crystal candlesticks. It really was stupid. Money was the main cause of his resentment, yet he was careless with the little they had left.

This was why May had to get married. The alternative was living under her father's roof forever, letting him inflict petty cruelties on her because it made him feel powerful.

Sometimes she wished that England had stayed Catholic, because then, at least, she could have gone to a convent. May would have made quite a good abbess; she sensed that she had a knack for managing things, if only someone would let her.

The Tecks no longer employed a butler: their house-keeper, Mrs. Bricka, answered the bell if it rang, but like all their staff, she was overworked. Their gardener, Charles, had been forced to start driving the carriage when they let their coachman go, and their cook had long since begun washing bedsheets.

May lifted a hand as she stepped into the sunlight, thinking she would just stroll around the yard for a moment—avoid the chaos inside—but then she saw Charles kneeling by a bed of gardenias. An idea rapidly formed in her head.

"Charles, could you bring the carriage around, please?"

He cast her a dubious stare. They both knew that there were few places a young lady could venture unchaperoned.

"Where are you headed, miss?"

Not for the first time, May wished she had a close friend, someone she could trust. Of course, she could never have actually told this mythical friend about the sordid details of her life. That kind of thing simply wasn't talked about. But it would have been nice to have someone she could visit at times like this, when White Lodge felt claustrophobic. When the pressure and panic roiling in May's chest threatened to boil over.

For some reason she thought of Alix of Hesse, and what she'd said at the wedding last night: that they should all come have tea sometime. Alix probably didn't expect May to actually come over, but no matter. The invitation had been issued.

She tipped up her chin as she looked at Charles. "I'm going to Buckingham Palace."

MAY BEGAN TO DOUBT HER DECISION THE INSTANT HER CARRIAGE rolled through the palace's iron gates.

A footman sprang forward to help her step down. She couldn't help noticing how pristine his white gloves were: even crisper than hers, and this was her nicest pair.

"I'm here to see the Princess Alix," she informed the footman, handing him her card.

His gaze flitted from the card to her dress, a three-year-old one that had been darned twice in an attempt to make it over for this year's fashions. Thankfully, skirts were getting narrower rather than wider.

After an awkward beat, the footman relented and opened the palace doors. "Please wait here, Your Serene Highness." He managed to pronounce *Your Serene Highness* with a touch of skepticism, sniffing as she followed him inside.

May tried not to dwell on how unfair it was that Alix and Ernie stayed at the palace when they were in London, yet May hardly ever set foot here. Alix was obviously Queen Victoria's favorite, because she was beautiful and because her mother had died. May might as well have been motherless too, given how little Mary Adelaide had ever done to help her—if anything, she had *hurt* May's chances on the marriage market. Yet Queen Victoria had never taken the slightest interest in May.

When the footman returned a few minutes later, his attitude was noticeably warmer. She supposed she had Alix to thank for that.

"This way, miss," he said, gesturing May up the stairs and into a sitting room with delicate hand-painted wallpaper.

Alix was inside, perched on an upholstered couch with a book in her lap. A Thomas Hardy novel, May noted dismissively. She never bothered with fiction; there was plenty to worry about in the real world without wasting time on made-up people.

"Oh, May! I'm so glad you could come by!" Alix stood, her dress rippling around her in soft folds. It was a buttery yellow, trimmed in lace at the shoulders and set off by a pair of pearl earrings.

Her smile was so warm, so genuine, that May felt herself thawing a little. Perhaps her idea hadn't been harebrained after all.

"It's good to see you," she said tentatively. "When do you leave for Darmstadt?"

"In two days." Alix led her to a tea table set up near the windows. Envy stabbed into May's chest at the sight of the pressed white tablecloth, the fresh-baked scones and ramekins of clotted cream, the silver pot of tea. Everything was embroidered or embossed with the palace's coat of arms.

"You're not going to Balmoral this summer?" May asked.
"Not this year."

Alix took a bite of buttered scone. May broke off a few pieces but didn't eat any. She had to be constantly vigilant, or she might wake up one day and look like her mother.

"I do love it there, though," Alix went on. "It's nice to be secluded, away from the bustle of the city."

"But the bustle is the best part of the city!" May burst out, unthinking.

Alix smiled. "To you, perhaps. I prefer the quiet."

May saw it, now: that elusive quality that made everyone trip over themselves falling in love with Alix. Her shy sweetness wasn't feigned, the way May's was. It almost made May feel protective, except that the very concept was laughable. How could she help a girl who possessed so much more than she ever would?

To her surprise, May found herself wanting to open up. "I understand what you mean, even if I don't wholly agree. I used to love the weeks my family spent at Chiswick with the Waleses."

A shadow passed over Alix's face at the mention of the Waleses, so quick that May almost didn't catch it. "Chiswick? Is that near the sea?"

"It's west of London. There's a lake, but no ocean."

Alix nodded distractedly. "I've always wanted to visit the ocean. Have you heard of this new trend of sea bathing? They say it cures anything, even—"

She broke off before finishing the sentence, leaving May to wonder what she'd been about to say.

There was an awkward silence; May felt the sudden need to fill it. "Will you come back soon? Perhaps for the holidays?"

"I'm afraid not. I need to be home with my father."

May twisted her fingers around a fistful of napkin. "I suppose you'll miss Prince Eddy quite a lot."

"What do you mean?" Alix asked, blood draining from her face.

This was why May didn't have any friends; she never quite knew how to phrase things. "I'm sorry if I overstepped," she fumbled. "I just thought—I mean, isn't it—don't you two have an understanding?"

Alix drew in a breath, tucking a strand of light blond hair behind her ear. "It would seem that everyone knew about this understanding except me."

May paused, sensing that she should give Alix space to continue.

"This morning, after breakfast . . . Eddy asked to court me," Alix added softly.

They hadn't been courting already? "Congratulations," May began, but her words faltered at the sight of Alix's face. "Alix—are you all right?"

There was a moment of struggle on Alix's perfect features, her desire for privacy warring with a need to confide in someone. "I don't know." She swallowed. "I hadn't really considered . . . When Eddy brought it up, I wasn't . . ."

"You don't want Eddy to court you?"

Her cousin stared down at her delft plate, blue-and-white figures dancing around its rim. "Apparently, Grandmama has always expected us to marry. I don't know." Alix swept her gaze downward, her lashes casting shadows on her cheekbones. "We don't love each other."

There was a moment of silence that seemed to last a lifetime.

May's heart skipped, a wild storm of thoughts racing through her head. Was Alix really dismissing Eddy's courtship because she didn't *love* him?

And if Alix had no interest in getting engaged to Eddy— if she, unbelievably, told him no—was there a world in which he might propose to May instead?

It wouldn't be easy, but stranger things had happened. Anne Boleyn had married a king, and she wasn't even a little bit royal, just the daughter of a lord.

After all, without Alix in the picture, who was Queen Victoria's next best option for Eddy? The only other princesses of their generation worth considering were that Mecklenburg girl and a few scattered cousins—Aunt Vicky's daughters, or perhaps Uncle Alfred's? Princess Hélène of France could have been on the list, except for the major issue of religion. Queen Victoria might let a younger son marry a Catholic, but it would never do for a future king.

Alix had been the clear choice since they were all children. If she stepped aside, it would be open season on Prince Eddy.

May wasn't as purely royal as some of the other contenders, but she was royal *enough*. And she was demure and soft-spoken, a very active member of the Anglican church, and had an airtight reputation, all of which were crucial requisites for a future queen. She was like Alix in that regard: both of them rule followers, tea sippers, writers of embossed thank-you notes. Both were quiet, elegant believers in the Way Things Were Done.

Besides, May had something those other princesses lacked— desperation.

She was determined, and she was here, and she was willing

to do what it took to marry Eddy, without letting something as nebulous as *love* stop her.

May needed to get out from under her father's roof, and if she could trade it for the roof of a palace, so much the better. She'd spent her entire life in the shadow of those who were richer or higher born. But if she could find a way to marry Eddy, everything would change. And all those people who'd found her wanting? May would relish the moment they came to her on their knees, begging favors, and she would have the delicious pleasure of telling them no.

She looked back up at Alix, who was watching her closely. Somehow, May sensed that she could tip this situation one way or the other. She could reassure Alix that she and Eddy would be good together, convince her to give the courtship a chance. Certainly that was what Queen Victoria would expect May to do, out of family duty.

Or she could act in her own self-interest.

It was in Alix's interest too, she reminded herself. If Alix really did want to marry for love, who was May to dissuade her?

She leaned forward. "Are you having reservations because of Eddy's women?"

"I— What?"

"I'm sorry; I thought everyone knew." May pretended to hesitate. "Please, forget I said anything."

"Tell me." For the first time there was a blade of strength in Alix's voice.

"Eddy keeps a Gaiety Theatre girl at a flat in Haymarket. And they say he's been . . . involved with some of his fellow officers' wives." May felt a little guilty, but everything she had said was true, and Alix might as well know sooner rather than later.

"I had no idea," Alix said faintly.

"Like father, like son, I'm afraid."

Surely even Alix had heard about their Uncle Bertie. Throughout his marriage he had juggled an endless cast of aristocratic mistresses, all of them high-ranking: countesses at the very least, if not duchesses. May had heard that each of the women got an ouroboros tattoo around her wrist, so wisp-thin that she could hide it beneath a diamond brace-let. The tattoo was her symbol of membership in England's smallest and most elite club—the club of women who'd slept with the Prince of Wales.

Alix's mouth fell open in a delicate O of shock. "Uncle Bertie, too?"

She really had no idea? May had underestimated Alix's naivete. "I'm sorry, I shouldn't have said anything. But I imag-ine that it's been hard on you, navigating all of this alone. With your mother gone and your sister in Russia . . . I know it's not the same, but I'm family too. I'm always here if you'd like to talk."

Honestly, she was doing Alix a good deed. If Alix was frightened off by Eddy's indiscretions, then she wasn't cut out to be queen. May was worldly enough to know that you couldn't marry a prince, ascend to the highest of heights, without any sort of trade-off.

She dared to reach across the table, laying her hand over Alix's. Shockingly, her cousin didn't pull away. "Forget about those women. Think of all the other exciting things you'll do as queen, meeting sultans and leading parades and having your picture on postage stamps!"

May would love all of that, but as she'd expected, shy Alix flinched at the prospect. She was just as dreamy and introspective as she'd been as a child, when she sat outside braiding daisies into a chain.

"If Eddy and I ever do get married, it won't be for any of those reasons," Alix said hesitantly.

"Of course. You'll marry Eddy so that you can spend the rest of your life here in England! Just think," May added warmly, "when you live in London, we can have tea once a week! You'll never have to go back to the cold of Darmstadt again!"

At that, Alix's expression crumpled, and May felt a twinge of guilt. Perhaps she shouldn't have laid it on so thick; she knew how homesick Alix was in London.

"I love Darmstadt." Alix's voice wavered. "I would miss it."

A clock echoed through the room, chiming twice, thrice, a fourth time. May stood. The table before her was covered in half-empty plates, crumbled scones and smears of butter glinting in the afternoon light. It all had an atmosphere of luxurious exhaustion.

"I should be going," she announced, ignoring the regret she felt at having manipulated Alix. Did it count as manipulating if all you'd said was the truth?

Alix gave a reflexive smile. "Of course. I'll see you at the theater tomorrow?"

"The theater?"

"Grandmama is taking us to *La Traviata* to celebrate our last night in town."

Grandmama. It struck May yet again how different her reality was from Alix's. She would never dare call Queen Victoria anything except *Your Majesty*, especially not a pet name like *Grandmama.*

"Have a wonderful time at the opera. I wish I could be there."

Alix's blue eyes were wide and guileless. "Surely your parents have a box for the Season?"

She might as well admit the truth; it wasn't much of a secret anyway. "Not anymore. We haven't taken a box at the opera in years, not since . . ."

May didn't complete the sentence, but she saw Alix's sudden comprehension. Even in far-off Darmstadt, word would have spread of the Tecks' financial ruin.

"You should come with us—you and your mother," Alix hurried to add. "I'm sure Grandmama would be happy to see you."

"Thank you. We would love to join," May said graciously.

If nothing else, a night at the theater would give her one last chance to dissuade Alix from marrying Eddy.

Maybe May was reaching too high; maybe marrying Eddy was impossible. But she had to at least try. She couldn't afford to sit back and passively let the future hurtle toward her. She had no grandmother arranging brilliant matches on her behalf, no help from her parents.

If May of Teck wanted something done, she had to do it herself.

CHAPTER FIVE

Hélène

IT WAS SUCH A SHOCK, SEEING LAURENT WALK INTO HER FAMILY'S formal dining room, that at first Hélène didn't process it.

The mahogany table before them was scattered with their breakfast plates: baguettes sliced in half, terrines of butter, carafes of steaming cocoa. Her parents had never converted to the heavy British breakfast of cold ham and venison pies.

"*Majestés.*" Laurent bowed to Hélène's father, then to her mother. They seemed pleased by the gesture; out in public, in England, they were so rarely addressed as king and queen.

"Are you leaving?" her father asked cheerfully. He was speaking in French, which he considered the language of everything elegant and dignified.

Hélène stared at Laurent, who looked painfully out of place in the rococo dining room, with his callused hands and his simple collared shirt.

Laurent kept his eyes trained on Hélène's parents, ignoring her. "I want to thank you again for the many opportunities you have given me. It has been an honor to work for you. I have trained Michel as much as I can, and I know he will do an excellent job."

"What are you talking about?" Hélène exclaimed.

Hélène's mother, Marie Isabelle, frowned from across the table. "Hélène, you know better than to interrupt anyone who is speaking, even—" She broke off before saying *even a servant* and turned to the coachman. "Laurent, I take it you haven't shared your news with the princess?"

Laurent stared resolutely at the space above Hélène's shoulder. "I've been offered the position of Master of Horse for the Marquis de Breteuil."

"All the way in France," Hélène said flatly. Her parents both sighed with longing and a touch of envy, because France, of course, was the one place they couldn't go—not unless the Third Republic changed the terms of their exile.

"It's a great opportunity for me," Laurent replied.

The position was undoubtedly a step up in the world; as the Orléans family's coachman, Laurent shepherded them around town and managed their eight horses. But as Master of Horse—especially for someone like the Marquis de Breteuil, who kept a massive stable—his life would be far bigger in scale. He would attend horse auctions and manage a team of grooms and stable hands; he wouldn't sleep on a mattress up in the eaves but would be granted a real room in the servants' quarters, perhaps even a cottage of his own near the stables.

This was clearly the news he had meant when he'd said that he had something to tell her.

She waited in a trancelike state as Laurent and her parents exchanged more pleasantries. Finally, when he started to leave, Hélène stood with him.

"Laurent, would you escort me to the stables before you go?" She fought to keep her voice even, though hurt coursed through her veins. "It's such a lovely day; I was thinking I might ride."

It was gray and overcast, not a lovely day at all, but Philippe and Marie Isabelle were too distracted to contradict their daughter. Laurent visibly flinched as he followed Hélène down the hallway and onto the back lawn.

"So. You're moving to France." She marched with angry steps, the heels of her boots digging into the grass. "When did you make this decision?"

"I'm sorry, I should have told you sooner. But you must agree that this is for the best," he breathed. "Things were getting too risky."

Hélène drew to a sudden halt. Not caring that they were in full view of the kitchens, she whirled to face Laurent, grabbed his shirt with both hands, and tipped her face up to his.

"Take me with you."

He blinked at her. "What?"

"I'll come with you. I'll use a new name." The words tumbled out of her, fierce and insistent. "We'll tell everyone I'm your wife. Better yet, we'll get married at some small country church along the way and I really will be your wife! Then we can live together, like we always wanted—you, me, and a stable full of horses—"

"No."

The finality in Laurent's tone was like the crack of a whip. He detangled Hélène's hands from his shirt and stepped away, putting a healthy distance between them.

"Be reasonable, Hélène. You can't run away with me."

"Why not?"

"Because you're a princess!"

"I'm the princess of nowhere," Hélène shot back. "What does it matter if I run away? My parents have no country to rule!"

"Aside from the fact that you're not allowed in France—"

"No one there even recognizes me!"

"If your parents caught us together, they would kill me!" Laurent exclaimed.

"That's not true; it isn't the Middle Ages. They would just have to accept the inevitable." Give up on whatever foreign prince they had hoped to match her with.

Laurent shook his head fiercely. "They would accuse me of abduction! I would go to prison at the very least. And besides, you would be ruined!"

"I already am ruined, and I don't care!"

"But no one knows it!" he said hoarsely. "We have to stop, now, while we still have a chance. While *you* still have a chance."

Hélène reached up to brush tears from her eyes. There was sense to his words, though she wasn't ready to hear it. "Don't leave me. We can figure this out. We can figure *anything* out, because we love each other."

Laurent's silence spoke volumes.

The realization hit her then, in all its bleak ugliness. He didn't love her. He was fond of her, yes; he enjoyed her company on horseback—better yet, when Hélène was on *her* back. He probably got a thrill out of breaking the rules with her. But what they shared wasn't love.

"I see," she said slowly, her voice cold. "Then I suppose this is goodbye."

"I really am sorry, Hélène." Laurent started toward her, as if to embrace her one last time, but Hélène flung up a hand in warning.

"*Don't* use my Christian name. You forfeited any right to

that when you decided to leave." Some long-buried regal instinct prompted her to tip up her chin, hold back her tears. "I am an Orléans, and to you I'm Your Royal Highness."

Laurent hesitated, then bent forward into a low, courtly bow. "Your Royal Highness," he said heavily.

She turned on one heel, the great volume of her skirts spinning around her like a bell, so that the last thing he saw would be her retreating back. She was Hélène d'Orléans, and she refused to let any man be the one to walk away from *her*.

Her movements were taut with anger as she stomped to the stables and asked one of the grooms to saddle her mare, Odette. The horse gave an impatient huff, her ears flicking forward and then back again.

The groom cleared his throat. For a moment Hélène thought he might criticize her for using the regular saddle rather than a sidesaddle, but he was frowning at the horizon. "Mademoiselle, may I suggest you stay close to the house. It's going to rain."

Hélène glanced at the storm clouds, low and ominous. "I'll be fine. That looks several hours away, at least."

Before the groom could reply, she vaulted onto Odette and gave a kick of her heel. The mare jerked eagerly into the wooded parkland.

Wind raked through the trees that lined the path. It whipped at the fabric of Hélène's skirts, which were balled up around her waist, spilling over her left leg and leaving her right stocking shockingly bare. It didn't matter. No one was ever out here to see.

When she was little, Hélène used to wear her brother's breeches and ride in a boy's saddle, until her governess locked the breeches away. Hélène, undaunted, had figured out a way to ride in skirts. It was why her daytime dresses were always cut so wide. Sidesaddle was a useless position, invented by men to keep women off-balance—to prevent them from riding quickly, or really, from riding *away*.

Of course, a princess should know *how* to ride, but she wasn't meant to enjoy it the way Hélène did. A princess wasn't expected to enjoy much of anything, not food or alcohol or a raunchy joke, and certainly not sex.

Perhaps that was Hélène's problem. She took too much pleasure in everything, the way a man would.

Hélène urged Odette faster, her thighs and calves straining pleasantly. The thudding of the horse's hooves echoed the frantic pulse of her blood. For a moment she imagined running away, just riding Odette on and on through the countryside until she reached the coastline, boarding a ship to Greece or Istanbul and never looking back.

But there was nowhere for Hélène to go; not really. The boundaries of Richmond Park pressed in on her, constricting the air from her lungs. Droplets of rain began to cascade onto the surrounding parkland, yet she pushed Odette onward, through the mud.

Laurent had never loved her. The realization stung. Except . . . had she loved him?

Or had she just *wanted* to love him, infatuated with the idea of being in love?

Hélène realized with a start that it had grown dark; storm clouds curled overhead like black ink spilling onto parchment. The rain was so hard it stung her bare skin. Around her, the forest was a sodden blur.

She wiped the rain from her eyes, exhilarated. Something

about the storm made her want to tip her face up to the thunder and shout a reply.

A dim shape rose up on the path before them.

She yanked at the reins, but it was too late; Odette was lurching wildly to one side. Hélène managed to slip her boots from the stirrups as the world flipped brutally on its axis. For a moment everything seemed to freeze—disorientingly, the ground was overhead, and hurtling closer. She closed her eyes as someone cried out in alarm—

HÉLÈNE BLINKED. DARKNESS SWIRLED AROUND HER. SHE WIPED at her eyes, and it resolved itself into the rain-soaked darkness of the storm, not the heavy black of unconsciousness.

"Are you all right?"

She looked up, startled, into the brilliant blue eyes of Prince Eddy.

So it hadn't been a deer that spooked Odette. Hélène struggled to sit up and immediately gasped, emitting a string of curses that would have made her roguish great-uncle Henri proud.

"Miss d'Orléans?" Eddy asked, surprised. "What are you doing out here?"

Hélène realized, a bit angrily—which was a stupid emotion in light of the circumstances—that Prince Eddy hadn't recognized her at first. Though she didn't look like much of a princess with wet hair plastered to her face. And even though they periodically crossed paths at parties, it wasn't as if she and Eddy spent any meaningful time together.

"You're hurt," he observed.

Hélène ignored him, twisting despite the pain. "Odette . . ."

"Your mare? She's hurt, too. Just a sprain, I think," Eddy said swiftly, at Hélène's expression. "But I doubt she can carry you back right now. Not that you're in much shape to ride."

Hélène followed his gaze to her legs. Her skirts were still twisted to one side, revealing a dangerous amount of bare stocking, but she had bigger problems. Her right ankle was swelling rapidly, already the size of a small melon.

She braced a hand on the mud behind her, trying to stand, and Eddy gave a huff of protest. "You can't put any weight on that."

"Then I suppose I'll hop back on one foot," Hélène snapped. The rain was coming down harder now, but there was no use trying to find shelter when she was already soaked through.

"Let me help." The prince hooked his hands beneath her armpits and hoisted her to her feet.

Hélène tried to hobble a few steps, leaning her weight on Eddy and using only her left foot. He moved slowly, letting her set the pace—until lightning shot through the night-dark sky. An instant later, thunder cracked, loud enough to make them both jump.

"This is getting ridiculous," Eddy muttered. Before Hélène could react, he reached a hand beneath her knees and swept her into his arms.

She was so shocked that she said nothing at first, just blinked up at the Prince of England as he held her to his chest. A very firm, solid chest. He smelled of damp wool and soap and, underneath, something else: something indefinably masculine and warm.

Then the reality of her situation sank in, and Hélène tried to wriggle from his grasp. "What are you *doing?*"

Eddy tightened his grip. "I'm trying to *help* you, not that you're making it particularly easy. If I lift you up, do you think you can ride?"

"Yes," Hélène said sullenly. The rain was already abating. Typical English fickleness. At least in France the weather picked a side, good or bad, and stayed there for more than an hour.

They started toward Eddy's horse, a massive bay that had been waiting to one side of the path, untethered. "Ares!" he called out, and the stallion trotted over, obedient as a dog. Hélène made a mental note to practice that with Odette.

"Ares?" she repeated drily. "You named your horse after the god of war? What, because you're both so intimidating and strong?"

"Are you always this grateful when accepting help from gentlemen?"

"I wouldn't know. I never need help."

"Of course not," Eddy muttered. Ares came to stand next to them, and the prince set her gingerly on her left foot. Hélène gritted her teeth.

"Ready for me to lift you up?" Eddy asked. She nodded, and he settled his palms around her waist.

For a foolish moment, it seemed to Hélène that they were suspended in time. There were droplets of rain in Eddy's lashes, trailing down his jaw, on the corner of his lower lip: which, on closer inspection, was full and sensuous.

Then Eddy lifted her into the saddle, and Hélène arranged herself on his massive horse with both legs to one side. The moment she sat back, she winced. It wasn't easy trying to ride sidesaddle under the best of circumstances, with a proper saddle, and now with her swollen ankle . . .

"Don't ride sidesaddle on my account," Eddy observed. "It looks painful, especially with your injury."

He was right, of course; her right ankle was pressed against the tooled leather of his saddle in an unnatural position. "Are you suggesting that I ride astride?" She tried to sound horrified at the suggestion.

A smile tugged at the corner of Eddy's mouth. "I saw you earlier."

Well, there was no use playing coy. Hélène tucked her skirts up around her knees and swung her right leg over the side of his horse. Her ankle felt so much better that an involuntary moan of relief escaped her lips.

Eddy looked over with curiosity, and something that might have been interest. Hélène bit her lip. That moan had been too raw, too intimate a sound for a lady—the sort of sound that Hélène used to make with Laurent, when their bodies had been wound together. It wasn't the sort of sound a well-bred girl should even know *how* to make.

As he looped her horse's reins around a branch, she frowned. "Are you sure we should leave Odette here?"

"We'll send the grooms back for her. Right now we need to get you home. You're shivering."

"It's too far for you to walk," she said dubiously, and Eddy barked out a laugh.

"I'm not walking. I'm riding with you."

Hélène spluttered. "You can't—I wasn't—"

Eddy hooked a foot into the stirrup and vaulted up behind her, looping an arm around her torso to pull her against him. "Ready?"

When Hélène nodded, he nudged his horse into a slow canter. Hélène tried not to think about the feel of his thighs behind her, shifting against the leather of the saddle as he guided Ares down the forest path.

"What is it?" he asked, after a few minutes.

She whipped her head around, and Eddy's lips grazed her wet curls with the movement. *Mon dieu*. This entire situation was woefully indecorous, even for Hélène: worse than what she'd done with Laurent, in some ways, because Eddy was the future king. And she was currently touching him in so many places—his long lean thigh pressed against the length of hers, her buttocks flush against his groin, the back of her head tucked beneath his chin as if they were lovers.

When she said nothing, he jerked his head in the direction of Sheen House. "I'll drop you near your stables, if you think you can manage to get inside."

"Hopping on one leg?" Hélène asked, though she understood what he meant. No one could know they had been out here, alone, together.

Eddy was clearly fighting to keep the laugh from his voice. "They might believe you made it all this way on your own. I get the sense that you're rather stubborn."

Hélène's traitorous body was softening in response to him. There was something disarmingly nice about this sensation— feeling like she was cocooned in a warm, steady strength. Like she was safe.

It was just the feeling of being *held*, Hélène reminded herself. She'd certainly felt it often enough with Laurent. Before he abandoned her.

"What were you doing out here, anyway?" She meant it

as a question, but she was hurt and irritable and it came out like an accusation.

"I could ask you the same thing," Prince Eddy replied.

"I *live* here."

His hands tightened on the reins. "Richmond Park is a royal hunting ground, so I have as much right to be here as you do."

"I haven't seen you riding here before."

"I have a lot of royal hunting grounds to choose from."

Hélène stiffened. Just when she'd thought that Eddy might not be as arrogant as she'd assumed, he had to make an entitled comment and confirm all her worst suspicions.

"And you came out here alone?" She waved a hand to indicate his surprising lack of groom or attendant. "I thought princes always traveled with an entourage."

"You sound like you're talking from experience. Have you met a great number of princes?"

"Enough to develop an opinion on them."

She felt Eddy shrug against her back. "Then you must know how rare it is for princes to be alone. I'm sure you can relate."

"But I'm not a princess, not *really*," she reminded him. "Haven't you heard? The French got rid of us."

There was a strange note in Eddy's voice as he replied. "I don't think losing your throne makes you any less of a princess. Royalty is a permanent condition. When you're born to it, there's no changing or undoing it, not even if your family is living in exile. Not even if you *wanted* to change it."

Before she could reply, he drew to a halt.

"This is where I leave you," Eddy announced, sliding off Ares. He reached to help Hélène down.

Her heart gave a confused thud as he let go of her and stepped back. For a moment their eyes locked.

"Thank you for helping," Hélène mumbled.

As she hobbled back to the barn, she sensed the weight of his gaze, as warm as the brush of his skin had been when his bare palm touched hers.

CHAPTER SIX

Alix

AT HOME IN HESSE, ALIX'S FATHER KEPT A DECIDEDLY MODEST household. Things were quite different at Buckingham Palace. Here, when Alix woke, the fire in her room already crackled; someone had slipped in to light it while her bed-curtains were drawn, a luxury that always left her feeling slightly unsettled. Breakfast was summoned at the touch of a bell, and fresh flowers materialized in vases as if by magic.

At home, Alix could visit her father simply by walking downstairs and knocking on the door to his study. A conversation with her grandmother was far more complicated. She had to ring for a footman and ask to see the queen, then wait for the message to travel through a spiderweb of servants and ladies' maids, until an entirely different footman finally appeared to escort her to Her Majesty.

She followed the footman down one soft-carpeted hallway after another. The closer she got to her grandmother's quarters, the more awed and hushed the palace felt, as if she had entered a religious sanctuary.

"Your Majesty." The footman rapped at the final set of carved wooden doors. "Her Royal Highness, Princess Alix of Hesse."

"Come in, my dear!"

Grandmama sat in an armchair by the window, dressed as usual in a black silk gown. She gestured for Alix to take the neighboring chair. "Are you excited for *La Traviata?*"

Alix sat, lacing her fingers nervously in her lap. "Of course. It's the perfect outing for our last night."

"Stay another month," the queen said automatically. She did this each time Alix and Ernie were about to leave. "We're heading to Balmoral soon, and you love it there!"

"That sounds delightful, but I need to get home."

Hurt flashed in Grandmama's eyes. "I've always hoped that you would think of England as your home, Alix. You're just as much British as you are German, like my own dear Albert."

Actually, while Alix was half British and half German by birth, Grandpapa Albert had been wholly German—and had given it all up to marry her grandmother, because he loved her so desperately. Even now, almost thirty years after his death, Grandmama never took off the black of mourning. It was a story Alix had heard a thousand times since she was a child, and each time, she was struck by the romance of it.

Alix hesitated. "Grandmama . . . yesterday Eddy asked if he could court me."

Victoria clapped her hands together. "Oh, I'm so glad! It was about time!"

About time? Eddy had been right; the queen clearly wanted them to marry.

"I'll write to your father at once," Victoria went on, smiling broadly. "Given this news, there's no question of you going home tomorrow. You must stay and spend some proper time with Eddy, not just at Balmoral but here in London. So-ciety will need to get used to seeing you together."

Alix hurried to interject. "But I'm not certain that Eddy and I are a good match."

"Of course you're not certain yet," her grandmother said blithely. "That's what the courting period is for! You've known Eddy your whole life, but as your cousin; now you must consider him as a husband. I have such fond memories of my own courting period, with Albert," Victoria added, a bit wistfully. "We spent much of it at Windsor, you know. Perhaps you'd like to go there with Eddy."

Alix knew she was expected to let go of her objections, but they kept rising, blocky and sharp in her throat.

"Were you aware that Eddy keeps women on the side?"

She hadn't planned to throw down the card May had dealt her yesterday, but to her surprise, her grandmother didn't flinch at the statement. She had obviously known.

"My dear, those women mean nothing. Chorus girls and artists' models! Eddy is just a young man in the military, act-ing his age. *You* are the one he intends to make his wife."

"I doubt Grandpapa ever behaved like that," Alix dared to say.

She was probably asking too much, hoping for fidelity in a royal marriage—more than that, hoping for love. Yet Alix couldn't help it. As outlandish as it was, she'd hoped that she and her husband might build a life *together*, instead of carv-ing the world into domestic and social spheres and spending their days apart.

She wanted someone who knew every last part of her, even the darkness at her core that Eddy had never seen—and if he did see it, he wouldn't understand. He would be appalled at her illness, disgusted by it. How could he ever love her when he didn't see the guilt that constricted her every breath, woven around her rib cage like one of those tropical snakes?

"I will admit that Eddy is not perfect," Grandmama said, with surprising bluntness. "But he is a good boy at heart, and means well."

There was something irritating about the indulgent way Victoria spoke of Eddy, as if he were a misbehaving child and not a full-grown man.

"Be that as it may, I fear that Eddy and I are not well suited. Our dispositions are so different. How would we ever come to love each other?"

"Just as my disposition was so different from my dear Albert's!" Victoria exclaimed, undaunted. "We *understood* each other, of course; we were cousins, as you and Eddy are. But we did not love each other at the beginning. To be truthful, we did not even *like* each other very much."

Alix blinked, startled by the admission. Her grandmother had only ever spoken of Albert in the most glowing terms.

"Albert couldn't stand me when we first met. He was resolute and calm where I was impulsive; he was serious where I was emotional. But that was what made our partnership so successful," Victoria insisted. "We each had different strengths. As for love, that grew over time, from the children we raised together, the shared goals we worked toward."

Alix tried, and failed, to imagine working with Eddy toward a shared goal. She shook her head. "I'm sorry, Grandmama, but I'm not staying. Ernie and I will leave town tomorrow as planned."

The queen frowned. "I hope this isn't your sister's

influence. Don't you follow her example and marry one of the Romanovs."

"Ella and Sergei are happy together," Alix protested, confused by the change of topic.

"And you and Ernie are visiting them later this year, yes? Please, just promise me you'll be careful." The queen sounded suddenly distraught. "Russia is dangerous."

"I don't think Ella is in danger." From her sister's letters, it sounded like her life consisted of summer picnics and masked balls.

"They are *all* in danger! That country is teetering on the edge, with anarchists loose in the streets, trying to assassinate the tsar and his family. Truly, the Romanovs' wealth is too much. To be so spectacularly rich in a country with so much poverty—" Victoria broke off, shaking her head. "We aren't like the Russians, who *bomb* their kings, or the French, who exile them. Britain is a glorious empire, and being its queen is the highest and most exalted position on earth."

Except that Alix didn't want to be queen. And even if she did, she wasn't worthy of it.

She realized, shocked, that her grandmother's eyes were brimming with tears. Alix stepped forward and hugged her, closing her arms around her grandmother's back. Victoria stiffened, unaccustomed to the physical contact, but after a moment she relaxed into the embrace.

"If you don't want to stay, I won't insist upon it. You can go home to Darmstadt tomorrow as planned," Grandmama said, once they had pulled apart. "But you must assure me that you won't make any rash decisions about Eddy. Let him keep courting you from afar, by letter. Then, when you visit again next summer, you and Eddy can pick up where you left off."

Somehow Alix doubted that Eddy would prove a diligent correspondent. "Very well. We can write to each other."

"And you promise that you'll come to Balmoral next summer?"

Alix almost smiled at her grandmother's insistence. "I wouldn't miss it."

"Good." Victoria nodded crisply, as if everything was now decided. Alix had a sudden fear that she'd set too much in motion—that by agreeing to visit Balmoral next year, she'd signed away her future. But she hadn't gotten engaged to Eddy, hadn't made any real promises except to write him some letters over the coming months. A courtship conducted at a distance hardly counted as a courtship at all.

At least, that was what Alix told herself.

THANK GOODNESS SHE'D INVITED THE TECKS TO THE OPERA THAT evening, Alix thought gratefully; she needed the extra buffer between herself and Eddy. Ernie was here too—along with Eddy's mother, the Princess of Wales—but there was something different about having the company of another young woman, especially one who knew your romantic troubles. One who was almost a friend.

If only there were a tactful way to lend May a new dress. Even Alix, who cared little for fashion, could tell that her cousin's mauve gown was hopelessly outdated, and had been recut to fit the current trends. Alix had the horrified suspicion that May had altered it herself.

When May caught her staring, Alix flushed. "Thank you for coming tonight," she said softly.

May whipped open her fan, holding it before her mouth to hide her reply. Of course, Alix thought numbly, she hadn't even considered that someone might be peering through a lorgnette at them, reading their lips. In the royal box, you were always being watched.

"Have you made a decision?" May whispered.

Alix paused, uncertain. "I'm still leaving tomorrow."

"So you rejected him?"

Below in the orchestra, the aria swelled to a loud crescendo. "Not exactly," she admitted. "I suppose we'll be courting from a distance?"

May's eyes darted to Queen Victoria, who was seated at the opposite end of the box with Aunt Alexandra. Somehow, Alix sensed that May knew what had happened—that Alix had tried to get out of the courtship, and that Victoria had refused to hear of it.

The entire theater burst into applause as the curtain fell. Audience members began to stand, eager to stretch their legs or visit neighboring boxes.

"Alix." Eddy came behind her, bracing his hands on the back of her chair. There was something casually proprietary about the gesture that irritated her. "Shall we head to one of the other boxes? The Lansdownes are in number twenty."

He'd phrased it as a question, but it hadn't been intended as one, had it? Alix was supposed to say *oh yes, of course.* To be led from one box to the next like some kind of show pony, quietly signaling to the world that she was his.

Well, she wasn't his—not yet, anyway. And Alix found that she wasn't ready to let their courtship start in earnest.

In an uncharacteristic gesture of defiance, she twisted

around and shook her head. "Why don't you go without me? I'm going to stay and catch up with May."

There was a momentary break in conversation around the rest of the box. Alix looked over at her grandmother, but Victoria was pretending to study her program, as indomitable as ever in her opera glasses and black gown.

Eddy shrugged good-naturedly and turned to Ernie. "Care to join me in the lounge?"

As their steps retreated into the hallway, Alix turned back to May. A heated sensation was building in her chest, which she strove valiantly to ignore. "I must admit, I've never seen *La Traviata*," she chirped. "We don't often make it to the opera, except once in Vienna."

Thankfully, May understood her need for small talk. "In Vienna! You don't mean with Emperor Franz Joseph and Empress Sisi? I've always wanted to meet them."

Alix nodded, grateful when May kept talking, some nonsense about the empress's legendary skin-care routine. To their left, May's mother began asking questions of the queen while the Princess of Wales stared in stoic silence out at the theater.

Every modern princess knew the story: how, as teenagers, Alexandra and her sister Minnie had been legendary beauties, sought by every foreign court. One of them had married the Tsar of Russia, the other the future King of England. The two princesses of Denmark, somehow sitting on the world's two greatest thrones.

Alexandra was still as stunning as ever, but Alix couldn't help feeling that there was something tragic about her beauty now—something quiet and long-suffering. Like a flower that had been pressed between wax paper and dried up.

Was that what would happen to Alix if she married Eddy?

She felt feverish, as if a thousand spotlights were trained on her skin. People were staring, weren't they? They had seen the way Eddy leaned over her chair and were already speculating, gossiping. The old paralyzing sensation grabbed hold of Alix, fear slinking like a sordid worm into her insides. *No*, she thought, trying to stave it off.

When the house lights finally dimmed and the music started up, signaling the end of the entr'acte, Eddy and Ernie still hadn't returned.

The episode came on slowly, as it always did.

It started with a prickling over Alix's arms, spots dancing at the edge of her vision. This had happened to her for years, ever since her brother Frittie had died of the bleeding disease, something no one in her family was permitted to speak of. In the months afterward, these dark spells had begun to haunt her. At first her family thought they were nightmares, except that they struck when Alix was awake.

She felt dizzy and weak and at the same time she pulsed with adrenaline, as if some primordial monster were chasing her, raking its claws over her skin. Alix looked at her hand, half expecting to see blood. But her skin was unblemished.

May glanced over. "Are you all right?"

Alix stumbled to her feet in a murmur of silk. "I . . . I'm feeling faint. I think I should head home."

"Do you want my mother to come with you?"

In her swirl of panic, Alix hadn't even thought of a chaperone. She momentarily hated society. Just this once, it would be so nice to behave like a man—to get into a carriage after dark and let the driver take her home, without worrying about her sullied reputation.

"I'll find Ernie," she gasped, then hurried through the inner box and out the door.

The hallway that curved around the boxes was mercifully empty, save a few guards outside the royal box, who shot her curious looks. Alix stumbled onto a bench upholstered in shining red damask. Tears pricked at her eyelids, and her chest heaved.

She sank her head into her hands and closed her eyes. The darkness that roared at her was an old darkness, pulled from the very depths of her. The kind of darkness that came from doing something unforgivable and having to live with the consequences. The kind of darkness born of searing regret.

She tried so hard to fight it off, but the memory wrapped its tentacles around her mind, dragging her back to that warm May afternoon. She heard a childish giggle, saw the sunlight streaming in through the open window. Her brother reached for her with his chubby toddler hands. . . .

No, she thought. *Not now. Not again.* Yet no matter how hard Alix tried to wrestle it into submission and lock it away, this memory always found a way to the surface.

And then it broke her.

CHAPTER SEVEN

Hélène

THE OPERA WAS EXCRUCIATINGLY BORING. NOT THE MUSIC, which spoke to an unnamed yearning in Hélène's soul, but the people. At every performance they were the same—the same families shuffling into the same boxes, recycling the same stories, trading the same rumors and petty complaints.

Hélène tried to ignore them. She draped her elbows over the brass railing of her parents' box, closing her eyes as the sounds of the orchestra reverberated in her body. Until Clothilde, her mother's lady's maid, came over and tapped her with a fan.

Princesses were not supposed to *lean*. They were supposed to sit with their hands clasped demurely in their laps, silent mannequins to hang jewelry and tiaras on.

"Sit up straight," Clothilde hissed. "And stop staring at the royal box."

The royal box? Hélène hadn't even glanced that way. Unlike most people, she was here for the show onstage rather than the sideshows playing out in all the society boxes. But for once, the mention of the royal box piqued her curiosity.

She looked over, only to find that Prince Eddy wasn't there. Of course he wasn't. He probably had no tolerance for something as high-culture and serious as opera. But his mother was seated next to the queen, along with Princess Alix and May of Teck, both looking as stiff and proper as Hélène was *supposed* to be.

She'd felt strange and restless all day, probably because of Laurent's betrayal. Hélène still couldn't believe he'd left her, just walked away from their relationship as if it meant nothing at all.

Except that it had never been a relationship, had it? It had been a liaison, an affair. Hélène repeated the word again in her mind: *affair.* It sounded tawdry and yet, oddly thrilling.

Perhaps that explained why she wasn't all that sad about Laurent's departure. Since she clearly hadn't meant anything to him, she refused to feel anything at his loss.

When her restlessness became an itch she couldn't ignore, Hélène murmured to no one in particular that she was going to the ladies' lounge. Clothilde sniffed in protest, but Hélène's parents, busy entertaining Lord and Lady Fleming, hardly noticed.

The hallway that curved like a horseshoe around the private boxes was empty. Everyone was seated right now; Hélène had walked out in the middle of the second act, instead of waiting for the entr'acte, when most people socialized.

She had no real desire to visit the ladies' lounge, a crush of warm perfumed bodies and rustling fans. Perhaps she would just walk the length of the hallway and back again. She started forward, only to pause at the sounds of sobbing.

Hélène turned back the other direction, then gasped.

Princess Alix of Hesse sat on a bench, her hands balled into fists as she sucked in heaving mouthfuls of air. The folds of her gown were crumpled around her like a pitiful flag of surrender.

"Your Royal Highness!" Hélène swept forward, alarmed by Alix's stillness.

When the other girl said nothing, Hélène tentatively sat next to her, putting an arm around her shoulders. She felt Alix flinch, but after a moment she relaxed, her breaths steadying.

"Shhh," Hélène murmured, the way she might soothe a skittish horse. "Shhh, it's all right."

Slowly, as if she'd been carved from a block of ice and was melting, Alix moved again—her hands first, then her head. Warmth returned to her skin.

"Thank you," she whispered at last. "And . . . I'm sorry."

"You have nothing to be sorry for!" Hélène scanned the hallway with wary eyes. "What happened? Did someone hurt you?"

"Not really."

"But the way you were moaning just now . . ."

"It's nothing like that. I just—I get this way sometimes." Alix flushed, and Hélène knew she hadn't meant to reveal something so intimate.

Hélène softened as understanding dawned. "My maman used to suffer from the same thing. She called it her malaise. She said it felt like fear had seized hold of her body and paralyzed her, that she couldn't move until the dark spell passed."

It happened less often these days, but Hélène caught glimpses of it every now and then, usually when the Third Republic extended her parents' exile. Her maman wasn't as homesick as her father—she'd been born a princess of Spain, after all— but she still longed to get off this rainy, dreary island, back to the civilization of the Continent. Every time Hélène's father got another letter rejecting his plea to come home, Marie Isabelle would descend into her malaise—gasping for air and going frighteningly quiet, as Alix had done.

Alix looked pale, but she nodded. "What did your maman do to get rid of the malaise?"

"I don't know if she ever found a way to get rid of it. Only to get through it."

The German princess said nothing in reply. She just stared down at her gloved hands, pensive.

"Shall I walk you back to the royal box?" Hélène offered.

"*No!*" Alix cried out, then lowered her voice. "No, I just want to leave."

"Fair enough. I can't stand the final act of *La Traviata*, either." Hélène attempted to sound lighthearted. "Why is it that all operas end with the woman's death? I don't mind tragedy, but it's never the *man* who dies in these stories. Probably because they were all written by men," she added ruefully.

For a moment it seemed like Alix might smile at that. Then she seemed to recall where she was, and sighed.

"I'm waiting for my brother Ernie to return from the gentlemen's lounge. He'll escort me to Buckingham Palace."

"I can find him for you. Just . . . wait here."

"Thank you." In the dim light of the hall sconces, Alix's eyes had turned a deep, mercurial shade of violet.

Hélène hurried down the hallway toward the gentlemen's lounge. There was no placard on the door, nothing to distinguish this room from a broom closet, except for the fact that everyone in this building knew precisely what it was.

She lingered outside for a few minutes, foot tapping as

she waited for a man to emerge. From within she could hear the low roar of voices, the tantalizingly indistinct sounds of clinking glassware and raucous laughter.

Eventually her impatience got the better of her, and she threw open the door.

It was exactly as she'd always imagined. Men in jackets and cravats reclined in armchairs or bent over card tables, gambling. On the walls hung portraits of even more men, who looked eerily similar to the ones they frowned down upon, save the occasional addition of a hunting dog. At a bar in the corner, a white-haired man poured amber liquid into a pair of tumblers. The entire scene was cast in the glow of bronze lamps, a haze of cigar smoke hanging over it all.

Hélène's heart leapt. This was nothing like the ladies' lounge, where everyone perched on settees with their backs ramrod-straight and spoke in low voices. Here, the room crackled with laughter and lewd jokes and thrilling male energy. This room felt alive; it felt . . . *fun.*

"Miss!" A portly, red-faced man near the door gasped in horror. "The ladies' lounge is at the other end of the hall. This room is reserved for gentlemen only."

He stepped forward, using his massive bulk to herd her toward the door as if she were an unruly farm animal, but Hélène dug in her heels. "I'm not lost. I'm looking for Prince Ernest of Hesse!" She called out the name, craning her neck as she searched for Ernie in the crowds. More gentlemen turned toward the door, curious as to what had caused this unprecedented and highly inappropriate female intrusion.

"Miss, you really cannot be inside," the attendant protested. He clearly longed to drag Hélène outside by the wrists, yet manners forbade him from touching a lady without her express permission—a fact that Hélène would use to her advantage. She deftly sidestepped the man and raised her voice.

"Prince Ernest, are you in here? Your sister is looking for you!"

"Hélène?" called out an all-too-familiar voice.

Obediently, the men in the room parted to reveal Prince Eddy.

"Your Royal Highness." Hélène inclined her head but didn't bother curtsying, though technically, since they were in Eddy's country, she should have. He smirked, seeming amused by her breach of protocol.

A young man next to Eddy stepped forward, and Hélène blinked, noticing him for the first time. He had the same blond hair and pale blue eyes as Alix.

"Prince Ernest of Hesse, at your service," he said quickly. "You said that Alicky sent you here? Is she all right?"

Hélène heard the nickname for his sister, the concern and affection in his voice, and immediately warmed to him. "She's not feeling well, and wants you to escort her home." *Not feeling well* hardly did justice to the vortex of panic gripping Alix, but Ernie's eyes flashed in understanding. He'd obviously seen this happen to his sister before.

"Thank you." He nodded to Eddy and left.

Hélène stole one last glance around the forbidden male sanctum of the gentlemen's lounge, since she would never get another look. Then she turned back into the empty hall, her skirts snapping around her ankles.

"Hélène! Wait!" Prince Eddy trotted to catch up. Hélène tried to quicken her steps but nearly tripped on her hurt ankle.

"Careful," Eddy exclaimed, grabbing her elbow to steady her. Hélène sucked in a breath, and he let go.

"I'm sorry. Can we talk?"

"I don't know what we possibly have to talk about." She felt prickly and defensive; somehow, she couldn't shake the sense that their meeting in the woods had put her at a disadvantage.

Or maybe she just didn't like showing weakness before anyone.

"I would like to spend more time with you." Eddy didn't seem to have noticed her rejection. "May I ask your father for permission to court you?"

"You . . . *what?*"

Eddy smiled. The part of Hélène that was a teenage girl registered how dazzling a smile it was—how breathtakingly attractive he looked in his navy jacket and crisp white shirt, which fit perfectly over his lean, muscled frame. But it was also an indulgent, pleased smile, as if Eddy felt inordinately proud of himself for doing Hélène this favor.

The sad thing was, he was right. Most men wouldn't have bothered checking with Hélène; they would have gone straight to her father. Exchanging her like a piece of property, man to man, the way these things were always done.

"May I ask your father for permission to court you?" he said again.

"What, to *marry* me?"

Eddy's grin widened. His gaze traveled over her with deliberate slowness, from her face all the way down to the hem of her gown, making Hélène's breath catch.

"Yes, to marry you," he drawled. "I'm hardly courting you to be my mistress, Hélène."

There was a hint of challenge in that statement. Hélène sensed that Eddy was trying to get the measure of her: to gauge just what sort of princess she was, exactly. He would never have said that word, *mistress*, to Alix of Hesse— would never have spoken to her in this low, taunting tone.

But then, Alix of Hesse wouldn't dream of riding astride, or marching into the forbidden sanctum of the men's lounge.

Hélène's eyes flicked up to meet his.

"It won't work. They will never let you court me."

Eddy leaned against the wall and crossed his arms over his chest. "Who, your family?"

"Or yours! I'm *Catholic*."

She'd expected that to put a swift end to things, but Eddy waved away her remark. "I'm not bothered by that. I promise to let you practice your religion in peace."

"Your Royal Highness—"

"Eddy," he corrected, his voice low and meaningful.

"Eddy. You're the future head of the Church of England," she reminded him. "You can't marry a Catholic."

"I don't see why not." He spoke with the easy confidence of someone used to getting his way.

"Because! The last time your country had a Catholic queen, it brought down an entire *dynasty*!" Hélène hissed. Anne Hyde, the wife of James II, had been so devoutly Catholic that she had converted her husband—which ended in the Stuarts being sent into exile.

Eddy stepped forward. She was startled when he ran his hands down her arms, from her shoulders all the way to her palms, which he caught in his own. She had, typically, left her gloves in the box, and the feel of his skin on hers sent shivers down her spine.

After all the ways they had already spurned propriety, she supposed this one didn't really matter.

"Please, Hélène. I just want to spend more time with you. Don't you feel the same way?"

"Your family is probably planning your engagement to someone else," she forced herself to say.

A sheepish expression darted across his face. "There's no formal understanding between me and Alix, if that's what you're worried about. Grandmother expects us to start courting, but in truth . . . I'm not sure it will work out."

It took a moment for his words to sink in. When they did, Hélène yanked her hands away, stung.

Eddy was the reason that Alix was in hysterics tonight.

"I can't believe you." Her voice was trembling with outrage. "You rejected Alix, then came straight to proposition me?"

"No! As I said, nothing has been agreed upon, or even—"

"Do you think that princesses are interchangeable, like coins or cigarettes? That if you lose one, you should just grab the next one within arm's reach?"

They were standing very close now. Hélène felt her breaths coming fast and shallow, making her wish that her corset wasn't so tightly hooked. She should put some distance between them.

Instead, she leaned in.

It wasn't much, just an inch or two, but that was all the invitation Eddy needed. His mouth was swiftly on hers, and Hélène didn't hesitate; within an instant she was kissing him back.

Eddy nudged closer, his hands closing around her waist. A pulsing, drugging heat seemed to swirl through Hélène's bloodstream; her hands roamed up over his shoulders as if of their own volition. This was nothing like kissing Laurent. It felt headier, more electric, probably because it was so wildly reckless—

The feel of Eddy's desire, pressing very firmly through his trousers against her belly, brought Hélène abruptly to her senses.

She stumbled back and cast a swift glance in both directions, then let out a relieved breath. Somehow, no one had seen them.

"That was a mistake," she began, but Eddy was smiling again.

"It didn't feel like much of a mistake," he said simply. "It felt like you enjoyed it."

Maddeningly, foolishly, she *had* enjoyed it. Which wasn't the point. A polite young woman would never have kissed Prince Eddy in the first place; she would have slapped him, or at least retreated a step.

Hélène wasn't a polite young woman at all. She had *leaned closer.*

"Please, forget this ever happened," she insisted.

Confusion darted over Eddy's features. "You can't expect me to walk away, not after this. Hélène, I want to see you again."

"To what end?" Her voice was tight with emotion. "Do you really think your family would approve of your courting me? Be honest," she commanded.

There was a long, drawn-out silence. "Perhaps not," Eddy said at last. "But—"

"Then we have nothing else to say to each other! I know

better than to get involved in another meaningless—" She broke off before saying *fling,* but it was too late; the damage had been done.

If Eddy hadn't figured it out from their kiss, then he knew now. Hélène was no innocent.

"Please, just leave," she said coolly.

She hated herself for doing this: using her formal princess voice to draw etiquette around her like a wall, shutting him out. But what other choice did she have? She couldn't afford to be vulnerable with another man, not after what had happened with Laurent. Especially not with a prince.

Registering her tone, Eddy stepped back, his expression hardening. "Good night, Miss d'Orléans. I'm sorry to have troubled you."

CHAPTER EIGHT

Alix

COVERED IN A FRESH DUSTING OF SNOW, THE ROOFTOPS OF St. Petersburg glittered like rows of iced cakes. Alix stared out the window of the carriage, which was the most opulent one she'd ever set foot in: a golden coach drawn by matched white horses, with oversized gilded plumes on their harnesses.

She recalled what Grandmama had said, about the Romanovs being too ostentatious for their own good, and shivered in foreboding.

"Are you all right?" Ernie asked.

Alix hurried to smile. "I'm excited to see Ella. I miss her so much."

For years the two sisters had been inseparable. They had slept in the same room, their beds pushed close so that Alix could reach for Ella's hand when her nightmares were at their darkest. The episodes that had started after Frittie's death only got worse after their mother passed, which was when Ella, eight years her senior, became the maternal figure in Alix's life.

It was Ella who brushed Alix's hair at night, whispering stories of enchanted forests and star-crossed lovers. When Alix got her first blood and wept in fear—she thought she was dying of the same disease that had killed Frittie—it was Ella who explained everything, and showed her how to fit a cloth belt beneath her petticoats. Last fall, Ella had come back from St. Petersburg to oversee Alix's coming-out party: pinning lilies of the valley to Alix's white muslin gown, selecting the music for her first dance. Ella had been both sister and mother to Alix, and when she'd married the Grand Duke Sergei and moved to Russia, it had left a gaping hole in Alix's heart.

As their carriage pulled into the courtyard of the Anichov, the Romanovs' official residence in St. Petersburg, Alix's chest constricted. Sunlight glinted blindingly off the hundreds of windows. And on the front steps stood row upon row of guards and servants, all of them wearing the Romanovs' crimson livery trimmed in gold braid.

All those eyes on her—weighing her, judging her, finding her wanting.

"Alicky?"

She tried to nod, though she could barely hear Ernie's voice through the roar in her ears. "Alicky, are you having one of your episodes?"

Her *episodes*, her *condition*—Alix's family had never known how to refer to her strange illness. Alix herself didn't really know what it was. All she knew was that her body would, without warning, descend into a whirlpool of grim panic. Her limbs would freeze up as dark spots exploded behind her eyes.

She should have known this might happen today. The attacks usually struck when Alix was in a highly public setting or facing a weighty decision. Her most recent episode had been that night at the opera, back in London, when she'd collapsed into such a trembling heap that Princess Hélène had been forced to go fetch Ernie.

How shameful, that someone outside her family circle had seen Alix in the grip of her affliction. Yet, oddly enough, Alix sensed that Hélène wouldn't tell anyone.

"Alicky?" Ernie repeated, as the carriage drew up to the front steps. He reached out and shook her by the shoulders, yet Alix hardly noticed; her mind was hurtling back to that awful day, to the nursery with its woven blue rug—

A postilion leapt from the back of the carriage and walked around to open her door. *Just step outside*, Alix willed herself, but her body refused to obey her commands; she felt like she'd been turned to stone, like one of the carved figures on the enormous stone pillars.

And then she saw him.

Nicholas, the tsar's oldest son, bounded down the stairs in a flagrant violation of protocol. He was taller and more broadly built than Eddy—why was she comparing him to Eddy?—yet despite the imposing bulk of him, all muscled shoulders and powerful thighs, he was light and graceful on his feet.

"Ernie! Alix!" Nicholas reached the bottom step and held out a hand. He spoke in French, the official language of the Romanov court, though she knew he could just as easily have chosen English. "Welcome to St. Petersburg."

He wore a scarlet coat over dark trousers, with leather boots that stretched almost to his knees. His dark hair was cut short, emphasizing the bold lines of his jaw. His deep blue eyes met hers, seeming to thaw her from within.

Alix placed her gloved hand in Nicholas's and stepped down from the carriage.

For a moment they stood there, gazes locked, like dancers frozen mid-waltz. There was something warm about Nicholas, something that made Alix feel like she'd been tossed in a storm and now she'd found safe harbor.

A soft tut from one of the equerries recalled her to her senses. Alix withdrew her hand and sank into the most reverential curtsy she knew how to make, so low that her gown swept over the stones of the courtyard. She wasn't required to make this curtsy to anyone except the tsar himself, but something in Nicholas's presence, the strength and solidity of him, made her do it on instinct.

Alix hadn't seen the tsarevich since Ella's wedding five years ago. Back then she'd been an awkward and uncertain thirteen-year-old, and while Nicholas had treated her with kindness, he hadn't really noticed her.

"Thank you for having us," she breathed, as servants began collecting their luggage from the back of the carriage.

"Of course. I'm sure you're eager to see Ella," Nicholas offered. "She's upstairs with my mother; they were hoping you could join them for tea, if you're not exhausted."

Alix wished that protocol required him to take her hand again. "We would be honored."

Asking questions about the journey, the tsarevich led her and Ernie through the hallways of the Anichov. It was magnificent, every surface covered in gold leaf or lapis lazuli or snow-white marble. Everywhere there were mirrors, lush Aubusson carpets, display cases of Fabergé eggs, whimsical Chinese tables. And it was all so vast—it seemed to Alix that her father's entire house would fit in the frescoed dining hall alone.

Buckingham Palace, which a few months ago had felt like the height of sophistication, suddenly seemed outdated and old-ladyish by comparison.

"My mother and Ella are in the blue salon." Nicholas made eye contact with a footman, who threw open a set of double doors.

"His Royal Highness Prince Ernest Louis Charles Albert William of Hesse. Her Royal Highness Princess Alix Victoria Helena Louise Beatrice of Hesse," the footman announced.

Alix always found it a bit silly, hearing herself referred to by that endless string of names. Clearly, the Russian imperial court was particular about etiquette.

She took a hesitant step through the doorway, and her years of training seemed to melt away, because there was her sister.

"*Ella!*" Alix sprinted forward and threw her arms around her. "Oh, how I've missed you!"

She was still Ella, Alix noted with relief. She smelled like Russia now, like warm furs and spicy perfume, and her gown and upswept hairstyle were painfully Russian—but underneath it all, she was still her sister.

Ella laughed softly. "Alicky, my darling," she murmured, a note of reproof in her tone.

Alix spun about and curtsied to the tsarina. Nicholas's mother sat in a chair by the window, staring at her and Ernie as if they were a pair of ignorant country bumpkins. "Forgive me, Your Imperial Majesty," she said self-consciously. "I was so excited to see my sister again. Thank you for having us."

The Tsarina Maria—Minnie, her family had always called her—pursed her lips together in disapproval. Alix sensed that she should remain in the curtsy, though her thighs ached from holding herself in that position. Behind her, Ernie bowed and politely greeted the tsarina.

Finally Minnie flicked her hand, a gesture that Alix took to mean she could rise.

Nicholas cleared his throat. "Enjoy your tea."

"You're not staying?" Alix blurted out, then winced. Her second violation of protocol in two minutes. She wasn't acting like herself.

Nicholas smiled, unbothered by her lapse in manners, and Alix's stomach tugged at the sight. He glanced at Minnie. "I'd love to join, if you don't mind, Mother?"

"Oh, very well." The tsarina waved at a footman, who hurried to bring over another antique chair.

Alix took a seat, her heart fluttering strangely when the tsarevich sat next to her.

A steaming gold samovar of tea stood at the center of the table. The porcelain dishes held a mishmash of traditional English foods—scones, clotted cream, bread and butter—and others that must be Russian delicacies: crystal bowls of nuts, poppy-seed cakes, unfamiliar crescent-shaped cookies.

"I'm so glad you two are here," Ella exclaimed, smiling at her siblings. "I can't believe it's been five years since you last came to Russia. To think that you haven't visited since my wedding!"

Alix had longed to come sooner. She would have visited every year if her father had allowed it, but he and Grandmama had insisted she wait. *Sergei won't want his new wife's sister underfoot. Wait until they're no longer newlyweds,* Alix's father had told her.

In royal circles, a couple was usually considered newlyweds until the birth of their first child, but so far Ella hadn't gotten pregnant. Alix wanted to bring it up with her sister, but she feared it was a sensitive subject, so she never mentioned it in her letters.

"Your wedding was so beautiful. I think of it all the time," Alix replied.

To her surprise, the tsarina looked over. "You do?"

"I miss Ella; she feels so far away. And of course the wedding ceremony was breathtaking," Alix hurried to add.

Her sister had seemed like a princess from a fairy tale, dressed in a white dress sewn with pearls, the Romanovs' famous pink diamond tiara on her head.

"We had the most magical time on that trip," Ella agreed. "Walking in the gardens, staying up half the night waiting for the sun to set over the water."

"Russia is at its best in summer, isn't it?" Nicholas chimed in.

Alix nodded. "I've never seen skies like that. It felt like they would keep glowing all night, like it would never turn dark at all." Dimly, she noted that the rest of the table had detoured into another conversation, leaving her and Nicholas in a temporary bubble of intimacy.

There was that smile again, the one that lit up his whole face. "'In the afternoon they came unto a land in which it seemed always afternoon,'" he quoted softly.

"You read Tennyson?" She hadn't expected that.

"I find that reading poetry helps me practice my English.

My father disapproves, though. He considers poetry a waste of time."

"Does he feel that way about all the arts?" Alix wondered how someone too impatient for poetry could own so many spectacular paintings and sculptures.

"My mother collected most of the things in this palace," Nicholas replied, guessing the direction of her thoughts. He lowered his voice. "She's the one who helps me get books of English poetry, too. Aunt Alexandra slips them into the packages that Eddy and George send from England."

Alix blinked. It was disorienting, hearing Nicholas talk about Eddy, but royalty was a very small circle. Especially at these elevated levels. And, after all, Eddy and George were Nicholas's cousins: their mothers, Minnie and Alexandra, were sisters.

She wondered if Nicholas had heard anything about her and Eddy. What if he had some mistaken idea that she and Eddy were planning to marry? Could she find some tactful way to let him know it was nothing—that they'd each only written a single letter since her departure from England?

"We have nothing like Tennyson in Russian," Nicholas was saying. "And the few poems we do have . . . they don't capture that same sense of quiet peace."

"Recite one for me."

"A Russian poem?"

"Yes," Alix pleaded, just wanting to hear his voice.

Nicholas spread his hands on the table before him and began to speak. The Russian language sounded harsh at first, almost guttural, yet the longer his poem went on, the more Alix sensed something else to it. A fluidity underneath all those rasping consonants. A feeling of melancholy, perhaps even wistfulness.

"That was very moving," she said, after he'd finished. "What is it?"

"An old folk song about a man who goes away to war. When he returns, his wife has run away to join the tree spirits. I heard it during my time in the army." He shot a glance across the table, to where the tsarina and Ella were laughing at something Ernie had said. "My mother says it's demeaning for me to know peasant songs, but I believe there's value to it. As monarchs we should understand what motivates our people, the things they hope and fear."

"I agree." Again Alix marveled at how different Nicholas was from Eddy. She broke off a small corner of bread and buttered it, trying to keep from staring. "When did you serve in the army?"

"I was in the Preobrazhensky Regiment for a few years. Under Sergei's command," Nicholas added, naming Ella's husband.

"And you saw active combat?"

"I saw enough to make me dislike it." He shook his head. "Forgive me, we should speak of happier things. How long will you be staying with us?"

"Six weeks." Suddenly Alix wished it were longer.

"Well, I hope you find Russia as captivating in winter as you did in summer."

Alix glanced out the window. It was snowing again, great flakes swirling behind the glass pane in a gentle dance. "It's beautiful."

"Yes, it is," Nicholas agreed, though his eyes were on her.

CHAPTER NINE

May

MAY NODDED, PRETENDING TO LISTEN AS HER MOTHER AND THE Duchess of Abercorn debated the merits of French versus British ladies' maids (so far the verdict was British, though French superiority in hairstyling had been much discussed). She dared a quick glance at Prince Eddy, tracking his slow progress through the ballroom. Soon enough he would be near the buffet table and the entrance to the front hall, and then she could make her move.

Thank god she was finally out in public again—and at Prince Eddy's investiture, no less. Today he'd been formally granted the titles Duke of Clarence and of Avondale, and now most of London was crammed into the ballroom at Marlborough House, celebrating.

May had hardly seen Eddy since that strange night at the opera a few months ago. When Alix had stumbled out of the box, May had followed, worried that Alix might chase after Prince Eddy and change her mind. But the German princess had just collapsed onto a bench and cried. These weren't ordinary tears, May had seen at once. They were something far more sinister, something—what was that word that people used now?—*psychological*.

For a moment May had stood there, watching Alix heave great lungfuls of air. Perhaps she should go comfort her? But what if May said the wrong thing, as she was wont to do, and somehow made it all worse? What if Alix was embarrassed and preferred her solitude?

When she heard footsteps coming from the opposite direction, May quickly retreated to the royal box.

Eddy had reappeared half an hour later, and May knew at once that something had gone wrong. The prince had seemed hurt by Alix's rejection, far more than May had anticipated.

But surely he was ready to move on. He hadn't seen Alix in the months since the opera; she'd been in Darmstadt, and then visiting her older sister in Russia, while the Waleses had spent the shooting season at Balmoral. Only May had been stuck here in London—and even if Eddy *had* been in town, she couldn't have seen him, because her grandmother had died.

The Duchess of Cambridge had been the sort of stern, uncompromising woman who insisted on being laced into stays and starched petticoats even after a stroke left her half paralyzed. "*This* is her?" the duchess had demanded the last time May visited, then turned to May's mother with a plaintive "Mary Adelaide. Really."

May knew better than to complain about her grandmother's brusque dismissal. The duchess was the only person who occasionally took pity on the Tecks and helped stem the tide of their colossal debt; no one dared speak a word against her in their household.

As etiquette demanded, May and her parents had spent the last ten weeks in mourning, and were only now reemerging into society. May was just glad to have left the house, though her joy had dimmed a little when she entered the ballroom and was met by a sea of fashionable new gowns. She'd gone to such pains selecting her dress for tonight, a rose-colored silk with full sleeves, but it was from last Season, and now seemed pitiful.

"Mama. Why don't we visit the buffet?" she suggested once the Duchess of Abercorn had left them.

"Of course." Mary Adelaide's eyes drifted eagerly toward the table, which was laden with sweetmeats—sugar-dusted tarts, biscuits, candied chestnuts—as well as an enormous bowl of champagne that a footman ladled into crystal flutes.

When they were close enough, May stepped near Eddy with a deft maneuver, then pretended she'd only just noticed him.

"Oh! Your Royal Highness!" She sank into a reverential curtsy, knowing that the gesture would gratify any of the family members who happened to glance over—Eddy's mother, or especially the queen. They might be family, but it was never wise to skip over the formalities.

The various courtiers or aristocratic young men who had been hovering near Eddy retreated. Thankfully, even May's mother was perceptive enough to step away. From the corner of her eye, May saw her heaping candied walnuts onto one of the filigreed gold plates from the sideboard.

"Congratulations!" she exclaimed. "I so enjoyed the investiture today."

He didn't seem to have heard her. "It was all a bit tedious, wasn't it? Ceremonies always are."

"Yes," May hurried to agree, though really, Eddy should

have known that the tedium was the *point*. How else would mere mortals know that their royal counterparts were elevated so far above them?

"How have you been? I haven't seen you in months," she added, then regretted the remark; it sounded needy.

"Has it been that long?" Eddy's careless question made it clear just how little time he'd spent thinking about her.

May cast about for a change in subject. "You must be very busy with the cavalry. And with your horses! I hope you have one entering the races," she said quickly. "It was such a shock when Lorne won last year's Ascot."

Eddy's interest sparked, and May said a silent prayer of gratitude for her sharp memory; she hadn't even *been* at Ascot, just read about it in the papers.

"Exactly! I was so surprised when Dante didn't win. He's a magnificent horse—the Duke of Beaufort let me ride him at Badminton House." Eddy glanced over her shoulder again, then back at May. "Do you ride?"

"A little." She hadn't ridden since she was a child on a pony, but if Eddy invited her on a hunt, she would say yes and figure out the details later.

"May. I need to ask you a favor." Eddy placed a hand on her forearm and tugged her aside, toward the archway that led to the front of the house. May should have been thrilled that he was touching her, except that something told her Eddy hadn't even registered it. His eyes were darting in the direction of the balcony.

She resisted the urge to follow his gaze. It was a cold, dank evening, and no one had ventured outside; the lamps weren't even lit. What was he looking at?

"Anything," she told him.

"I need to step away and . . . take care of something," he fumbled. "If Mother is looking for me, tell her I went to the smoking room?"

The entrance to the smoking room was on the opposite side of the ballroom. No doubt it was crowded in there, this far into the party; May was quite certain Uncle Bertie had retreated there half an hour ago to drink brandy with his friends. Leaving the hosting to his wife, as he always did.

May nodded. "Of course."

"Thanks," Eddy said warmly. "I knew I could count on you. You're a good sort."

A *good sort?* Wasn't that the sort of thing men said when they clapped each other on the back?

Then Eddy was gone, his scarlet uniform vanishing through the archway that led to the front of the house.

May closed her eyes. She stood there for a moment, swallowing back the ache that threatened to burn in her throat. All she had done was say yes and be agreeable, yet in some way she didn't understand, she had failed. Again.

"In America, we call that being relegated to friendship."

May whirled around to see a young woman standing nearby. She couldn't help registering the expensive details of the stranger's gown: the rich gold braid along the cuffs, the detailed embroidery, and the vibrant green of the silk, which matched the young woman's emerald-colored eyes.

"Excuse me." May started to brush past her, but the newcomer kept talking.

"It's not very enjoyable, is it, when you're interested in a man but he's completely unaware of you?" She sighed sympathetically. "I can't believe His Royal Highness asked you to cover for him while he went off to a liaison in a coat closet."

May was so shocked that she nearly stumbled. She glanced back over her shoulder and remarked, in her iciest tone, "That was a private conversation."

"Don't worry, I won't tell anyone," her companion chirped.

May should have left it at that, but for some reason she added, "And the prince wasn't sneaking off for a *liaison*. I'm sure he just needed a moment away from the party."

She didn't like the notion that Eddy had asked her to lie for him while he met up with another woman. But even if he had, what did it matter to May? Whoever he snuck off with wasn't her competition; it would have to be a servant, or perhaps some nobleman's wife. No unmarried woman could behave that way, at least no one of quality.

The stranger shrugged, making the emerald droplets in her ears shimmer. There was a deliberateness to all her motions, from the way she tilted her head to the click of her heels on the floor, that conveyed a forceful personality.

"Perhaps. Personally, I'd put my money on the coat closet. Shall we peek inside and find out?"

"Are all Americans appallingly coarse, or just you?"

May had never spoken like that before. But then, she'd never been spoken *to* this way, with such blunt disregard for propriety or appearances.

She expected the young woman to blanch at her rudeness, but the stranger only laughed.

"Don't worry, I can be as opaque as you British, who say

lots of beautiful words without ever saying what you *mean*. I just reserve that for the men. We need to protect them from our real opinions, because if they knew what we actually thought, they would run the other direction!"

How many times had May thought the exact same thing? Though she was wise enough to keep such convictions to herself.

The young woman smiled warmly as she added, "Surely we don't need to be so disingenuous with each other. Don't you agree, Your Serene Highness?"

May hesitated, curious. "You have the advantage of me, since you evidently know who I am, but I haven't had the pleasure of making your acquaintance."

"Agnes Endicott." The girl bobbed into a curtsy—belated, certainly, but perfectly executed. There was a sound like rain falling on gravel. It took May a moment to realize that Agnes's gown had a train sewn with delicate gold beads, which were dragging over the parquet floors with the movement.

"Endicott. As in the steel company?" May asked.

Agnes nodded approvingly. "I'm so glad you know of us. Most women aren't even aware how steel is used, let alone who produces it."

To her own surprise, May admitted the truth. "I read the newspapers in the mornings, before my father wakes up." And then she folded the pages neatly back in order, so that when Francis finally tripped down the stairs, stale with a hangover, he wouldn't realize that anyone had been there before him.

May wasn't sure what would have angered Francis more, the realization that his daughter was intelligent, or that she'd taken something that he considered his property.

"Good for you! I read the newspaper as well, starting with

the society pages, of course. I find that I only have the stomach for business and world affairs after I've consumed at least one cup of coffee."

May eyed Agnes's outfit with new understanding. The Endicotts' fortune might be new money, but it was surely immense.

"Miss Endicott. Why are you here?"

"My father met the Prince of Wales at a shooting party hosted by the Keppel family—you must know them? He and His Royal Highness hit it off." Agnes lowered her voice conspiratorially. "They gambled for great sums of money. Daddy said the prince is such an awful whist player that it took tremendous skill to lose on purpose! But once he did, he was able to hint that we would love an invitation to tonight's event."

Well, that explained why an American commoner was at the investiture party. Since he was technically the host, Uncle Bertie could alter the guest list, something he would never have been able to do at a Buckingham Palace event.

"I meant, why are you in England?"

"Why else do wealthy Americans come abroad these days? I'm here to get the one thing I cannot buy at home—a title. My mother has her heart set on a prince, but I'm not a fool; I know that's not an option for me." Agnes spoke flippantly, with a mischievous, teasing smile. "Perhaps for you, though."

"I don't . . ." It was surreal, hearing another woman talk so frankly about May's secret hopes.

"I'm afraid I'll have to settle for an impecunious earl, if I'm lucky. Unless you know any dukes with run-down castles looking to renovate?" Agnes went on.

May knew she should walk away from this conversation,

back to the familiar circle of society women and their talk of bonnets and marriages and who had offended whom. She and Agnes had veered into dangerously personal territory. Yet something about the American was . . . refreshing. She had a bright, New World zest for life, so at odds with the sense of defeat that May was used to. And her frankness made May want to sigh with relief.

"Do you?" Agnes prompted, causing May to blink in confusion.

"Do I what?"

"Do you know of any dukes with run-down castles?"

When May said nothing, Agnes sighed. "I'm sorry if I'm overstepping, Your Serene Highness—"

"You are," May cut in.

Agnes ignored her. "You and I could help each other! I know about your family situation." She said this without an ounce of judgment. "You clearly think I'm an ignorant American, but I'm also a quick study. I've read all about the aristocracy—I can spot the Spencer red hair, the Cavendish temper, the Grosvenor family curse. Yet the moment I arrived in London, I realized that I'm still unprepared."

"What makes you say that?" May couldn't help asking.

"Because it's no good knowing the players when you can't understand the rules of the game!" Agnes's eyes were downcast. "Nothing here is like it was in Chicago, and the stakes are far too high to allow for defeat. I need someone to teach me all the things they *don't* write in books."

May sighed. "You're at the investiture of the future king. I don't know if you need any help."

"Please. I'm not such a fool as to think I'll get invited to another event like this. The doors have opened to me for this rare, fleeting moment, and if I don't make the most of it while I have the chance, the opportunity will be lost! I can't be reliant on my father," Agnes added, the bold command in her voice faltering.

May softened in spite of herself. She knew better than anyone what it felt like, wanting to escape the shadow cast by one's father.

"It won't be easy."

"Because I'm American?"

"Because it's as you said; you need to learn the rules! You showed up tonight looking like you're dressed for a ball in—in—" She struggled to think of somewhere typically American and flashy. "Newport! Even at a royal event, you don't need so much gold embroidery. Or such large jewels. I assume you have wonderful diamonds, too, but I hope you never wear them during daylight hours. And no dark furs until you're married."

The other girl glanced self-consciously down at her gown. "I wanted to stand out."

"You will stand out by reputation. People will talk about your money, even without you literally wearing your fortune on your sleeve." Without thinking, May had adopted Agnes's forthright way of speaking. "And you'll need to keep your opinions to yourself."

"What opinions?"

"All of them! If you want to marry a future earl, let alone a duke, you'll need to impress their mothers. No society mama wants her son to marry a modern girl."

"Then they aren't *so* different from American mothers."

Agnes flashed that bright, hopeful smile again. "So you're going to help?"

"Oh no—I was just giving you some friendly advice." May couldn't afford to be seen with an American husband-hunter. If she wanted to marry Eddy, there was no room for mistakes.

Agnes clapped her hands in sudden excitement. "But of course, we haven't discussed your payment!"

"*Payment?*" May wasn't a tradesman for hire, or someone who accepted bribes.

"You must understand that Americans don't accept anything for free. So, to thank you for your generous advice, I must insist upon buying you a new gown."

"I couldn't possibly accept that."

"Why not? It's such a small thing. Please," Agnes pressed. "I don't like feeling like I owe anyone, or am in their debt. Let me do something to even the scales between us."

May was well aware that a new gown far exceeded the value of the advice she had just given. And yet . . . How glorious it would feel to arrive at a party not in a turned-over dress with recycled lace, but in something new.

She felt her convictions wavering. Men didn't go to war without armor; how could she wage the greatest campaign of her life, a campaign to marry a prince, without being dressed for battle?

"I don't know how I would explain a new dress to my father," May muttered, half to herself.

"Didn't you just lose your grandmother? I'm sorry for your loss, by the way," Agnes added hastily. "But could you say that the duchess left you a bit of money and you used it to buy the dress?"

May studied the American girl with new thoughtfulness. If Agnes knew how May was related to the late Duchess of Cambridge, then she really *had* studied the aristocracy. Maybe she could hold her own in a drawing room or two.

"What do you need from me?"

"Not much!" Agnes said swiftly. "Just make a few introductions; give me suggestions about my attire or behavior, as you did just now. And warn me about the people I'm going to meet."

May's eyes drifted once more over Agnes's gown. Though it was far too ostentatious, with the train and the gold stitching, it was also so *new*, its fabric rich and expensive-looking. She thought of her own drab wardrobe, the way everyone at these receptions looked at her with such pity in their eyes.

"Very well, Miss Endicott. I will introduce you around."

Agnes squealed in delight. "Thank you!"

"You're welcome," May told her, already hoping that she wouldn't regret this decision.

CHAPTER TEN

Hélène

IT WASN'T EASY IGNORING THE GUEST OF HONOR AT HIS OWN party, but if anyone could, it was Hélène.

She'd been in the ballroom of Marlborough House for most of the night, and she'd managed not to make eye contact with Prince Eddy once. Even if some stupid part of her *wanted* to talk to him, just to find out what he'd meant by his mysterious gift.

After the opera, Hélène had done her best to forget about Prince Eddy. He was a rogue and a libertine, and there was no use getting entangled with him when it would end in heartache. She had almost convinced herself of this—until the package arrived at Sheen House.

Her lady's maid, Violette, had brought it to Hélène's room with evident confusion. The packages her mistress received were usually tied with the silk ribbon of a high-end boutique, not wrapped in unmarked brown paper. Violette had stood in the doorway, clearly hoping Hélène would open it in front of her, but Hélène could tell that this was private. She waited for Violette to leave before ripping off the paper.

Inside was a folded plum-colored outfit, the likes of which Hélène had never seen. She'd hurriedly unhooked her day dress and shimmed out of her petticoats to try it on.

The first piece—she supposed they were trousers, though they certainly looked nothing like the ones men wore—was loose and billowing, gathering at the ankles with gold-stitched cuffs that matched the cuffs at her wrists. The blouse was the same rich material, its hem falling to just above the waist of the pants, leaving a pale strip of her stomach bare.

Looking at her reflection, Hélène almost didn't recognize herself. She felt feminine and beautiful—yet also powerful, and a bit dangerous.

It was a heady, intoxicating sensation.

She'd fumbled in the box, wondering who could have possibly sent her something so gorgeous and exotic. The enclosed note was only a single line of text.

Now you have something to wear the next time you ride without your sidesaddle.

Hélène had reread the note a hundred times since that day, wondering what Eddy meant by it. Tonight was the first time she'd been in a room with him since.

The music ended. Hélène smiled and took a step back from her partner, whose name she'd already forgotten, and glanced toward the front of the ballroom.

In a wooden armchair sat Queen Victoria, several ladies-in-waiting hovering around her like a cloud of moths. Her Majesty was dressed as usual in all black, though half a dozen strands of pearls hung from her neck: and then, as if she had too many pearls to know what to do with, she had also hung a few from her chest, fastened with an enormous diamond pin. She didn't wear a tiara (in her old age, she complained of the weight of it), but the profusion of so many milky pearls against her black silk gown was striking enough to remind everyone she was queen. As if they were in any danger of forgetting.

Beyond her stood Prince Eddy, still wearing his uniform from today's investiture ceremony. He was talking with May of Teck, who gazed up at him with wide, worshipful eyes—the same way most women had been looking at him all night. Apparently Eddy was even more appealing now that he had a few more meaningless titles to string onto the end of his name.

"I'm getting some air," Hélène told her dance partner, and headed onto the back patio of Marlborough House. Technically she wasn't doing anything illicit; the terrace was in full view of the ballroom, with gas torches along the wall. It was just too cold for anyone to have bothered lighting those torches.

Hélène wandered to the railing and leaned her gloved forearms on it, kicking one heel behind the other.

Several minutes later, a voice sounded behind her.

"I should have known I'd find you hiding out here."

"I don't hide from anything," she insisted.

Eddy came to stand next to her, staring out at the dark gardens. "Well, that makes one of us. I came outside to hide from everyone."

She clucked her tongue in mock sympathy. "You gained two new titles today, the eligible young women of London are fighting over you, and still you're having a bad night? Should I be worried?"

"The eligible, utterly *boring* young women," Eddy corrected. "As for the titles, they don't mean much, do they? It's not as if I did anything to earn them."

Hélène was so startled by that remark that she opened her mouth, then closed it again. "That was a rather tedious ceremony," she said at last. "So much bowing and protocol, so many ermine-trimmed capes. I would be tired, too."

"My thoughts exactly."

A silence fell between them, but it felt less hostile than before. Hélène cleared her throat.

"Thank you for the outfit, by the way."

A smile teased the corner of Eddy's lips. "You like it?"

"It's beautiful. It feels like something a *real* princess would wear," she exclaimed, at which he chuckled. "And it fits perfectly."

"Oh, good. I had to, um . . . guess at the size."

"You guessed accurately," Hélène said drily. "Where did you find clothing like that?"

"The Shah of Persia visited last month. When he told me that his wives wear trousers every day, I asked if I could trouble him for a set."

"His *wives*? How many does he have?"

"I didn't ask him for the exact number, Hélène."

She drummed her fingers over the iron railing. "I suppose all men wish they could have multiple wives. Just trade one woman for the next whenever you tire of one, is that it?"

"Not me," Eddy said adamantly. "I'm daunted enough at the prospect of marrying just once, thank you."

Hélène glanced over, but his expression was unreadable. "What did the shah say when you asked for a set of women's clothes? Did he wonder who it was for?"

"Of course not." Eddy sounded horrified. "Men don't get involved in one another's affairs, if they can help it."

She lifted an eyebrow. "This is hardly an affair, Your Royal Highness."

"I'm well aware. In an affair, I wouldn't have to constantly dodge your insults."

"But the insults come so naturally to me—" Hélène began, as a door opened on the terrace behind them.

"Your Royal Highness? Are you out here?" someone called.

Eddy grabbed Hélène around the waist and tugged her swiftly downward, so that they were both crouching behind a massive stone urn.

"Hiding from your adoring public?" she whispered sarcastically.

"We're hiding for your sake! I'm trying to protect your reputation."

Hélène said nothing, because she knew he was right. It was one thing to have been standing on the terrace alone, another thing entirely to be out here with a man, unchaperoned.

When the door to the ballroom had shut again, they rose reluctantly to their feet. "We should go back inside," Eddy murmured.

But a wild, eager restlessness prickled through Hélène. The night seemed to unfurl before her, full of possibility.

"Let's take a walk through the gardens first."

Eddy frowned down at the pathways between the hedges. "We can't go in there."

"Why not?"

"Because," he spluttered.

"Because of convention? Because of propriety? As you've gathered, I'm not particularly fond of either." She shrugged, causing the sleeve of her dress—a deep blue velvet with resplendent silver detail—to slip lower. "I'm taking a tour of your family's gardens. Feel free to join me or not."

Hélène spun on one heel, wondering just how many people in Prince Eddy's life had turned their back on him. Probably not many.

She trotted down the curved staircase and turned onto a gravel path. The limestone fountains and sculptures glowed eerily in the shadows, like ghosts.

Eddy rushed down the steps after her. "Hélène, you can't just run around in the dark like this."

"I wasn't running, but that's an excellent idea. See if you can catch me." She cast him a gleeful smile, then grabbed two handfuls of her heavy skirts and took off.

After a moment, Eddy laughed and followed.

She marveled that she'd never seen it before: his bold vitality, his streak of childlike joy. Running around the garden like this, she wondered how much of Eddy's libertine reputation was real and how much was just that—a reputation. He'd had affairs, yes, but she sensed now that he wasn't malicious or callous about it, as some men could be. He was just passionate.

Perhaps that was why Her Majesty had sent Eddy into the military. She'd seen the uncontrollable spark within Eddy and wanted to stamp it out. *A future king cannot act like a child*, Hélène imagined her saying.

It was essentially what Hélène's governess used to say about her.

She kept running, aware that Eddy could have caught her long ago. He let her reach the farthest corner of the garden, near the stone wall that marked the edge of the Waleses' property, before he finally sprinted forward to touch her shoulder.

"Tag. You're it," he teased, and Hélène fell still.

They were both breathing heavily. Eddy stared down at her, his blue eyes luminous. Hélène curled her hand into the lapel of his jacket and tugged him close.

This time, she was the one who kissed him.

His tongue slid into her mouth and she moaned, arching her back. His hands skimmed slowly downward, caressing the sides of her breasts and her waist before settling around her hips to pull her closer. Hélène released his jacket and looped her arms around him, tangling her fingers in the soft hair at the nape of his neck.

God, she wanted him. She had wanted him since that moment he'd picked her up in the rain-soaked forest and held her against his chest. She didn't *want* to want him, but she did, and her reasons for telling herself no felt increasingly flimsy.

Eddy must have sensed the direction of her thoughts, because his breath caught. Their kisses grew faster, almost mindless. Hélène's thoughts dissolved into shadows and Eddy's pulse and the heat radiating from his body and the urgency of his mouth on hers. When his thigh pressed between her legs, she opened them without a second thought.

To her surprise, and delight, Eddy reached around her buttocks to hitch her up closer to him. Hélène felt the stone of the garden wall against her back, as hard and unyielding as Eddy felt pressed against her. Small noises escaped her lips as she pulled him closer, kissing his jaw, his neck, the corner of his mouth.

Hélène tugged at her skirts, pulling them higher up around her waist, her intent unmistakable. She had never felt this way with Laurent, like her entire body was molten and aching all at once. Laurent had always been so careful with her, almost hesitant, handling her as if she were made of glass.

She liked that Eddy didn't seem to think of her as fragile or delicate, that he seemed untroubled when her desire roared up to match his.

When Eddy pulled away, Hélène blinked in confusion.

He took a careful step back, unhooking her legs from around his back and gently lowering her to the ground. The cool air felt sharp on her skin.

"Hélène." His voice was hoarse. "We can't do this."

Though her experience was limited to a single man, she knew enough to know that men rarely turned down a willing woman.

"But I want you," she said baldly.

"You think I don't want *you*? God, Hélène, you're driving me to distraction." He ran a hand through his hair, mussing it at the edges. "I take responsibility for all the lines that were crossed tonight. I'm sorry."

Hadn't she chastised Eddy at the opera—expecting him to be sorry, angry when he wasn't? Now he'd given her an apology, and Hélène had no idea what to do with it.

Eddy laced his fingers in hers, and she looked up to meet his eyes.

"I spoke to my grandmother about you," he confessed.

Hélène's heart skipped a beat. "And . . ."

"And she told me that courting you was out of the question. She said that marrying a Catholic would provoke a constitutional crisis, and I was a fool to even consider it. She still wants me to—"

He broke off, but Hélène could guess the rest of the sentence. Victoria still wanted Eddy to marry Alix.

"I suppose that settles that." She tried to sound nonchalant, but failed.

"I keep thinking there must be another way. I could talk to Lord Salisbury," Eddy began, but Hélène just sighed.

It surprised her, how upset she was at the prospect of giving him up. But she was an Orléans; she knew a lost cause when she saw one. Her country had been in quiet, desperate conflict, republicans versus monarchists, for her entire life. She'd been in exile since she was fifteen. She had always known that she was a princess without a throne, a princess whose entire worth would be determined by one single thing—the man she married. She was a living, breathing parcel that her parents would send to some other family, hoping to gain more allies for the Orléans cause.

Princesses were born to be pawns in their parents' political ambitions. They didn't get to marry according to their own desires.

But that didn't mean they never *felt* those desires.

Eddy turned toward her one last time. He brushed a kiss over Hélène's lips—a featherlight, tender kiss that felt like an apology, filled with yearning and regret—and then he stepped back.

"I'll walk around the side of the house to the kitchen entrance. You can go through the terrace without anyone seeing us together. Again, I'm sorry," Eddy said gruffly.

It was the sight of his retreating back that made Hélène cry out, "Wait!"

Eddy turned around slowly.

She swallowed. "I'd like to see you again. In private," she clarified.

There was a beat of silence as they both processed the magnitude of what she'd suggested.

"Are you sure?" Eddy asked, eyes fixed on hers.

There was no way they could court formally. No chance that they could get married. They had no future together—but they could have something now, in the present. If Hélène was willing to risk it.

"I'm sure," she assured him, wondering if she was out of her mind. It had been dangerous enough getting involved with her family's coachman. Having an affair with a future king was something else entirely.

"When?" Eddy asked, and Hélène smiled in relief.

"Soon. But it can't be at my house—"

"Of course not," he cut in. "Don't worry, my valet will arrange everything. Can you find a way to leave the house undetected if I send a carriage?"

"Yes."

"Then I'll see you soon." Eddy reached for her hand.

Hélène laced her fingers in his, tugged him closer, and planted one more kiss on the side of his jaw. "*Soon* can't come soon enough," she told him.

CHAPTER ELEVEN

May

AGNES'S LETTER HAD ARRIVED EARLIER THIS WEEK, ON STATIO-
nery embossed with a family crest that must have been
sketched by some artist for hire. *Shall I pick you up on Thurs-*
day at noon and we can get started? Let me know if that day is
agreeable to you.

May had thrown out the note without replying. Of course
she couldn't actually go out with an American, the daughter
of a steel baron. What had she been thinking, agreeing to
Agnes's preposterous bargain?

But when Thursday morning arrived, May caught herself
glancing at the clock every few minutes. Agnes wouldn't actually come, would she? Surely she would realize that May's
silence had been a rebuke.

At the sound of carriage wheels crunching over gravel,
May's heart skipped a beat. Her father was home; he could
not see this. In a flurry of motion she pulled on her gloves,
tied a cloak around her neck, and ran unceremoniously down
the front drive. She had every intention of telling the coach
to pull away.

Agnes flung open the door, taking in the scene at once.

"Oh, you're sneaking out? You should have warned me!"
She reached for May's hand.

To her own surprise, May allowed herself to be pulled into the warm interior of the carriage. Agnes rapped twice on the roof and they started off at a brisk trot.

"I'm glad we are doing this." Agnes smiled, settling back onto the velvet-upholstered seat. "I have to admit, I wasn't sure you'd want to go through with our partnership."

"Neither was I," May said frankly.

She let out a long breath, feeling her pulse calm, and kicked her feet onto the foot warmer in the middle of the carriage: a wooden box filled with coal. Simply *owning* a foot warmer was luxurious, and the Endicotts' was engraved with that same family crest. May wondered if they'd brought it over from Chicago with the rest of their luggage, or just commissioned a new one in London.

"So, where should we start?" Agnes asked.

May was surprised to find that she had an answer to this question. Despite her hesitations, the gears of her mind must have been turning all week, considering the best way to bring an American into the heart of society.

"We'll start with church. You'll come to services with me and my mother next weekend. I don't care if you're Anglican or not," she added, before Agnes could protest. "The whole point is that you're there, sitting in one of the back pews, holding a prayer book. You can borrow mine."

Agnes looked a bit miffed at the reference to the back pews. "I can buy my own prayer book."

"Absolutely not. You want an old one that looks like it was handed down through your family. The more battered the cover, the better." May's had belonged to her great-aunt, and smelled like aged paper and faded sachets. If only it actually worked to answer her prayers.

"How typically British," Agnes said drily. "You only think things are valuable if they're old, or if they were made by old men."

May pursed her lips against a smile. "If you do well at church, I might bring you to a musical evening or an afternoon at home. Lady Wolverton is having one soon."

"At homes are only for ladies, though, aren't they?"

"Agnes, you can't be seen directly pursuing men! You'll never get anywhere until the women in society accept you. Or at the very least, until they tolerate you."

It took a moment for May to realize that Agnes was smiling. "When I asked where you wanted to start, I meant what boutique you wanted to visit first. But I'm glad to hear that you've formulated our social plan of attack." Her grin broadened as she added, "I knew I was right to choose you as a friend."

A *friend*. The word shot like a beam of sunlight through May's loneliness.

Their carriage slowed, and she realized belatedly that they had pulled up outside Linton & Curtis. "We aren't going to your house?" she asked, as the driver came down to open the door.

"We can do that later! Come on," Agnes wheedled. "We need to get you something to wear to all these events you're bringing me to!"

May said nothing as she followed Agnes inside, trying not to stare. Rolls of fabric were stacked along every wall: butter-soft silks and crisp taffetas, deep velvets for winter day dresses and floral poplins for spring. One entire wall held selections of lace, which glimmered like enchanted snowdrifts.

Toward the back, glass display cases revealed neat arrangements of buttons—mother-of-pearl buttons, brass buttons, even enamel ones—as well as leather gloves, brooches, feathers. An arched hallway led to what May assumed were private fitting rooms. It was all so bright, and new, and beautiful.

May and her mother never shopped at places like this. When they did purchase new dresses, they ordered them from Madame Renault, a wizened old Frenchwoman who took their measurements at her house and smelled like she hadn't bathed in weeks. She and May's mother inevitably haggled over the prices in angry French before they finally settled the bill. Once, Mary Adelaide had even brought the dressmaker a pheasant that May's father had shot, insisting that its feathers could be used in a hat. The end result had looked atrocious. But then, feathers were expensive.

"Miss Endicott!" A salesclerk emerged from the back of the store, her arms laden with bolts of fabric. She hurriedly set down her burden and adjusted her apron. "My apologies, we didn't know you were joining us today."

Agnes smiled and gestured to May. "We're not shopping for me right now; we're here for Her Serene Highness, Princess Mary of Teck."

Predictably, the salesgirl startled at the use of May's title. "It would be an honor, Your Serene Highness." She hesitated as if uncertain whether to curtsy—it wasn't required, since May wasn't a true royal—then apparently decided to err on the side of caution, and curtsied anyway. "Please, right this way."

"I'm thinking a lot of blues for Her Serene Highness," Agnes declared, as she and May followed the salesgirl into a fitting room. "A deep blue velvet for a riding habit, a blue-gray for a day dress. And then something different for a tea gown—what happened to the carnation-colored silk you showed me last week? With the Alençon lace?"

The salesgirl nodded frantically. "The Alençon has been rather overdone this Season, Miss Endicott. Might I suggest the guipure?"

"Why don't you bring both. With a few silks for formal evening gowns, of course."

May ran her hands nervously down her skirt, an old serge gray one that she'd paired with a simple white blouse. Surrounded by all this luxury, it felt even dowdier than usual. "We won't be needing so many things. I'm only here for one gown," she explained to the salesgirl, who cast a bewildered glance at Agnes.

"Why else did we come, if not to try different dress options?" Agnes said blithely. "This is the fun part!"

The fun part. May couldn't remember the last time she had done something for fun, instead of obligation or guilt or her own desire for self-improvement. The very idea felt childish, selfish.

And yet . . . maybe she could afford to have a little bit of fun, just this once.

"*One* dress," she repeated.

"One dress, with a matching hat and gloves," Agnes negotiated. May threw up her hands in defeat, and Agnes laughed and ducked out of the fitting room.

When May was standing there in nothing but her petticoats and corset, the salesgirl pulled out a cloth measuring tape and knelt to wrap it around May's waist, then her torso, then on and on from her elbow to wrist, knee to ankle. She took far more measurements than Madame Renault ever did.

"Tell me about Lady Wolverton's at home," Agnes asked through the curtain that separated them.

"She's an old friend of my mother's." *One of the pillars of London society,* May should have said. "If you can win her over, the invitations will keep coming."

"Do you think the Princess Maud will be in attendance?" Agnes asked, naming Prince Eddy's younger sister.

"Maud?" Surprised, May twisted her neck to look at Agnes's silhouette. "Why do you ask?"

"She's your cousin, isn't she?"

"A distant cousin. Technically a second cousin once removed," May explained, though Agnes probably didn't care.

The salesgirl took one last measurement and stood, disappearing into the back of the store. The moment May was dressed, Agnes tugged the curtain aside.

"I think you should spend more time with Maud. Getting closer to her can only help you with Prince Eddy."

May froze. It had been strange enough discussing Eddy at the investiture party, but here at the dress boutique, in broad daylight, the topic made her feel foolish. And very exposed.

"Oh, don't be bashful!" Agnes exclaimed. "Can't we talk about it? I want to help see you happy."

"I don't think women *can* be happy."

May immediately winced; she shouldn't have said that aloud. Yet Agnes was staring at her with something like approval. "Why not?"

Perhaps it was the look in Agnes's eyes—a look of intelligence that she was forced to stifle, of eager curiosity she was wise enough to keep hidden—a look that May knew all too well from glancing in the mirror. Whatever the reason, she admitted the truth.

"Safety, position, money: these are the reasons a woman should marry. Not for something as fleeting and insubstantial as happiness, which can evaporate at any moment, leaving you with nothing."

Agnes nodded in agreement. "Which is why you want to be queen. The position with the most safety and wealth of all."

If you knew what my family was like, you would understand, May thought. She pursed her lips and said nothing.

"In that case," Agnes went on, undeterred, "you should absolutely pay more attention to Maud. She's your ticket to the inner circle."

"What do you mean?"

Agnes picked up a soft green moiré from a stack of fabrics and drummed her fingers over it. "How are you supposed to attract the prince's interest if you only ever run into him at crowded receptions? Becoming friends with Maud gives you more opportunities to see His Royal Highness. The more time you spend near him, the better chance you have of convincing him that you are the right choice."

There was an indisputable logic to this. And yet . . .

"Maud and I have never been close. Trust me, I've tried." May had always assumed that Maud and her sister Louise had inherited their parents' snobbery. Uncle Bertie certainly made no secret of his feelings toward the Tecks; he tolerated them with weary reluctance, the way you might resign yourself to a stain in the wooden floorboards that you could never remove.

"Then try again," Agnes commanded. "I suspect that Maud has changed since you were children. No one ever pays her much mind, do they? She seems lonely, constantly overshadowed by her siblings."

It was a bit unsettling how easily Agnes had taken the measure of Maud. The youngest of the Wales children, two years younger than May, Maud had always been ignored in favor of her brothers—the ones who mattered, the heir and the spare—and her vivacious, headstrong older sister.

"You really think it might go differently this time?" May mused aloud.

"Of course. Last time you tried to befriend Maud, you didn't have *me*."

May couldn't help chuckling at the sheer audacity of it. Then her laughter died down, replaced by a puzzled confusion. "Agnes. Why are you helping me?"

"I like a challenge." Agnes smiled, a bit naughtily. "And of course, I wouldn't mind being friends with the future Queen of England. If you marry Prince Eddy, you can help me track down one of these bankrupt dukes that my mother has her heart set on."

SEVERAL WEEKS LATER, THE ENDICOTTS' CARRIAGE PULLED UP outside the Wolvertons' home in Mayfair. The fence surrounding the property seemed unusually frightening, as if the iron spikes were sharper than normal, turning the house into a fortress. And here was May, bringing an interloper inside like the Trojan horse.

She glanced over as they headed up the front steps. Reading the concern in May's eyes, Agnes slowed. "Should I remove my muff?" She gestured with her hands, which were tucked into a roll of fluffy white fur. "I know you said no sables, but you didn't say anything about lynx."

"No—it's fine," May assured her.

She and Agnes had met up a few times since their excursion to Linton & Curtis, always at the Belgravia townhome the Endicotts had rented for the year, because May could never risk bringing Agnes to White Lodge. They would sit in the drawing room, sipping tea, as May did her best to explain the Rules of Behavior.

So far, Agnes had proven an apt pupil. She listened carefully as May warned her about the various women she would encounter, explaining whom to befriend and whom to be wary of. She practiced curtsying to various degrees, because of course one must sink to a different depth for a king versus an earl versus a mere baronet. May had laid a place setting for a full banquet and drilled Agnes on the correct use of every utensil, from the fish fork and oyster fork down to the demitasse spoon.

May hoped she'd done enough, because there was no turning back now.

"Good afternoon." The butler opened the front door before they had even knocked, gesturing to a footman to take their coats. "Lady Wolverton's guests are gathered in the drawing room."

Inside, a dozen or so women of various ages were seated on arrangements of sofas and ottomans. A few of them held cups of tea, and a tray of iced cakes sat on a side table, though they looked untouched. The point of an at home was the conversation, not the refreshments.

Lady Wolverton swept forward. "May, I'm so glad you could join us! You look lovely today."

"Thank you." May resisted the urge to shoot a grateful smile at Agnes. She was wearing the dress they had bought together, a soft blue with navy trim around the wrists and hem. Nothing showy or ostentatious, but it was cut according to the most current styles and fit like a dream.

She gestured to Agnes. "Lady Wolverton, may I present Miss Agnes Endicott, recently arrived here from Chicago." To her relief, Agnes executed a perfect curtsy.

"And how did you meet Miss Endicott?" Lady Wolverton asked May, with distinct coolness.

"Her father is a hunting companion of the Prince of Wales," May said swiftly.

"And who is her father?"

"Mr. Robert Endicott," Agnes offered. "He works in steel manufacturing."

May shot Agnes an incredulous glance. She shouldn't have spoken until she was spoken to; they had reviewed this countless times. What was she thinking?

"Mr. Endicott." Lady Wolverton repeated the name as if it were in a foreign language. More loudly, for the benefit of the room, she added, "I've always thought how trying it must be to grow up in America: all of you clumped together like chickens in a coop, without titles or rank. How on earth do you know which young men to address and which to avoid?"

"We don't, of course."

May closed her eyes. Agnes's words sounded impertinent, even dangerous.

"We rely on our mamas to tell us," Agnes went on sweetly, "as proper young women should."

To May's vast relief, Lady Wolverton took Agnes's statement at face value, unable to even dream that someone might address her with a hint of sarcasm. Only May seemed to have heard the amusement in her friend's voice.

"Yes, a proper young woman should obey her mother in all things. A sentiment that my own daughters have, sadly, failed to internalize," Lady Wolverton said slowly. "Welcome to London, Miss Endicott."

It was a far more ringing endorsement than May had expected.

Recognizing the dismissal, May led Agnes away, and conversation hummed through the room once more. May couldn't be certain, but she heard snatches of words like *fifty thousand a year* and *stands to inherit everything*. If Agnes heard it, too, she revealed nothing.

Then May glanced up and realized, surprised, that Princess Maud was here.

She was seated at the piano, her fingers drifting over the keyboard as she played a gentle background piece—Beethoven, maybe?

Agnes wandered closer. May reached out to pluck at her sleeve, but her friend ignored the warning. She stood there, waiting patiently, until Maud's hands finally came to a rest.

"That was lovely, Your Royal Highness." Agnes sank into her lowest curtsy, tipping her head forward so that her twist of chestnut hair was visible.

"Thank you." Maud paused, and May hurried to step in and make a proper introduction. She expected the princess to turn aside once she realized she was speaking to an American commoner, but Maud studied Agnes with curiosity. "Do you play?"

"Not so well as you! Which has always been a disappointment, as I love listening to music. Your rendition of Schubert was so moving."

So it hadn't been Beethoven after all. May didn't play the piano very often anymore; she only dared practice when her father was out of the house.

"Have you heard his duets? They are even more powerful than the Andante." Maud scooted over on the bench. "We could attempt one now, if you like."

Agnes smiled dazzlingly. "I fear that Schubert is far beyond my abilities. Perhaps Her Serene Highness might play with you?"

May tried to hide her frustration at Agnes's interference. She looked at Maud with a smile that probably came out like a grimace.

"Of course," Maud agreed, seeming bemused.

"Thank you." May sat next to her on the bench, tucking her skirts about her legs. A few other guests glanced over, then quickly lost interest when they saw that it was just May and Maud—the two overlooked, unremarkable princesses.

Maud flipped through the music atop the piano. "What about this one?"

May quickly scanned the page. Neither part looked easy, semiquavers dancing wildly up and down across the bars. Was Maud trying to intimidate her?

"I'll take the top part," she decided, choosing the slightly less terrifying of the two.

Maud held her hands over the keys. May drew off her gloves and set them carefully atop the piano next to Maud's—at least they were new ones, she noted with relief.

The piece began with a disingenuous calm, as Schubert was wont to do, but it escalated quickly. There were several moments when May's hands danced over Maud's, but after a minute she no longer noticed; the music required every ounce of her concentration.

May was aware that she lacked the innate talent of a truly great musician. But she'd always appreciated the piano for rewarding diligence: if you kept at it with enough stubbornness, you could muscle your way into a level of competency. As a child, she used to chain herself to the bench for hours, practicing various pieces over and over until she could perform them with her eyes closed. She might as well be good at something ornamental, she had thought, since she wasn't destined to be a great beauty.

When the duet drew to a close, she and Maud struck their final chord at exactly the same moment. May looked up, meeting Maud's gaze, and was surprised to see a smile there.

Perhaps Agnes was right; perhaps Maud wasn't as pretentious as May had assumed. It was unnerving, realizing that she had likely misjudged her cousin the way everyone was always misjudging her.

But how was anyone supposed to know the truth about another person when society forbade you from revealing your true self? When all you spoke about was insignificant gossip and trivial details? May realized with a shock that she knew more about Agnes after a matter of weeks than she knew about most people in her life—because Agnes had peeled back the veneer of polite conversation and spoken frankly.

"I enjoyed that," Maud ventured.

May smiled. "We should do it again, though I would prefer to practice before performing in public once more."

For a moment she worried she'd overstepped, but Maud nodded in agreement. "Why don't you come over next week? Mama receives on Tuesdays at three."

An invitation to Marlborough House, after just a single duet at the piano?

If she had known it would be this easy, May would have attempted it long ago.

CHAPTER TWELVE

Alix

IT FELT SURREAL, ALMOST MAGICAL, WEARING BLACK TO A FORmal party. Staring around the ballroom of the Winter Palace, Alix thought that the world had been temporarily leached of all color, the entire scene drawn in shades of white and black, shadow and light.

She reached for Ella's hand and squeezed it. "I can't believe I'm leaving tomorrow."

"It's gone by too fast!" There was the slightest quaver to Ella's voice as she added, "I'll miss you and Ernie so much."

They both glanced at their brother, who was whirling about the dance floor with one of the Romanov cousins, looking quite debonair in his black tailcoat and bow tie. There were no mirrors in the ballroom, just gilded tracery on the walls and a profusion of flowers—imported at great expense from the Crimea—on every surface. But Alix could look at Ernie and know that she was the same: the dark fabric making her blue eyes glow, turning her long hair into a blaze of gold.

"Thank you for lending me the dress," she added softly. She hadn't brought anything black because she wasn't in mourning; all her evening gowns were bright with color.

"A *bal noir*," Ella mused. "Isn't it a unique idea, making

everyone wear the same color? I only wish it weren't black," she added, in a rare display of disloyalty to her in-laws. "Think how enchanting this might feel if we all dressed in white. Or red!"

Alix smiled softly. "If you throw such a ball, I promise to come back for it."

"Even in the winter?"

"Especially in the winter."

Having grown up in Darmstadt, Alix thought she knew cold, but she'd never felt anything like a Russian winter. The bitter wind off the Neva River sank its claws through her layers of fur, bit searingly at her skin. Yet Russians didn't let the temperature slow them down. At home in Germany, and in England, the social season stretched over the summer months; Alix was used to spending the winter in bed, with a hot water bottle at her feet.

Yet this was the height of St. Petersburg's Season, which began on New Year's Day and lasted until the start of Lent. Night after night, at Ella and Sergei's urging, Alix and Ernie had bundled into their furs and gone out in a sleigh, skimming over the snowy streets to the theater or the opera, to balls and banquets.

Every aristocrat in Russia must have spent a small fortune hosting parties that Season—on entertainment, on groaning tables of food, and most of all on the fuel: wood for the stoves and gas for the chandeliers, not to mention the long wax tapers that burned in silver candelabra. It was as if they thought they could hold the long Russian nights at bay if only they had enough light. Often Alix and Ella didn't come home until dawn streaked the sky, though Alix resolved never to tell Grandmama this fact.

"Oh, here comes Nicholas," Ella said brightly.

Alix's heart skipped at the sight of the tsarevich, who was moving unmistakably in their direction.

She'd seen him a little over the past six weeks, though she wished it had been more. As the heir to the throne, he had other demands on his time, other people flocking about him asking for favors or advice. Whenever his eyes met Alix's, he would flash her one of his rare, brief smiles, and she would glow from within.

When Alix was lucky enough to be seated near Nicholas, she inevitably threw etiquette to the winds and ignored the partner on her other side so that she could talk to him. He was full of stories—lighthearted ones that made her laugh, like the time he and his brother Misha had climbed onto the roof of the Winter Palace and gotten stuck there, as well as serious ones about his time in the army, or his grandfather. He made a point of asking Alix about herself and always listened with careful attention.

He was so achingly handsome, but that wasn't what drew Alix to him. Nicholas was wholly and completely himself, without the bluster or bravado that characterized most men. He made his opinions after much gathering of facts, and then, when he acted, his movements were consistent with those opinions. He was like an arrow, straight and true.

"Alix," Nicholas said when he'd reached her. "Would you like to dance?"

"I— Of course."

She placed her palm in his and let him tug her to the center of the ballroom, where couples swirled over the polished wood floors. Normally, Alix tried to avoid dancing; no matter how gracefully she waltzed with her dance instructor, she inevitably tripped or forgot the steps in public.

Dancing with Nicholas would be just as bad as it had been when she danced with Eddy in London. Already she could feel everyone staring at her, whispering about her. *That awkward German girl*, they were probably saying, *she's nowhere as stylish or confident as her sister. . . .*

Nicholas's left hand clasped her right, his other arm settling around her waist. The feel of him was steadying. As they launched into the first steps of the dance, Alix tried to focus on that—the sensation of his hand, separated from her skin by only a few layers of fabric. But the old panic began to stir in her chest.

"Are you all right, Alix?"

She attempted a smile, though it came out wobbly. "I'm all right."

The ballroom was a black-hued blur. The cacophony of gossip and music receded in her ears, replaced by the haunting sound of childish laughter.

Alix fought off a wave of dizziness. Not here, not *now*. She had managed to avoid an episode throughout this entire visit; surely she could make it one more day.

Nicholas drew to a halt, nearly making her stumble. "You're unwell," he observed, frowning. "I'll get you a glass of wine."

Alix shook her head. She couldn't bear to go into the neighboring salon, where women in low-cut dresses and men with loud voices picked over the late-night feast—chicken in cream, stuffed eggs, and six different kinds of caviar.

"I just need some air," she managed.

Nicholas nodded. "Follow me."

Wordlessly, Alix let him lead her out of the ballroom and down a hallway, until they turned down another hallway she didn't recognize. The cacophony of the party was suddenly very distant.

"Thank you," she breathed, her steps slowing. "I'm not sure what came over me."

Nicholas shrugged. "This party makes one feel oddly claustrophobic, doesn't it? Everyone looking the same, like a horde of ghosts dressed in black."

She was startled to hear him echo her own thoughts. "It *is* rather difficult to locate someone when we are all wearing the same color."

"But I found you, didn't I?"

Alix was unnervingly aware of her pulse, of how acutely alone they were. She hesitated, glancing over her shoulder as if a chaperone might materialize out of thin air. "We should probably head back. . . ."

"Of course." Nicholas hesitated. "But . . . I won't tell if you won't."

Alix gave a hesitant smile, finally taking in her surroundings. Gas sconces illuminated a hallway lined with oil paintings, most of which depicted bearded, scowling men dressed in ermine cloaks and crowns.

"I haven't seen this part of the palace."

"It's easy to get lost in. Mother and I prefer staying at the Anichov," Nicholas explained, naming the palace where they had welcomed Alix for tea at the start of her visit. It still boggled her mind that the Romanovs had so many palaces they could afford to live in one and use another just for entertaining and state events. "Though when Misha and I were little, we loved playing at soldiers in these halls. My parents had given us wooden toy swords, which actually proved quite destructive."

"Ernie had one of those! My father took it away when Ernie knocked over a crystal candlestick."

Nicholas chuckled. "Misha shattered his fair share of candlesticks and porcelain vases. Once he splintered the entire leg of a wooden side table."

"And he wasn't punished?" Alix asked, surprised.

"Oh, you know how my father is. He just laughed and clapped Misha on the back—said he was glad that one of his sons, at least, was a true Romanov."

Nicholas spoke casually, but Alix sensed that he was hurt. She felt touched that he'd shared something like this with her.

"I don't think your father was being fair. What defines a true Romanov if not someone brave and intelligent?"

"A Romanov shows only strength, and never reveals weakness." The words came out so automatically that Alix knew they had been drilled into Nicholas from a young age. He gestured to a portrait on their left. "Like Peter the Great, who refused to accept defeat. Did you know he built this entire city from nothing? The whole area was swampland, but Peter insisted that it would be his legacy. He lived here for two years, in a shack no better than a hut, laying stones alongside the laborers until the main streets of St. Petersburg were paved."

Alix stepped closer to the painting. She had heard the story of St. Petersburg: how Peter the Great had brought it into existence through brute strength. Not to mention the suffering of countless people.

In the portrait, Peter stood in full armor, a red-plumed

helmet cradled in one arm. Yet he didn't look warlike or even particularly dangerous. His face, cast half in shadow, was etched with lines that suggested sorrow.

"He looks unhappy," Alix murmured.

"He *was* unhappy. Despite all his victories for Russia, he lost both his sons, leaving the succession in question upon his death."

"Who succeeded him?"

"His second wife became empress, though she only lived another two years. Apparently they were very much in love, and once Peter was gone, she died of a broken heart."

Alix glanced over, surprised at the romantic nature of the story, but Nicholas had started walking farther down the corridor. She trotted to keep up, listening as he gestured to each portrait in turn. "Then we had a series of brief rulers—Peter II, Anna, Ivan, Elizabeth, *another* Peter—until Catherine the Great."

The full-length portrait depicted Catherine in her later years, dressed in full court attire. The Romanov Imperial Crown, its surface encrusted with diamonds, sat atop her head.

"Peter the Great, Catherine the Great. The only other 'Great' I can think of is Charlemagne," Alix observed.

"It's not an epithet that is frequently bestowed." Nicholas hesitated before adding, "When I was little, I told my tutor that I would be remembered in history as Nicholas the Great. He said it was impossible."

"Why?"

"He told me that 'the Great' was a term used for people who changed the world, and that Russia was done changing.

That it was no use trying to modernize Russia any more than it already had been."

Alix wasn't quite certain what Nicholas meant by modernization—building more factories? Changing the political structure?—but decided that the details weren't relevant. If anyone could change this great giant of a nation, it was the young man before her.

"Of course Russia can change," she said adamantly. "But it won't happen the traditional Romanov way, through stubbornness and sheer force of will."

Nicholas stared at her. "What do you mean?"

"Russia is vast. It may have been enough for Peter the Great to live in a hut and pave the roads alongside his men, but that kind of action won't work any longer. In Hesse it might," she added, with a self-deprecating smile. "Did I tell you that every Christmas, I distribute baskets of bread around the village? That's *our* way of combating poverty."

"You distribute baskets of bread," Nicholas repeated.

Alix reddened. She hadn't meant to remind him of the disparities in their positions—the fact that her father led a small German duchy, while his father controlled one-sixth of the earth's surface.

"Yes, every Christmas," she said firmly, determined not to be embarrassed by something so important to her. "That kind of charity would never succeed in Russia. It would be like trying to stop a torrential flood by laying a single row of bricks."

"I'm afraid I would run out of bread." Nicholas flashed her a teasing smile, which gave Alix the courage to continue.

"What I mean is, Peter the Great's approach won't work for modern Russia. To change things now requires more than action; it requires *ideas*. And you have plenty of those. It will be difficult, certainly, because everything is more extreme in Russia—your nights are longer, your cold is more bitter, your parties are more . . . dramatic. You cannot do things by half measure here. But it's no use trying to make the present along the same lines as the past."

She flung out a hand, indicating the painted faces of all the long-dead tsars and tsarinas. They were meant to inspire awe, but they suddenly seemed so flat and dull compared to the living, breathing man before her.

"You are here, and *you* are the future of Russia. It's time to look forward, not back," she finished.

Nicholas was watching her, an unreadable expression on his face. "You know, Alix, you're more Russian than you realize."

"There are certain things I would enjoy about being Russian," she agreed: a bold declaration, though it came out in a whisper.

Nicholas's eyes met hers. Alix felt something stirring inside her, pulling her forward and terrifying her at the same time.

She took an unconscious step toward him—and as she did, her heel caught in her hem.

For a terrifying moment Alix thought she might crash to the floor; she flung her arms out and closed her eyes, praying she wouldn't knock over some priceless bronze bust. Then a pair of hands closed around her waist.

Alix should have just let Nicholas pull her upright. But she was flustered, and whipped her head toward him as he turned his cheek away—causing her mouth to brush against his.

For a fraction of an instant, Nicholas's lips softened, before he set her on her feet.

Neither of them spoke. They just stood there for a moment, the only sound the echo of Alix's heart thudding wildly and frantically in her chest.

Nicholas's gaze dropped from Alix's eyes to her lips. The almost-kiss hovered between them, as gossamer and fragile as a butterfly. Alix found that she wanted to snatch it up and hold it close.

Then the tsarevich's expression shuttered. "We should return to the party."

Alix hurried to step back, forcing a smile. "Clumsy me! I always trip when I borrow Ella's gowns, since she's slightly taller." Somehow she managed to hide the bitter sting of his rejection, or whatever had just happened between them.

Really, nothing *had* happened, she told herself. Alix had tripped, and Nicholas had stepped forward like a gentleman to help her; that was all.

He obviously thought nothing more of it, so neither would she.

CHAPTER THIRTEEN

Hélène

HÉLÈNE HAD ALWAYS LOVED THE RACES AT EPSOM DOWNS. SHE was aware that few women shared her opinion; they preferred the social parade of Ascot, where no one seemed to care about the horses at all. It was just a fashion show to them, an excuse to gossip about everyone else in the Royal Enclosure.

Epsom Downs was positively shabby by contrast. The stands surrounding the racetrack were constructed of simple white deal board; even here in a box, the only sign of exclusivity was the fringed red baize that swagged along the walls.

Hélène braced her palms on the railing of Lord and Lady Hardwicke's box, vaguely listening to the chatter of the guests behind her, including her parents. Down on the course, men with brooms and shovels were smoothing out the divots made by yesterday's racers. The first race would start soon; she could see grooms walking the horses behind the starting gates.

"Who do you favor?"

A thrill shot through Hélène as Prince Eddy came to stand next to her. In the sultry heat of early June, he wore a gray morning suit like all the other gentlemen, yet to Hélène he shone as if lit by a spotlight.

"I wasn't sure I would get to see you today," she said under her breath. Eddy was always at Epsom—his father was a racing enthusiast, or more accurately a gambling enthusiast—but it was hard to know whether Eddy would be able to sneak away at events like this.

"And miss the chance to watch the race with the one person whose opinion I value?" Eddy's mouth lifted in a smile. "You haven't answered my question. Which horse do you favor?"

"Galahad," Hélène declared.

"Really? My money is on Orlando."

"The Earl of Sackville's horse? But *Sporting Life* magazine ranked him near the bottom of the entrants!"

Eddy chuckled at her admission of having read a men's magazine. "Well, I disagree with the *Sporting Life* editors. Orlando was sired by Mortimer," he added, naming a famous racehorse from ten years ago, "and lineage inevitably plays a role when it comes to racing."

Not just racing, Hélène thought. Her own lineage seemed to cause her nothing but problems.

Out of unspoken agreement, she and Eddy had drawn farther along the railing, away from the crowds that would soon begin to press forward. He stepped closer, his shoulder brushing hers in a movement that might have looked accidental to a bystander. "Are we agreed upon a wager, then? Orlando versus Galahad?"

"I suppose it depends on the stakes."

Eddy lifted an eyebrow. "What are you suggesting?"

"Oh, I'm sure I can find a way to make you pay off your debts," Hélène replied, her tone deliberately, deliciously, vague.

But Eddy's next words weren't light or teasing at all. "If I win, will you come to Balmoral with me?"

Her heart skidded. "What?"

"I can't actually host you at Balmoral Castle," Eddy explained. "But I asked Louise if you could stay with her, and she agreed. She and Alexander are close by at Mar Lodge."

He had involved his *sister*? "Eddy. What did you tell Louise?"

"The truth. That I can't face Balmoral without you there."

When Hélène stared at him, he hurried to add: "We can trust Louise, I swear. I wouldn't have dreamed of mentioning this to Maud or George, but Louise and I . . . we've always understood each other. She supports us."

Hélène's heart seized at the searching, pleading look in his eyes. He leaned a hip against the wooden railing in a deceptively casual gesture, but his attention wasn't on the racetrack. It was on her.

"Eddy," Hélène whispered. "Turn around." The trumpeters were gathering near the starting gates; the race would begin soon.

"Just—tell me what you're thinking," he insisted.

She was thinking that things had escalated further than either of them had anticipated. That seeing Eddy in London, illicitly, was nowhere near as risky as sneaking around under his family's noses.

"You will love Scotland, Hélène!" Eddy had turned to face the racetrack, but his hands gripped the railing with uncharacteristic tightness. "I want to show you everything—the hills so steep that you can only navigate on horseback, the loch where I learned to swim, the way the brush looks at twilight."

Oh, this was dangerous. If they were ever exposed, *she* was the one who would suffer for it, not him. She stood to lose so much.

When she'd begun their affair last year, she'd never dreamed that it would go on this long. Or that the stakes would grow so high.

"I will come," she heard herself say, and Eddy broke into a smile. Hélène realized, then, just how much she adored those smiles—how thrilled she was to be the cause of them.

So much had changed since the first night they had met in secret.

Hélène had waited until the house was still: the fires in the kitchen banked, footsteps creaking along the upstairs corridor as the last few maids went to sleep. Then she'd slipped into one of her simplest gowns, a charcoal-colored one that laced up the front instead of the back, and padded on silent feet down the servants' staircase. It was eerily similar to what she used to do when she'd visited Laurent, except that instead of turning toward the barn, Hélène started toward the front of the house. In her dark gown, a heavy cloak swirling around her, she was as fleeting and insubstantial as the wraiths her old governess used to tell stories about.

The carriage Eddy had sent was waiting around the bend in the road. When Hélène slipped into it, the driver said nothing, just clucked at the horses and started off.

The apartments he took her to were surprisingly simple: just a room that served as both kitchen and footman's quarters, which led to a massive bedroom. Hélène darted her gaze from the four-poster bed with gold-fringed hangings that dominated the space. The purpose of these apartments was abundantly clear, especially now that Hélène had seen how smoothly it all went—the carriage pickup, the bottle of red wine waiting on a side table with two glasses.

Eddy was in an armchair by the stone fireplace; at the sound of her footsteps he hurried to stand.

"Hélène. You came."

"Yes," she said softly, twisting her hands together to fiddle with her rings. Eddy's gaze drifted from the gesture to the pulse that must be fluttering wildly at her neck. He took a step forward and caught one of her hands in his, lacing their fingers.

"You're nervous," he observed.

Hélène's protests died in her throat. She *was* nervous, a ridiculous emotion since this was hardly her first time, yet this felt more monumental than anything she'd done with Laurent. Eddy was a future *king*.

He let go, and Hélène resisted the urge to snatch his hand back; somehow she felt braver and more centered when he was touching her. He poured two glasses of wine and handed one to her, then gestured to the opposite armchair.

Confused, she glanced toward the bed. "You don't want to . . ."

"Would you mind if we sat for a moment?" He phrased it as if she'd be doing him a favor, though she suspected that he was slowing down for her sake. "And I should have asked— when do you need the carriage to take you home?"

"The kitchen maids wake at dawn. I just need to be upstairs before that."

"Perfect. Dawn is hours away."

Hélène leaned back and took a sip of her wine. Already this encounter was drastically different from her hurried, frantic couplings with Laurent. If she hadn't known better, she might have said that Eddy was *wooing* her, but she was already here, ready to bed him, so that didn't make sense.

To her shock, the prince leaned down to grab one of her feet. He tugged it up onto his lap, and then—slowly, with great gentleness—unlaced her boot and tossed it aside.

Hélène went very still as his hands skimmed beneath her dress, all the way up to her inner thigh. She let out an involuntary gasp of pleasure, yet Eddy didn't venture higher. He grabbed her garter and peeled off her stocking.

"What are you doing?" Her words came out in a whispered gasp.

"Setting us both at ease." Eddy began massaging the arch of her foot, almost absently. His eyes gleamed in the firelight.

"I hardly think this is setting *you* at ease." It should have been impossible for Hélène to relax, with a prince massaging her feet the way a lady's maid would after a long evening. Yet the tension was, in fact, seeping from her body.

"I don't make a habit of taking women to bed when they're wary of me."

Hélène couldn't hold back the giggle that escaped her lips. "I'm not a skittish horse, Eddy. You don't need to groom me before you ride me."

A lady should never have *thought* such a sentence, let alone spoken it aloud, yet Eddy just gave an appreciative laugh. "I never underestimate the importance of grooming. Sebastian—my father's Master of Horse—taught me how to stable my ponies when I was five. He said that if you can't care for an animal, you have no business being its master."

"My father's groom said the same thing! He was always trying to teach my brother how to pick out hooves or use a round brush. Philippe never had the patience for it, but I did. I was sneaking out to the stables and braiding the horses' tails long before I learned to ride."

Eddy's expression softened. "Do you miss France?"

It was the type of question that no one ever asked in society, because no one ever talked about anything *real*. Yet Eddy had cut straight to the paradox that dominated Hélène's existence. France was everything to her, yet at the same time nothing at all—a cipher, a symbol, a repository of half-forgotten memories that often felt like they belonged to someone else.

"Sometimes," she admitted.

Eddy waited for her to continue. He'd pulled his chair closer and let his hands slide higher, gently massaging her calf muscles. His fingers were rougher than she would have guessed, scratchy with calluses, but his grip was warm and certain.

"When I miss Paris, it's mostly the small things. The scent of rosemary outside my window, the sound of the church bells all chiming the hour at the same moment," she recalled. "But more than that, it's the haunting feeling that there is this other life I could have led, if things had gone differently. I would have been a *real* princess, one whose father was a true acting king."

Eddy's fingers fell still. "I can't pretend to understand what you and your family went through, being forced to flee your homeland. But I know that feeling of rootlessness, of not knowing where you belong."

Hélène stared at him. "You're the future king. You belong here more than anyone."

"Yet my family would exile me, given half a chance." Eddy said it flatly, the way he might remark upon the weather. "Grandmother is disappointed in me. I'm not as clever as George, with his books and all his endless correspondence.

Did you know he wrote Mother a five-page letter every week while we were in the navy?"

"I never have the patience for long letters, either," Hélène admitted. "There are better ways to spend that time."

"Exactly! Grandmother is always scolding me for what she calls my 'lack of attention.' She says that a king who can only speak English is an embarrassment. But no matter how hard I tried at Latin or German, it never stuck."

Hélène nudged her foot playfully into his chest. "Would it help if I taught you some French?"

"It can't hurt." A slow smile spread over Eddy's face. "All I've managed thus far is *Enchanté, mademoiselle,* and *Vous êtes très belle.*"

"An auspicious start," Hélène teased.

"*Très belle,*" he repeated, his eyes lifting to meet hers.

The air in the room was suddenly heavy with significance, with anticipation.

Hélène rose to her feet and crossed the two paces to Eddy's chair. Slowly, she lowered herself to sit on his lap—not the way a child would, with her back to his chest, but wantonly. Face to face.

Eddy held himself very still as she reached around his head to play with the curls at the nape of his neck. His eyes were like pale blue flames.

Hélène dipped her head, lowering her mouth to his.

The kiss was soft at first, surprisingly tender. Eddy's hands resumed their quest over her body, gliding down her back to settle around her hips. Hélène made a sound of pleasure deep in her throat.

When he pulled back, a question in his gaze, she just nodded. For once, she had no words.

Eddy scooped her up in a single motion and carried her to the bed, where he deposited her atop the coverlet, stretched out alongside her, and resumed their kiss.

Afterward, when Hélène tilted her head onto his chest, she was surprised to feel Eddy momentarily tense—but then his arm folded around her, tugging her closer. She realized that he wasn't accustomed to this part, that most women he slept with were probably too awed to curl up next to him as if he were an ordinary man.

Princes, it would seem, were quite solitary creatures. Like the wolves that used to roam around her family's house in Normandy.

Well, that ended now, Hélène thought, twirling a hand over the spot where his heart beat. Eddy might be experienced, but he had a thing or two to learn about intimacy. And she would be only too happy to teach him.

THE SOUND OF CHEERING INTERRUPTED THE FLUSHED HEAT OF Hélène's memories. That first night felt so long ago now, though it had only been six months. Six months of illicit moments, of furtive glances at crowded events, of nights that always ended too soon.

The horses stood at the starting line, prancing as the course clerk climbed up to his podium. The trumpeters played a short fanfare, and the roar of noise in the stadium fell abruptly still. The clerk lifted a red-and-yellow flag overhead—then, when the music stopped, he swung it down.

A cloud of dust exploded from behind the starting line.

Hélène heard Eddy's shouts to her left and glanced over, amused; he was as enthusiastic as the laborers in the stands below. The other guests in the Hardwickes' box began to press around them, leaning on the railing in their curiosity. Epsom Downs was a fast race, usually over in two minutes.

"Orlando!" erupted through the stands when a bay Thoroughbred tore across the finish line.

"Looks like I was right, and *Sporting Life* was mistaken."

Eddy was deliberately looking away from her, the words spoken under his breath, but Hélène was far too attuned to his presence not to hear.

"I suppose I owe you, then." She matched his casual posture.

"I'll see you in Scotland," he replied, unable to hide his smile.

One of the other guests came over to grab Eddy's attention. Hélène stepped back as if they'd been talking about nothing of importance, forcing herself to glance down at the field. Already grooms were leading the sweating horses away to be curried.

That was when she saw Laurent.

He stood in the open space along the edge of the racetrack, where the cheapest tickets were sold for standing room only. It was clear that he'd been watching her. When their eyes met, he jerked his head to the side with unmistakable intent.

What was he *doing* here? Hélène wished she could turn aside, pretend that she hadn't seen him, except that then Laurent might cause a scene. She had no choice but to go down and hear him out, whatever he wanted.

Hélène started toward the back of the box as if she were

headed to the lavatories. No one questioned her; within moments she'd clattered down the staircase, holding the hem of her skirts to keep from tripping, and surged out into the crowds at the back of the stands.

As she'd expected, Laurent was there, waiting for her. The collar of his shirt had fallen open, revealing that his neck was sunburned. Hélène looked away.

It was strange: the version of herself that had loved him, or thought she loved him, felt so young. Seeing him again was like trying on a gown from last Season that no longer fit, constricting and itchy.

"I'm surprised to see you," she admitted.

"The Marquis de Breteuil is thinking of buying one of the horses from today's race. Or, failing that, of putting one of his mares to stud with the winner."

Of course. The marquis was a notorious racing fanatic; Hélène should have seen this coming. It showed how little thought she'd given to Laurent over the past months that she hadn't even considered the possibility of seeing him.

"Hélène," he added—then, at her glare, quickly amended, "Your Royal Highness. May I have a moment?"

She gave a reluctant nod, allowing him to lead her in the direction of the stables. While this wasn't ideal, it was a public enough setting not to be wholly improper, either; there was nothing wrong with a former groom showing her the stables in broad daylight.

Laurent waited until they were sheltered behind a storage shed before clearing his throat. "I'm sorry to do this here, but I don't know when I'll see you again." He stared at her pleadingly. "I miss you. Letting go of you was the biggest mistake I ever made."

Hélène felt the blood drain from her face. Taking her silence as encouragement, Laurent kept going.

"I'm sorry I didn't run away with you last year, when you wanted to elope. If your feelings haven't changed . . ." He shocked her by reaching for her hands. "I can't give you everything you're accustomed to, but I keep thinking about what you said: that all we needed was each other and a stable full of horses. The life I've built in the marquis's service is a good one. We could be happy there."

Hélène blinked and tugged her hands away.

"Laurent, no," she said gently.

"Why not?"

Because she was involved with someone else. And yet, even if nothing had ever happened with Eddy, Hélène knew she wouldn't have gone back to Laurent. She couldn't trust someone who had left her so carelessly, so callously.

"It's too late for us, Laurent. I gave my heart into your keeping and you treated it carelessly."

"It's never too late." He hesitated. "Unless you have fallen for someone else."

Was she falling for Eddy? It was something Hélène didn't dare admit, not even in the privacy of her own mind. *Affair, relationship, liaison*—she used all kinds of words to explain it to herself, everything but that single, infinitely dangerous word. *Love.*

Laurent must have seen the truth on her face. "This man . . . does he know about you and me?"

"He knows enough, but not the details." *Not who you are,* Hélène didn't need to say. Eddy was aware that there had been someone else before him, but he was too much a gentleman to probe.

Laurent let out a breath, understanding. If Hélène was involved with someone who knew she was no innocent, then either that man didn't especially care about her—or he loved her enough not to be bothered by it.

"Who is he?"

"You can hardly expect me to tell you that."

"I'm sorry." Laurent braced a palm on a hay bale, tugging absently at a few strands of straw. "Well . . . I suppose this is goodbye."

Hélène looked at him then: the sort of searching look that takes inventory of a person's strengths as well as their flaws. She and Laurent had been over for a long time, yet there was something bittersweet about hearing him say the word *goodbye*, as if she were closing a chapter of her past. So much had changed since they parted. Back then she'd been such a child. What was that Bible verse? *For then I saw through a glass darkly, but now face to face.*

Hélène wasn't a child anymore; she was woman enough to look at her past, face to face, without flinching. And then to let it go.

"Goodbye, Laurent," she said simply.

He nodded and started toward the stables. Hélène stood there for a moment, watching him walk away, letting her heart settle back into its normal rhythm. She hadn't anticipated how much it would unsettle her, confronting the ghosts of her past. And yet, as she made her way back to the box where Eddy waited, she couldn't help feeling that she was moving toward her future.

CHAPTER FOURTEEN

May

IT WAS SHOCKING, REALLY, THAT THE ROYAL FAMILY PATRONIZED an event like Epsom Downs. The stands below were full of laborers in shirtsleeves, their mouths full of sausage rolls and oranges, the peels and wax paper strewn carelessly over the seats.

Certainly this was nowhere as civilized as Ascot, where everyone at least *dressed* appropriately. Where gambling was done discreetly, among gentlemen, instead of with ragged shouts at the betting post.

"He's not in the royal box," Agnes remarked, so quietly that only May could hear. "Where do you think he went?"

There was no need to clarify which *he* she meant. They both knew Agnes was talking about Prince Eddy.

"He's probably just visiting someone." Or placing a bet, or watching a cockfight out on the grounds.

The other guests of Agnes's parents—mostly wealthy Americans, with a smattering of British aristocrats—milled about the box, holding glasses of lemonade and staring down at the racetrack. May's gloved hands closed over the railing as she dared a quick glance around the stands.

The Posonbys' box was to the right, filled with the sort of

second-rate nobility May would expect from them. Further along was Lady Leticia Dreier, looking absolutely terrible in an *eau de Nil* hat—really, someone should tell her that color made her skin look positively green—and who was she talking to? May couldn't tell from this distance, but she suspected it was one of the Cubitt boys: all four of them were tall and lanky, with that reddish-blond hair. As Agnes had said, the royal box yielded no sign of Eddy, just the red-faced Prince of Wales and his wife.

Then, a few boxes further, she caught sight of Eddy.

"He's in the Hardwickes' box," she told Agnes. Not all that surprising; Charles Hardwicke was the sort of nobleman Eddy gravitated toward: poorly educated and charmingly ill-behaved.

Agnes adjusted her hat, refastening the silk bow beneath her chin. "You're going to the royal box soon, aren't you?"

For a panicked moment May thought her friend was fishing for an introduction, but Agnes just sighed longingly. "Surely you want to thank them for inviting you to Balmoral? Please, promise you'll write me with every last detail!"

"I'm only there as a guest of the Princess Maud. I'm not really part of the royal party," May pointed out, but Agnes waved away the protest.

"It doesn't matter how you got there! The important thing is that you'll be there at all!"

May still couldn't quite believe she'd been invited. Ultimately, she had Agnes to thank, since without Agnes's prompting she wouldn't have ever grown close to Maud. Over the past months, May had slowly built up a relationship with Eddy's sister. It had started with the occasional "surprise encounter" at church or in Hyde Park—encounters that were carefully staged, of course—but the real turning point had come when May devoted more time to the Needlework Guild.

Like all gently born young women, May had stitched a shirt or two for the guild every year since she was a child; it was the sort of token charity work that was expected of her station. But once she'd learned how deeply Maud was involved with the guild, May had started volunteering there, too. Now she spent several days a week at the Imperial Institute in South Kensington, checking lists and sorting clothes into enormous cloth bags, with Maud at the table next to her. It was tedious work, but every last stitch had been worth it when the invitation to Balmoral arrived.

Though Queen Victoria rarely wrote to White Lodge, May had recognized her stationery at once. The royal crest bloomed at the top of the page: a blue *VR* for Victoria Regina, the letters overlaid one atop the other with the emblem of a crown on top. Curlicues swirled out from the letters like tendrils of a creeping blue vine.

My dear Mary Adelaide, the letter had begun; typical of Queen Victoria to send the invitation through her mother rather than directly to May.

I should be most delighted if May and Adolphus could join us at Balmoral soon. We shall have a merry party with the Wales family in attendance, and it would be a delight to have your two children along as well.

May had been horrified at her mother's response: that Dolly couldn't make it, but she, Mary Adelaide, would be utterly delighted to accompany her daughter to Balmoral.

The queen had blatantly ignored the suggestion, and replied that May could journey with Princess Alix of Hesse by train, chaperoned by one of Victoria's ladies-in-waiting. The queen and the Waleses would already be at Balmoral when they arrived, having gone up to Scotland earlier in the month.

"What are you going to pack? Do you need to borrow anything?" Agnes offered.

"I'll be all right, thank you." May had accepted far too much of her friend's generosity already. Agnes had bought her several new gowns—now that Linton & Curtis had May's measurements on file, it was easy for Agnes to keep ordering them—not to mention all the small gifts she kept bestowing: a set of cream-colored gloves, a newly trimmed hat with gleaming dark feathers. *I bought it by mistake; it's not my color,* Agnes would say, or *I'm tired of it and want the space in my wardrobe, please take it off my hands.* May knew she should refuse, but it was just so lovely seeing the warm concern in Agnes's eyes. The look of a *friend.*

And each time she put on one of the new dresses, May felt a touch braver, as if some of Agnes's American boldness had rubbed off onto the fabric.

"At the very least please borrow some of my trunks! You'll need them for the train," Agnes was saying. "You're going with Alix, right? I wonder how long the journey is."

"It should take a day. We'll sleep on the train and arrive in the morning," May explained.

Her friend lifted an eyebrow. "Plenty of time for you to find out how the long-distance courtship has been going."

"Poorly, I would imagine, given what a notoriously bad correspondent Eddy is." May sighed. "Not that it matters.

We both know why Alix will be there." Unlike May, who'd barely scraped herself an invitation through Maud, Alix had been asked to Balmoral by the queen herself. May suspected that Victoria had been waiting for this trip since last summer, when she'd first suggested that Eddy and Alix start courting. She would keep shoving Alix and Eddy together every chance she got—which meant that May would have to work a thousand times harder than Alix if she wanted a fighting chance.

"Perhaps Alix will break off the courtship herself. Didn't you say she isn't very interested in His Royal Highness?"

The hot sun was making May uncharitable, or perhaps her own long-simmering resentments had bubbled to the forefront, because she blurted out, "Alix isn't cut out to be queen. She can't even handle a performance at the opera without collapsing into hysterics!"

A trumpet blared down on the course; the race would start soon. The other guests began pressing forward, eager for space along the railing. Agnes seized May unceremoniously by the elbow and tugged her backward.

"What did you just say?"

May hesitated, guilt threading its way through her stomach, but then she told Agnes what had happened at the opera last year—how she'd seen Alix in the grip of something that definitely wasn't a normal fainting spell. When she'd finished, Agnes stared at her in quiet shock.

"You haven't told anyone?" Agnes whispered.

"Not until just now."

"But, May, Her Majesty deserves to know! She is trying to groom Alix for a public role, one that Alix clearly isn't suited for!"

"She is certainly shy," May agreed, but Agnes cut her off.

"*Shy* is being reluctant to dance with a man you've just met. No, Alix is something more than shy; she sounds . . . damaged."

Agnes might as well have used the word *ruined*. To be on the marriage market and be branded *damaged*? Why, you would never marry at all.

"I don't see what I can do," May whispered.

Down on the racetrack, the horses took off in a thunder of hooves. Neither of the young women glanced their way.

"I'm just surprised you don't want to tell Her Majesty, or at least tell *someone*. You are trying to marry a prince, and you are in possession of critical information about your greatest competition! Oh, don't look at me like that," Agnes went on, throwing up her hands. "You obviously think I'm being heartless. But this is to Alix's benefit too, isn't it? If she's as romantic as you say, if she really does want to marry for love, then she would never be happy with His Royal Highness."

May's mind was lurching from one confused thought to the next. She reached up to tuck a damp strand of hair behind one ear, shaking her head. "Please, let it go. And do not speak of this to anyone."

"Don't worry, I won't. I have my own campaign to wage; I cannot be managing yours too. Even if I think you're mistaken." Agnes crossed her arms, which were covered to the wrist in floating white chiffon, over her chest.

Hoofbeats thundered below them; the horses were entering the final stretch. Agnes glanced at May one last time before stepping forward to watch the end of the race. May smiled automatically when the stands erupted in a cheer, not really knowing who had won. As if she cared about the out-come of a horse race.

"I'm going to step away for a moment," Agnes announced.

May looked over, startled at the odd note in her friend's voice. Was Agnes upset that May had ignored her advice? She realized with a pang how much she'd come to rely on Agnes at these events—her jovial presence, her frank remarks. She had been so unbearably lonely before Agnes's friendship. "Is everything all right?"

"I just need to say hello to someone. I'll be back." Agnes's eyes were fixed on another box as she started off. Probably going to flirt with some baronet that May wouldn't approve of. That was Agnes, always scheming. How had she put it? *I have my own campaign to wage.*

As her friend headed off, May smiled to herself. "Good luck," she whispered, not that Agnes could hear.

They both needed a healthy dose of luck. Yet for the first time in years, despite the odds, May felt . . . hopeful.

Perhaps both their campaigns might prove successful after all.

MAY ALWAYS FELT A FLURRY OF ANXIETY WHEN BOARDING A train. Her mind inevitably flung her back in time to *that* train, to the night of her family's ultimate disgrace.

The creditors had descended like a pack of locusts, and no one—not even Queen Victoria—was willing to help the Tecks anymore. Mary Adelaide and Francis had borrowed too many times for even their families to trust them. They had no choice but to flee the country, to run away from their debts like the ragged vagabonds they were.

It had rained that night, as if God himself wanted to add to their punishment. May would never forget how it felt to stand on the platform of Victoria Station with her parents and Dolly, rain battering mercilessly at her umbrella. They had taken the midnight train to avoid seeing anyone they knew, and had traveled under the false name of Count Hohenstein and his family. As if anyone abroad gave a fig about the Tecks.

It was a vastly different experience traveling in broad daylight, on the royal train.

May was well aware that the train had been summoned for Alix's sake, not hers, but that didn't dim her enjoyment. Afternoon sunlight shone through the windows on both sides of the car, gleaming on the polished hardwood floors. Aside from the gentle rattle as the train sped along its tracks, you might have thought you were in a well-appointed living room. Everything in here was expensive, from the blue watered silk lining the walls to the pillows stitched with the Scottish thistle.

They had been traveling all day; May knew that they would cross into Scotland overnight, speeding past Edinburgh at dawn before finally arriving at Balmoral's own Ballater Station. Through the windows she saw rugged northern forests interspersed with the occasional town, smoke drifting up from chimneys.

May's eyes darted from their chaperone, Miss Cochrane—asleep in a blue armchair—to Alix, who was curled up with a novel. It was irritating how incandescently beautiful she was, her blond curls framing her face, her expression luminous. Whatever silly story she was reading, she seemed engrossed in it.

May must have been staring too forcefully, because Alix looked up and met her gaze.

"Come sit with me?" she offered.

"Oh—of course," May said quickly. The two young women had spoken a bit at lunch, but Miss Cochrane had been hovering over them, and they hadn't really mentioned anything of consequence.

The train shook a little as May moved down its length, holding back her skirts to keep from tripping. She tried to think of a tactful way to bring up Prince Eddy.

"Aren't you excited to be going back to Balmoral? I always love it there," Alix said, when May had settled onto the seat next to her.

"Actually, this will be my first time there." May tried to hide her annoyance, and embarrassment, but Alix clearly picked up on it and smiled apologetically.

"I hadn't realized; you and your parents have traveled so much. You've been to Italy, haven't you? I've always longed to go."

Yes, they had been to Italy. That rain-soaked night at Victoria Station had launched the Tecks on several years of wandering, when they'd made their way through Europe like well-bred beggars. They had stayed with Princess Catherine of Württemberg, with May's awful uncle Willy—and then, in one of Mary Adelaide's masterstrokes, they had lived for almost two years in Florence without paying a penny in rent. The owner of the villa had evidently loved the thought of hosting royals, not realizing how tangential the Tecks' royal status was.

"We lived in Florence for a year and a half," May agreed.

Alix sighed at the prospect. "That must have been so lovely. Did you see Botticelli's *Venus?*"

"Botticelli's *Venus* is one of the few lovely things *about* Florence," May confessed. "I actually found the city rather trying. It was so dirty."

"Dirty? Really?"

"The river is rancid, there's trash in the streets, and the Italians all chain-smoked black cigars. Even the women!"

May had expected to shock Alix, but to her surprise the Hessian princess nodded. "The women in Russia smoke too, though cigarettes, not black cigars. The most high-ranking grand duchesses are the worst offenders! Even the tsarina smokes," she added in a conspiratorial whisper. "I saw her pulling cigarettes from a monogrammed case as carelessly as you or I might pull out a handkerchief!"

"The tsarina?" May repeated, surprised.

"I know! Before my visit to St. Petersburg, I thought only actresses smoked!"

May was surprised to see a glint of amusement in Alix's eyes. How unexpected, that Alix of Hesse should have a sense of humor. The shock of it made her bark out a laugh.

Then Alix was laughing too, the two of them giggling like a pair of schoolgirls.

Was it possible that they were having fun?

"Tell me more about Balmoral. I really don't know what to expect," May admitted.

Alix eagerly began talking, explaining how "Grandmama"

often had breakfast served outside near the garden cottage, while a piper marched back and forth playing the bagpipes. Most days a party would go out hunting, while everyone else stayed at the main castle, walking the grounds or catching up on correspondence.

That didn't sound very promising, at least not in regard to Prince Eddy. How was May supposed to get any time with him if he was out in the woods with a rifle every day?

"What about the evenings? Does Her Majesty do any entertaining?" May pressed.

"Usually just a small dinner. Though I believe Grandmama is hosting a ball for our final night. You did pack your tartan, didn't you?" Alix added. "We always wear tartans over our gowns at Balmoral, pinned at the shoulder."

"My tartan?"

"Surely your mother and father have their own plaid? Most branches of the family have designed one at some point. . . ." Alix trailed off, her blue eyes wide with understanding.

Normally, May hated that look. There was nothing she despised more than being pitied. Yet Alix was so obviously guileless that for once May didn't feel that resentful; she was just weary.

All her hard work getting here, and she would still look like an outsider because she didn't have a *plaid shawl*.

"I didn't pack a tartan. Will I be terribly out of place without one?"

"You can borrow one!" Alix said hastily. "There are always extras of the Stuart tartan in the linen closet at Balmoral. That's the classic red print."

"Is that what Her Majesty wears?"

"No, she wears her own personal print, a gray-and-black pattern. The Waleses will all be in it too."

Great. Now May would look every inch the poor relation—which she was, of course—wearing some drab old tartan that had been sitting in mothballs for the last thirty years.

Her dismay must have shown on her features, because Alix cleared her throat. "You're welcome to borrow one of mine, if you don't mind dressing like the Hessian branch of the family."

"You have another tartan?" It struck May as unbelievably extravagant to have extras of a custom-made fabric that you only wore once a year.

"Yes. I have mine, and my mother's. She designed the pattern, actually," Alix added softly.

May drew in a breath. "I'm sorry, I didn't mean to . . ."

"It's all right, Mama would have loved that her tartan was being used."

Alix's features were bright with heartache. Talking about her mother made her seem so childlike, so vulnerable; May was torn between a desire to protect her and another, equally strong urge to shake some sense into her. *The world isn't a fairy tale,* she wanted to say. *Stop thinking that it is!*

They both swayed a little in their seats as the train curved along its track. May adjusted the cushion behind her, then asked, "What was she like? Your mother, I mean."

"My biggest fear is that I will forget her. Already she is blurring with Ella in my mind—because after Mother died, Ella became like a mother to me, too. I'm terrified that one day I'll wake up and have forgotten her face completely."

Alix's voice broke, but after a moment she continued. "One thing that I do remember is how much she loved music. She was always singing, making up nonsense songs, or changing the lyrics to some popular song so that it was actually about us. 'Those aren't the words, Mama!' I would protest, and she just swept me into her arms and laughed that it didn't matter. She said that the words could be whatever we wanted them to be, that the song was ours for the writing."

"She sounds very special." May couldn't imagine how it might feel, having a dreamy and imaginative mother like that. Her own mother could hardly be called practical, given how overdrawn their accounts were, but she had never been the type to make up words or games. The only stories she'd told May were real ones about their family history.

"I miss her so much," Alix murmured. "But as hard as it was on me, my father took it the worst. He never really recovered from her death."

"Really?" May didn't know much about Louis of Hesse; he kept to himself in Darmstadt. Come to think of it, how had he managed to marry a princess of Great Britain? His duchy was nothing special by German standards, hardly better than her own father's home of Württemberg.

"They were so in love, you know, that they married only six months after Grandpapa Albert's death. Everyone was still in mourning," Alix offered.

That didn't sound like an auspicious start to May, but it did explain things. In the wild throes of her grief over Albert, Queen Victoria might have agreed to a marriage she would never have let her daughter make under normal circumstances.

Alix kicked off her slippers, then pulled one foot up onto

the upholstered cushion, tucking it behind her knee in utter defiance of etiquette. "For years people kept telling my father to remarry, but he always refused. He said that there was no one in the world like my mother."

It was true: most men would have remarried within the year, simply for a pair of hands to raise their children and run their household.

"That's the kind of love I'm looking for," Alix added, almost in a whisper. "I know it's foolish to think that I might find it, but I can't help hoping."

"Excuse me, Your Highnesses." A maid emerged from the neighboring railcar and began lighting the oil lamps on the walls. May noted in surprise that the sun had set, its golden rays disappearing behind the distant hills.

"When shall I tell the conductor to halt the train for your supper?"

They both glanced at the figure of the elderly Miss Cochrane, who was still dozing in her armchair on the opposite side of the railcar.

"Perhaps we don't need to pause," Alix suggested, surprising May yet again.

The maid frowned. "Her Majesty always has the train come to a full stop before dining. She says that it is messy attempting to eat while in motion."

"But Her Majesty isn't here. Why don't we attempt to eat while moving, and that way we can arrive at Balmoral a bit ahead of schedule?"

When the maidservant retreated with a nod, May lifted an eyebrow.

"Eating while the train is moving? A bit reckless, to be breaking Her Majesty's rules before we even get there."

"If I shatter a plate, promise me you'll help me sweep it under the rug?" Alix asked lightly.

"Of course. We're quite good at that in our family," May heard herself reply.

Alix gave an appreciative smile. They were teasing each other, May noted in surprise, sharing jokes known only to the two of them. Acting the way that *friends* would.

The realization made her think of Agnes, who was a very different sort of friend, cunning and defiant where Alix was soft-spoken. Yet May had shared hidden pieces of herself with each of them.

After all these years of being on her own, it was rather a nice sensation—letting people in.

CHAPTER FIFTEEN

Hélène

"EDDY!"

Hélène thundered after him, her horse's hooves kicking up dirt as they galloped around the pine and birch trees. In the distance rose heather-covered hills that turned to mountains, their craggy peaks still capped with snow. Emerald lochs gleamed in the afternoon sunshine, occasionally narrowing into the frothing ribbon of a waterfall.

The rest of the group—the Prince and Princess of Wales, Princess Louise and Alexander Fife, and a few neighbors from the surrounding countryside—had gone uphill, hoping to scout locations for tomorrow's stag hunt. Hélène and Eddy had drifted away from the others and met up down here, far below the rest of the group.

Hélène loved riding alone with Eddy. It was thrilling, getting to race as fast as she could—which was surprisingly fast, given that she had to ride sidesaddle in polite company. She felt unbound and electric, as free as if she'd released every last hook in her corset and let the whole wretched thing fall to the floor.

Finally Eddy slowed to a walk, and she followed suit, letting her mare amble alongside his. Both horses were breathing heavily through their nostrils, their necks gleaming with a sheen of sweat.

"I'm so glad you agreed to come," Eddy declared.

"Me too." Hélène had been here a week, and already the trip was slipping by too quickly. Eddy had been right when he'd claimed she would love Scotland. It was wonderful and harsh, with a wildness that called to that answering wildness within Hélène: to that part of her that she always tried, unsuccessfully, to keep hidden.

So far the Fifes had proven ideal hosts. They wanted to spend each day outdoors, and didn't stand on ceremony for meals. It made Hélène wonder why she and the Princess Louise—now Duchess of Fife—hadn't been friends before. Louise was bright and exuberant in a way that young women rarely were, an avid participant in the typically male pursuits of hunting and fishing. And while she'd never said anything to Hélène, she kept finding ways to leave her alone with Eddy: pairing them together on the hunt, or asking Eddy to show Hélène the paintings in the gallery, though he clearly had no idea who the paintings were of. Hélène couldn't help wondering, sometimes, whether Louise would be so indulgent if she knew the extent of their affair—because of course Eddy hadn't told her *everything*, just that they'd fallen in love despite Queen Victoria's wishes.

Louise may have loved someone unbefitting her station, but Hélène doubted the princess had given her virginity to Alexander Fife before they were married, let alone that she'd slept with anyone else.

Hélène and Eddy had only discussed Laurent once—and even then, she knew better than to admit the whole truth. It came up one night while they lay in bed, her palm on Eddy's chest, feeling it rise and fall with his breath.

"Who was he?" Eddy had asked, very softly. When Hélène flinched, he turned on his side to study her with those intense blue eyes. "I'm sorry; you don't have to tell me if you don't want to. It's just . . . I have been worrying that you . . ."

"What?" she had whispered, confused. Eddy had known all along that he wasn't her first; that had been clear from the beginning, hadn't it?

"Was it of your choosing, everything that happened between you?"

Hélène blinked, and Eddy drew in a nervous breath. "You're experienced, but you've never even been engaged. If you were harmed . . ."

Hélène found that she was oddly touched by his protectiveness, by the careful but determined way he'd brought up the subject.

"We did not part amicably, but no, I was not harmed. Everything that we did, I wanted to do," Hélène assured him.

Eddy relaxed. "I'm glad. I was about to offer to have him killed, and that would have been messy to deal with." He was teasing now, but she heard the affection beating beneath his words.

Hélène strove to match his light tone. "No need. And anyway, he's French, which would make killing him rather complicated."

She immediately longed to swallow back the words—what was she thinking, revealing any kind of detail about Laurent? But Eddy only laughed softly.

"That's hardly fair. I can't compete with some French prince who wooed you with macarons and châteaux."

"I assure you, neither of those was involved—"

"Does he have a mustache? I bet he curls it with tongs, and wears heeled shoes, and—"

Hélène reached for a pillow and began pummeling Eddy before he could say more. She was laughing, a bright, easy laugh that fizzed up from her chest like champagne, and to her delight Eddy was laughing too.

Then he flipped his body atop hers, and they both fell silent.

"Don't give him another thought. I never do," Hélène had whispered.

Now Eddy reached over to lay a hand on her horse's reins, interrupting her thoughts. "Should we stop?" He gestured ahead, to where an offshoot of the River Dee trickled over uneven stones.

Hélène nodded and slid down from the saddle.

"You look like the goddess Diana," Eddy observed, which made her smile.

"And what does that make you, a hunter attempting to seduce me in a woodland grove?"

"I'm not the most assiduous pupil of mythology, but I'm quite certain that Diana was never seduced. If anything, she did the seducing."

"Is that so?"

They stood next to each other at the edge of the water, their horses' heads lowered to drink. Eddy reached to lace his fingers in hers.

"For the record, I'm happy to be seduced," he said softly.

Hélène tugged him closer, letting her lips brush lightly against his. The kiss was languid at first, her blood pulsing contented and slow through her veins.

But it took only a moment for their kisses to grow fever-ish. Eddy's nearness sent a flood of heat through her body, making her feel molten and shivery, a delicious contrast to the cool air on her skin. It had been far too long since she'd felt the simple pleasure of touching him. After all, she was a guest in his sister's house right now; there had been no sneak-ing around late at night.

Hélène reached for Eddy's shirt and tugged it impatiently from his belt, then slid her hand beneath its hem and up over his skin.

Who knew how far things might have gone. They might have tethered their horses and made love right there in the forest of Ballochbuie, except that they both went still at the same moment, their hunter's instincts on sudden alert. They were no longer alone.

When she saw the creature a short distance to their right, Hélène gasped.

The horses had turned to living statues; even the huff of breath from their nostrils seemed to have stilled. Their eyes were trained on the majestic gray figure that stood atop a boulder, watching them.

In the mottled shade of the forest, the wolf's eyes glowed a fierce amber. Hélène felt pressure on her wrist: Eddy was grabbing her in silent warning, urging her to stay still, not that she needed any convincing.

The wolf drew her lips back in a growl. Hélène wasn't sure why she felt so convinced it was a female, but she would have put money on it. They all stayed as frozen as figures in a tableau.

Finally, the wolf nodded in something resembling

acknowledgment, then turned and darted off in the opposite direction.

With that, the spell was broken. The sounds of the forest seemed to descend around them again: the horses whickered nervously and stomped their feet, and birds resumed their chirping in the trees.

Hélène glanced to Eddy. His expression was alight with wonder.

"I can't believe that just happened. It's so uncommon to see a wolf in the middle of the day; they usually only come out after dusk." Eddy shook his head. "In medieval times people would have considered it an omen. The question is, what kind of omen—a good one, or bad?"

"She nodded to us. It must be a good omen," Hélène declared.

"You think so?"

"Who cares! We live in modern times; we can make our own luck."

"That's what I love about you: the sheer force of your convictions," Eddy told her. "When you get passionate about something you are so . . ."

"French?" Hélène offered, with a laugh.

"You are wondrous."

Hélène drew in a breath, startled by the sincerity in Eddy's voice. It was the first time either of them had used the word love—*That's what I love about you,* he'd said, even if it wasn't *I love you.*

To hide her confusion, she walked over to her horse and reached for the reins. Eddy came to stand next to her, bending over to lace his fingers into a makeshift stirrup.

"I don't need your help getting into the saddle," Hélène pointed out.

Eddy smiled, boyish and mischievous again. "I'm aware."

She rolled her eyes but placed her boot in his hands, allowing him to lift her. "If you wanted to look up my skirts, all you had to do was ask."

Eddy barked out a laugh. Within moments they were cantering, heading toward the mountains where the rest of the group had disappeared. Hélène urged her horse faster, her body pulsing with adrenaline, her heart still thrumming in the aftermath of Eddy's words.

A WEEK LATER, SEATED IN THE GRAND SALON AT BALMORAL, Hélène clung tight to those words.

Things had changed the morning after she and Eddy saw the wolf, when Alix and May arrived.

Now each time Eddy tried to come out hunting, his grandmother insisted he do something else instead—take a carriage ride to a nearby town, have tea in the garden—always with Alix at his side. Just yesterday Victoria had tasked Eddy and Alix with fetching bluebells from the fields, though the entire castle was already bursting with bouquets.

Hélène glanced around the grand salon; its furniture had been rearranged for tonight's theatricals, chairs lined into rows before an empty rug that served as a stage. As she watched, Louise emerged from the next room wearing a set of priest's robes. They looked genuine, making Hélène wonder if they'd been borrowed from a local curate. Normally that sort of request might have been sacrilegious, but of course, no one would deny the head of the Church of England.

These amateur performances—vignettes, Queen Victoria called them—were yet another of the inscrutable traditions tied to this house. Eddy had explained that they did them every year. One summer they had re-created classical paintings; another, they had reenacted famous moments in British history. *That was my favorite,* Eddy recalled; *I got to play Wellington at Waterloo, slashing about with a wooden sword.*

Who was Napoleon? Hélène had replied, and Eddy laughed.

Louise, of course. She kept cursing at me in French because, of course, curses are the only words she really learned.

This year, the theme was some kind of tribute to Prince Albert, with a different theatrical sketch for every letter of his name. *A* for *abundance* had been a harvest scene, with Maud dressed in a toga-like gown as Demeter; *L* stood for *leisure,* a scene where Eddy and George had napped on a tiger skin from India.

Thank heavens only Queen Victoria's grandchildren were forced to take part in this. It struck Hélène as bizarre, and a bit childish, like when Amélie used to flounce about the house in their mother's dressing gowns, the embroidered hem trailing after her.

"Our next letter is *B*," Louise announced, as if no one in the room knew how to spell Albert.

Hélène tried to catch her gaze, hoping to coax a conspiratorial smile, but Eddy's sister was looking pointedly away.

"For *bride,*" Louise finished.

Something hot and sticky twisted in Hélène's stomach as she realized what was happening.

Eddy emerged from the door to the hall and came to join his sister, who stood at the front of the room like a priest at a wedding. And then Alix began processing toward them.

Oh god. This was a fake wedding—with Eddy as the groom and Alix as the bride.

Someone had acquired a costume for Alix, a genuine Scottish peasant's dress made of simple cream-colored fabric with red detail, and in her hands she clutched a bouquet. She walked slowly, unsmiling, her back straight and her color heightened.

"Dearly beloved," Louise said, a bit awkwardly, "we are gathered here in the sight of God, to join together this man and this woman in holy matrimony. . . ."

In a nearby armchair, Alexander Fife leaned toward the Prince of Wales. "Painfully obvious, isn't it?" he murmured to his father-in-law.

"You know how Her Majesty can be." Bertie chuckled and spread out his hands in a gesture of amused surrender.

Hélène gripped her hands tight around the chair's armrests. She wanted to run away, to escape to the stables or her bed—she would even take the ladies' lounge right now—anywhere but this drawing room, where she had to watch this ridiculous wedding play out before her.

"Wilt thou have this man to be thy wedded husband?" Louise was asking Alix. "Wilt thou love him, comfort him, honor and obey him, in sickness and in health?"

"I will," Alix mumbled.

Eddy fumbled in his pocket for a ring (there was a *ring?* Hélène thought wildly) and slid it onto Alix's finger, his jaw tight. Hélène's breaths felt shallow against her stays, her blood pounding. But she forced herself to keep watching, because she might as well get used to it. *Alix* was Eddy's future, not Hélène. A fact that she had conveniently let herself forget.

Hélène wasn't wearing a costume, yet she had engaged in a game of pretend far more dangerous than the theatricals onstage, imagining that her affair had no consequences. That it wouldn't cost her.

Because that was all it was—an affair. She had known precisely what she was getting into, Hélène reminded herself. This was always supposed to be a meaningless distraction.

Yet, without her realizing, it had begun to mean something.

Far too much, actually.

CHAPTER SIXTEEN

May

MAY HAD RESENTED THIS RIDICULOUS EVENING FROM THE START.

Several days ago, Queen Victoria had asked her grandchildren to perform "amateur theatricals," pointedly leaving May out of the assignment. May knew she was being snubbed, forced to sit in the audience with the likes of Bishop Cameron and Hélène d'Orléans while the Wales children and Alix were onstage.

And that was *before* May had seen the fake wedding. It was almost laughable, the lengths that Victoria would go to in order to push Alix and Eddy together. Except that May was in no mood to laugh.

She glanced around the drawing room, which was heavy with all the scents so distinctive to Balmoral—woodsmoke and leather and something else that might have been old wood, or old stone, or old everything. The theatricals had just ended, and the "actors" were still in costume, making them stand out awkwardly from the other guests. Uncle Bertie might have found the whole display as frustrating as May did, because he'd immediately retreated to smoke on the terrace; but everyone else was milling about near the fireplace, clutching glasses of brandy or sherry.

"I have to admit, I'm jealous that you were allowed to be part of the audience," remarked a voice to her left.

May turned, startled to see Prince George standing next to her.

Belatedly, she realized that she needed to reply. "You didn't enjoy acting tonight?"

"I loathed it. And I imagine that you would have, too."

"I'd have preferred not to be left out." Perhaps Agnes was rubbing off on her; May normally didn't speak so bluntly.

George cast her a curious glance. They were standing near the edge of the oriental carpet, near a claret-colored tufted sofa.

"Perhaps you're right," George agreed. "At least if you were onstage with us, no one would have to worry about you forgetting your lines as Louise did."

May was puzzled, though a bit gratified by the disloyalty to his sister. "What do you mean?"

"Just that you have excellent powers of recall. I'll never forget that summer we were all children, when Grandmother offered a prize to whoever would be first to recite the catechism."

May couldn't believe he remembered; it was so long ago. "She promised that whoever could do it first would get a Bible embossed with his or her name."

"Except that we were children, and not particularly motivated by the Bible as a reward. Chocolate would have been a better choice."

Not to May. She had been enamored by the prospect of owning something marked with her name: the letters pressed into the cover by a stamp, never to be erased or undone. Something that was clearly, undeniably *hers*.

"You learned the catechism within a matter of days, while

the rest of us were busy playing at pirates," George went on. His eyes lit on hers as he asked, "I hope you still have that Bible."

"Oh . . . I never got one, actually," May admitted.

"That's not fair." George was positively indignant as he added, "I have half a mind to tell Grandmother that she owes you a Bible."

She owes me far more than that for ignoring me my whole life, May thought. "It's all right. I'm sure she just forgot."

Except that if it had been Eddy, or her beloved Alix, Victoria would never have forgotten.

May steered the conversation back to a safer level. "Tell me, why did you dislike the theatricals? I think you may have had the best part of anyone."

"Because I had no speaking role and just napped on a tiger skin?"

"Was it comfortable?" May asked, and to her surprise, George laughed.

"Extremely. Have you ever seen a tiger? Eddy claims he shot one in Nepal, but I'm not sure whether to believe him."

"I've never traveled to Nepal, of course, but I did see the tiger at the Zoological Gardens in Regent's Park." May hesitated, then added, "I have to admit, I much preferred the hippopotamus."

"The hippopotamus? You must be the only person in London who feels that way."

"It's not the hippopotamus's fault that he was poorly named, and looks more like a hog than a Thoroughbred!" May protested. "One can hardly blame him for splashing people in retaliation."

There had been such a fanfare when the animal had first

arrived in London, newspaper headlines proudly announcing the GREAT AFRICAN RIVER-HORSE. Then when people saw it—expecting some kind of Pegasus with fins—they were sorely disappointed. Within a week, children were throwing hunks of old bread at the hippopotamus, shouting insults in its direction.

May loved that the hippo ignored their criticisms, just gave a huge yawn of indifference and then jumped back into its pond, spraying water up onto the children. She wished that she could do the same when society threw barbs her way.

"Of course," George said evenly. "I would splash people, too, if they kept me locked up in that pond with only the giraffes next door for company."

He was smiling, May noted: a shy, almost playful smile. The remark was a *joke*.

"Giraffes seem rather stuck-up, don't you think?" she replied. "The way they've always got their noses in the air?"

It was a silly, nonsensical thing to say, but George chuckled appreciatively.

How strange, that May had never really paid him any mind. As a child George had always trailed along in Eddy's wake, watching the older, more rambunctious cousins. Yet there was clearly a sense of humor beneath his placid surface.

"You know what animal should have been named the hippopotamus? The dolphin. They are incredible—so fast, and as playful as frolicking puppies," George told her, still smiling.

"You saw a dolphin? Was this in the navy?"

"Off the coast of Malta. Missy and I saw them, right alongside the yacht."

Right. Missy.

When they were children, George had always been overly solicitous of their younger cousin: holding the lead rope when Missy learned to ride a pony, helping her try to catch fireflies at dusk.

The oldest daughter of Uncle Alfred and Aunt Marie, Missy was pretty in a bright, vivacious way, nothing at all like shy Alix of Hesse. Honestly, Queen Victoria might have considered Missy as a bride for Eddy if she weren't so young.

And George was clearly still infatuated with her.

"George!" Maud bustled over, relieving May of the need to reply. "Father is looking for you."

"Very well." George cast an inscrutable glance at May, then nodded his goodbye and disappeared.

Maud watched him leave. "What were you and George talking about?"

May couldn't explain the unexpected, almost whimsical turn their conversation had taken—or that the mention of Missy had acted like a dash of cold water to her face. "We were just discussing the theatricals. Did you enjoy them?"

"Not really." Maud shrugged. "But you know how Grandmama is. It's easier to agree to her demands than to put up a fight."

Of course. Queen Victoria's will went unquestioned, at least within her family.

A burst of laughter across the room caught Maud's attention. May couldn't help glancing over as well—to where Alix of Hesse stood with Prince Eddy.

They should have looked like a couple; they were standing so close together, both of them wearing those bizarre peasant wedding costumes. And they were certainly both attractive. In her cream-colored dress, her golden hair shot through with firelight, Alix looked ethereal, angelic. Yet there was something stiff about the way they moved around each other, neither of them quite meeting the other's gaze.

What was it Alix had said on the train? *That's the kind of love I'm looking for.* The romantic, adoring devotion of a spouse who never stopped grieving you: the way Alix's father had done for her mother, the way Victoria still did for Albert.

Alix would never find that kind of love with Eddy, May felt certain of it.

But Alix wasn't brave enough to extricate herself from the situation. If nothing happened to change their course, she and Eddy would get pulled into an engagement through sheer inertia—swept along by everyone's expectations, by the force of Queen Victoria's will. Alix would say nothing in protest, until one day she looked up and realized she was married to Eddy after all.

May had her own reasons for wanting to sabotage things, but was it really sabotage when you were *saving* someone from a fate they didn't want? May tried to think of what Agnes would say if she were here.

She knew the answer as clearly as if Agnes had whispered it to her all the way from London.

Agnes would want her to tell Maud the truth about Alix.

"The marriage vignette surprised me a bit," May heard herself say. "I take it that an engagement is already in the works?"

Maud blinked at the directness of the question. "Nothing has been announced yet, but if Grandmama had her way, it would be in the papers tomorrow."

"Perhaps it's for the best that no formal announcement has been made," May murmured in reply.

"What do you mean?"

Wordlessly they both took a step back, settling onto an ottoman upholstered in scratchy blue fabric. It meant they had to sit ramrod-straight, but at least this way they could see the entire room.

May sighed. "I worry about Alix, with all her ailments."

"Ailments?"

This was the point of no return. May could still take it all back, pretend that she'd only meant Alix suffered from harmless headaches. But then she would be lying. Besides, Alix's panicked episode had happened out in public; for all May knew, other people had seen. The truth would come out eventually, with or without May's help.

Once more, she glanced over at Alix's face—pale, strained, uncertain. It lent her the resolve she needed.

"Alix suffers from the vapors," May explained. "Or, really, it's like the vapors but far worse. I saw it happen last year at the opera. Her hands were paralyzed, clenched into fists so tight that she couldn't open them. She couldn't even *talk*."

Maud lifted a hand to her mouth in surprise. "I've never heard of such a thing."

"And then, of course, there's the bleeding disease."

"The bleeding disease?" Maud repeated, in a near whisper.

"You know it runs in her family. A disease that causes uncontrolled bleeding." *It runs in* our *family*, May could have said; it had killed Queen Victoria's youngest son, Leopold. Though no one ever, ever mentioned that.

"Alix's brother Friedrich died of it," May went on. "And the doctors say it's carried through the female line."

"Really?" It was a mark of Maud's inexperience, or perhaps her privilege, that she didn't pause to consider whether she might be a carrier of that same disease.

May had wondered, of course. That was how she'd come by this highly sensitive information in the first place: she'd eavesdropped on her parents as they discussed the family curse, debating whether May might pass it on to her own children.

But unlike Alix, May didn't have a brother who had bled to death. Her own brother was in perfect health.

"Alix is troubled, and . . ." May hesitated, then spoke the word Agnes had used. "And damaged."

That word had sounded so perfect in her head—so confident, so definitive—but falling from her lips, it seemed unbearably harsh. May thought of Alix, smiling at her across the railcar, and felt queasy with regret.

Maud's eyes widened. "How terrible for Alix. Do you think Grandmama knows?"

"Probably not." May had always sensed that Alix's family was tight-knit. Especially after Alix's mother died, the Hesse siblings had closed ranks against the rest of the world, even their own cousins. They would have gone to great lengths to keep Alix's paralyzing episodes a secret.

Thanks to May, it was a secret no longer.

"I'm so glad that you told me, May. I just want what's best for Eddy." Maud shook her head in concern.

Now that she'd dealt her blow, May felt the energy that had coursed through her rapidly drain away. She had been *helping* Alix, she reminded herself, because Alix wasn't bold enough to help herself.

But the fact remained that she had also traded Alix's secret for her own gain.

CHAPTER SEVENTEEN

Alix

THE NEXT MORNING, ALIX STUDIED EDDY ACROSS THE BREAKFAST table. He tucked heartily into a Scottish breakfast—eggs, smoked haddock, roasted tomatoes—while deep in conversation with his father. From the sound of things, they hoped to ride out hunting later this morning with Louise and her husband, who were hosting a small party down the road at Mar Lodge.

Alix wondered what Eddy thought of their prospective engagement. They hadn't discussed it, not even after that awful fake wedding.

For her part, she'd half forgotten that they were supposed to be courting, until she arrived back in England at the start of the summer. It wasn't as if she and Eddy had been assiduous correspondents. What was she going to write him about—the blankets she'd helped stitch for the local hospital, her thoughts on the various books she'd read?

Those were things she would have loved to share with Nicholas, if they were in the habit of exchanging letters. When she'd finished *Le roman du prince Eugène*, her fingers had itched to write the tsarevich and ask if he'd read it—the novel raised so many questions about family, about how to respect your parents while still escaping the shadow they cast.

Of course, she didn't dare write to him. They hadn't spoken since that almost kiss, or whatever it was, the night of the *bal noir.*

"What is everyone planning for today?" George asked, glancing around the table.

"Maud and I were just saying that we'd love to sit in the garden and work on our cross-stitching," May declared. "Alix, will you be joining us?"

"I will be riding out to Glassalt Shiel this morning, and would like some company," the queen cut in, before Alix could reply.

Everyone stared down at their plates or out the window, like children willing a schoolteacher not to call on them. Most of the queen's family considered her carriage rides unbearably tedious. She went out every day, no matter the weather, stopping at various places of interest on the Balmoral property or delivering gifts to nearby farmers. Occasionally she ventured into the neighboring town, where she would purchase sweetmeats or a new quill pen from the flustered clerk at the general store.

"Alix, you will come, won't you?"

Despite the phrasing, there was no mistaking the queen's words for anything but a command. Alix stole a guilty glance at Maud and May, who had so obviously been excluded from the invitation. She wished she could explain how much she hated it when Grandmama played favorites. It seemed particularly unfair to May.

"Eddy," Victoria added, and he looked up, squirming. "You will join us."

Alix tried not to let her dismay show. First the onstage wedding, and now this?

"I was supposed to ride out with Louise and her party— you know, Ivo and Caroline, and Hélène d'Orléans. . . ." At the look in the queen's eyes, Eddy faltered. "But of course, they shall be fine hunting without me."

"Then it's settled." The queen stood, and everyone quickly bobbed up like puppets and pushed back their chairs. It would seem that breakfast was over.

Half an hour later, Alix, Eddy, and the queen climbed into an open carriage, as if Victoria were willfully daring the overcast skies to rain on her. To Alix's relief, no one spoke much on the drive uphill.

If anyone had been around to see them, their party would have made a strange sight: the queen forbidding in all black, Alix at her side in a blue dress with full sleeves, Eddy in an olive hunting jacket and matching cap. The horses were groomed to such a sheen that they seemed to glow in the ambient Scottish light, as if they were parading through Belgravia and not alone in the Highlands.

Alix tried her best to enjoy their surroundings. This was the Balmoral she loved: the shade-dappled forest, its ancient trees lined in moss. The air was heavy with woodsmoke and the cool, clean scent of the river.

But it was hard to focus on Scotland's natural beauty in such tight quarters, with Eddy's knees periodically brushing against hers.

"I have been waiting for the two of you to ask me for a private audience," Grandmama said at last. "Yet you remain maddeningly silent. Do you not have any news to share?"

Alix's heart thudded, and she glanced at Eddy.

"Grandmother, we are still courting," he began, but the queen cut him off with an impatient gesture.

"You've been courting all year—what more is there to learn about each other? I invited you to Balmoral for the express purpose of aiding said courtship, yet you've spent no time together at all! Even when I wrote you a sketch where you *got married* onstage!"

Well, at least the queen had admitted the motives behind last night's shameless theatricals.

Alix leaned forward. "I'm sure I speak for Eddy when I say that we need more time." She wasn't actually sure she spoke for Eddy at all, but it was hard to catch his gaze, and she felt the need to say something.

"Time is the one thing we no longer have! I'm not exactly getting any younger!"

Alix drew in a sharp breath, reaching for her grandmother's hand. "Why do you say that, Grandmama? Is there an issue with your health?"

"Of course there is! I'm an old woman! I might drop dead at any moment!"

In other words, no. Alix should have known that her grandmother was fit as a fiddle.

"Eddy," Victoria said angrily. Alix noted that his hands were closed tight around his knees, his neck muscles straining. "I cannot let you leave the succession undecided any longer. I want to see my great-grandchild before I die!"

At the mention of children, Eddy looked like he'd been hit by a dash of cold water. His eyes lifted to Alix, but she got the unnerving sense that he wasn't seeing her at all—that he was thinking of someone else. "I'm sorry, but Alix and I haven't discussed this."

"That's why I'm insisting you discuss it now. You are the future king, and you have a duty to marry!" Victoria rounded on Alix. "As for you, your mother was my daughter, a princess of Great Britain! You have duties to this country, too!"

Alix's throat felt dry. "Grandmama, we have much to think about—"

"What on earth is there to think about? No princess could dream of a better marriage than to the British throne! All that's left is for *you* to propose"—she told Eddy, then turned expectantly to Alix—"and for *you* to accept. Once that's settled, we can plan a wedding for next summer."

"Next summer?" Eddy repeated.

"Yes, and then hopefully Alix will have given us another future king within the year!"

Alix had always known this was what princesses were meant for: that their aspirations were supposed to begin with marriage and end at motherhood. That they were nothing but beautiful, well-bred vessels meant to bear beautiful, well-bred heirs. But hearing her grandmother say it so explicitly made a new resentment simmer in her chest, like rising steam.

"Very well," Victoria declared, when it was clear that neither of them would say anything. "If you won't do it, then I'll manage the whole thing for you. I propose marriage in Eddy's name, and Alix, I accept on your behalf. Congratulations!" She reached for both their hands, tugging them together until Alix's gloved palm was pressed against Eddy's. "We can notify the papers when we return to London, start planning some joint events for you two. Why don't you go to the Cadogans' ball together next month?"

Alix stared numbly at their intertwined hands, struck by the utter strangeness of touching Eddy like this.

"No." Eddy spoke with surprising determination, pulling his hand away. "We can't make an announcement."

"We cannot make an announcement *yet*," Queen Victoria corrected. "I will let you delay the news, as long as you assure me that you're going through with the marriage."

Eddy's eyes were dark with emotion, something quiet and profound that Alix had never seen in him before. It made her realize just how little she knew him.

And perhaps that wasn't entirely his fault.

"I ask that you wait a month. There are some . . . there are things I need to sort out before this news becomes public," Eddy said softly.

He was talking about another woman, wasn't he? Alix knew she should care, but she was too bewildered by the speed at which things were progressing: the fact that Eddy had just agreed, at least implicitly, to marry her. Were they engaged? She hadn't said yes, but this was hardly a typical proposal. Eddy hadn't gotten down on one knee, hadn't even been the one to ask her.

"Very well. We shall wait a month," Queen Victoria agreed, her lips pursed in disapproval.

They rumbled on for several more minutes, the excruciating silence broken only by the clatter of the horses' hooves. Alix gripped tight to the side of the carriage to keep from accidentally being jostled against Eddy.

When the pointed stones of the prince consort's cairn came into view, Alix found her voice. "I thought we were going to Glassalt Shiel."

"Change of plans. We shall pay our respects to Albert

first." Her grandmother waited until they had drawn to a halt before letting the coachman help her out. Eddy started to disembark, but the queen shook her head. "Eddy, you stay. Alix will accompany me alone."

Apprehension twisted in Alix's stomach. She half wished that Eddy would insist on remaining with them, if only to have another voice protesting this engagement, but he just nodded and crossed his arms, his expression dark.

The queen reached for Alix's hand, leaning on her granddaughter in place of a cane as they made their way to Prince Albert's cairn.

Alix had always thought the monument seemed out of place in the wilds of Balmoral, its stones formed into a triangular pyramid like the ones in Egypt. She supposed that was the point, to make it stand out from the surrounding landscape so that one couldn't help but notice it. The inscription on its side read TO THE BELOVED MEMORY OF ALBERT, THE GREAT AND GOOD PRINCE CONSORT.

"I wonder, sometimes, what my dear Albert would think of all this," her grandmother said quietly.

Alix's reply came out sharper than she meant. "What he would think of the cairn, or the fact that you're forcing us into an engagement?"

"About you and Eddy, of course. Albert would have loved the cairn." Victoria sighed. "He was always building little ones when we went out on a walk, to mark places he thought we should revisit. He stacked the stones atop one another in the traditional Scottish way, like this."

Alix watched as her elderly grandmother bent down and stacked three stones in a makeshift tower. It looked surprisingly sturdy.

"The word is Gaelic, you know. *Càrn*," the queen went on. "Albert may have been German, but he constantly learned bits and pieces of other languages. He was very intellectually curious, like you." She sighed. "I know he would have agreed that England needs you."

"Please, don't," Alix cut in helplessly.

"I'm afraid that Eddy isn't much like Albert. Neither is Bertie, for that matter," the queen continued, with shocking bluntness. "George is the one who inherited Albert's curiosity, his patience. The only trace of Albert I can see in Eddy is his love of this place. Scotland always seems to bring out the best in him. When he's here, he's more decisive, more purposeful."

"Perhaps he just needs more to do." Alix had always been baffled by Eddy's tendency to spin from one party to the next, but what alternative had he been given? Grandmama guarded her duties jealously, and refused to share any power with Uncle Bertie, let alone with Eddy. He wasn't just in the shadow of the throne, but in the *shadow* of its shadow.

"Of course Eddy needs more to do. Which is precisely why he should marry you, to keep him from being so . . . aimless."

"I'm not a compass," Alix burst out.

The queen took another step forward, her black skirts swishing heavily. "I beg to differ, my darling. A woman is always a compass, a guiding force, to the man she marries."

"Grandmama, nothing has changed since last year. Eddy and I are still not suited for each other."

"This again!" Victoria exclaimed. "Alix, the purpose of the courtship period was to find ways you *are* suited for each other. Yet the two of you still behave like strangers!"

Alix stared up at the stones of the cairn, its outline a stark gray against the softer gray of the skies. She felt her palms growing damp inside her gloves.

"I know you don't love Eddy. I'm not asking you to do this for love of him, or even for love of me, as much as I adore you." To Alix's surprise, Victoria's voice cracked with emotion. "Do it for your love of England. Eddy will make a wonderful king, as long as he has a woman like you to ground him."

When Alix said nothing, her grandmother added softly, "You need him, too, you know."

"I . . . what?"

"You need his proposal as much as he needs your agreement. Strange rumors have been circulating about you, my dear. Just this morning I heard a ridiculous story about how you suffer from crippling fainting spells—that you passed out at *La Traviata* last year."

Alix's blood ran cold. People were gossiping about her episodes?

"I put a stop to the rumor at once, of course," Victoria was saying. "It's nonsense. And I made it very clear that anyone who repeats it risks angering me."

Well, that was one unmistakable perk of being queen. You could protect the people you cared about. *Like Ernie*, Alix thought, unbidden. Or her father.

"Thank you, Grandmama. I do occasionally need smelling salts, but that hasn't happened in quite some time," she said as calmly as possible.

Her mind whirled back to that night at the opera last year, when she'd dissolved into panic before Hélène d'Orléans. How stupid she'd been to assume that Hélène wouldn't tell anyone.

Alix had spent her entire life hiding the ugly secret of her condition. If people found out, she might never marry; no man wanted a wife who came with unknown complications. And while Alix might not care so much about marriage herself, it would cast such shame upon her family, make things harder for Ernie—even for Ella, all the way in St. Petersburg.

Alix might be an idealist, but she was no fool. She knew that as much as society adored young women like her—beautiful, highborn princesses—it relished their destruction even more. If the truth became public, all the people who had once lifted her up would sharpen their knives, just as eager to tear her down.

"Marry Eddy, and you'll have a powerful shield protecting you from all this nonsense," Grandmama said urgently. "Besides, think of the life you can build here in Britain: coming to Balmoral every summer, spending your days surrounded by people you love! Married to Eddy you would hardly have a public role at all. This is England, not Russia," she added disparagingly. "Our queen consort isn't like the tsarina, who takes part in all their ceremonial proceedings. Look at what a quiet life your aunt Alexandra leads. You could have that, too."

It sounded like Grandmama realized there was truth to the rumors. Alix should have focused on that, but her mind snagged on the reference to Russia.

"What do you mean, it's not like being the tsarina?"

Her grandmother made an exasperated *pshhh* noise. "You think I don't know about you and Nicholas?"

"There's nothing to know," Alix said quickly.

Her grandmother didn't seem to have heard. "I'm sure that St. Petersburg seemed very glamorous when you visited, that Nicholas was dashing and handsome in his regimental uniform—"

"Please, we don't need to—"

"Did I ever tell you that the Tsar Alexander came to court me when I was a new queen?"

Nicholas's *grandfather* had wooed Victoria? Alix had never heard this story.

"I was your age, just nineteen. Alexander came to London for the Season and squired me about to balls, to the theater, on carriage rides. It was really quite scandalous; he took such liberties when he danced." The queen sighed wistfully, then blinked as if emerging from a trance. "And now he's dead, smashed into pieces by an anarchist's bomb!"

"It was tragic," Alix said cautiously.

"Tragic? It would never have happened in England! My dear, this is precisely why you need to steer clear of Russia!"

"It's not an issue!" Inadvertently, Alix had raised her voice. "Nicholas has no romantic intentions toward me, of that I can assure you."

If Victoria heard the implied subtext—that Alix had romantic intentions toward *him*—she was too tactful to reveal it.

"I see," the queen said simply, with deliberate calm.

For a long moment they just stared at each other, grandmother and granddaughter, each strong-willed and stubborn. Then Victoria sighed.

"Why don't you take a moment to collect yourself. I'll be waiting at the carriage."

As the queen walked off, admirably steady without her cane, Alix wrapped her arms around her torso and stared at the horizon. She thought of something her mother used to say: that when you have a question, it's always best to ask in the morning light, because that's when answers are easiest to find. She realized now that her mother had likely said that to stop Alix's endless questions at bedtime. Still, it was hard to shake the old belief.

This still counted as morning light, even if was gray and Scottish and damp.

"Mother," Alix whispered, her eyes stinging with tears. "Please, tell me what to do."

THE LETTER WAS WAITING IN ALIX'S BEDROOM WHEN THEY AR-
rived back at Balmoral.

She recognized the seal at once, a double-headed eagle clutching a shield in its talons. Still, she didn't really believe it was from him until she opened it and saw his signature at the bottom of the page—*Nicholas.*

Alix let out an actual yelp, dropping the letter as if it had burned her fingers, then scrambled to pick it back up. The note had been forwarded from London and was dated several weeks ago.

Alix,

> *My mother just told me your joyous news, and I want to be the first to congratulate you. I am so excited for you and my cousin. Eddy is lucky to have you as a wife. I know that he will make you happy, and of course you must be delighted to stay in your beloved England. . . .*

There was more in the same vein, but Alix set the letter down, her hands trembling. Beneath her outrage—this was clearly the work of the Princess of Wales, who'd written her sister, Nicholas's mother, about an engagement that hadn't even *happened* yet—she felt a flicker of confused hope.

What did it mean, that Nicholas had written to her about Eddy?

Throwing everything she knew about etiquette and proper behavior to the winds, Alix reached for a sheet of her stationery.

Your Imperial Highness,

No, that felt wrong. He had called her Alix; surely she could use his name.

Nicholas,
I was delighted to receive a letter from you. However, I am afraid I must inform you that your mother has fallen victim to a rumor. There is no news about me and Prince Eddy, except that I am staying at Balmoral with Her Majesty, and the Waleses are also here.
If anything is agreed upon, you will learn of it when a formal announcement is made.
I hope you are in good health and continuing to recite poetry.
                              Respectfully yours,
                              Alix

The line about poetry might have been a bit much, but she wanted to remind him that they weren't strangers. They had a shared history, too: maybe not as extensive as her ties with Eddy, but one that could be built upon. If Nicholas was willing to try.

Alix folded the letter, sealed it with hot wax, and handed it to a maidservant before she could change her mind.

She hadn't lied to him. Grandmama had tried to coerce her and Eddy into an engagement today, but while Eddy may have consented, Alix had never given *her* agreement. She didn't consider herself engaged—at least not yet.

And if Nicholas thought she was, then Alix needed to correct him.

CHAPTER EIGHTEEN

May

MAY CAUGHT A GLIMPSE OF HERSELF IN THE BALLROOM MIRROR
and bit back a sigh. Like everything else at Balmoral, the evening
attire seemed especially designed to show her at a disadvantage.
Her red-and-black tartan, borrowed from the Balmoral stock,
hung despondently over her shoulders, refusing to stay put
despite the brooch May had pinned it with. Really, it was ab-
surd of the queen to insist they dress like this; no one actually looked *good* in tartan.

Except, of course, for Alix, who looked stunning in a soft
blue pattern interwoven with navy and gray, which brought
out the impossible blue of her eyes. No one else in the ballroom was wearing that print; it must have been the one she'd
mentioned on the train, designed by her mother, Alice, for
the Hessian branch of the family. May would have loved to
take Alix up on her offer and borrow her extra—it would
have been so much more flattering than this old, mothball-
ridden one—but it didn't feel right, making any demands on
her budding friendship with Alix. Not after May had gos-
siped about Alix to Maud.

The ballroom was full to bursting. The guests, and all the
neighbors from the nearby estates of Birkhall and Abergeldie,

jostled for position with the castle's staff: this was Queen Victoria's annual Ghillies Ball, held at the end of every summer to thank the servants.

The final night of their visit, and May had nothing to show for her efforts toward Prince Eddy.

She couldn't be sure whether Maud had spread word about Alix's ailments, but if the queen had heard, the news clearly didn't perturb her, because she kept throwing Eddy together with Alix. And as if that weren't enough of an obstacle, Eddy seemed to have forgotten May's existence altogether.

He never paid her more than the most cursory attention, his gaze constantly sliding over her as he searched for someone else. At first she'd assumed that someone was Alix, but after ten days of discreetly watching them, May was convinced that they didn't care about each other. Their courtship had continued only from a sense of inertia, or obligation.

Still, there was something out of place about Eddy, a restlessness or emotion that May couldn't quite identify. Just this morning while standing at her window, she'd seen him wander distractedly to the edge of the gardens, where he knelt down for a bright yellow flower and tucked it in his pocket. Perhaps he was plagued by money troubles, or an issue with his family? Given his ambivalence toward Alix, May doubted it was romance.

She stole another glance across the ballroom at Alix, who had drifted away from Eddy to stand alone. "Maud, shall we take a turn around the room?" May suggested, looping an arm through her cousin's. Enormous iron candelabra hung overhead, their gas lamps casting the room in a cozy amber glow. May tried not to look at the boars' and stags' heads mounted above the ornate stone fireplace. Apparently they could never be removed, as they had all been shot by Prince Albert.

When they reached Alix, May smiled as brightly as she could. "Hello, Alix. Are you enjoying the dancing?"

"Oh yes! This is always my favorite night at Balmoral."

It was a surprising statement from shy Alix, given the rambunctious atmosphere. The male servants in particular seemed indefatigable, hurtling through dance after dance with hoarse, rowdy cheers. Already two glasses had shattered on the floor. May suspected that the men were sneaking off to drink something stronger than the wine and sherry served by the queen.

"Look at Grandmama! She's enjoying herself," Maud observed, gesturing to a line of dancers. Sure enough, the queen was beaming. "It's almost as if she recently got some good news."

Alix colored at that, but all she said was, "I do love seeing Grandmama dance. She never does so at home."

Because it would be vastly inappropriate for the queen to toss aside her cane and dance a quadrille in a London drawing room! To May's utter shock, Victoria—wearing her tartan sash over her usual black gown—had joined in tonight's jigs and reels, clapping vigorously to the music of the piper. Her limp seemed to have temporarily vanished, and there were spots of color on her cheeks, as if she'd shed decades along with her dignity.

"I'm sure it's easier here," Alix added, almost to herself. "So many of the Scottish dances are done in a group, rather than requiring a partner—which probably makes her think of Grandpapa, and how much she misses him."

Alix, always the sappy romantic. "You're right," May agreed.

As one song ended and the lines of dancers bowed to each other, Prince Eddy started toward them. He glanced back over his shoulder at his grandmother, as if checking to make sure she was watching, then beelined for Alix.

See, his actions seemed to say, *I'm doing as I was bidden, are you happy?*

"Would you join me, Alix?" he asked, holding out a hand.

"Of course." Alix paused as the opening bars of the next song filled the room. "But it's the Dashing White Sergeant! Maud, come with us?"

"I was just about to get some air," Maud demurred, retreating a step.

"May?" Alix prompted.

May stared at her blankly, and Alix repeated, "It's the Dashing White Sergeant! Dance with us, please?"

"It's a dance of three, typically performed with two women and one man," Eddy clarified. "Alix is right; we need a third."

Two women and one man—how utterly Scottish. If someone tried to introduce this dance in London, the society matrons might die of shock.

"I would love to, though I don't know the steps." May hated that she was once again drawing attention to her outsider status, to the fact that they all knew these Balmoral quirks and traditions, while she was behind a veil of ignorance.

"The steps are easy!" Alix exclaimed, with evident relief. It was so strange how she didn't seem to want to be alone with Eddy. "First you make a circle in one direction, then you spin with your right-hand partner . . ." Alix kept going, rapidly listing a series of dance steps, though May had given up listening.

She would learn the movements on the fly; she was good enough at following someone else's lead. God knows she'd been doing it with her father for years now.

Everyone raised their hands to clap over their shoulders as the music sped up. Eddy and Alix each reached for one of May's hands, and the three of them began spinning: first one direction and then, as May began to feel dizzy, the opposite way. After a few bars of music, their circle merged with another circle—composed of George, Louise, and Hélène d'Orléans—and the six of them began wheeling ever faster.

May was half a step behind the others, always struggling to catch up to what they had just done, but it didn't seem to matter. She felt buoyant, seized by an unexpected and utterly childlike joy. It was all so silly, as if she and her cousins had gone back in time and were playing ring-around-the-rosy on the lawn. Eddy was just as lanky and laughing as he'd been at age ten; across the circle, George furrowed his brow, focusing intently on the steps. The sight struck May as endearing.

She met Alix's gaze and ventured a smile as the other three-some broke apart, then began a funny little jig in their direction, all of them prancing and pointing their toes.

And then May saw it. A single yellow blossom was tucked behind Hélène's ear.

It had been discreetly done; May would never have noticed if the heated dancing hadn't slipped Hélène's hair from its pins. But it was there, as unmistakably gold as when Eddy had plucked it from the gardens this morning.

Logically, of course, May knew this could be some other flower. There were certainly thousands on the grounds of Balmoral. But some primal feminine instinct made her feel certain that it was not.

Eddy had picked this flower specifically, and secretly, for Hélène.

It all fell into place, stray questions resolving themselves in May's mind. Eddy had been distracted at Balmoral, but as she'd suspected, it wasn't because he loved Alix—it was because his grandmother wanted him to marry Alix while he had feelings for *Hélène*. Who was at best an erstwhile princess: a royal without a throne, without a country. It also explained the puzzling fact of Hélène's presence at Mar Lodge, which May had been curious about, since Louise and Hélène weren't exactly friends.

Of course, Hélène could never be considered as a bride for Eddy. Aside from her family's exile, there was the insurmountable issue of religion. A Catholic queen? No, May assured herself. Hélène would never get Queen Victoria's stamp of approval.

Still, she was a complication.

It had been hard enough when May thought she was up against Alix, the queen's clear favorite. Now she had *another* princess to contend with? Hélène might be unsuitable as wife material, but Eddy clearly cared for her—which was far more than he'd ever felt about May. And if Hélène was wearing his secret love flowers, then his sentiments were returned.

Stomp, stomp, spin, spin: the dance kept whirling about her, breathless and relentless. May stumbled, the pin of her brooch digging into her skin, her good mood viciously deflated. She'd been smooth enough when her mind was focused on following the others, but now she'd lost her rhythm and couldn't get it back. She kept tripping over Eddy or turning the wrong direction. Shame clouded her vision, and bitter tears stung her eyes. Stupid of her to think that she might have ever had a chance at Eddy—at *freedom*. May would be stuck with the Tecks for the rest of her life, forever relegated to the fringes of the royal world, a poor relation only invited to events out of pity or obligation.

If she didn't feel so miserable, she might have laughed at the circumstances of this dance, which placed Eddy between two women as if he were the prize they were fighting over.

Except that there weren't just two women who wanted him: there were three.

CHAPTER NINETEEN

Hélène

SEVERAL WEEKS LATER, HÉLÈNE WALKED SLOWLY THROUGH THE gallery, snatches of conversation floating around her.

I never imagined that photography might be an acceptable hobby, but I suppose if the Princess of Wales is doing it . . .

What are you wearing to the Cadogans' ball? I was thinking of going as Madame de Pompadour, except there are sure to be so many of those . . .

Her Royal Highness really captured the spirit of the dogs, don't you think?

Hélène paused before the portrait in question: a photograph of a mournful-looking basset hound, nestled on a tasseled and fringed pillow. LOCKEY AT HOME, BY HER ROYAL HIGHNESS THE PRINCESS OF WALES, read a plaque below the photo. If she weren't in such a rotten mood, Hélène might have burst out laughing.

Her parents had dragged her to today's gathering at an art gallery on Regent Street. Though they weren't in the palace, this was to all intents and purposes a court function: the unveiling of a series of photographs taken by Alexandra, Princess of Wales.

So far, Hélène had successfully managed to avoid a

conversation with Prince Eddy, as she'd done ever since their return from Balmoral.

Belatedly, she realized that the Princess of Wales was approaching, and sank into a curtsy. "Your Royal Highness."

Alexandra looked impeccable as usual in a dusky pink dress, her smile bland. "Thank you for coming. What do you think of the photographs?"

"Oh! Your work is so . . ." Hélène scrambled to find a fitting adjective. "So interesting! I'd love to hear more about the process. Have you set up a darkroom at Marlborough House?"

"I don't actually develop the photographs. That would be the work of Mr. Helsby."

At his name, a man with a black mustache stepped forward and bobbed his head. "Thomas Helsby, of the London Stereoscopic Society, at your service."

"Mr. Helsby has been giving me private photography lessons, and of course, he handles the development process. I find that it's more pleasant just to take the images."

"Silver nitrate solution is quite noxious. Hardly appropriate for a lady to be handling," Mr. Helsby said officiously. "And of course I help Her Royal Highness to carry the camera and the tripod."

"Yes, the implements are quite heavy," Alexandra agreed.

It sounded like the Princess of Wales hadn't done much to produce these images at all, except perhaps to arrange her various dogs in front of Mr. Helsby and his tripod.

Eddy's mother turned aside to greet someone else, leaving the photographer with Hélène. "Are you interested in photography, miss?" he asked politely. "We've had a number of young ladies of quality taking lessons at the institute, as a modern alternative to painting and sketching. And we have the loveliest garden out back."

"A garden?" Hélène repeated.

"So that you can photograph the flowers." He gave what he probably thought was an encouraging smile. "The Countess of Erroll is quite enamored of our rosebush. She took a charming series of pictures there, featuring her Siamese cat."

Her cat. Of course.

"Mr. Helsby, are all the cameras very heavy, or is there one that I could carry on my own?" At his blank look, Hélène added, "There must be some research into reducing the camera size. I would love to be able to bring a camera with me."

"Bring it with you? Where?" he asked, bewildered. "Surely you have a manservant or a brother who can assist you with the tripod, even at your country home."

Mr. Helsby probably thought he was being tactful, avoiding any mention of a husband or fiancé, but it didn't matter. He'd made his point. Photography was yet another activity that a woman couldn't engage in without the help of a man.

Hélène had no desire to sit placidly in a garden, photographing rosebushes. She wanted to sail down the Nile and drink tea in Ceylon and ride horses across a sand dune, wearing the outfit Eddy had given her. And she wanted a camera that could record it all, so that when she was old and bedridden she could look at the images and remember how full and adventurous her life had been.

Not that such a life was even an option for her.

Hélène murmured a goodbye to Mr. Helsby and started to turn aside—only to freeze at the sight of Prince Eddy. He was over by the windows with his father and Alix of Hesse.

Hélène's body felt still, and cold, and heavy, as if she'd

plunged into a frozen lake and was being dragged down into its icy depths.

Alix and Eddy looked so maddeningly perfect together, like the set of matched dolls that Hélène had been given as a child. Alix's docile sweetness, her perfect blond hair, the way her every gesture was underscored with etiquette and forethought—she was exactly what a future queen should be, as if she had been custom-designed to stand next to Eddy and show off his kingliness.

Alix looked up, apparently feeling the weight of Hélène's gaze. Then, to Hélène's surprise, she said something to Eddy and started over.

God, it would be so much simpler if Hélène could hate her. She *wanted* to hate her. Yet there was a good-natured earnestness to Alix, a sweetness that shone through her shy reserve. Ever since that episode at the opera last year, Hélène had felt oddly protective of Alix: the way an older sister might feel, though Hélène was hardly a year older.

In other circumstances—if Alix weren't publicly courting the man Hélène secretly loved—perhaps they could have been friends.

"I'm glad to see you today, Miss d'Orléans," Alix began, a bit coolly. "There is something I'd like to ask your advice on."

Hélène nodded, caught off guard. "How can I help?"

The two young women drew aside, away from the photographs that lined the walls. Hélène realized that Alix was thrumming with tension like a newly strung bow.

"What would you do," Alix demanded, "if someone betrayed your trust in a cruel and hurtful way?"

Oh. This was no rhetorical question; it was an accusation.

Alix knew about Hélène and Eddy.

Hélène's mind whirled. She could deny it, of course: insist that Alix had the story all wrong. But that would only add a lie to the wounds she'd already inflicted.

"I'm sure that the person in question didn't set out to hurt you," she said swiftly. "Any damage done must have been inadvertent, not malicious."

"Then this person was thoughtless, which is as condemnable as outright cruelty."

So much for Alix being a shy wallflower. It would seem that when push came to shove, she was ready to defend her ground.

Hélène nodded, chastened. "You are right. A lack of foresight is no excuse for harming others, no matter how unintentional the damage was."

At that, the anger seemed to deflate from Alix, and she gave a weary sigh. "I just . . . I had hoped you might be more discreet."

Before Hélène could reply, Alix turned and walked away, her face smooth and sphinxlike. You would never know from looking at her that she'd just confronted her fiancé's lover.

Hélène stared after her, regret curling in her stomach.

She needed to find Eddy. But she wasn't like Alix; she had no claim on him, couldn't just march over and grab his elbow. Hélène was forced to head over slowly, chatting with other guests along the way, weaving around swishing petticoats as various people pretended to admire the Princess of Wales's handiwork.

When he saw her approach, Eddy nodded to a picture of Alexandra with her daughter Louise. The two of them had posed on the terrace at Sandringham, parasols perched over their shoulders.

"I must say, I'm not sure Mother should get credit for this one."

Hélène's breath caught. She couldn't help it; the moment she saw him, the old familiar longing pulsed through her body, to pool warm and hungry in her core.

Unaware of her distress, Eddy kept talking. "She can't have taken the picture if she's in it. Which raises the question: what does self-portraiture mean in photography?"

"Eddy . . ." Hélène meant it as a warning, or a reprimand, but it sounded more like a sigh.

He took an imperceptible step closer. It was reckless, having him this near to her—so close that she could almost feel the heat of his body.

"You haven't come over since Balmoral," he whispered. "Is everything all right?"

"Of course not!"

It came out harsher than she'd meant, but the image of Eddy and Alix together was still branded onto the back of her eyelids like the aftermath of a photographic flash.

Eddy stiffened. "So it's true? You've been avoiding me?"

Yes, she'd been avoiding him since Balmoral, stung by the way he'd publicly courted Alix—dancing with her, sitting next to her at every meal, *marrying* her onstage—then giving wildflowers to Hélène in secret, as if an illicit flower could somehow fix everything.

And that was *before* she'd realized that Alix knew about them.

"Eddy, we need to talk," Hélène said heavily.

The change that came over him was swift and awful: his eyes darkened, his body tensed with anxiety. "Who told you?"

"What?" she asked, confused.

"Never mind." Seeming relieved, Eddy nodded toward a doorway that led to an alcove: an extension of the gallery, technically speaking, but no one had ventured in there because the walls weren't hung with the Princess of Wales's portraits. It was half-lit and empty and certainly not where a young woman should walk with a prince unchaperoned.

Hélène nodded, letting Eddy lead her into the shadowed silence.

When they were alone, he spun her around to face him. "I've missed you," he murmured gruffly.

"Me too."

Even though she shouldn't, Hélène let herself nestle closer. When Eddy lowered his mouth to hers, she kissed him automatically, unthinkingly.

Then she tore away and took a step back.

"Eddy—did you tell Alix about us?"

The shock on his face was genuine. "Of course not."

"If you didn't tell her, then someone did. She knows. Her exact words were, 'I wish you had been more discreet'!"

"I trust Jonathan, and you said that Violette would never betray you. Who else knows?"

"No one! But maybe Alix saw us together at Balmoral, or figured it out somehow?"

"We've been careful—"

"Not careful enough!" Hélène shook her head. "All I know is that she just confronted me, accused me of betraying her trust."

Eddy had the grace to look deeply uncomfortable. "I'm sorry. I can speak to her if you like." He sounded like he would rather go into battle unarmed.

Hélène remembered what he'd said earlier—*Who told you?*—and a horrible, sinking feeling seized her in its grip.

"What is the exact nature of things between you and Alix?"

His expression fell, confirming her worst fears. Her throat closed up, and she wanted to scream, but somehow, impossibly, she held his gaze. "Are you engaged?"

The bleak truth was written on his face. She nodded and turned away, but Eddy caught her wrist in his grip.

"Hélène, please! Don't leave me because of who I am—because of what's expected of me."

She tugged her hand away, stung. "Congratulations. I'm sure you'll be very happy together."

"You must know that I don't want to—"

"It's quite all right; you don't owe me any explanation." Her words were wooden, stilted with formality. "We both knew this would end eventually."

"No," he said swiftly. "Nothing has to change. We can continue just as before!"

"Until when? Until you are *married?*" Hélène challenged. "What are you going to do, sleep with Alix for an heir and then come to my bed straight from hers?"

He winced at her bluntness. "We could find a way to make things work."

"Alix would hate us for it."

"If she knew—"

"Eddy. The wife always knows."

They fell silent, both of them thinking of Eddy's long-suffering mother. Most recently, the Prince of Wales had gotten involved with the Countess of Warwick—and the count was one of his close friends. It was a pattern that Bertie seemed to prefer, sleeping with his friends' wives.

Was that what Eddy planned to do with Hélène? Marry her off to one of his friends to make their affair more convenient?

"I'm so sorry," Eddy said softly.

She knew what he meant by those words. He was sorry he was a prince, and not free to follow his heart; he was sorry that she wasn't an appropriate choice for a future Queen of England. She knew, too, that he didn't say *I'm sorry* very often in his life.

Hélène looked back up at Eddy and saw her heartache mirrored on his features. He reached up to graze her cheek with his fingertips, and the sensation shivered through her whole body.

How deeply foolish she'd been, going to Balmoral, letting herself fall in love with him. Because she did love him, despite all her promises to herself.

It would hurt to leave him, yet this affair would end in hurt no matter which road she chose.

The only thing Hélène could do now was protect herself as best she could.

"I'm sorry, too," she said, before walking away from the future King of England.

CHAPTER TWENTY

May

THE PROBLEM WITH FANCY-DRESS PARTIES, MAY THOUGHT IN frustration, was that it grew quite difficult to recognize the other guests. And if you were on the hunt for a husband, you really needed to know who was who.

She glanced around the ballroom at Culford Park, where Roman centurions waltzed with medieval damsels, and men in doublets strolled with women in the wide panniers and be-ribboned wigs of the *ancien régime*. In spite of the costumes, May had successfully identified several dukes and at least one earl, though unfortunately most of them were already married. Well, she would settle for a divorcé at this point; she would settle for a *marquess* if push came to shove.

She needed to get out of her father's house, and fast.

Earlier this afternoon, she'd been starting to curl her hair with heated tongs—a difficult process that involved sitting by the fireplace, trying not to sweat, while constantly studying one's reflection in the mirror—when she heard the crunch of wheels on their gravel driveway. A glance out the window revealed that it was the Endicotts' carriage.

May hurriedly dropped the tongs and ran down the stairs, taking them two at a time, but she wasn't fast enough.

Inexplicably, her father had risen from his lethargy to answer the door.

If only he'd stayed put. It wasn't as if they were in the habit of greeting unexpected guests; the only people who ever showed up at White Lodge were creditors, or the occasional woman dropping off Needlework Guild shirts for May.

When May reached the entry hall, she found her father staring bemusedly at one of the Endicotts' footmen, who was holding a massive box in both hands.

"Your Serene Highness," the footman called over Francis's shoulder, recognizing May from all the afternoons she'd spent with Agnes. "I was instructed to bring this to you."

May winced, silently cursing as she tiptoed forward to accept the box. It was clear from its size and shape that it contained a gown.

Ignoring the footman, Francis turned to his daughter, his voice dangerously cold. "May. Have you been shopping?"

"Oh no . . ." May felt herself becoming smaller, as if she were one of those tropical turtles retreating into its shell— as if by taking up as little space as possible, she might encourage her father to forget her. "It's an old dress," she lied, "but the fringe on the hem needed to be repaired. Thank you for delivering it," she added pointedly, in the direction of the footman. To her relief he bowed and retreated, hearing the dismissal in her words. Within moments he was snapping the reins over the Endicotts' matched bay horses, which started off at a crisp trot.

Francis watched the carriage depart, his eyes narrowed as he took in its expensive details. "Whose carriage is that? It hardly looks like it belongs to a tradesman."

"It belongs to a friend." Before her father could ask which friend, May went on: "She's the one who stepped on my dress and tore the hem, so she sent it out for repairs at her expense."

Francis nodded, pleased by this explanation. "I'm glad to hear that you stood up for yourself, made her clean up her own mess. If only your mother could do the same."

May's arms ached from holding the box, but she didn't dare set it down. "I'm sorry?"

"You haven't heard? Your mother's cousin has once again denied my petition to be styled as a Royal Highness."

It was one of Francis's absolute favorite things to do, call-ing Queen Victoria *your mother's cousin*. Emphasizing and underscoring his tenuous royal connection.

"I'm sorry," May murmured, though he wasn't listening.

"It's an outrage, frankly. A grave insult. After everything I've been through!"

Everything he had been through? In other words, his com-plete inability to live within a budget and spend according to his means, which had landed them in such debt that May had spent years in exile?

Of course the queen had refused his request to become a Royal Highness. Francis had asked the same thing half a dozen times before, as if sheer persistence might wear Victo-ria down. May didn't share his optimism.

She took a tentative step toward the staircase, causing Francis to glance at her again. He must have finally noticed that her hair was half-curled, because he asked, "Are you going somewhere?"

"We've been invited to the Cadogans' fancy-dress party."

The invitation had been extended to the whole family, though May wasn't sure whether her parents planned on attending.

"Fancy dress." He sneered. "It's ridiculous, grown people dressing up as if they're children playing at make-believe."

That sounded like a resounding no.

Still clutching the enormous box to her chest, May started up the stairs, but her father's next words stopped her in her tracks. "You know, when the doctor came out of the birthing chamber and told me your mother had delivered a girl, I was delighted."

The burst of sentimentality was so unexpected that May nearly stumbled. "You were?"

"I thought to myself, a girl, now that's something. A girl could be the making of this family—provided she married well."

The smile that had started to form on May's face evaporated.

Francis snorted in derision. "What a fool I was. You . . ." He waved a hand in her general direction, indicating her dowdy outfit, the curls of hair already growing limp and straight, her plain face.

"You are not the daughter I expected, not at all," he'd said dismissively.

Now May blinked and stared around the party, trying to shake off the memory. She was grateful for the distraction when Agnes looped an arm through hers.

"I thought you said the prince was coming?" Agnes asked, her voice low and conspiratorial.

"I believe so." Though May had seen Agnes a few times since she'd returned from Balmoral, she hadn't explained everything that had happened. Namely, that she had given up hope on Prince Eddy.

May liked to think of herself as clever and resourceful, but even she knew her limits. What good was it continuing on this path when Eddy was publicly attached to Alix and privately enamored of Hélène?

No, May thought wearily, she couldn't afford to waste time on lost causes. She needed to resign herself to her dwindling prospects and look elsewhere.

Lord Weymouth was here, dressed as Emperor Augustus. He might be old enough to be her father, but May wouldn't let a consideration like that stop her. Should she go over and make a remark about how they were both dressed as ancient Romans, or would he think it too forward?

Oblivious to May's distress, Agnes squeezed her arm. "Well, I for one cannot *wait* until His Royal Highness sees you! You look stunning."

May was wearing the gown Agnes had sent, a deep green silk with velvet brocade down the skirt. Agnes had remarkable instincts when it came to these things—May would never have selected this shade for herself, but it was undeniably flattering. The emerald color emphasized her skin, making her unremarkable face seem almost pretty, or at least unblemished, and it caught the darker strands of her blond hair, enriching its normally ashen color. Thoughtfully, Agnes had instructed the dressmaker to include a woven crown with artificial leaves, adding a vaguely Roman touch.

"Thank you for the dress," May said warmly. "Though, really, you shouldn't have bought it."

"Please! It's the least I could do, after you saved me from the social suicide of coming here as Guinevere." Agnes looked around. "I wouldn't have noticed it, but of course you're right. I see a thousand French and Spanish kings, but not a single Tudor."

When Agnes had announced that she would dress as Guinevere, a horrified May had quickly explained the unspoken mandate ruling British fancy-dress parties. One could *never* dress as a British king or queen, even a fictional Arthurian one, if real royalty might be present. It was a gross example of lèse-majesté.

Forced to abandon her Guinevere plan, Agnes had commissioned a Cleopatra costume instead. The billowing white fabric of her dress was shot through with gold, and a snake-like headpiece fastened back her chestnut-colored hair.

"*You're* the one who looks stunning. You were born to be Cleopatra," May said loyally, at which Agnes brightened.

It was a bit surprising that the Endicotts had been invited tonight; the Earl Cadogan and his wife always entertained on a grand scale, but May had never known them to befriend Americans before. Good for Agnes, she thought. May might have launched her career, but Agnes seemed to be moving along quite well on her own.

May hadn't realized how much better it would be to attend this sort of party with a friend, instead of languishing on the side with all the other unmarried women. Agnes might be unmarried, too, but she was constitutionally incapable of sitting still.

"Look, there she is!" Agnes whispered excitedly. May followed her gaze to where Alix of Hesse stood across the ballroom.

Alix had dressed in a white shepherdess dress and matching bonnet, apparently opting for simplicity. Though she wasn't standing with Eddy—she was talking with a pair of rather dour-looking women dressed as nymphs, or were they dryads?—countless guests stared at her, as if they had heard the rumors, and already considered her their future queen.

The unfairness of Alix's beauty struck May all over again. The whole premise of fancy dress was that everyone mutually agreed to look ridiculous. Yet despite the rustic nature of her costume, Alix was resplendent.

"You never told me what happened at Balmoral," Agnes prompted. "Do you think Alix and Eddy are still courting?"

"If they are, it's at Queen Victoria's insistence. She seems determined to see them married."

"Ah," Agnes said meaningfully.

May hesitated, then stepped past the dance floor to a pocket of silence near a window. Agnes followed eagerly in her wake.

"I tried what you suggested. I told Maud about Alix's bizarre fainting spell, about how Alix was damaged," May whispered.

That word, *damaged*, echoed cruelly in the silence. But Agnes beamed at May with unmistakable pride. "I'm so glad! I knew you had it in you!"

"I don't know." May swallowed against a roughness in her throat. "Don't you think it was a little . . . harsh?"

"All you did was tell the truth," Agnes said evenly. "Of course it would be different if you had lied; that would be slander. But you really *did* see Alix in the grips of a psychological attack. If I were Her Majesty, I would want to know such a thing about a potential future queen." She hesitated. "Are you certain that Maud told her?"

"I assumed she would, but the queen never seemed to

change her opinion about Alix." Perhaps she simply didn't want to hear something negative about her favorite grand-child.

Agnes digested this thoughtfully. "You could tell some-one else . . . the Princess of Wales?"

"To what end? Eddy has shown no interest in me." May sighed. "He hardly even knows I exist!"

"You didn't manage to speak with him alone? You were gone for almost two weeks, in a remote castle in the Scottish highlands. If that doesn't give you the space for a bit of flirta-tion, then nothing will," Agnes replied, slightly teasing.

"There may have been flirtation, but it wasn't with me."

A pair of men dressed as knights shuffled past, the light gleaming on their false armor. Agnes and May drew further back into the alcove.

"Flirtation? I thought you said he and Alix didn't seem interested in each other."

May hesitated. Now she really was dealing in unfounded rumor; she had no proof of her suspicions save an incrimi-nating flower. Still, she'd been dying to tell *someone* since the moment she saw it tucked behind Hélène's ear.

"I think Eddy and the Princess Hélène are secretly in-volved."

Agnes gave her a startled look. "That French princess? The one with dark hair and a loud voice?"

May wouldn't have thought to call Hélène loud, but perhaps it was true. At Balmoral she had certainly laughed more heartily and ridden more eagerly than any of the other young women. There was a restlessness to her that May recognized—because, like May, Hélène seemed to chafe against society's bonds. Except that May kept her frustrations hidden.

And May knew better than to engage in flirtations with men who could never marry her.

She told Agnes about the flower in Hélène's hair, and how she'd seen Eddy plucking it from the garden earlier that day. "I could be wrong, of course. Perhaps it's just a coincidence. But it explains the feeling I had that Eddy was hiding something. . . ."

"Coincidences are rarer than you think." Agnes's fingers drummed absently on the windowsill. "No, I would wager that you are right. You are clever, May; your instincts about these things are rarely wrong."

A small part of May must have hoped that Agnes would call her ridiculous, because she sagged in defeat. "If it really is true, then I must give up my hopes for Eddy. There's no use trying to compete with Alix *and* Hélène."

May's eyes cut across the ballroom to Prince Eddy. As if on cue, he stole a furtive glance at Hélène, who was dancing with the Earl of Hertford.

Now that May knew what to look for, the attraction between Hélène and Eddy felt almost obvious.

"Do you think Alix knows?" Agnes asked, after a moment.

"About Hélène?"

"Yes! Do you think she suspects that the prince who has been publicly courting her is flirting with another woman, right beneath her nose?"

May realized, a bit guiltily, that she hadn't considered this from Alix's perspective. "Surely you aren't suggesting that I should tell her?"

"If not you, then who?" Agnes asked pointedly.

"It's not my place!"

"Don't you think she deserves to know? I thought you said that Alix was a romantic, and wanted to marry for love."

"I don't want to get involved! This is between Eddy and Alix."

"But you already are involved! If you ignore this, then you're making a choice on Alix's behalf, without her consent," Agnes said bluntly. "Don't pretend that doing nothing frees you from any responsibility. Doing *nothing* is as much an action as doing *something*."

Not to mention that if Alix found out about Hélène, it might end things between her and Eddy. Then, at least, May would be rid of one of her rivals.

It was a tempting prospect—but May thought of everything she'd already done to Alix, and shook her head.

"I'm done interfering in other people's relationships. I tried it at Balmoral when I told Maud about Alix's sickness, and it accomplished nothing."

"I think you're making a mistake," Agnes insisted.

"That's because you don't understand how things operate here!" May snapped, more tersely than usual. "If I'm not careful, I could get a reputation as a gossip. No one wants to be known as the woman who's always airing other people's dirty laundry. It is so . . . tawdry. So low."

Agnes drew in a sharp breath at the implication that *she* was tawdry and low. May winced, seeing the unmistakable pain in her friend's bottle-green gaze.

"I'm sorry," she blurted out, but Agnes interrupted.

"No, *I'm* sorry. You're right, I shouldn't have mentioned it." Agnes gestured toward the terrace, where colorful Chinese lanterns led down into the gardens. "I heard there might be fireworks later. Should we make our way outside?"

May nodded, though she still felt guilty. This was why she'd never managed a real friendship—because she didn't know how to navigate the difficult conversations that came with letting someone in. With *trusting* someone.

But lately, May had lost so much: her chance at befriending Alix, the prospect of winning Prince Eddy. She was determined not to lose Agnes, too.

AN HOUR LATER, MAY STEPPED INTO THE BALLROOM ALONE; Agnes's mother had stolen her daughter away, hoping to introduce her to some of her new acquaintances. May was scanning the crowds for a friendly face—Princess Maud, perhaps—when she was startled by the approach of Prince George. She couldn't place his costume; was he a Renaissance king, with those slashed sleeves and the ruff around his neck? He was wearing a crown, because of course *he* was exempt from the silent ban. You were allowed to dress as British royalty when you already *were* British royalty.

"Good evening, May." He wasn't smiling, but there was a softness to his expression that gave the impression he *wanted* to smile.

"George—hello." For some reason she didn't curtsy the way she would have for Eddy. Not because George was the younger brother, but because she sensed it would put him ill at ease.

He surprised her by holding out a hand. "I was wondering if you'd like to dance?"

"With me?" May winced at her own clumsiness; what was wrong with her? "I just meant, after our dances at the Ghillies Ball, surely you don't want to risk it. I'm afraid I stumbled all over your feet."

"Those dances are a bit wild for my taste, too," George admitted. "Which makes sense, given that they were invented as a martial exercise."

"Martial exercise?"

"Warriors used to perform them as training for battle. All that complicated footwork of the jigs? It traces back to swordplay."

"That explains why I was so abysmal at it; I have no experience in swordplay." May was surprised to hear how light-hearted her words came out, almost teasing. She placed her hand in his, and George led her onto the dance floor.

As the music started up, May realized with a flush of self-consciousness that it was a waltz. Waltzes were nowhere as scandalous as they once were—thirty years ago a young woman needed her parents' permission before she could dance one—but it was still the most physical dance on offer. Unlike the quadrille or the minuet or any of the other assembly dances, a waltz required the gentleman's hands to fully encircle his partner's waist. And stay there.

In other words, the waltz was the perfect dance for sneaking a few illicit touches between lovers, especially on a crowded dance floor like this one, full of warm bodies in crushed proximity.

George's hands settled a bit hesitantly over the green boning of her gown. "You make a wonderful Livia," he mumbled.

"Livia?"

"The Roman empress—Octavian's wife, deified after her death. She's not your costume?"

"I didn't actually have anyone in mind. I just wanted to wear this gown, and then I thought a laurel wreath might look nice with it. . . ." May trailed off self-consciously.

"Better a laurel wreath than a crown. Those are heavy," George said, gallantly changing the subject. The music shifted and they drifted toward the center of the dance floor, George's hand pressing a bit more steadily on her waist.

"I'm just grateful that I didn't come as Marie Antoinette." May nodded to where two different women were dressed as the French queen, each glaring at the other's costume.

"They rather look like they want to guillotine each other, don't they?" George asked, following her gaze.

"I wonder what the real Marie Antoinette would say, if she could see us now. Probably she would be insulted that we hadn't *all* dressed like her."

" 'Thus we play the fools with the time, and the spirits of the wise sit in the clouds and mock us,' " George said softly.

May wasn't one to moon over fictional characters like Alix, but even she recognized the cadence. "Is that Shakespeare?"

"*Henry IV, Part Two.*" George nodded down to his costume.

"Oh. Of course." May couldn't remember the last time she'd seen Shakespeare performed.

The steps of the dance pulled them apart for a brief moment. When they came back together, George bent his head. The small movement brought their lips dangerously close.

May blinked, flustered. George pulled back, leaving an appropriate amount of space between them.

"I actually wanted to be a highwayman tonight, but Mother refused to let me," he said gruffly, clearly trying to resume their normal conversation.

May chuckled. "I'm sure the Countess Cadogan would faint if she saw a highwayman in her ballroom! Though I have to imagine you'd have been more comfortable. Your ruff looks like an ordeal."

"It does make me grateful for modern fashion."

"At least you're not wearing a sword. That might have caused safety concerns."

"Funny that you say that. Eddy wanted us to borrow prop swords from the Shakespeare Memorial Theatre, but I told him it was more trouble than it was worth."

That sounded like Eddy, still eager to play with toy weapons.

"Besides, if you were a highwayman, you would have been forced to wear a mask," May went on.

George nodded emphatically as he spun her into one of the turns of the waltz. "Exactly! I wanted to wear a mask. It's so rare I get an excuse to keep my face hidden."

"Really?" Why on earth would George, a prince, want to walk around as an anonymous nobody?

"It would have been nice to escape notice for once. People are always talking to me because of who I am—because they want to use me to get to Father, or to Eddy." George attempted a cavalier tone, but May heard the hurt beneath.

She had never considered that aspect of his position, had she? George's entire self was defined in relation to someone else: his grandmother, his father, or most of all his brother. Eddy was the heir, the One Who Mattered, while George was just the *other* prince, brought into the world in case, god forbid, anything ever happened to Eddy.

The laws of succession weren't meant to be cruel; they were an incontrovertible part of life, as impersonal and unchanging as the turning of the planets. Still, they meant that George was imprisoned by his own identity. Just as May was.

"Well, I don't want to *use* you to reach someone else. I'm glad to talk to you for your own sake," May declared.

It shouldn't have been a bold statement, yet it somehow came out that way.

George smiled, not so shyly this time. "I feel quite the same."

Long after the party was over, May kept replaying those words in her mind. Her quest for Prince Eddy had reached a dead end, but maybe she shouldn't have gone after Eddy in the first place.

Maybe she had focused all her energies on the wrong brother.

CHAPTER TWENTY-ONE

Alix

ALIX TAPPED HER SHEPHERDESS STAFF AGAINST THE FLAGSTONES, wondering how much longer this party would last. She had come out to the terrace for a reprieve from the dancing—and from all the stares. It felt like everyone in England was watching her, wondering when she and Eddy would officially be engaged.

As the queen had promised at Balmoral, there was still no formal announcement, but the month Eddy had requested was rapidly dwindling away. Alix could only assume he'd spent the time arranging things with his mistress, or whatever else he'd needed to do.

Meanwhile, Alix couldn't stop thinking about the letter she'd written Nicholas at Balmoral, letting him know that she and Eddy were not engaged.

No reply had come.

The letter should have reached St. Petersburg within a matter of days, meaning that the tsarevich could have replied two weeks ago. Alix marshaled up one excuse after another: Nicholas was at Livadia and his mail hadn't been forwarded, or the maidservant at Balmoral had never posted it in the first place, or the railway car carrying it to Russia had crashed in a fiery explosion.

She clung to the belief that he hadn't gotten it, because it was far worse to think that he'd read it and disapproved of her forwardness—or, worse, that he simply didn't care.

The terrace was growing more crowded, fairies and Greek warriors and Valkyries spilling outside in anticipation of the fireworks. This might be a good time to fetch a glass of lemonade, or to seek out May of Teck. After Balmoral, Alix felt like May was the closest thing to a friend that she had in England. Certainly she *trusted* May, which was more than she could say for most people. Just look at what Princess Hélène had done, telling everyone about Alix's fainting spell. She'd as good as admitted it when Alix had confronted her at the photography exhibition. At least she'd had the decency to seem regretful.

There was a burst of noise near the doors that led inside. From the eager tone of the voices, Alix knew it could only mean one thing: royalty. The Prince of Wales must be approaching, or maybe Eddy.

Alix drew a breath into her rib cage and smiled, bracing herself for the onslaught of stares. But when she turned, she didn't see Eddy or his father.

Nicholas.

It couldn't be, Alix thought faintly. The Tsarevich of All the Russias was not at a house party in Suffolk. She had simply thought about him so much lately that she'd begun to hallucinate. Yet the figure before her looked startlingly real.

His cousin Tino—Prince Constantine, future King of Greece—stood next to him, wearing an old-fashioned doublet. Nicholas, on the other hand, hadn't dressed in costume at all but was wearing the formal version of his Russian dress uniform. His military jacket fit snugly over his shoulders, medals gleamed on his chest, and at his hip was a gleaming saber. A real one, not like the painted wood weapons that some men were carrying tonight because the real thing was too heavy to dance in.

Alix sensed that Nicholas didn't care all that much about dancing, and that this saber was far more than a prop—that, if necessary, he could wield it.

When he saw her, a smile touched Nicholas's features. Alix's heart picked up speed as he began threading through the crowds toward her.

"Alix. It's good to see you," he said in greeting.

"What are you doing here? I mean—" She flushed and recalled herself with a quick curtsy, which Nicholas waved away. She forced herself to try again. "I hadn't expected to see you tonight." *I hadn't expected to see you at* all.

In answer, he held out a gloved hand. "Walk with me?"

Alix was powerless to resist. She placed her palm carefully atop his and let him lead her into the gardens, which were a patchwork of shadow and colored lantern light.

The moment was surreal, yet at the same time Nicholas's presence was substantial and solid. It felt like the rest of the party had become a bright, elaborate dream and he was her only link to reality, the only person she could cling to.

"I've been traveling with Tino," Nicholas began, as they started down a gravel path. "He wanted a grand tour before his wedding to Princess Sophie, and my father suggested I join him."

Alix nodded distractedly. If Nicholas had been traveling, maybe her letter had never even reached him? "Where did you and Tino go?"

"We started in Ceylon, Singapore, Japan—I had a bit of

an incident with a sword there, actually." Nicholas lifted a lock of dark hair from his forehead.

Alix gasped at the red gash beneath. Her hand itched to reach up and trace it, but she resisted the highly inappropriate urge.

"That looks like it might scar," she said carefully.

"It's actually quite shallow. Nothing to worry about," Nicholas said swiftly. "Japan is fascinating, Alix. Did you know that they have an order of knighthood that dates back over a thousand years, with the same traditions and oaths since the very beginning?"

"No change for a thousand years? Sounds a bit like Russia."

To her relief, he grinned at the joke. "Probably explains why my father sent me there."

Alix's steps slowed as they approached an iron railing bordering one of the parterres. "Where else did you go?"

"We came up through the Suez Canal and have been visiting some cousins. The Greeks, the Italians—and we saw Franz Joseph and Sisi in Vienna."

"It sounds like you've had quite the adventure. Why, you've probably met more royal families than anyone I know except for Grandmama."

"Oh, it was all for Tino's sake." A funny expression darted over Nicholas's features, but Alix couldn't quite parse it out.

"Did he enjoy his grand tour? I imagine you were there to keep things calm," Alix said tactfully. A woman never did anything to mark the occasion of getting married, except perhaps for a tea with friends when she returned from her honeymoon, but it was different for men. Apparently on his own pre-wedding tour, Uncle Bertie had left a string of angry husbands and gambling debts all over Italy.

"Something like that," Nicholas said vaguely.

Alix's hand rested on the iron railing. Nicholas put his hand next to hers, close enough to touch without quite daring to do so.

"You look lovely tonight," he said quietly.

The air felt cold against her overheated face; she looked down at her feet to avoid Nicholas's gaze. "It's a silly costume. I don't really care for fancy-dress balls."

"Neither do I." Nicholas made a self-deprecating gesture that encompassed his military uniform. "We only arrived in town this morning; we're staying with Eddy and George at Marlborough House."

It was as jarring as always, hearing Nicholas refer to Eddy. The two of them occupied such vastly different roles in Alix's life.

"How long will you be in London?" she ventured.

"That depends." He cleared his throat. "I was disappointed when Ella told me that you and Ernie weren't coming to St. Petersburg this year. I had been hoping to see you—I have quite missed your conversation."

Her *conversation*?

"It has been a long time since we said goodbye," Alix agreed, heart pounding.

"Alix." One of Nicholas's hands had strayed to the handle of his saber, as if he might draw it and run someone through. "What you wrote in your last letter . . . is it true?"

At that, the world seemed to stop.

"You got my letter?" she whispered.

"Why else do you think I'm here? We were supposed to head back after Austria, but I convinced Tino to extend our tour. I needed to see you." Nicholas swallowed. "Are you engaged to Eddy?"

"No!"

The word escaped her lips in a single cry, like a plea.

"No?" the tsarevich repeated. "Because everyone in England seems to think that you are. Why, Aunt Alexandra told me just this morning that you and Eddy would be making an announcement soon."

"Grandmama wants us to get engaged, but I have not agreed to it," Alix insisted—because she hadn't, not technically. "Nothing has been decided."

The world felt unnaturally sharp around her, Nicholas's eyes a gleaming blue against the dusky night sky.

"So you are not promised to Eddy?" he asked again.

The sounds of the party felt impossibly distant; there might as well have been no one on earth but the two of them, together in this garden, beneath the star-flecked sky.

"I am not promised to Eddy, or to anyone."

Nicholas did not draw in a breath, or reach for her hand, or even smile. But there was a new brightness in his gaze as he turned to her, his breath fogging little clouds in the air.

"Do you remember your last night in Russia, at the Winter Palace?"

"Of course," Alix said softly.

"I thought for a moment that we almost kissed, but I wasn't sure . . ."

Wasn't sure if he'd meant to? If he ought to?

"I wasn't sure if you wanted me to."

Her reply was as quiet as his. "I did want you to. Very much."

Nicholas sighed at that, a deep sigh that Alix could feel in her own chest, and then he reached his hands around her torso and pulled her close. Alix had never been kissed before, but some instinctive part of her knew exactly how to tip her face up and press her lips to his.

The kiss was soft, and tender, and infinitely sweet. Alix knew they were being reckless, embracing like this in public—at a crowded party, no less—but she could no longer bring herself to care. She was drowning in the moment, in the feel and taste and scent of him, allowing her body the closeness it had craved since the moment she first saw Nicholas, all those months ago. Her hands crept up to settle around his shoulders, drawing his body even nearer to hers. It all felt so utterly *right*, as if her palms had been seeking those shoulders for years and now, at last, knew where they belonged.

Alix had no idea how long they might have spent entwined like that if a staccato sound hadn't flung them apart.

Her hands flew to her mouth. *Oh god*, she thought, someone had fired a gun—but then she realized that it was nothing to worry about; the pyrotechnics expert had begun setting off the fireworks down the lawn.

"I'm sorry." Nicholas took a hasty step back. "I should never have—it's my fault that—"

"Please, don't," Alix said breathlessly. "I do not regret anything that has happened, nor should you."

She only regretted that it hadn't happened sooner.

"Still, I am determined to do this right. Which means that we should get back to the party," Nicholas insisted.

Alix reluctantly started back toward the terrace, toward the other guests in their garish costumes and headgear, all of them transfixed by the colors in the sky. She knew he was right; they needed to return before their absence was noted.

Still, as they walked, Nicholas held her hand in his. His thumb traced small, delicious circles over her glove, sending shivers across her skin. It felt like a promise that whatever was between them had only just begun—that everything she felt for him, he felt, too.

CHAPTER TWENTY-TWO

Hélène

HÉLÈNE WISHED SHE HADN'T COME TO THIS STUPID FANCY-DRESS party. She'd done such a good job avoiding Eddy since that day at the photography exhibit: she'd ignored the notes he sent to her house—which were on unmarked stationery, though her parents had never screened her mail as some young women's did—and had stayed home from any events he might attend.

But there he was, wearing a navy tunic with a cape and a wide-brimmed hat, both decidedly French in style.

Hélène felt him trying to catch her eye and deliberately ignored it, dancing with one nobleman after another without registering their names. As usual, Eddy was surrounded by admirers of his own; the women around him were constantly batting their eyes or thrusting out their chests in their ridiculous spangled costumes. Hélène wished she could prowl circles around Eddy like some kind of territorial jungle animal. *Back off,* she wanted to tell them all. *He is mine.*

Except he wasn't hers, and never had been. He was Alix of Hesse's.

"Is that Hélène? My god, it's been too long!" The booming voice of Prince Constantine sounded behind her. He held out a hand, grinning. "Please, say you'll dance with me."

Dance with Eddy's cousin, known in the newspapers as the "rake of Greece"?

"I would be delighted." Hélène just hoped that Eddy was still watching. If he felt jealous, all the better. Maybe he would begin to understand what it was like for her, constantly watching him with Alix.

She and Tino swept onto the dance floor. The Greek prince looked wickedly handsome in his slashed doublet, as if he'd stepped straight out of a Titian painting. He nodded appreciatively at her plum-colored riding habit.

"Look at you, attending a fancy-dress party dressed for a hunt. You remind me of an Amazon," he declared. "One of the beautiful ones, of course, from the statues in our garden in Athens." He winked in a way that somehow implied he meant nude statues.

Normally Hélène would have laughed at that; she'd always liked Tino. He was easygoing in the way that men so often were but women never seemed to be. Because women could never *afford* to be.

Instead she stole a reflexive glance across the ballroom to where Eddy stood. He was watching her.

Something shivered between them, a flash of heat so palpable that Hélène almost worried the other guests might sense it.

Eddy tilted his head toward the terrace in a slight but unmistakable gesture.

Hélène knew she shouldn't follow, yet without a second thought she mumbled an excuse to Tino and turned away. It was as though Eddy were the sun, exerting a bodily gravitational pull on her.

She stepped through the double doors and saw that he was

heading into the grounds, his head tucked down beneath his hat to avoid notice. Hélène hesitated for only a heartbeat before following in his wake, edging along the manicured garden with its neatly trimmed parterres. Groups of people strolled along the gravel paths, which were lit by torches every few yards to maintain the illusion, at least, of propriety. Though Eddy and Hélène were sticking to the shadows along the far wall.

Ahead lay the orangerie, an enormous stone structure topped with a glass cupola. Eddy cast another glance back at Hélène before opening the door.

The air inside felt damp, heavy with the scents of earth and water and growing things. Vines and climbing plants trailed up the walls. Potted palms stood near the entrance, giving way to trees that grew in blithe disorder, their branches lacing overhead. It felt lush and erotic, pulsing with heat, completely unlike the rigid gardens Hélène had just walked through.

When he saw her, Eddy swallowed and pulled off his hat, running a hand through his hair. The warm lights drew out its tawny notes, making him look younger than usual.

"Have you read my letters?"

When she shook her head, he sighed, seeming unsurprised. "I want to talk to you—"

"I don't think we should be speaking at all, not when you're going to marry Alix," Hélène cut in.

"But that's just what I want to talk to you about! I want to marry you instead!"

His words reverberated wildly through the space, echoing off the trees, the fallen leaves. Hélène stared at him mutely.

"I'm sorry, I'm doing this all wrong." Eddy cursed under

his breath, then sank to one knee, right there in the damp earth. "Marry me, Hélène."

Hélène had always felt dismissive of women who needed smelling salts, but right now she felt as dizzy as any society lady. She gave Eddy's hands a gentle tug, trying to draw him to his feet.

"Eddy . . ." Her voice broke before she could say more.

After a painful moment he stood and let go of her. Hélène was acutely, achingly aware of the empty air between her body and his.

"Marry me," he said again. "I know there are obstacles, but I also know that I won't be happy with anyone but you."

Obstacles was putting it mildly. They were more like enormous boulders blocking the path forward: her religion, his position, her *lack* of a position.

"When was the last French and English royal marriage?" she prompted. Eddy frowned, puzzled, and Hélène answered her own question. "Four hundred years ago! When Catherine of Valois married Henry V!"

"Then it sounds like we're overdue for one." When Hélène didn't smile, Eddy abandoned the attempt at levity. "Look, I'm not pretending that it won't be difficult, but surely we owe it to ourselves to try?"

This was not how a princess's engagement should be decided. It should have been debated by her parents, in a drawing room, with her dowry and trousseau negotiated down to the last lace handkerchief. If her fiancé proposed at all, it was supposed to be a stiff and formal question, posed somewhere public like a garden party.

It should not be anything like this: a question asked in

warm, sultry darkness by a man you had already been to bed with, his face lit by flickering torchlight. There were small marks on Eddy's trousers from where he'd knelt on the ground.

In his fancy-dress ensemble, Eddy looked almost ordinary, but it would be foolish to think that there was anything ordinary about him.

"No matter what we do, they may not let us marry," she warned.

"Then we'll elope," Eddy said swiftly. "Actually, it's not a bad idea—we could do it tonight, find a local priest and get married in a chapel somewhere, with a few witnesses from a tavern to sign the certificate! Instead of asking my grandmother for her permission, we'll give her an existing marriage—a done deal. What is everyone going to do," Eddy added indignantly, "insist that I divorce you? No, once it's binding and legal, they'll have no choice but to live with it."

Hélène couldn't help thinking back to a year ago, when she'd said much the same thing to Laurent: that she wanted to run away and elope, and to hell with the consequences.

How odd that she'd wanted to elope with someone she didn't truly love, and now that she *was* in love, she couldn't go through with it.

"You know we can't," she said softly.

Eddy's expression darkened. "Why not? Just because we're royal, we have to be bound by laws and precedence?"

"In this instance, yes."

"You sound like Alix! I thought you were braver than this."

"I love you too much to pretend that I'm ashamed of you!"

Eddy drew in a breath. He realized as well as she did that it was the first time either of them had said *I love you.*

"Oh, Hélène. Surely you know that I love you too."

He held his arms open and she stepped forward, letting him fold her in an embrace. Hélène rested her cheek against his chest, reassured by the steady thump of his heartbeat.

"You still haven't given me a real answer," he said, his voice a rumble in her ears. "Will you marry me?"

The significance of this moment struck Hélène like a thunderbolt. Her reply would change everything. *It's too complicated*, she should tell him, except that every atom of her being wanted to shout instead, *What took you so long?*

She couldn't lie to him; it would be like trying to lie to herself. There was only one answer to give.

"Of course I will."

Eddy broke into a relieved smile. Hélène expected him to kiss her, but instead he tugged her deeper into the orangerie, as if hungry for more time alone. She pulled off one of her gloves and laced her fingers in his, relishing the sensation of touching him.

To their left was a bed full of plants she didn't recognize, with spiky leaves that stretched toward the glass ceiling. Following her gaze, Eddy asked, "You like pineapples?"

Was that what a pineapple plant looked like? Hélène had only ever seen the inner fruit, cut into golden segments on a dessert platter. Pineapples were a rare delicacy, imported from the colonies for the very wealthy.

"They're so ugly," she blurted out, at which Eddy laughed.

"I don't know if I would say ugly. They're sharp on the outside and sweet within. Not unlike a French princess I know." Before Hélène could argue, he'd reached for one of the spiky fruits and plucked it.

"Eddy!" she hissed. "You can't steal one of the Earl Cadogan's pineapples!"

"Why not? I highly doubt he'll notice." To her surprise, the prince pulled a small penknife from the pocket of his doublet. He expertly cut and cored the fruit, then held the knife toward her, a segment of pineapple speared on its tip.

Hélène lifted an eyebrow. "Impressive."

"I picked up a few tricks in the navy." He was back to his usual cheeky, mischievous grin. "Let it never be said that I don't provide for the woman I love."

Hélène leaned forward to bite the pineapple off his knife. "It's magical," she murmured, though she wasn't sure to what she was referring.

Eddy took a bite, too, then let the rest of the fruit fall into the dirt. He tucked back a loose strand of Hélène's hair and cradled her face in his hand. At the tenderness in his eyes she couldn't take it anymore; she tilted her chin up and kissed him. Eddy tasted warm, and sweet like the pineapple, and beneath it all something else, something that was indefinably *him*.

"We're getting married," he declared, when they finally pulled apart.

Laughter bubbled up out of Hélène, and she shook her head wonderingly. "We're getting married," she repeated.

CHAPTER TWENTY-THREE

Alix

IN THE WEEK SINCE THE CADOGANS' FANCY-DRESS BALL, ALIX had seen Nicholas nearly every day. It was always in a group setting—a musicale evening, a ride in Hyde Park—but whatever the occasion, the two of them would find a way to dance, or sit together, or simply talk.

She relished Nicholas's stories about his family, and most of all about Russia. His words painted a vivid picture of his vast empire: from the barren reaches of Siberia to the windswept mountains of the Caucasus to the glittering waters of the Black Sea. He told her of the *chyerti*, the magical beings of Russian folklore: "Mother would have been angry if she knew, but our nurse always left out a sip of milk for the *domovoi*. The house spirit," he explained, with a wink.

In exchange Alix told him her own stories, of drinking mulled wine at Christmas and playing blindman's bluff at the lake, of how Ernie used to bang at the family's organ to wake her up.

"You have an organ in your house? Do you live in a church?" Nicholas had teased.

Alix explained that the organ was located directly beneath her bedroom; Ernie delighted in blasting it when it was still dark out. "That organ is worse than the bagpipes at Balmoral," she added, which only made Nicholas laugh harder.

She loved his laugh, a bright, easy chuckle that felt so at odds with the polite laughter of society. She loved it most when *she* had made him laugh.

There was no more sneaking around; Nicholas didn't even reach for her hand unless the steps of a dance required it. But sometimes she caught him looking at her with a smoldering heat in his gaze, and Alix would shiver, thinking about their kiss. She wanted more of it—more of the delicious, illicit sensation of his mouth on hers, but also *more*. She wanted to be touching him in all ways possible.

It was a terrifying thought, and yet thrilling, too: the realization that kissing him didn't seem to be enough. She had never felt this way about anyone, hadn't even known she was capable of such a feeling.

Yesterday at breakfast, Grandmama had informed her that Eddy would be stopping by Buckingham Palace on Monday. "You will join us, Alix," she'd said crisply, as she tapped a spoon against the side of her soft-boiled egg. "We have much to discuss."

Alix couldn't let this engagement become official. Which meant that she and Eddy needed to be on the same page, and face Queen Victoria together.

Accompanied by one of the Buckingham Palace parlormaids, whom Queen Victoria had assigned to be Alix's lady's maid during her stay, she began the short walk down the Mall. It was a misty afternoon, and the few people she passed—other women strolling with their maids, or stern-looking nurses pushing perambulators—hardly seemed to notice her.

"I'm here to see His Royal Highness, Prince Eddy," Alix told the butler of Marlborough House, presenting her card. Though Nicholas was staying with the Waleses, she knew he would be out; he always spent the mornings riding with Tino. But Alix still feared she might run into Aunt Alexandra or Maud, and would be forced to explain why she was visiting her so-called fiancé unannounced.

The butler hesitated, clearly thinking along the same lines. "His Royal Highness is in his study. If you'll accompany me to the salon, I shall send for him."

"There's no need; I will call upon him directly," Alix declared. A new energy crackled through her, a bold and uncharacteristic sense of daring.

The butler had no choice but to point her down the hall. Technically Alix wasn't breaking the rules; she had a maid with her, and besides, couples were allowed unchaperoned time together—within reason—once they were engaged. Which everyone apparently thought she and Eddy were.

Outside Eddy's office, Alix turned to the maid, Amelia. "Would you mind waiting in the hall? I shall leave the door open," she offered, in concession to propriety. Then she knocked once and, without waiting for a response, pushed open the door.

Eddy was seated in an armchair, one leg crossed over the other knee as he studied a leather-bound tome. Without looking up he said, "Can it wait, Jonathan?"

"I'm sorry, but it can't."

Eddy startled, nearly dropping the book. "Alix?"

"I know you weren't expecting me, but I was hoping we could talk," she explained, taking a few cautious steps into the room.

Unlike his father's study, which occupied a whole corner of the ground floor, Eddy's was an extension of the Marlborough House library. A pair of double doors connected it to the main space, though they were currently shut. It was a handsome room, despite the half-eaten meat pie on the desk and scattered papers on the tables, the faint hint of tobacco smoke lingering in the air.

Eddy obviously hadn't planned on receiving company here. Especially female company.

"Of course." Eddy stood and took a few steps forward, glancing toward the windows. Storm clouds hung low and ominous in the skies, mist fogging the glass. Still, he half-heartedly asked, "Shall we head outside?"

"I'm quite all right here." Strangely enough, Alix rather liked that she'd caught Eddy off his guard. She was in no mood for artifice and social niceties.

The door to the hall was still open. Eddy kicked it partially shut—*don't kick at doors like a common innkeeper,* their grandmother would have said if she were here. Seeming to decide that leaving it half-open was good enough, Eddy gestured to the pair of armchairs near a bookcase. "Shall I ring for some tea, or . . ."

"I only need a few moments of your time." Alix settled onto one of the armchairs, a heavy, masculine thing that seemed to swallow her up. She shifted so that she was perched on its edge.

"Of course," Eddy agreed, bemused. He lifted the book he'd been reading and set it on a small wooden table. Alix stole a glance at the title: *The Old Regime and the French Revolution,* by Alexis de Tocqueville. Not what she'd have expected Eddy to be reading.

"Did you receive a summons from Grandmama?" she asked, cutting right to the chase.

A nervous expression darted over Eddy's features, and he ran a hand through his hair so that it stood up like a dark halo. "Actually, Alix, I'm glad you stopped by. I wanted to discuss it with you. That is . . ." He fumbled, started again. "I will always have the utmost respect for you, and I meant the sentiments that I expressed to you last year—or at least I meant them at the time—"

He looked so utterly miserable that Alix decided to interrupt. "If you're saying that you would rather not announce the engagement, I am in agreement."

"Oh. Yes—exactly."

A strange silence fell between them. Alix was acutely aware of the hiss of the wind outside, the rustle of her skirts as she shifted in the enormous chair.

"Should we formulate a plan?" she suggested. "We could still go to Grandmama's for tea, as she requested, and then together we can explain that the wedding is off."

When Eddy nodded morosely, Alix let out a breath. "I don't understand. Are you upset?"

He leaned forward, head in his hands. "It's just that . . . even without being engaged to you, I hardly expect Grandmother to approve of Hélène."

"Hélène?" Alix repeated the name slowly. "You mean Hélène of France?"

Eddy looked at her in surprise. "I thought you knew about us."

Eddy was interested in *Hélène*? Now Alix understood why he'd wanted to delay the engagement announcement. "What? How would I know about you two?"

"I have no idea! Hélène was very upset that you'd figured it out," Eddy proclaimed. "She said that you spoke to her at Mother's photography show. You told her that she should have been 'more discreet.'"

"I was angry that she'd been gossiping about me!" Alix burst out.

It all made so much more sense. Alix had never understood why Hélène had started talking about that fainting spell a year after it happened, but now she saw: Hélène was trying to undermine her, to break off Alix and Eddy's engagement in the hope of getting Eddy for herself.

Eddy frowned. "What do you mean, Hélène has been gossiping about you?"

Every fiber of Alix's being screamed at her to stop, to keep the awful truth of her illness hidden. Yet she'd already broached the subject—and she felt an unexpected urge to be honest, for once.

"I have a . . . condition," Alix said haltingly. "Hélène knows, and has apparently been telling people about it." Briefly, Alix explained that she'd suffered from a crippling panic ever since her brother died. She told him how Hélène had found her having an episode last year at the opera, and was now spreading the word about Alix's illness.

Eddy listened to her confession thoughtfully, without judgment. Perhaps she'd never given him enough credit.

When she'd finished, he shook his head. "Someone else must have spread those rumors. It wasn't Hélène."

"No one else saw me!"

"That you know of," Eddy insisted. "You said it yourself: you were out in the walkway of the opera house. Anyone might have been watching. I swear, Hélène would never hurt you like that. Actually, she's always liked you, in spite of . . . um . . ."

"In spite of Grandmama's plans for us?"

"Yes." He lifted his deep blue eyes to hers. "I realize that I'm in no position to ask a favor, but will you agree not to tell anyone about me and Hélène? I want to protect her reputation."

Oh. Alix had assumed that Eddy and Hélène were engaged in a secret courtship, that they had exchanged whispers and flowers and perhaps even a scandalous moment like her kiss with Nicholas. But if Eddy was genuinely worried for Hélène's reputation . . . Well, Alix highly doubted that they had left it at longing glances. Or even at kisses.

"I won't tell anyone," she assured him.

"Thank you." Eddy looked relieved, but then he sighed again: an angry, helpless sigh. "Though as I said, it's not as if Hélène and I can get publicly engaged, even once you and I break off our . . . understanding."

The future King of England marrying the Catholic princess of a former, deposed throne? No, Alix didn't see Grandmama agreeing to that.

"You really want to marry Hélène?" she asked.

"I've already proposed, and she said yes. I love her." The frankness of Eddy's reply caught her off guard.

"If you love her, then you'll have to find a way."

"But how? *You* are the gold standard, Alix. You're the one that Grandmother wants, and no one else will satisfy her. If only you weren't so perfect," he added, with a touch of sarcasm.

"I'm hardly perfect, Eddy." Hadn't she just told him about her shameful illness?

"Well, you do a damned good job convincing everyone that you are. Why do you think I originally asked to court you?"

Before she could swallow it back, a *laugh* bubbled out of Alix's chest.

She lifted her hands to her mouth, horrified. Eddy stared at her for a moment, and then, to her surprise, he was chuckling too.

It was strange to think of it—the life they might have built together, if they had followed Queen Victoria's mandates. For a moment that future seemed to shimmer in the air between them, as incandescent as a ghost.

"You're right. Looking back, it's clear that I did an appalling job of wooing you," Eddy agreed.

"I'm sure there have been worse courtships," Alix quipped, testing a joke.

"Undoubtedly. Uncle Alfred's, for starters." Eddy stood and walked to a side table, where he poured amber-colored liquid into two crystal tumblers, then handed one to Alix.

She eyed it with some skepticism. "Is this brandy?" A lady shouldn't drink anything but wine, or the occasional glass of sherry.

Eddy shrugged. "I know it's not really proper, but then again, neither are our circumstances."

"I suppose not." Stealing a glance toward the half-open door—the hallway seemed mercifully empty—Alix lifted the glass to her lips. The liquid burned down her throat, and she coughed.

"Alix. I know you have no reason to believe me, but I swear, Hélène wouldn't spread cruel gossip about you," Eddy said again, his tone low and earnest. "I just . . . I don't want there to be bad blood between us. At least, not about that."

"I do believe you," Alix decided.

Feeling brave, she took another sip of the brandy. This time its warmth felt almost pleasant, curling like a fire deep within her belly.

It must have been the brandy that made her blurt out, "You should know that you aren't the only one to blame for our broken engagement. I have also given my heart to someone else."

"Ah. Well, that explains why you marched in here demanding to see me." Eddy grinned and sprawled back in his oversized armchair. "Who is it? Can we expect an engagement announcement soon?"

"I highly doubt it."

She must have looked forlorn, because Eddy's smile faded. "You haven't fallen for an American, have you? Or a Catholic?"

"Possibly worse." She hesitated, but she'd already told him about her episodes. What was one more confession? "It's Nicholas."

There was no need to specify which Nicholas she meant.

Eddy was silent for a moment, then posed the same question that Alix had asked him; which, she supposed, was only fair. "You want to marry him?"

"Yes."

Alix hadn't even dared admit that aloud. All she knew was that Nicholas had stolen his way into her heart and mind, that she wanted to see him first thing in the morning and last thing at night. To share his hopes and his dreams and his innermost fears.

Eddy shifted. "Surely it's not impossible. Didn't your sister marry Nicholas's cousin?"

"His uncle. A very young uncle," she clarified, not that Eddy would care.

"So what is the issue? You don't want to move to Russia?"

"Nicholas hasn't asked," Alix admitted. "I do think he cares for me, but he hasn't proposed. And even if he did, Grandmama would not give her permission."

She couldn't believe she was saying these things aloud, and to Eddy, of all people. Yet Alix found that she quite liked this new honesty between them. It was refreshing—bracing, even, like a gulp of clean air after you had been shut in a stuffy room.

"Not to mention that you'll have Nicholas's parents to deal with," Eddy added.

"You think the tsar and tsarina will be an obstacle?"

"Aunt Minnie isn't friendly under the best of circumstances. She will have plans of her own for Nicholas—plans that don't involve you, or else you'd know about them." Eddy looked Alix square in the eye. "Which means that you'll need to convince her otherwise."

"How?"

"The way you did today! You marched in here, hackles raised, and demanded a straight answer about our engagement. Harness that energy, and show Aunt Minnie what a great tsarina *you* could be."

"I don't think I *demanded* anything," Alix protested.

"Trust me, I've been in the military. You could lead men into battle with that glare. You should use it more often."

They weren't flirtatious words, yet Alix couldn't help thinking that it was the greatest compliment Eddy had ever paid her.

Since propriety already lay in shreds around them, she kicked her dress unceremoniously to one side and tucked her feet up onto the leather armchair. It was too bad that women weren't ordinarily allowed to sit in furniture this comfortable.

"You need to tell Grandmama about you and Hélène," Alix mused aloud. An idea was forming in her mind, of a way that they just might get what they wanted—all of them.

"And have her forbid us from ever seeing each other?" Eddy set down his glass of brandy. "There are too many reasons for her to say no: Hélène's religion, her family's complicated status, the fact that France keeps having *revolutions*."

"Those are all valid, logical obstacles," Alix agreed, "which is precisely why you cannot use logic to sway Grandmama. You need to appeal to her sense of romance."

She thought of the cairn at Balmoral, of the queen's incessant black mourning, of the catch in her voice whenever she mentioned Albert. "You know that Grandmama was deeply in love with Grandpapa. *That* is the side of her that you need to appeal to. Speak to her as your grandmother, not as the queen. Tell her that you and Hélène never planned to fall in love—"

"We didn't!" Eddy cut in.

"Explain that you couldn't help falling for Hélène, that you can't imagine life without Hélène. Isn't that what Louise did when she asked for permission to marry the Duke of Fife?"

"Louise was just a princess. I'm the heir to the throne," Eddy pointed out, stating the obvious.

"Then you'll need to be twice as persuasive as she was! *Beg* Grandmama for her permission on bended knee. I mean that literally, not as a figure of speech," Alix clarified.

Eddy sat there for a moment, digesting her words. Then he shook his head in slow admiration. "It just might work."

"You could go on Monday," Alix suggested, thinking of the appointment that she and Eddy already had with the queen. "Grandmama is expecting to discuss your marriage, after all. Just bring Hélène instead of me."

Eddy lifted an eyebrow, skeptical. "You don't think Grandmother will be angry? I doubt she likes being ambushed."

"There is a fine line between an ambush and an impassioned plea, as long as you stick to the romantic script." Alix suspected that Grandmama might actually respond well to the spontaneity of it all—to the notion that Eddy was showing initiative, taking decisive action.

"It's worth a shot, if nothing else. Alix . . ." The prince's eyes met hers, as earnest as she'd ever seen them. "Thank you."

How odd that this conversation—where they were putting an end to things between them, once and for all—was the most relaxed Alix had ever been with Eddy.

He must have been thinking along the same lines, because he smiled. "I'm glad you came to see me today. And no matter what happens, I hope that we can stay friends."

Friends. It was a strange way for things to end, after their almost-engagement had dragged on for so long, yet it felt right.

"Friends," Alix agreed. "I would like that very much."

CHAPTER TWENTY-FOUR

May

IT WAS ONE OF THOSE GLORIOUS AUTUMN DAYS WHEN THE SUN felt as high and warm as summer, but with a hint of the coming winter in the wind that tugged at May's hair. The air was filled with the jangle of bridles and the crunch of wheels over gravel. Five o'clock on a Sunday—the peak time to see and be seen at Hyde Park, with all the sporting gigs and broughams looping through the ring, men on horseback weaving around the carriages at a crisp trot.

The first time May had brought Agnes here, her friend hadn't understood; apparently there was no such social hour in the parks of Chicago. But Agnes quickly came to realize that Hyde Park was like an outdoor ballroom. Rotten Row was really just one long parade where society showed itself off.

A group of men on horseback cantered into view, and May immediately sat up straighter. They weren't just society, but the peak of society—the princes Eddy and George, with their cousins, the Tsarevich Nicholas and Prince Constantine of Greece. A pair of grooms trotted behind them, dressed in the livery of Marlborough House.

"I'm so glad you suggested we come out today," Agnes murmured, following May's gaze.

May could only nod. Her heart had leapt strangely at the sight of George; she hadn't seen him since the Cadogans' ball.

"It's remarkable how much the tsarevich looks like Their Royal Highnesses," Agnes went on, her eyes flicking to the group of young princes and then away again.

"They *are* cousins," May said absently. Really, the most striking resemblance was between Nicholas and George. Eddy's coloring was fairer, his build slimmer, while George and the tsarevich shared the same chestnut hair and deep blue eyes, the same broad torso and square jaw. *They* were the ones who looked like brothers.

As May was pondering this, a gust of wind tugged her hat loose and sent it billowing into the breeze.

"Oh no!" she cried out, unthinking. The hat was her favorite: a gift from Agnes, made of navy felt and trimmed in deep blue feathers.

"By all means, you must go retrieve it. You look far too fetching in that hat to lose it," Agnes remarked. There was a funny note to her voice, but May was too preoccupied to fully register it.

She hesitated for an instant, because young women typically didn't leap down from their carriages in the middle of Hyde Park, but the sight of the hat careening toward the pond decided her. May wasn't Agnes; she didn't have enough beautiful things to give one up without a fight. She quickly slid out of her seat and began running in the direction the hat had disappeared, down the bright green slope of the lawn. This section of the park was clearly not intended for foot traffic— the grass was untended and wild—but May's crinolines protected her legs from getting too scratched.

"May!" a voice behind her called. It took a moment for May to register the pounding of hoofbeats.

She turned in surprise, lifting a hand to shade her eyes. George had come after her, still mounted on his dappled gray horse.

"You didn't have to follow me." May immediately longed to swallow back the words; she hadn't meant to make George feel unwanted. "I just feel a little silly, losing my hat like this."

"One of the hazards of Hyde Park," George said generously, because they both knew it wasn't a typical occurrence. He vaulted down from his horse with surprising ease, looping the reins around a branch before starting down the slope toward May. "Do you know where the hat ended up?"

May pointed to the edge of the pond, where it was curled in a sodden heap, the dark blue ribbon trailing over a lily pad in a pitiful gesture of surrender.

George nodded. "I'll fetch it for you."

"Are you sure?" The water looked brackish, a few beetles hopping over its surface.

But George was already picking his way along the grass. "I'm not sure you want to put this back on," he warned, once he reached the hat. "It might need to be cleaned first."

The wind whipped at May's hair again, tugging a few ashen curls loose from their pins. She reached up to tuck them back. "Thank you. I still can't believe I lost it like that."

"I saw the hat fly away; I know that this wasn't your fault." A smile touched George's lips as he added, "Unlike Louise's hat."

May drew in a breath. "You remember that?"

It was back when they all used to vacation together at Chiswick, where brightly colored pebbles lined the shores of the lake. One summer when she was nine, May had spent days collecting her favorite stones, working tirelessly, silently, like a machine. And then when the bucket was nearly full, Louise had seized it and thrown the whole thing into the water. Simply to prove that she could.

Hurt and bewildered by the random act of cruelty, May had yanked the hat off Louise's head and tossed it into the lake.

"Of course I remember. I always pay attention to . . ." He trailed off, leaving May to wonder if he'd been about to say *pay attention to you.*

"I was young and immature," May began, but George shook his head.

"It's so rare that Louise suffers any consequences for her actions. I'm glad you did it." He hesitated a beat before adding, "Aside from that, we had fun at Chiswick, didn't we? I miss those days."

"As do I." May's family had stopped sharing holidays with the Waleses when their financial straits became too dire. She found herself wondering how things would be different if her parents hadn't spent beyond their means. Would she and Maud have become friends sooner?

And where would things stand between her and George? Not that there was anything between them at all . . . was there?

"We should head back." The prince gestured to his horse. "You're welcome to ride, of course, though I doubt you want to?"

"What do you mean?" May asked, and he shrugged.

"Just that you didn't seem very keen on outdoor sports at Balmoral."

It was true; May had hated the traditional Balmoral

activities. She'd complained of this in a letter to Agnes, who had replied that May needed to set aside her discomforts and do it all. *You aren't fishing for salmon; you're a fisher of men—of a prince!* Despite the sacrilegious nature of the joke, May had smiled in amusement, and gamely rode out with the group once or twice. But it was hopeless. She just wasn't built for the outdoors, especially not the wild domain of Scotland.

May nodded. "Yes, I'm more suited to city pursuits than to the country. You seem to enjoy riding, though."

George gallantly placed her hat atop the pommel of his saddle, then tugged at the reins, leading his mount uphill while May walked alongside him.

"I love riding," he agreed. "There is something about it that makes me feel braver. Why else do you think men through history have commissioned portraits of themselves on horseback?"

"I thought it was just to make them seem taller. Napoleon being the best example," May joked, and George chuckled.

"Taller, braver: those are often the same thing. It really is too bad we can't ride horses into a ballroom; then perhaps I wouldn't be such a disappointment at parties. Especially to Father," George added, almost under his breath.

May was startled at the vulnerability of the admission. "I'm sure that's not true," she protested.

"He's not malicious about it. I just know that our relationship would be easier if we had common ground." George kept his gaze aimed downward, picking his way carefully back up the slope. "I'm sorry. This is hardly a topic for polite conversation."

"It's quite all right," May said quickly.

"You must have no idea what I'm talking about. There's no way your family could find fault with *you*."

It had been clumsily phrased, yet May recognized the statement as a compliment. She found herself longing to tell George the truth—that she knew all too well what it was like, struggling endlessly for parental approval you would never get. It was like fumbling around in the dark without knowing what you were looking for, struggling to answer a question you hadn't been asked.

"I understand more than you might expect. I often fear that I am a source of bafflement to my parents. Even to Dolly," she admitted.

"Really?"

May decided not to broach the subject of her father. "Like you and the Prince of Wales, my mother and I are . . . not very similar."

George nodded, considering this. "And it must be harder on you as her only daughter. At least I have Eddy. Father spends so much time with him that he tends to forget how dissatisfied he is with me." *He tends to forget me altogether* was the unspoken subtext. Yet George still soldiered on, trying to forge his own path forward.

In his quiet, steadfast way, George might be the strongest of them all.

"Sometimes I wish I had a sister." May wished she could explain why—that she longed for someone with whom she could weather her father's cruelty. Someone who could have held her hand, all those nights when Dolly was at school and May huddled at the top of the stairs, listening as her parents shouted at each other in the living room.

Maybe it was better that there wasn't another Teck girl who had to endure all that. May certainly wouldn't wish it on anyone.

"At least you'll have Maud now. I mean—perhaps—now that you've grown closer, maybe she can be like a sister to you," George said clumsily.

Like a sister, or a sister-in-law? May's heart skipped a little, and she told herself not to read too much into it.

"Of course. I have loved getting to spend more time with Maud," she hastened to reply.

They were drawing closer to the main ring; May heard the cacophony of horses and shouted greetings up ahead. She cast about for a topic that might delay their return to the group.

"How long will Prince Constantine and the tsarevich be staying with you?"

As she'd hoped, George's steps slowed. "I'm not sure. Tino should be getting back to Greece soon, preparing for the wedding, but he and Nicholas keep delaying their departure."

"Of course, the wedding! I'm so glad for Tino and Sophie," May said automatically.

Everyone had been a bit surprised when the wild, rakish Tino got engaged to quiet Princess Sophie of Prussia. Their upcoming wedding in Athens was the talk of Europe.

George glanced over. "Will you be going?"

"I'm not certain," May replied evasively.

The Tecks would almost certainly receive an invitation, which May expected her father to decline, grumbling that he didn't want to be surrounded by his pompous relatives. The real reason, of course, was the expense. Traveling to Athens meant train tickets, and renting a house, not to mention new gowns for the wedding itself: all costs that they could ill afford.

"Mother and Father are insisting that we all come." By *we all*, George clearly meant his siblings. He smiled shyly as he added, "I hope you'll be there, too."

It wasn't a proposal, or a declaration, but May recognized that George didn't say such things often. It suddenly felt crucial that she get to that wedding.

"I'll talk to my parents," she assured him.

She would find a way, somehow, because she was nothing if not resourceful.

George smiled, then looked up and paused. "That is your companion, is it not?"

May noted with surprise that he was right. Agnes seemed to have followed her example and climbed out of the carriage; she stood with a pair of grooms along the fence that lined Rotten Row, speaking in urgent, rapid tones. The grooms shook their heads and Agnes crossed her arms over her chest.

"I wonder why she's talking to the coachmen?" George asked, voicing May's thoughts.

"Agnes?" May called out.

When Agnes saw her, she quickly smiled, then hurried over, holding out her hands palm up in a gesture of puzzled amusement.

"May, I was so worried about you! You ran off and I had no idea where you'd gone! I was asking everyone if they'd seen you," she explained breathlessly.

What? May wanted to say in confusion. *You're the one who told me to chase after the hat.* But Agnes had already turned to George and executed a perfectly elegant curtsy.

"Your Royal Highness, I'm so glad that you went to May's rescue! What a knight in shining armor!"

George colored and retrieved the hat from atop his saddle, handing it back to May. "It was my pleasure." Then, with a nod to May, he vaulted back onto his horse and started off.

May waited until he was out of earshot before turning to Agnes. "What were you doing with those coachmen?"

Agnes hesitated for a fraction of an instant, then waved her hand in a dismissive gesture. "It's as I said; I was looking for you! You really did a vanishing act, chasing after that hat. Though it seems it was well worth it," she added, teasing. "Now look, here is Jacob!" Agnes waved a gloved hand to hail her family's driver.

Once Jacob had helped them back into the landau, May balanced her hat on her lap. She felt abuzz with a tentative new feeling that might have been hope.

She had gone after Prince Eddy because he was a means to an end, an escape from the dismal fate of remaining a spinster in her father's house. Marrying Eddy would have kept her safe: from her father, from a life in debt, from anyone or anything that might hurt her.

But what if she could have it all, security *and* affection?

As she thought of George, May wondered if she might still end up with a prince . . . not just because he made her feel safe, but because he made her happy.

CHAPTER TWENTY-FIVE

Alix

WITH THE WALESES, A "FAMILY DINNER" COULD MEAN ANYTHING, a casual gathering of five people or a formal meal for forty. Tonight's family dinner, hosted by Uncle Bertie and Aunt Alexandra at Marlborough House, veered toward the latter. The official reason for celebrating was that Uncle Alfred and his family were visiting from Coburg, though everyone knew that Bertie needed no excuse to host a party. Sometimes he gathered his friends for an eight-course dinner on a Monday evening for no other reason than boredom.

Alix stole another glance around the massive dining table, which was nearly at capacity. The light from the chandeliers cast the guests in a golden glow, setting off their profiles against the deep blue wallpaper. Technically speaking, this *was* a family dinner, since nearly everyone was related to someone else at the table. Half of Queen Victoria's nine children were here—Uncle Bertie, Uncle Alfred, Uncle Arthur, and Aunt Beatrice—along with their spouses and children. Not to mention Nicholas and Tino, who were still staying at Marlborough House.

The queen herself wasn't in attendance, and Alix sensed that Bertie was secretly relieved by this. It meant he got to pour more wine, laugh louder, tell off-color jokes—all the things he so rarely got to do with his younger brother, who'd moved to Coburg a decade ago.

"I once saw a black-billed thrush in the woods outside Rosenau," Alix's companion remarked in German. Alix managed a distracted nod, hyperaware of the fact that Nicholas was on her other side. In just a few short minutes, when the soup course ended, she would finally be allowed to turn and speak with him.

She and Nicholas hadn't originally been seated together. Apparently Nicholas had solved this before the dinner, when Aunt Alexandra was lamenting the number of guests in Alfred's entourage ("They're bringing Coburg cousins who don't even speak English!"). At which point Nicholas had pointed out that Alix spoke German, and rearranged the place cards himself.

Now here she was, with one of the Coburg cousins—a Baron von Stockmann, or was it von Stockmar?—to one side, and Nicholas on the other.

Realizing that the baron was staring at her expectantly, Alix smiled in apology. "Forgive me. You were saying?"

"I would love to know if you've seen any robins yet." At her blank stare, he pushed his glasses further up his nose and added, "They migrate during the winter, many of them coming from Russia or Scandinavia all the way to England. Some even make it as far as Spain! They cannot stand the harsh northern winters."

"A tiny robin flies all the way from Russia to Spain?" Alix asked, surprised.

"They do indeed! They are small but mighty."

He was so earnest that Alix found herself warming to

him. "How marvelous. I feel a kinship for them, for I too have only migrated here for the season."

The baron nodded assiduously. "And, like the robin, will you stay throughout the winter?"

They were speaking in German, so she didn't expect anyone to understand, yet Alix felt Nicholas tense next to her. It would seem that he, too, was waiting for her reply.

"I suppose it depends upon a number of factors," Alix admitted.

At that moment, an army of liveried footmen materialized to whisk away the guests' soup tureens. This was the moment that, as etiquette dictated, a lady should break off conversation with the gentleman on her left and turn to the one on her right.

"Nicholas," she said eagerly, beaming.

His blue eyes fixed on hers. "What factors does your decision depend on?" he asked, in English.

"I didn't know you spoke German."

"I wouldn't say I *speak* it, but I understand a little. Enough to follow the gist of important conversations."

"I suppose one of the factors is sitting next to me." Emboldened by her own daring, Alix ventured, "And you? When will you be headed back to Russia?"

"I don't know. I have many reasons to go home, and one very crucial reason to stay," he said softly.

Alix could only nod in reply. As she'd suggested, Eddy would go to their meeting with Grandmama tomorrow—bringing Princess Hélène with him instead of Alix. She prayed that it would all go smoothly. Not just for her own sake, although Alix needed the queen to accept that she and Eddy were done, but because she genuinely wished them well.

Alix believed what Eddy had said, that Hélène hadn't spread those rumors about her. Which made her wonder . . . who did?

Under the table, Nicholas's foot nudged the hem of her skirts, and she drew in a breath.

"Sorry," he muttered. "I didn't—"

"No," Alix said quickly, before he could move his foot away. She flushed, but held his gaze. "I'm sorry, what were we discussing?"

A mischievous note entered Nicholas's voice as he replied. "Birds, I believe. Or at least, that's what you and Baron von Bird-watching were talking about."

"Alas, I know very little about birds."

"I know a bit, actually. My grandfather was a bird enthusiast," Nicholas explained, as a pair of servers placed the next course before them: a glazed partridge stuffed with foie gras. "He used to take us out in the mornings to look for birds, usually when we went to Livadia."

"Livadia?" Alix carved a small sliver of meat with her knife but didn't eat it, too intent on his story.

"Our summer palace."

"I thought Peterhof was your summer palace," she said hesitantly.

"Peterhof is our summer palace in Russia. Livadia is in the Crimea," Nicholas explained, as if it were perfectly reasonable to have multiple summer palaces.

The closest thing Alix's family had was an open-air cottage on the grounds, where they used to do lessons on hot days.

She felt a stab of self-consciousness. Talking to Nicholas, it was so easy to forget his family's staggering wealth, their immense reach and power. Compared to his, her life was provincial, almost quaint.

"Livadia is beautiful," Nicholas went on, sensing her discomfort and changing the subject. "I wish you could see it in the mornings, with the sun rising over the water; the skies are such an impossible blue. I know everyone says the south of France has the prettiest beaches in the world, but I challenge France to find a prettier view than the one from our back terrace."

Alix loved this about him: his unabashed love for his homeland, his unshakable pride in being Russian.

"What birds did you see there?" she asked.

Nicholas looked sheepish. "Gulls? Or maybe ospreys? All I really remember is sitting outside with Grandfather while he drank his morning coffee. It was the most peaceful I ever saw him."

Alix hesitated. This would be hard to say, but it felt crucial that she acknowledge his loss openly—instead of skirting around it, the way people always did when her mother was mentioned.

"I'm sorry about your grandfather. I know it must have been a shock, losing him so suddenly."

Nicholas stared down at his dinner plate. "I miss him. All of Russia misses him."

"You must hate the anarchists," she blurted out.

"My father does." The tsarevich sighed. "I obviously wish that they had found another way to make their point, instead of reverting to violence. It made things so much worse in the end. My grandfather was on their side."

Alix knew that Alexander II had been the most liberal tsar

in Russia's history. He had emancipated the serfs and modernized the judiciary, and he had been working to reform the National Assembly when the terrorists blew him up.

Nicholas's father, in retaliation, had promptly undone many of his father's reforms.

"I was there, you know, on the day he died." Nicholas's voice was barely a whisper.

Alix blinked, shocked. "Not in the carriage, surely?"

"No, but they summoned me to his bedside immediately after the bomb exploded. Misha and I were walking to the pond to ice-skate. They sent Misha home, but as for me . . . Father said I needed to see it." Nicholas's face looked pained at the memory. "There was so much blood. And Grandfather's legs were just . . . gone."

Alix could picture the scene: a frightened twelve-year-old Nicholas, dressed in a scarf and coat for an afternoon of ice-skating with his younger brother, dragged to the bedside where his grandfather lay legless and dying. She could practically smell the incense they would have brought into the room, could hear the hypnotic chants of the priest reciting his last rites.

"I'm sorry, I shouldn't speak of such things, especially not at a dinner party," he amended.

"No, I'm glad you did." Alix clenched her hands in her lap to keep from reaching for Nicholas.

It felt like the more he shared, the more desperate she felt to keep listening. She wanted to understand every last part of him, to see the way his mind worked.

"I know it must have been hard on you, but at least you got to say goodbye," she offered, in a small voice. "I never got that with my mother. They refused to let me look at her afterward; they said the illness had ravaged her body, and they wanted me to remember her as she was before. But it made it harder to digest, somehow."

Nicholas nodded sympathetically. "I'm sure it felt less real to you, which is hard on a child. Did you secretly imagine that it was all a mistake, that they'd gotten the wrong person and your mother would come back and laugh about the misunderstanding?"

"All the time," Alix confessed.

There was movement around the rest of the table—people exchanging stories about hunting or fashion or ocean voyages, women clapping in delight, Uncle Bertie's raucous laugh underpinning it all—but Nicholas held her gaze as steadily as if they were alone. Through the skirts of her gown, Alix felt his leg pressing against hers again. Not in a flirtatious way, but in something like support, or solidarity.

It felt like he *saw* her—really saw her, through the facade she showed the world, all the way to the insecurities and regrets that twisted like snakes at her core. He saw, and he wasn't afraid. If anything, he understood.

AFTER THE DINNER CONCLUDED WITH A SELECTION OF ICED chestnuts and orange wedges, the men retreated to the smoking room. Alix and the other ladies swept along to the card room, where a few of the older women poured discreet glasses of sherry. Princess Maud settled at the piano as usual, but Alix's gaze traveled to her cousins Missy and Victoria Melita.

Victoria Melita—known by her childhood nickname Ducky, since there were a half dozen Victorias among the cousins—stood near the fireplace, her slippered foot impatiently tapping the floor. Her sister Missy seemed just as restless, repeatedly retying the sash of her gossamer pink gown.

"Missy, Ducky! It's good to see you." Alix pulled her cousins into an embrace.

"It has been far too long!" Missy agreed, then lowered her voice. "Ducky and I need your assistance with something. We have been begging Mama to let us go riding in Hyde Park, but she says we cannot. Even with a groom as an escort!"

"It is true that some women ride," Alix admitted. *Like Princess Hélène.* "But I usually go out in a carriage, if you'd like to join me?"

Missy gave a dramatic shudder that made her dark curls bounce. "I refuse to ride in a jostled, bumping carriage if I can be in the saddle instead!"

Alix couldn't help smiling at that. There was something so disarming about Missy, the unguarded way expressions flitted across her face.

Meanwhile, Ducky watched Alix with a guarded curiosity. "It's all right, Missy," she said slowly. "When we go to St. Petersburg with Mama, Kiril and Boris will take us hunting."

"You both go hunting? With the men?" Alix had seen how easily the sexes mingled in Russian society, yet she was still startled. Missy and Ducky were princesses twice over, granddaughters of the late Tsar Alexander and of Queen Victoria. They didn't belong in the bloody chaos of a Russian boar hunt.

"Mother raised us more Russian than English," Ducky replied with a shrug. "Speaking of Russia, Alix, is it true that—"

"Ducky, stop distracting your cousin with idle gossip."
Missy and Ducky's mother—Marie, Duchess of Edinburgh—
swept forward.

Marie's voice was low and husky, and even now, after all
her years as a British duchess, retained a Russian accent. It
was a distinctive voice, once as famous as her extravagant
wardrobe. Years ago, when she had come to London as the
bride of Queen Victoria's second son, people had talked of
nothing but her Romanov jewels and her gravelly voice.

Before her daughter could answer, Aunt Marie turned to
Alix with a forced smile. "Alix, my dear, may I borrow you
for a moment?"

"Of course," Alix agreed, a bit surprised.

"Let us take a turn around the room." Her aunt started
off, giving Alix no choice but to follow.

Marie was silent for a while. She led Alix past the enormous watercolor that dominated one wall, past wooden cre-
denzas topped with candles—though Marlborough House
had gas lighting, they were all lit, because nothing could re-
place the ambience of a candelabrum. Only when she was
halfway along the windows overlooking the garden did Aunt
Marie speak.

"Since your dear mother is no longer with us, Alix, please
forgive me for overstepping. But I need to ask what is going
on between you and the tsarevich."

"What do you mean?" Alix tried to sound innocent, but
her aunt wasn't fooled.

"Did you think your little trick with tonight's seating
would go unnoticed? Ducky clearly saw, and I doubt she's the
only one! Not to mention how much you and Nicholas have

been out together recently," Marie hissed. "I expect better behavior from a young woman who is engaged elsewhere, and if your mother were here, I know she would agree."

Bringing in Alix's dead mother as a negotiating tool was deeply unfair.

"If my mother were here," Alix repeated angrily, "she would remind you not to spread unfounded gossip. I am not engaged to Prince Eddy, and I'm sorry that everyone seems to think otherwise."

Aunt Marie made an impatient gesture. "Whatever is between you and Prince Eddy is none of my business. I just want to *help*, Alix. Nicholas is not someone to flirt with lightly."

"I'm not just flirting."

"I'm sorry, how else would you characterize your behavior: cavorting around London, making a fool of yourself?"

"Nicholas and I enjoy each other's conversation," Alix replied, stung.

"*Conversation*, is that all that's happened? I hope you know it can't go any further. Whatever promises he's made to you, Nicky is not free to make them."

"He hasn't made any promises—"

"Well, that's a relief—"

"He doesn't need to, because we're in love!"

The words were out before Alix could think them through. She'd spoken in a low tone, but she might as well have shouted; Aunt Marie's features were glazed in shock.

"You're in love?" she repeated, as softly as Alix.

Alix felt heat rising to her cheeks. "I love him," she replied, as steadily as she could.

"Oh, Alix." Aunt Marie sighed. She'd clearly noticed the

change in syntax, and understood what it meant—that Nicholas hadn't articulated the truth of his feelings.

"You say you love him," her aunt continued, "which means . . . what? You like attending parties with him, perhaps have even shared a kiss?"

Alix decided to ignore the bit about kissing. "Nicholas understands me; he makes me happy—"

"Let me tell you something about love, Alix. It is nothing like it seems in the novels: some elemental force that makes you dizzy and weak at the knees. That is physical attraction, and as wonderful as it feels, attraction will fade. If you want a relationship that will truly last, you need a foundation of shared responsibility. Of duty."

"That's not love; that's just a—a partnership!" Alix stammered.

Marie lifted an eyebrow. "And what would you know about either?"

"I have seen enough royal marriages to know that most are as you say," Alix admitted. "A practical relationship where husband and wife exist in different spheres. They come together as needed, for children or official duties. And you're right, those marriages function smoothly enough, but only because there is no common ground. There can be no conflict if husband and wife never share anything genuine! Love comes from living a joint life, with all the disagreements and ugliness that entails."

"Have you ever *seen* a relationship like the one you describe?" her aunt challenged.

Alix sensed that this was some sort of test—that a great deal hinged upon her answer.

"I have," she insisted.

"Your parents?"

"I was too young when my mother died to remember much about their marriage. I only know about it from my father," Alix confessed. "No, when I think of fierce, unrelenting love, I think of the tenant farmers I met outside Darmstadt several years ago."

"A Hessian peasant couple," Marie said flatly.

"They were bent down by age and hardship, yet their hands were clasped tight. As I spoke with them, I came to learn that no matter how little they had—food, medicine, firewood—each of them was determined to give it to the other. *That* is what I want my marriage to look like. A love so great that it puts the other person before oneself."

She and her aunt were still walking, their progress around the edge of the room slow and stately.

After a long moment, her aunt sighed. "How young you are. I forget how immediate and vivid everything feels at your age." She glanced over at Alix and added, "Did you know I was only sixteen when I met Alfred?"

Alix shook her head, waiting for her aunt to continue.

"He swept me off my feet, wooed me so beautifully. Oh, he came to St. Petersburg and recited sonnets, pleaded with my father, threatened to shoot himself if he couldn't have me! It was all terribly thrilling," Marie added wistfully.

Well, now Alix understood where Missy had gotten her flair for the dramatic.

"My father told me not to marry Alfred," Marie went on. "'You'll end up unhappy,' he told me. 'You'll miss Russia.' I hate to say it, but he was right."

"I'm sorry," Alix said haltingly. It was disconcerting, hearing her aunt admit to being unhappy.

Marie looped an arm through Alix's and gave her a squeeze—in support, or perhaps in warning. "I just hope you're right, and that you really love Nicholas with the selfless devotion of that peasant couple. Because if you continue down this path, it will require unimaginable sacrifice."

"We know it won't be easy." Alix spoke uncertainly; she hadn't really discussed this with Nicholas.

"Oh no, I'm not saying that he will sacrifice anything. *You* will." Marie drew to an abrupt halt, turning to face Alix. "If he proposes, if you find a way to get married—which will all prove difficult enough—Nicholas will go on living the life he has always led, while yours will be rocked to the core. My dear, surely you know that you will be forced to change everything. Your home, your language, your religion."

Alix breathed once, twice, in and out, trying to think over the skittering of her pulse. Hearing it stated so bluntly didn't make things easier.

"Ella is in St. Petersburg. If I were ever to move there, I would at least have my sister," she pointed out, as much for her own benefit as Marie's.

"And you would have me."

Alix looked up in surprise, and her aunt smiled. "I don't live in Russia, of course, but I am still a daughter of that court. You'll need me when trying to navigate its twists and pitfalls."

"Are you saying that you'll help?"

"I'm saying that you need all the help you can get. Even if you can get Her Majesty to approve the match, which would take some doing, Sasha will be harder to win over."

It was jarring, hearing Nicholas's father, the Tsar of All the Russias, referred to by a childhood nickname. But then, Marie was his sister.

"Thank you," Alix said fervently. "I am so, so very grateful."

"What can I say? I have a weakness for romance, in spite of everything," Marie said firmly. "And don't thank me just yet. You have a long road ahead of you."

"I know," Alix agreed.

Then she thought of Nicholas—of his steadiness, his warmth, the way his eyes lit up when he smiled—and her fears disappeared like morning mist burned off by the sun.

Alix knew one thing for certain: she loved him. And it was as the Bible said: love hoped all things, endured all things, believed all things.

She could hope and endure and believe anything, if it meant she had a future with Nicholas.

CHAPTER TWENTY-SIX

Hélène

"ARE YOU CERTAIN THIS IS A GOOD IDEA?" HÉLÈNE WHISPERED to Eddy, as their carriage pulled up to Buckingham Palace. He had explained the purpose of today's meeting, and the rather disconcerting fact that Her Majesty was expecting *Alix*, not Hélène.

Somehow Hélène doubted that the queen would take kindly to the last-minute change in leading lady.

"We were going to need Grandmother's permission eventually," Eddy insisted. "I know it's risky, springing everything on her like this. But it's also our best shot."

The butler who greeted them cast Hélène a curious glance, but said nothing as he led them upstairs. It felt like they passed through endless corridors, a series of doors opening soundlessly before them until they finally paused before Her Majesty's personal sitting room.

The butler rapped on the heavy wooden door. "Your Majesty, His Royal Highness Prince Albert Victor—"

Oh no, Hélène thought, but it was too late; he announced her too.

"—and Miss Hélène d'Orléans."

It was a bit galling to be announced that way, but her royal status wasn't officially recognized in England, no matter how often people referred to her as a princess.

The door swung open and there was Victoria, seated in a stiff-backed chair and wearing her customary black gown and white widow's cap. At the sight of Hélène, her lips pursed; then she deliberately turned to her grandson.

"Eddy, thank you for coming to see me. Where is dear Alix?"

Though she hadn't been acknowledged, Hélène sank into her most reverential curtsy and stayed there, frozen like a statue, until her knees felt like they might lock.

Eddy stepped forward. "I am sorry that I didn't send word, but Alix is not joining us today. I asked Hélène to come instead."

"And what are you doing here, Miss d'Orléans?"

"I am the one who begged her to come; it was all my idea," Eddy interjected, with surprising ardor. "Please, Grandmother, there is something Hélène and I are desperate to discuss with you."

Victoria nodded imperceptibly in Hélène's direction, which Hélène took as permission to stand.

Eddy walked over to his grandmother and sank to one knee, bowing his head like an Arthurian knight. "Hélène and I are in love, and have come to ask for your blessing on our marriage."

"Your marriage?" Now the queen's voice was distinctly cold.

Eddy remained kneeling, his words tumbling out in broken sentences as he explained that they had not planned any of this, that they had been swept away by the utter force of their emotion. In his words, their relationship was a chivalric love story—as if he and Hélène had fallen in love properly, at a respectful distance, by dancing together and sharing some laughter at Balmoral. Certainly he gave no indication of how scandalous their relations really were.

Hélène wished she could say something, but she knew that this was all better coming from Eddy. He was Victoria's heir.

"I must admit, I'd hoped you might come to feel this way about Alix," Victoria said at last. "She is a much more appropriate match."

Hélène had expected as much, but the queen's words still hurt.

"Alix and I are in agreement. We do not wish to be engaged," Eddy said firmly.

Victoria steepled her fingers, which were covered in silver rings. "If there is really no chance of you and Alix, then I hoped you might consider Marie of Anhalt. Or perhaps the youngest princess of Saxe-Altenburg—"

"I don't want to marry a German princess I've never met! I'm in love with Hélène!" Eddy cried out.

Well, now he'd done it. He'd broken one of the cardinal rules of royalty: you never talked over the monarch, and you *certainly* never shouted at them. Hélène winced, bracing herself for their dismissal.

At that, the queen gave a ponderous sigh. "You may as well stand, Eddy."

He rose to his feet and reached instinctively for Hélène's hand, lacing his fingers in hers. Victoria's eyes flew to the gesture.

"What do you have to say about all of this, Miss d'Orléans?"

Hélène swallowed. "Your Majesty, surely you remember

what it is like to be young and in love. If you have any sympathy for our plight, please help us find a way to be together."

The queen stared at her as if taking inventory. Hélène had agonized over what to wear today, and she was glad, now, that she'd chosen this gown: a simple plum-colored dress trimmed in matching velvet. Hélène had never been one for ribbons or fringe or endless lace flounces, and she sensed that Victoria wasn't, either. Still, she hadn't been able to resist a single adornment—an antique gold brooch shaped like a flower, the center studded with pearls. It was three hundred years old, and had supposedly belonged to the Marquise de Montespan.

She needed Victoria to remember that Hélène wasn't just some nobody. The Orléans family might not have a country to rule, but they still had a legacy, a dynasty.

As the queen's eyes flicked over her, Hélène had the frightening sense that Victoria understood all of this. That she read the intent in Hélène's outfit, and her actions, with uncanny insight.

The queen rose with stately calm, surprising them both. "Miss d'Orléans. Join me on a walk."

Eddy stiffened. "Grandmother, may I—"

"I would like to speak with this young woman alone, Eddy. You shall wait for us here."

He had no choice but to nod and step back. Hélène waited for Queen Victoria to move toward the hallway, her ivory-tipped cane clutched in her hand, before following at a discreet distance. She wasn't such a fool as to speak without being spoken to.

The footman outside the door stood to attention. Ignoring him, Victoria turned down a corridor lined with oil paintings and statues. She paused before a bank of windows to look out over the lawn. The lake at its center glittered in the sunlight, a few water lilies scattered over its surface.

Hélène braced herself for a barrage of accusations, even insults. What she didn't expect was for the queen to say, "My dear Albert designed the lake. It's man-made, you know."

"I hadn't realized, Your Majesty," Hélène said quickly.

"He brought in the swans, too. The black one was specially procured from a forest in Germany. Albert said we should always have at least one black swan in residence—that it was insufferably dull having only white swans to look at."

Hélène hadn't noticed, but the queen was right: all the swans floating on the lake were white, save a lone black one. "It's beautiful," she replied, still puzzled. Was *she* the black swan in this analogy, the one who didn't belong?

"Albert was always keeping busy like that: replanting the gardens, giving speeches at universities, sponsoring scientific research. I suspect that if these new automobiles had existed in his time, he would have learned to drive one." Victoria's smile faded. "He didn't have it easy. Being married to the monarch—being a queen consort, or a prince consort as my dear Albert was—is a difficult job, perhaps the most difficult job in the world. It involves all the hard work, yet none of the recognition."

"Your Majesty, I am a princess," Hélène said softly. "I have known since I was a child that I would marry a prince. I assure you that I am up to the task."

The queen turned her back on Hélène and resumed her walk down the corridor, the only sounds the tap-tap of her cane, the rustle of her heavy silk skirts.

"Eddy says he is in love with you," Victoria went on, as Hélène caught up. "But he is a future king. His marriage is an affair of state, not a matter of personal preference."

With daring boldness, Hélène replied, "I should hope that the two might go hand in hand, as they did in your own marriage, Your Majesty."

Victoria lifted an eyebrow. "And you love Eddy?"

"Yes."

"But he is far from perfect. Eddy has always been impulsive, easily distracted. He failed miserably at his studies with his tutor. The woman who marries him will need inner strength and conviction, in order to forge him into the king that England needs."

"Eddy is smarter than you give him credit for!" Hélène knew she shouldn't speak this way to Her Majesty, but she was tired of Eddy's family undermining him. "He may not be intellectual the way George is, but he is thoughtful, and empathetic. If he only had the opportunity to take on some responsibilities, you would see that—"

The queen held up a hand and Hélène fell silent, chastened. Then she noted with surprise that Victoria was smiling.

"You are defending him; I am glad of it. The primary job of a queen consort is to assist the king in all things. To quietly magnify his greatness without detracting from it. Why do you think I wanted Eddy to marry Alix? I knew there was no affection there," the queen admitted, with shocking frankness. "Alix is thoughtful, demure, soft-spoken. The qualities one should search for in a queen consort."

Hélène could hardly claim to be soft-spoken or demure. "Perhaps those qualities should only be sought for a certain kind of king. Perhaps Eddy requires a different sort of partner to balance his personality."

She held her breath, hoping she hadn't overstepped.

Victoria looked out the window again, her profile stoic. "You may be right. I had such great hopes for Alexandra, when I selected her for Bertie—I thought her quiet patience was just what we needed, the perfect counterpoint to his lack of focus. Yet marriage never seemed to change him."

Eddy is not his father, Hélène wished she could say.

"If you are serious about marrying my grandson, then you need to be prepared for everything that you must endure."

"I know," Hélène said quietly. Then she said again, in a firmer voice, "I love him."

Victoria's expression seemed to soften. "As a grandmother, I am not unsympathetic to your cause. But I am a sovereign, too, and must think in those terms. Our future king, allying himself with the daughter of a former royal house?"

"There are many countries where our sovereignty is officially recognized," Hélène pointed out. *Just not in England.* And, most importantly, not in France.

The queen didn't seem to have heard. "I remember when your great-grandfather Louis Philippe fled France under the alias of 'Mr. Smith,' with his mustache shaved! Your family has had safe haven in my country ever since, though you've gone back and forth to France as the tides of political opinion have turned."

Didn't Hélène know it. The Orléans had been exiled for two generations, then returned to France just after she was born, only to be exiled once more when she was fifteen. France never could make up its mind whether to welcome them or despise them.

"My country has a complicated history, but so does yours," Hélène ventured. "We shouldn't pretend that it never happened, but instead should recognize the ways we can learn from it. Isn't that what monarchy is all about?"

"Learning from history?"

"Providing a living link between the nation's past and its present, while also looking forward to its future."

The queen's eyes twinkled; she clearly liked that remark. "I am quite fond of you, and of your parents. But a match between a future king and the daughter of an exiled pretender . . . It poses a number of problems."

Hélène knew what Victoria was trying to say. It was the very issue that had plagued Amélie during her marriage negotiations with Carlos—namely, that the family she married into could never quite be sure what they were getting, a princess or a nobody.

France had renounced its kings before, only to invite them to return on two different occasions. Hélène's father might remain the Count of Paris his whole life, or he might sit on a throne again next year. The likelihood of each outcome depended on whom you asked.

"No matter which princess Eddy marries, you will inevitably offend those who weren't chosen," Hélène said carefully. "I would hazard a guess that all your choices come with complications of some kind. And since the Church of England only permits *one* wife for each husband, you will be forced to make a decision as to which complications are least objectionable."

"Albert would have liked you. He had the same habit of using logic against me." Now Queen Victoria was definitely smiling. "You are right in claiming that none of the choices is without obstacle."

"Perhaps they are all . . . How did His Royal Highness describe the swans? Insufferably dull."

Queen Victoria snorted with suppressed laughter, and Hélène felt distinctly pleased with herself. Her guess had been right; she *was* the black swan. Ah well. There were worse things to be.

They passed a series of landscapes. The queen paused as if considering a painting of a shadowed forest, though Hélène could tell that she was thinking deeply.

Eventually, she looked back at Hélène with a sigh. "There remains the question of your religion."

"I consent to raising my children in the Church of England," Hélène said quickly.

Victoria's expression didn't change. "Surely you know that the Act of Settlement of 1701 forbids any Catholic, or person married to a Catholic, from ascending the throne. If Eddy were to wed a Catholic princess, he would be forced to give up his position in the line of succession."

Hélène blinked. "I thought—"

"It would be different if you were marrying George, of course," the queen went on. "But George does not share Eddy's destiny. Only one of them is the future king."

Hélène should have known that agreeing to raise her children Anglican wasn't enough. "You're saying that I must convert?"

"Now that *would* solve this conundrum!" Victoria

exclaimed, as if she hadn't been the one to suggest it. "Though I wouldn't want you to take such a momentous step without consulting your conscience."

Hélène bit her lower lip. All her life she had been a Catholic, had counted rosary beads in church and prayed to the Virgin Mary. Catholicism felt like a core part of her, as deep-rooted and familiar as her own name.

She weighed her faith against her love for Eddy, and there was simply no question.

"I will convert for him." Her parents would be livid, but Hélène would deal with that later.

Feeling the slightest bit wicked, she added, "Will Your Majesty serve as my confirmation sponsor?"

Victoria chuckled at her boldness. "I would be delighted."

Then, to Hélène's shock, the queen looped an arm through hers and led them back in the direction they'd come, her cane apparently no longer needed. "You are a breath of fresh air, Miss d'Orléans. And to think you were under my nose this entire time! I had never considered you before because of your father's . . . complicated position," she said tactfully. "Not to mention the question of religion. But if you are willing to make such a sacrifice for Eddy's sake, then I have no choice but to give you my blessing."

Relief flooded Hélène's chest. "Thank you, Your Majesty."

When they reentered the sitting room, Eddy was pacing by the window.

"Eddy, my dear," the queen said warmly, "I find that I like your fiancée almost as much as you do."

That word, *fiancée*, spoke volumes.

Eddy's eyes widened, and he rushed toward them. "Grandmother! Does that mean we have your blessing?"

"Yes, but I'm not the only one you will need to convince. Parliament must approve of your marriage as well. Which means we need to start winning minds to our side. Eddy, you must come over for tea soon with Arthur Balfour, Lord Salisbury's nephew, and I'll ask Emily Russell to get her husband involved. . . ."

We *need to start winning minds*, Victoria had said, as if she was now fully invested in their relationship. Indeed, she looked positively twenty years younger at the thought of taking on her Parliament.

Hélène met Eddy's gaze and saw that he was smiling just as broadly as she was. It was really happening, she thought, in a dazed sort of wonder. They were getting married.

Which meant that Hélène was the future Queen of England.

CHAPTER TWENTY-SEVEN

Alix

ALIX DIDN'T NORMALLY MAKE A HABIT OF ATTENDING THE PRINCESS of Wales's Tuesday at homes; she saw enough of her family while she was in town without deliberately seeking them out. But her thinking had changed now that Nicholas was staying at Marlborough House.

Plus, she was eager to hear Eddy's account of his meeting with the queen.

Alix had deliberately left Buckingham Palace beforehand, fleeing with Amelia, the parlormaid, to wander the streets of Piccadilly. She had trailed along the sidewalks for several hours, studying the goods in store windows without really seeing them. So much depended on what happened between Eddy, Hélène, and Grandmama right now: her own future as well as theirs.

When she finally judged it safe to return, the palace butler greeted her with an opaque "Her Majesty is waiting for you."

Alix's heart pounded as she approached the sitting room. She had braced herself for the worst—but to her surprise, and relief, her grandmother merely peered at her over her spectacles and said, "I hear that it is all over between you and Eddy."

Whatever it was, it never really began, Alix thought. Aloud she said simply, "I am sorry to have disappointed you, Grandmama."

"You should be the first to hear that Eddy asked for permission to marry Hélène d'Orléans."

Alix gasped with the appropriate amount of shock. She understood that she wasn't supposed to know this yet—that Eddy's plea had hinged on Victoria's thinking she was the first to hear their secret. As Alix had hoped, Grandmama had clearly been swayed by the impulsive romance of it all.

"Hélène? Really?" she asked.

Her grandmother nodded. "I have decided to grant them my blessing. I always thought that *you* would be good for Eddy, but I am beginning to think that Hélène will, too. She is certainly headstrong . . . though perhaps that is not a bad thing. Already she has inspired Eddy to take the most drastic action I've ever seen him take. The way he stood up to me, the conviction with which he spoke . . ." Victoria trailed off, pensive.

Good for Eddy, Alix thought, trying to hide her satisfaction.

"Of course, you cannot speak of this to anyone until it is announced," her grandmother commanded. "And in the meantime, we must think of you. Now that Eddy is spoken for, we should consider other options. I was wondering if you had ever considered the Danish princes—Christian, or perhaps Carl?"

Alix must have blanched, because her grandmother smiled indulgently. "Denmark *is* quite far. Which brings me to Maximilian of Baden, a good German prince only a few years older than you. Of course, he is not as handsome as one might hope, but Vicky assures me that ever since he grew a beard, his nose does not seem so terribly oversized. . . ."

If the prospect of more arranged courtships hadn't terrified her, Alix might have been amused. Her grandmother was alarmingly shallow sometimes.

"I'm afraid I'm not ready to make such a choice," she said hastily. "Why don't we discuss it next summer?" She needed a stay of execution, at least until she knew how things stood with Nicholas.

Now, as she stepped into the gallery that ran the length of Marlborough House's second floor, Alix was quite grateful that Eddy and Hélène had bought her some time.

Etiquette demanded that she speak to the Princess of Wales first, so she obediently turned to the hostess, who gave her usual, politely bland smile. "Alix, it's such a treat to have you in town this long. You look lovely, as always."

Alix nodded and made an appropriate reply, but her eyes had drifted eagerly past her aunt. Normally an at home was attended exclusively by women, but there were always exceptions, especially when the hostess had out-of-town guests.

Sure enough, there they all were: George and Eddy, along with their visiting cousins, Tino and Nicholas. Uncle Bertie and Uncle Alfred were there as well, clutching wineglasses and laughing uproariously. The haze of male energy made the space, filled with gilded chairs and sofas, feel smaller than normal.

Nicholas saw Alix at once, his eyes lighting up. He said something to the rest of the group and immediately made his way toward her.

"Aunt Alexandra, I am having the most wonderful time," he murmured, inclining his head ever so slightly. Then he turned to Alix. "It's such a beautiful day that I was thinking of strolling the grounds. Would you care to join me?"

She beamed at him, ignoring her aunt's startled expression. Aunt Alexandra probably didn't know that she and Eddy had broken off their so-called engagement, but it wasn't Alix's place to tell her. And there was nothing improper about a walk on the grounds of a private home.

"I would love that," Alix told the tsarevich.

Outside, Nicholas led her onto a path alongside a row of clipped hedges. Sunshine glinted over the parterres filled with golden-brown chrysanthemums.

He cleared his throat. "I am so glad you came today, Alix. It feels like every day I don't see you is a day lost."

She knew exactly what Nicholas meant. They had been apart for less than forty-eight hours, since the dinner party two nights ago, but it had stretched on like an eternity.

Alix smiled. "I agree. Really, I owe Tino a debt of thanks, for going on a Continental tour before his wedding and giving you an excuse to visit."

"That is actually what I wanted to discuss with you." Nicholas let out a breath. "My parents have finally sent for me. I go back to Russia in two days."

Alix stopped in her tracks. Then, recalling all the people who could surely see them from the gallery—who might be snooping through the mullioned windows that looked out over the back lawn—she forced herself to keep walking.

"I understand. They need you with them, of course."

Hadn't she known that this would happen eventually? Nicholas couldn't keep pushing back his departure date the way she could. He had an empire to help run.

"I shall miss you," Nicholas said urgently. "Surely you know by now how much you occupy my thoughts."

They had come to stand near a thicket of beech trees, out of sight of the house. It was improper, perhaps, but Alix couldn't bring herself to care.

Nicholas must have realized the same thing, because he fell to one knee, right there in the gravel path, and clasped her hand in both of his.

"Marry me, Alix."

For a moment all she could do was stare at him. She had thought—had hoped—he might declare his affections for her, or ask if they could keep writing while he was gone. She certainly hadn't anticipated a *proposal*.

Reading her silence as indecision, Nicholas fumbled to keep talking. "I'm sorry that I don't have a ring; we can get one in Russia, if you like. I know this is a lot to consider. I am asking so much of you, hoping that you will move with me to Russia, say goodbye to England and to Darmstadt—"

"I love you."

Alix had dreamed of saying those words to a man ever since she first read an Ann Radcliffe novel at age twelve, yet the declaration didn't come out like she'd always thought. It wasn't histrionic and passionate, the way a romantic heroine might say it. Instead the words seemed to float out of her, escaping her lips of their own accord.

Nicholas's features flooded with relief. "I love you, too," he said softly. "So is that a yes?"

Her smile faded.

Seeing her expression, Nicholas went still. "You are going to say no, aren't you."

"No! I mean, I'm not certain, I just . . ." She tugged at

Nicholas's hands, pulling him to his feet. He stood slowly, hurt flashing in his eyes.

She loved him, but she also feared everything that came along with marrying him: the gowns, the grandeur, the endless state functions. How could a young woman who had suffered crippling anxiety at her own confirmation—which was only attended by a few dozen people, all of them family—handle the most excruciatingly public role on earth? Tsarina of All the Russias was the only position more prominent and vast in scope than Queen of England.

"I need to tell you something," she began.

All her life, Alix had hidden her illness behind a bland, social smile and polite words—and even though she'd lately begun lowering her shields, revealing her sickness to Hélène and then to Eddy, she hadn't dared confess the reasons behind it. Even her family, who knew the truth, would never say it aloud.

But she had to tell Nicholas.

It might change the way he looked at her, but that was a risk Alix needed to take. He deserved the truth.

"I have suffered from an affliction for years now."

Nicholas's eyes met hers in concern. "What sort of affliction? Have you seen a doctor?"

"I have, though it's not technically an illness. It can *feel* like a physical ailment, but it's more . . . emotional in nature." Alix drew in a breath, then said, "When I was five, my brother Friedrich—Frittie—died."

"I know. I'm so sorry," Nicholas replied, with infinite gentleness.

"His death was my fault."

A ringing silence followed her words. Alix couldn't bear

to see the horror on Nicholas's face, so she stared out into the distance, the trees a green blur, her eyes stinging.

"He had the bleeding disease. It runs in our family and for some reason seems only to affect men. Or boys."

Nicholas said nothing, so she swallowed and continued.

"My mother always said that Frittie was delicate, that I had to treat him gently, but I never really understood. I just wanted to play with him. One day in the nursery we were pretending to be knights. I told Frittie to climb up onto a chair, that I would be the dragon and he could slay me. But once he was standing on the chair, he saw something outside, and leaned out the window . . ." Her voice caught, wavered. "He fell out."

"Oh, Alix," Nicholas murmured.

"The nursery was on the ground floor; I had fallen out of that window before, trying to catch butterflies! It wasn't a great distance at all. But once Frittie fell . . . he couldn't stop bleeding. He wasn't even three years old," she added mournfully.

"I'm so sorry," Nicholas said again, but Alix shook her head.

"Don't you see? *I'm* the one who should be sorry! He died because of me!"

Her words were as sharp as knives. Knives she would turn upon herself, to plunge into her own anguished chest.

"You were both children," Nicholas reminded her. "Little boys always run around, and climb things, and fall. You cannot blame yourself for that."

"I knew he was sick! I should have pulled him down from the chair, should never have played with him in the first place. . . ."

"What happened was a terrible tragedy, but it was not your fault, Alix. No one could blame you for what happened."

She wrapped her arms around her chest, hunching forward. "I blame *myself*. That's why I can't marry you, Nicholas. Ever since the accident, I've been . . . different. I fall prey to sudden episodes of fear and anxiety."

"What kind of episodes?" he asked, without judgment.

"I feel dizzy and paralyzed with panic; I can't breathe. It usually happens when I'm somewhere crowded, or about to make an important decision. Then my mind spins me back in time and I'm in the nursery with Frittie again, watching him fall, hearing his little voice, so broken and weak . . ." She wiped at the tears on her cheeks, then closed her eyes. "Having to see his tiny body in the coffin."

A moment later, she felt arms encircling her. Alix hesitated, then let herself relax into the warmth of Nicholas's chest.

Her head was tucked beneath his chin, his arms a solid band around her torso. She listened to the steady beat of his heart, felt the rise and fall of his breath, inhaled the delicious scent of him. This was wildly inappropriate, but she didn't step away.

Slowly, the anguish drained from her.

"I'm sorry about Frittie. I can't imagine what you went through." Nicholas's words rumbled through her. "But you need to let go of all this self-recrimination. It wasn't your fault."

"Nicholas, I can't marry you! You deserve someone who can love you with a whole heart, not one that was broken years ago. Not someone who can't even look at a crowd without feeling like she might faint."

Nicholas took a step back but didn't release her; his hands stayed clasped on her shoulders, then slid down over her arms, to lace his fingers in hers.

"Maybe your affliction will never go away. Guilt can be stubborn like that," he said softly. "Still, I think that your episodes will become less frequent if you stop blaming yourself for Frittie's death. As for your heart," he went on, "I would rather have yours, no matter how bruised or broken, than any other."

"You still want to marry me, knowing all of that?" she whispered.

Nicholas placed a gentle kiss on her brow. "I want to marry you *more*, if that is even possible."

Alix looked into his eyes. She had never imagined that someone might see all the terrible parts of her and still want her. Still *love* her.

"In that case," she said through her tears—which were tears of joy, now, as much as grief—"I will marry you."

CHAPTER TWENTY-EIGHT

May

MAY HAD GOTTEN INTO THE HABIT OF ATTENDING THE PRINCESS of Wales's at homes this year, hoping to run into Eddy or at the very least see Maud. The first few times, Agnes had asked to come with her, though to May's relief she'd given up after May kept refusing—and besides, Agnes was in Paris now anyway.

Today, May had brought her mother with her. Mary Adelaide could be embarrassing, certainly, but she was also a living reminder that May was part of the royal family, too. That she *belonged*.

The butler directed them upstairs, and Mary Adelaide groaned in protest, muttering that one should always receive guests on the ground floor. May nodded, grateful that her mother had never paid her all that much attention, and therefore didn't notice her new hat: the same one that had blown away at Hyde Park. It was a bit overtrimmed for an at home, but May hadn't been able to resist wearing it, in case she saw Prince George.

Surely he would understand what she meant by choosing this hat. It was a silent reference to that day, and the moment of intimacy they'd shared.

The sounds of laughter and conversation floated down the hall; Mary Adelaide began walking faster, unable to resist the allure of a party. "It sounds crowded! I wish I'd known; I would have worn my butterfly brooch." At the doorway to the gallery, she straightened a little, then launched herself into the room like a ship at full sail.

May followed in her mother's wake, glancing around in search of George. Then her gaze lit on someone she hadn't expected to see: Hélène d'Orléans.

The French princess was standing near the window, talking to Prince Constantine of Greece. As always, there was something easygoing in her manner—perhaps in the way she was standing, her weight shifting restlessly from one foot to the other so that her skirts kept swishing and swaying, or perhaps it was the bright sound of her laughter. Other women kept their expressions neutrally polite, their smiles as lacquered as a mask, whereas Hélène allowed her emotions to run wild over her face.

Hélène looked up and, seeing her, flashed an unexpected smile. "May! How have you been?"

"I'm—um, I'm doing well, thank you," May said haltingly. It wasn't as if they had spoken much at Balmoral, and while she'd seen Hélène across the ballroom at the Cadogans' fancy-dress ball, she'd been too preoccupied to seek her out.

"Maud was telling me that you have a charity bazaar coming up?" the French princess asked, and May nodded.

"For the Needlework Guild. It's several weeks away, if you'd like to contribute anything."

Predictably, Hélène shook her head. "I'm useless with a needle, much to my mother's dismay. But I could always read to you and Maud while *you* sew? That counts as supporting the Needlework Guild, doesn't it?" she added cheekily.

"Read to us?" May repeated.

"Our governess used to read to me and Amélie while we were learning our embroidery stitches, though it was all quite tedious. You know, *Ruminations on Female Behavior* or other books about etiquette." Hélène made a face. "Surely you and Maud would opt for something a bit more enjoyable?"

"I'm not really a fan of novels," May replied.

"If you mean romances, then I wholeheartedly agree." Hélène lowered her voice. "I prefer the epics. You know, the classics. I used to steal Philippe's copies when he studied them with his tutor."

"I did the same with Dolly's books," May admitted, to her own surprise.

Hélène flashed a quick, conspiratorial smile. "Did you play at being Jason, too—sailing after the Golden Fleece? Or Hercules performing his labors?"

May nodded, though her favorite stories were actually those of Odysseus. The crafty, wily one, the warrior who got by on his wits rather than brute strength.

"I'd love for you to come read aloud during one of our sewing sessions. It would certainly help pass the time," she agreed.

Surely Hélène's offer had to do with Eddy? Hélène was already friends with Eddy's other sister; or at least, she and Louise had seemed close at Balmoral. Perhaps Hélène was trying to win over Maud now, too, just as Agnes had suggested that May do last year.

If May's suspicions about Hélène and Eddy were correct,

then gaining his family's support was a smart move. They would certainly need all the help they could get.

May decided to cast a line, see if Hélène took the bait. She lowered her voice and asked, "Is Alix of Hesse here? I was wondering if she and Eddy had announced their engagement yet. Surely the news will come soon, don't you think?"

There it was: a telltale flicker of significance on Hélène's face. She caught herself and smoothed it over, so quickly that a casual observer might not have noticed.

But May was no casual observer.

"I've heard that rumor too, and I think it might be just that. A rumor," Hélène declared. "Eddy and Alix do not seem particularly attached, don't you agree?"

May heard the proprietary pride in Hélène's voice as she spoke of Eddy. It was the tone you used when describing someone you cared about—someone you were bound to.

She nodded in cautious agreement. "Perhaps not. Are the princes here today?" Belatedly she realized it was an abrupt question, and strove to explain. "I need to find Prince George, to thank him for a service he rendered me. He recently rescued my hat." She reached up to touch the brim.

Hélène noticed the gesture. "The hat you're wearing?"

"Yes, it blew away at Hyde Park, and George fetched it back from the duck pond."

"It is quite a charming hat. I am glad for your sake that it did not become fodder for ducks. But . . ." Hélène hesitated, then reached her hands questioningly toward May's face. "Do you mind?"

Before May could reply, Hélène tipped the hat slightly forward, then reached up to comb a finger softly through the feathers. "That's better. It looks more . . ."

May glanced at a mirror that hung on the wall and nearly gasped. That subtle shift had changed the way the hat framed her face, softening the lines of her jaw and bringing out the gleam in her eyes.

"More sophisticated," she murmured, just as Hélène declared, "More *French*."

They both let out a tentative laugh. "I suppose those are the same thing, aren't they?" May asked, and Hélène gave an amused shrug.

"I would say so, but I'm hardly impartial."

May studied her reflection a moment longer. She had been startled when Hélène reached out to touch her, but that was what other young women did, wasn't it? They fussed over each other, plaited each other's hair while sharing secrets. And though Hélène hadn't technically confessed to a relationship with Eddy, May felt as convinced as if she had.

She found herself wondering what she would say to Hélène, if this moment of tentative friendship became something more—if Hélène confessed to the romance and asked May's advice.

Until recently, May would have said that Hélène was gambling dangerously with her future. She'd put her reputation on the line for . . . what, exactly? Passion? Love? Only fools believed in love, May reminded herself. Getting involved with Eddy was reckless of Hélène, and ill-advised.

Yet some unexpected part of May, a part that had newly stirred to life, couldn't help thinking that Hélène was also brave.

Braver than May had ever dared to be.

"I'm afraid that I must leave. I'll see you at Tino and Sophie's wedding?" Hélène said, with a little wave of farewell.

May murmured goodbye and stepped back toward the center of the gallery.

Then she met George's gaze across the room, and her heart skipped.

He took in her hat, newly French and sophisticated the way Hélène had styled it, and smiled in recognition. Eddy stood behind him, but for once, May didn't really notice much about the heir to the throne.

She thought of the sisterly way Hélène had tugged at her hat and felt a burst of sudden fondness. Maybe this was the way things were always meant to play out, Eddy with Hélène and May with George.

Maybe someday the four of them would all be friends—hosting events together, leading parades—Hélène as the Queen of England, May as Duchess of York.

Why not? Stranger things had happened than princes marrying for love.

"MAY, THANK GOD YOU'VE COME!" AGNES GREETED HER, WHEN May arrived at the Endicotts' house the following week. "We have so much to discuss!"

"It looks like you had fun in Paris," May replied, glancing around Agnes's bedroom with a mixture of amusement and envy. Her friend had been out of town for ten days, on a jaunt to Paris with her parents for no apparent reason except to shop. Her bedroom rug was currently hidden beneath an ocean of striped boxes, each marked with the coveted label RUE DE LA PAIX. Clothes were strewn over the four-poster bed and hanging from hooks along the wardrobe in extravagant, blithe disorder.

There were just so *many* things. Tea dresses and day dresses and riding habits in lilac and peach and moss, every last one of them with a hat to match. And that wasn't even including the gowns: floaty, frothy concoctions that shimmered with glass beads, silk bows, or swishing fringe.

"What do you think; is this appropriate for Athens?" Agnes held a gown up to her chest. It was gorgeous, its deep green silk covered in velvet scrollwork all down the bodice and skirt.

May blinked in surprise. "You're going to the wedding?"

"Not to the *actual* wedding, of course." Agnes smiled. "But you can hardly blame me and Mother for wanting to visit when so many crowned heads will be there! I've never seen a royal wedding," Agnes added, almost shyly. "It will be such a treat to simply be *near* one."

That made sense. Athens would be the most glittering place in the world that day, with so many royals and their retinues descending on the city for wedding festivities. The Endicotts were just one of countless wealthy families who, along with reporters and photographers, would flock to the city in the excitement.

"It's a beautiful gown. Just make sure you have a warm fur to go over it; Athens is cold this time of year."

"Thank you, I hadn't considered that. Lisette!" Agnes called out. Moments later, her lady's maid appeared from an interior door. Agnes nodded in May's direction. "Can you pull out the gowns we set aside for Her Serene Highness?"

May flushed as her friend's intent became clear. It was one

thing for Agnes to lend her gloves or a hat, even to buy her a gown or two from Linton & Curtis. But for May to accept a whole Season's worth of cast-off items? "Agnes, I don't . . ."

"Oh, please, just take these off my hands! We both know I won't wear any of them again, not when I have all my new clothes from France."

May watched as Lisette began pulling things from the depths of Agnes's wardrobe: a pale gray tea gown, an ivory silk blouse with pearl buttons, a velvet skirt with panels of black lace. A veritable treasure trove of expensive dresses, most of them hardly even worn.

"I can't accept these," May said again, but Agnes waved dismissively, pretending to misunderstand.

"I know they're not perfect. You'll have to adjust the length in a few places, since you're a bit taller, but you're resourceful—you can let out some hems, or wear flat slippers. . . ."

When Lisette had ducked back into the hallway, her arms laden with garments to fold and put into boxes, Agnes smiled. "You'll never believe what else happened while I was in Paris. I have *such* news."

"What?" May asked, curious.

"It's about the Princess Hélène."

"Princess Hélène was in Paris?" May frowned, leaning one hip on the side of Agnes's bed. "I thought her family were in exile?"

"No, she wasn't there, but I learned something about her. Something that will change everything." Agnes paused dramatically. "May, she had an affair with her family's *coachman*."

May was so startled that for a moment she could only stare at her friend. "What are you talking about?"

"Princess Hélène! She's been sleeping with the help!" Agnes exclaimed, with typical American bluntness.

May headed to a love seat along the windows, moving a hatbox onto the floor so that she would have room to sit. Agnes quickly came to join her.

"I know it sounds impossible, but I assure you that it's true. Hélène was involved with her family's coachman for nearly a year." Agnes proceeded to tell a preposterous story about how she'd seen Hélène sneaking off at Epsom Downs, and followed her, only to eavesdrop on a highly intimate conversation between Hélène and her former lover.

May shook her head, struggling to keep up. "You followed Hélène at Epsom Downs? Why? That was before Balmoral, before I had any idea about her and Eddy."

"I could tell she was *up to something*," Agnes insisted. "The way she was walking, all angry and tense, I sensed that something illicit might be going on. So I went to see what it was."

"But . . . you didn't even know her." *You still don't*, May thought dazedly.

Agnes's nose wrinkled. "I don't see how that matters. She is a princess, or a former princess, and if I could find a secret about her, then it might prove useful someday. Secrets always do," she said firmly. "When I heard what Hélène said to him, I knew at once that I had stumbled upon something *very* illicit. Though of course, I didn't have any reason to use it until you came back from Balmoral and told me about Eddy and Hélène."

"Is that why you were talking to the coachmen in Hyde Park?" May asked, comprehension dawning. "You were digging into Hélène?"

Agnes nodded, pleased. "I knew I needed to track down

this mysterious Laurent figure if I was going to have any hope of using what I knew. And I finally did."

Horror, and shock, twisted in May's stomach. "You didn't just go to Paris for the shopping, did you."

Agnes's green eyes flashed with satisfaction. "Laurent works for the Marquis de Breteuil, at a château just outside Paris. It was easy enough to tell Mama I was going on an excursion to a picture gallery, then pay him a visit instead."

"Whatever for?" May whispered hoarsely.

"What do you think? For an accusation like this, you need proof! And now I have it." Agnes walked over to a drawer in her bedside table, which she unlocked with a key from her pocket. Then she whirled around, brandishing a letter like a weapon. "Wait until you read *this*."

The letter was written in French, in a rough hand. May scanned the text and felt her cheeks grow hot. Laurent certainly didn't hold back; he referenced a night when he and Hélène had slept together in the back of a carriage, and were almost caught. He said he could not bear the thought of her with anyone else—

"I told him that I was a friend of Hélène's, delivering a note from her," Agnes explained, with distinct pride. "I said that she had asked me to wait for a reply. He immediately went off and wrote this. Isn't it incredible?"

It took a moment for Agnes's words to sink in. When they did, May felt slightly nauseous. "You forged a letter from Hélène?"

"It was simple; I knew the coachman wouldn't recognize Hélène's handwriting! I highly doubt they were in the habit of exchanging love notes." Agnes shrugged. "I told him that

Hélène was betrothed to someone else but having second thoughts. It worked like a charm—Laurent tried so hard to woo her back! Look at all the incriminating things he wrote!" She leaned forward to read over May's shoulder. "Have you gotten to the part where he mentions the birthmark on Hélène's shoulder?"

"Agnes. If you spread this around, it will ruin her." May was still staring at the letter in numb shock.

Agnes stepped forward and snatched it from her grasp, an eyebrow raised. "Don't be melodramatic. I'm not saying we have to ruin her."

May didn't like the sound of that *we*. "I don't want to be involved in this."

"But I've already done the hard part! All that's left is for you to pay Hélène a visit. Remind her that queens of England do not sleep with coachmen—that she should be wary of getting engaged to Prince Eddy, lest her sordid past come back to haunt her."

"You want me to *blackmail* her?"

Agnes walked to the side table and locked the letter back in its drawer. The skirts of her dress contorted around her body as she moved, making her look like a figure from a painting.

"*Blackmail* is such a terrible word. I'm just suggesting that you show Hélène this letter from Laurent," she said. "Let her know that a future queen must be beyond reproach, that it would be easier for everyone involved if she ended things with Prince Eddy. Then, with Prince Constantine's wedding in Greece coming up, you'll have the perfect opportunity to show Eddy what a good choice *you* are!"

In other circumstances, May would have corrected Agnes

for calling Prince Eddy by his first name, but she was too stunned.

"I won't do that to Hélène. She's a good person."

"And Alix isn't?" Agnes challenged. "How is this any different than when you told Maud about Alix's fainting spells? Hélène really *did* sleep with Laurent; she did this to herself."

May thought of Hélène's buoyant smile as she'd tugged May's hat forward, the way a friend might.

"No," she said firmly.

Agnes's green eyes widened. "You don't want to be queen?"

"Not if it means destroying innocent people along the way."

"Hélène is far from innocent! Come on, May," Agnes said emphatically. "We both know that the marriage market isn't some childhood game where everyone gets a prize ribbon at the end. For one young woman to succeed, there are inevitably others who lose."

Wasn't that precisely how May had always thought? Yet the mentality now struck her as callous, and senselessly cruel.

"It still doesn't mean I should tear someone else down for my own gain."

She and Agnes stared at each other for a long moment; then Agnes gave a heavy, disappointed sigh.

"Fine. If you want to give up when you are *this* close to achieving what you want, I can't stop you. It's your own future you're throwing away."

There was no possible reply except to say, simply, "Goodbye, Agnes," and head toward the door.

May knew she was doing the right thing, refusing to act on the explosive secret that Agnes had uncovered. She focused on that, to keep Agnes's words—*it's your own future you're throwing away*—from echoing insidiously in her mind.

CHAPTER TWENTY-NINE

Hélène

EDDY LEANED BACK ON THE SOFA OPPOSITE HER, ONE ARM flung carelessly across its top. "Grandmother wants us to hold the wedding ceremony in St. James's Palace; it's where she married Grandfather. Though she also said that we could use Westminster Abbey. I assumed you might prefer that, since it's a cathedral?" he added, phrasing it like a question.

"I would love that. Thank you," Hélène replied, touched by his thoughtfulness. With its soaring Gothic arches and stained-glass windows, Westminster Abbey looked more like the Catholic churches of France than it did the post-Reformation British chapels of Christopher Wren. Which made sense, since it had been a Catholic church for four hundred years before King Henry VIII seized it as Crown property.

Eddy was trying to make things at least somewhat familiar for her, since she would be converting to *his* religion. A detail that she still hadn't shared with her parents.

Last week, Queen Victoria had invited Hélène's father to Buckingham Palace to discuss the engagement. He'd come home hours later, ruddy-faced and jubilant, crowing that he wanted to open the finest champagne in the house and toast his daughter. *Queen of England! I never imagined you could do such a thing,* he kept saying, almost reverently.

Hélène knew what he meant. It had been achievement enough when Amélie married the future King of Portugal. Philippe had never imagined that his other daughter—the stubborn, willful one, who refused to ride sidesaddle and hardly acted like a princess at all—might make an even more illustrious marriage.

When he failed to mention the issue of religion, Hélène realized that Queen Victoria hadn't shared Hélène's promise to convert. It was considerate of her, letting Hélène be the one to tell her parents, but Hélène dreaded that conversation. Their Catholic faith was one of the strongest forces in her parents' lives.

She just had to hope that their ambition was stronger.

Eddy grinned and leaned forward to take an iced madeleine from the coffee table—his third in the course of half an hour. "These are wonderful, by the way."

She rolled her eyes, amused. "You speak as if you've never had French pastries before."

"Not like these, I haven't. Forget scones; these are far better."

"Don't let your grandmother hear you speak such treason." Hélène fought back a smile.

It was surreal, hosting Eddy in her family's sitting room in broad daylight: not sneaking around his bachelor apartments or stealing a moment at a crowded event, but inviting him over in his official capacity as her suitor. He had left his jacket and hat with their butler, and rolled up his sleeves before tucking into his tea, so that his bare wrists showed. There was something deliciously intimate about seeing him like this, more intimate in some ways than all their secret nights together.

Hélène's hand strayed to her pocket, where she'd tucked the yellow wildflower that Eddy had given her at Balmoral. It made her feel like a fairy. The flower was dead now, and too crumpled even to be useful as potpourri, but she couldn't bring herself to throw it away. Perhaps she would sneak it into her wedding bouquet.

She sighed in contentment, happy to just sit here in his presence. No one had ever told her that things could get this way. That after the frenzy of infatuation, your feelings for someone might deepen into something heavier and headier, the way a fine wine became more substantial the longer it remained in the bottle.

Footsteps sounded from the hall, as they had every twenty minutes since Eddy arrived. Hélène had been surprised when her parents allowed her and Eddy to sit here alone, though they had kept the double doors wide open in a nod to propriety—and kept sending their butler, Jean-Baptiste, to check on the couple.

"Your Royal Highness. Mademoiselle." Jean-Baptiste bowed to Eddy, then nodded in her direction. "May I bring you anything?"

"Just more tea," Hélène answered, wearily amused. He would be back in another twenty minutes for the same exact routine, but oddly, she didn't mind.

Jean-Baptiste held out a silver platter laden with envelopes. "Your mail, mademoiselle. I shall return with the tea."

Hélène scooped the letters off the top and began shuffling through them.

"Anything interesting?" Eddy asked, watching her affectionately.

"The usual." Most of the notes were invitations—

addressed by social secretaries, whose handwriting was never as loopy or irreverent as a lady's—or bills in brown paper envelopes. But when she saw an unmarked letter, Hélène paused.

The lack of return address wasn't unusual in itself; plenty of society women trusted their embossed stationery to indicate who they were. Yet something about the missive lifted the hairs on the back of Hélène's neck. A shadowy, ominous intent seemed to cling to it in a way she couldn't articulate.

Hélène stood and walked to the escritoire, where she found an enameled letter opener in the top drawer. She sliced open the envelope with a flick.

Hélène,

It pains me to write this letter, yet I cannot ignore the dictates of my conscience. As your friend—I hope you will think of me as a friend—I feel compelled to warn you.

I know about you and your former coachman, Laurent Guérard.

If you doubt my word, only see the enclosed page, one of several in Laurent's letter to you. I assure you that I came into possession of this letter quite by accident, but now that I have it, I have no choice but to speak.

Surely you realize the immorality of what you have done, as well as the danger. If you are reckless enough to move forward in your relationship with Prince Eddy, or worse, to announce an engagement, then people will start looking through your past. I fear that the truth will come out.

Don't you think it better to break things off now, before it's too late? You can still retreat from this situation without any scandal. You might even be able to marry someday, perhaps a Continental relative, someone with a less prominent position.

After all, the last thing you want is to become a cautionary tale like Marie of Mecklenburg-Strelitz. Not to mention what it would do for your family's reputation.

If you do not end things with Prince Eddy before Princess Sophie and Prince Constantine's wedding, I shall be forced to conclude that you have made the wrong decision. And, as much as it grieves me, I will have no choice but to show the rest of Laurent's letter to Her Majesty. She deserves to be warned of this scandal before it reaches her through some other avenue.

I hope it will not come to that.

Your friend,
May of Teck

The words were blurring in Hélène's vision. She braced a hand on the silk cushion to steady herself and quickly looked at the enclosed page, on plain rough paper.

She didn't actually know Laurent's handwriting—they'd never had cause to write to each other—but the note was unmistakably from him. She recognized the urgent pulse of his voice, his use of French colloquialisms. Her heart plummeted when she saw that he mentioned one of their more reckless afternoons, when they had nearly been caught in the back seat of her parents' carriage.

Queen Victoria could *not* see this letter. Hélène could always claim it was a forgery, that someone was trying to blackmail her by spinning falsehoods . . . but stories like the carriage were frighteningly specific, and hard to disbelieve.

She hadn't imagined that May of Teck was capable of such cruelty. Why, just last week they had shared a moment of understanding at the Princess of Wales's receiving hours. Hélène had actually been foolish enough to think of May as a possible *friend*. And the whole time, the other girl had been plotting her downfall!

I came into possession of this letter quite by accident, May had claimed. Hélène wasn't so foolish as to believe that. May had obviously figured out about Hélène and Eddy—perhaps she'd seen them together at Balmoral? So she'd gone digging, and uncovered the truth about Laurent, even going so far as to intercept his *letter*.

Clearly, she thought she could edge Hélène out of the way and marry Eddy herself.

Hélène drew in a breath with such anger that Eddy looked up, startled. "Did you receive some bad news?"

The worst. "I'm fine," Hélène said, and though it took every ounce of her willpower, she managed a smile. It must have been convincing enough, because Eddy nodded and changed the subject.

"I was wondering, how would you feel about announcing our engagement at Sophie and Tino's wedding next week? Most of our families will be there, and—"

"No!"

It came out too sharply; Hélène winced and tried to recover. "It will be Sophie's big day. I don't want to overshadow her with our news."

"I hadn't thought of that. You're right, of course," Eddy said ruefully.

Jean-Baptiste reentered the room with a pitcher of tea and began officiously refilling their cups, giving Hélène a much-needed chance to think. She shoved May's letter under the pile of other letters and stacked them all on a side table. She wasn't sure why, but she didn't dare let Eddy see it—didn't want to involve him in any of this until she had a plan.

It seemed unbelievable that quiet, demure May of Teck would stoop so low as to *blackmail* her.

Some girls would go to any lengths to wear a crown.

CHAPTER THIRTY

Alix

"ARE YOU READY?" NICHOLAS ASKED, WITH A SMILE THAT BE-trayed his nervousness.

No, Alix thought wildly. Of course she wasn't ready to tell the tsar and tsarina about their secret engagement.

Last month, after Nicholas proposed at Marlborough House, he'd suggested that they share the news with their families at Sophie and Tino's wedding. Or more accurately, they would share the news with *his* family, since Alix's father was sending Ernie to the wedding in his stead. Alix had agreed, because what other choice did she have? This sort of thing needed to be discussed in person, and the wedding provided a perfect chance to do so.

Yet now that the moment was here, a cold panic had sunk its hooks into her flesh. The tsar and tsarina were stern under the best of circumstances; Alix couldn't imagine how they would react when told that their oldest son, their *heir*, had gotten engaged without their knowledge.

She just had to hope they would accept the match once they realized how happy it made Nicholas. They loved their son; surely they would want him to love his wife, too.

"I'm ready if you are," she told Nicholas.

He nodded and began leading her through the crowded reception hall. Skirts hissed over the marble floors as guests exchanged gossip, their heads whipping avidly toward the entrance with each new arrival. Through the windows, the colorful houses and towers of Athens were silhouetted against the golden sky.

They were at the Greek royal palace, which had been filling up all week as foreign kings and queens arrived in town. Nicholas and his parents were lodged in the palace itself; but King George and Queen Olga simply couldn't host everyone, so lower-ranking guests—like Alix and Ernie—were shuffled into the homes of various bewildered aristocrats. Apparently King George had even commandeered carriages and extra servants from his court. Alix had already heard Emperor Wilhelm of Germany snickering about the footmen's mismatched livery.

But what the Greek royal palace lacked in size and scale, it made up for in antiquated ceremony. Alix and Ernie's carriage had pulled through the wrought-iron gates amid the fanfare of trumpets. A pair of footmen had then sprung forward to marshal them through the front doors, up a sweeping staircase into the great receiving rooms.

Nicholas found his parents near the windows, surrounded by a cluster of other, less important guests. The tsar was as sullen as Alix remembered; he stared imperiously around the room, as if this palace belonged to him rather than to King George. Next to him, the tsarina nodded in assiduous agreement with whatever he said.

Alix felt the room growing hazy. No, she thought fiercely, she could not afford to faint now, in front of all these people.

She focused on physical sensations, trying to anchor herself in the present—the feel of her leather gloves over her palms, the smell of the salt air, which seemed to permeate Athens, even indoors.

The tsar glanced briefly toward his son, then returned to his conversation without a flicker of emotion, as if determined to make Nicholas wait, or beg. Minnie noticed the standoff but made no move to intervene.

When Nicholas's patience had worn thin, he stepped forward and bowed his head. "Father, I'm sorry to interrupt, but I wanted to speak with you about something."

"Then speak."

Nicholas glanced sidelong at the other guests. "Could we have a moment in private?"

"You had plenty of moments in private, the whole time we were journeying here," the tsar said drily. The onlookers chuckled.

When his son made no move to step aside, Sasha let out a resigned breath.

"Oh, all right, if we must."

He turned without another word, leaving the tsarina to give their excuses to his companions. Nicholas cast Alix a pleading look, then hurried along after the tsar, leaving Alix and his mother to follow.

Their disjointed party made its way into a corridor, past guards standing at attention, until they reached a half-empty sitting room. Its gas lamps flickered as they opened the door, making shadows dance along the frescoed walls. The sight struck Alix as oddly sinister.

She wished she could reach for Nicholas's hand but decided

against it. No one had yet addressed her, or otherwise acknowledged her presence, though they were all obviously aware that she had joined their party.

"Father. Mother." Nicholas turned to each of his parents. "I wanted you to know that Alix and I are engaged."

There was a moment of hollow, echoing silence. Alix kept her eyes downcast, as a proper young woman should in this situation, though she itched to look up and see the tsar's expression.

"Oh, Nicholas." Minnie spoke in a forlorn breath, which was somehow more alarming than if she'd been angry.

It would seem that the tsar was angry enough for both of them.

"You are most certainly *not* engaged," he told Nicholas through clenched teeth. "When you are, your mother and I will inform you of that fact. You are in no way free to make such declarations for yourself, especially not about some backwater German girl."

At that, Alix couldn't help but look up sharply. All three sets of eyes were trained on her. Sasha grunted, dismissing her, then shifted his attention back to Nicholas.

"You are not some commoner who can marry at a whim. You are the future Tsar of All the Russias, and your marriage is an affair of state!"

"And Alix will be a wonderful partner when I take the throne someday," Nicholas said evenly. "I'm sorry if you had someone else in mind, Father, but it no longer matters. I have asked Alix to marry me, and she said yes."

Sasha stared at his son in acrid disbelief. "*I* didn't say yes. And my permission is the one you need."

Alix knew the tsar and tsarina would find her impudent, perhaps even ill-bred, for speaking up. But she couldn't stand here and let them discuss her future without comment.

She sank into an excruciatingly low curtsy. "If I may ask, Your Imperial Highness, why do you object?"

"Ah! Look, Minnie, the mouse can speak!"

Alix rose, her cheeks hot; the tsar must have seen her resentment, because he chuckled. "You hadn't heard that nickname, had you? It's what everyone in St. Petersburg has been calling you since you came to see Ella last year: the Hessian mouse. Speaking of your sister, she—"

The tsarina laid a hand on his forearm, and to Alix's surprise, the tsar fell silent.

"Alix," she said gently, "you are a lovely young woman, but you are not right for Nicholas."

"We need someone higher-ranking than the daughter of a German nobody." The tsar pretended to glance back over his shoulder toward the wedding. "Is your father even in attendance today, or was he not invited?"

Alix decided to ignore that question. Best not to get into the issue of her father, who had become reclusive—and, she had to admit, a bit eccentric—since her mother's death.

"Higher-ranking?" she repeated. "I am a granddaughter of Queen Victoria."

"Yes, and how many are there of those? Thirty?"

Twenty-two, Alix thought in frustration, but she knew better than to correct him.

To her relief, Nicholas cut in. "I'm sorry if you don't approve of the match, but Alix and I are engaged. We are in love."

"In love?" Sasha laughed—a great belly laugh, as if his son had made an uproarious joke. "I'm sorry, are you a peasant now, to marry according to your lusts?"

Minnie shot a warning glance at her husband, the enormous pear-shaped diamonds in her ears swaying with the movement. Then she looked back at Nicholas with what seemed to be an attempt at sympathy. It came out more like a grimace. "Please do not keep saying that you are engaged, Nicky. You have indulged in a bit of harmless flirtation, but that is all."

"It is not just flirtation! We made a pledge—"

The tsar stepped forward and struck his son across the cheek.

Alix gasped and stumbled back a step, hands flying to her mouth. The tsarina's expression flickered, yet she made no move to help her son.

Already a red mark was blooming on the tsarevich's cheek.

In the ringing silence, Minnie cleared her throat. Her eyes were now fixed on Alix. "I hope that a pledge is the only thing you've made, Alix. I hope you haven't been such a fool as to throw away your future on an engagement that can never be."

Alix blinked. What did that mean, *throw away her future?*

Minnie spoke slowly, as if addressing an ignorant child. "Have you lain with my son?"

"*What?*"

The tsarina continued in the same deliberate, dispassionate tone. "Because if there's a surprise coming in nine months, it won't change anything. It won't succeed in tying you to Nicholas. All it will do is ruin you."

Alix could only stare at the tsarina in bewildered shock.

"Mother, this is beneath you. Alix is a young woman of honor, and I will not allow you to besmirch her reputation!" Nicholas exclaimed.

"But, Nicky, *you're* the one besmirching it!" Sasha interjected. "If you keep saying that you are engaged when you are not, Alix is the one who will suffer. She has already been linked to one prince who didn't marry her. A young woman whose name keeps being bandied about, with no engagements announced . . ." He shrugged. "She might never end up marrying at all."

"Eddy didn't break things off with me!" Alix couldn't help herself; it was impossible to hear the tsar's words and not clarify. "*I* said no to *him!*"

Sasha smirked as if he found that distinctly unbelievable. "If you really turned down the future King of England, you're even more of a fool than I took you for."

"Nicholas, my darling, we just want what's best for both of you," Minnie pleaded.

"If you wanted what was best, you would *listen* to me!" Finally Nicholas reached for Alix's hand, lacing their fingers in defiance of his parents. "I'm sorry that we fell in love without consulting you, but your objections about Alix are unfounded. Our family has married foreign brides for centuries! Mother, you were a Danish princess before you moved to Russia, and you succeeded in learning our ways. You can help guide Alix, teach her to become a great tsarina."

A great tsarina. The phrase filled Alix with foreboding, but she told herself she could handle it. It was the only way she and Nicholas could stay together.

As difficult as it would be, finding a way to live with him, she couldn't bear the prospect of living without him.

"It's not just Alix's lack of position that concerns me. I'm sorry," the tsarina added, "but even in Russia, word has spread of your health problems. I fear that with your weak constitution, you would find the demands of being tsarina simply unbearable. Far better to stay close to home, where you will feel safe."

Alix went cold; Nicholas cast her a worried, protective glance. Minnie noticed and pressed her lips into a thin line, as if they had just proved her point.

"I don't know who has been spreading such gossip about me," Alix forced herself to say. "Surely I'm not the first woman to need smelling salts because my corset was laced too tight."

"Is that all it was? From what we've heard, you are afflicted with something much worse."

Alix breathed once, twice, trying to think over the skittering of her pulse. She felt the familiar darkness hovering at the corner of her vision like an unwanted guest.

"Nicholas needs someone who can give him strong, hardy heirs. Not a wilting German flower," his mother went on.

"I'm not—"

"The primary duty of a tsarina is to provide the next tsar," Sasha said bluntly. "The ceremonies, the public appearances— none of that is as crucial as the future of our family. And frankly, young lady, I'm not sure that you can handle *any* of it. You will never marry Nicholas, not while I have breath in my body."

Shame flooded Alix, white-hot and corrosive. Her eyes stung, but she blinked away the tears.

The tsar turned to address his son. "What happened on your grand tour with Tino? Your mother and I sent you on that trip—at great expense, I might add—because you wouldn't stop mooning after Alix after she left St. Petersburg last year. You were supposed to pay court to foreign princesses, to get this"—he waved a dismissive hand in Alix's direction—"this *infatuation* out of your system."

Oh. A tiny corner of Alix was pleased to learn that Nicholas had been thinking of her all last year, too. His feelings must have troubled his parents greatly if they'd sent him on a trip with Tino—who supposedly had no problem sowing his wild oats over multiple continents—to erase the memory of Alix from his mind.

Nicholas's jaw clenched. "I am nothing like Tino."

"To my eternal disappointment!"

The tsarina cut in, angling her body between Alix's and the two men as if steering her toward the door. "I'm sorry, Alix, but I think it's best you return to the party."

Alix cast a helpless glance back at Nicholas, but he had crumpled forward in defeat. Feeling her gaze, he looked up, and the hopeless expression in his eyes broke something in her.

"I know this may seem harsh to you," Minnie was saying, "but I promise that it's for the best. Moving to Russia, assuming the duties of a tsarina: it's not for everyone, even princesses who have trained to rule. Russia is a harsh land, full of violent contradictions and complicated history."

"I could learn," Alix said softly. She was a granddaughter of Victoria Regina; of course she'd been raised to manage palaces, to help her husband rule.

"I'm afraid not, my dear. If you persist in trying to marry my son, it will only end in heartache and disaster."

The words fell from Minnie's mouth like heavy stones,

like the ominous pronouncement of some ancient prophet-ess. They made Alix shiver.

She grabbed her skirts in both hands and began running back toward the ballroom, no longer caring about appear-ances. Her slippers tripped on the scrolling carpet; she nearly tumbled to the floor, but caught herself.

It didn't matter where she went, as long as she got *out* of here—away from these heartless people, from the cruelty and ambition and callousness that was at the heart of every royal court.

She tried not to think about the fact that her body, falling into a panic, was proving Sasha right.

Maybe she wasn't cut out to be Empress of Russia.

CHAPTER THIRTY-ONE

Hélène

"ALL RIGHT, HÉLÈNE. WHAT'S TROUBLING YOU?" HER MOTHER cast her a long, slow look, studying her in the way that only mothers can do.

"Nothing!" Hélène tore her gaze from the entrance; she'd been watching the arrivals of the various royalty and high-ranking aristocrats, keeping an eye out for May of Teck. Sensing her mother's skepticism, she added, "I'm just tired from the journey."

"We both know it's not that. You've been acting strangely since last week." Marie Isabelle put a hand on one hip, causing her bracelet to glitter. Tonight's reception at the palace in Athens was merely a prelude to the main event, so she'd worn only the single strand of diamonds on one wrist. Tomorrow, at the wedding, was when the tiaras and jewels and military medals would *really* come out, all the guests subtly vying to outdo one another.

"Are you and His Royal Highness in some kind of lovers' quarrel?" her mother pressed when Hélène didn't answer.

"No. I just . . ." Hélène caught a glimpse of ash-blond hair and drew in a breath, only to realize that it wasn't May, just another of the seemingly endless cousins in attendance.

Probably the girl was named Victoria—weren't they all?—but Hélène couldn't remember what ridiculous nickname this one went by. Ducky, Moretta, Mossy?

"I imagine the secrecy is weighing on you!" her father cut in, a bit gleefully. "How difficult to be at a wedding and not be able to share your own big news! Has Her Majesty decided when you'll be able to make an announcement?"

"I'm not sure," Hélène said vaguely.

Philippe grinned, oblivious to her anxiety, probably envisioning the support he would be able to muster—the monarchists who would rally to his cause—once his daughter had married into the greatest royal family of all. The Third Republic might even reconsider his exile once the British had declared themselves, at least implicitly, on the Orléans side.

If only Hélène shared his confidence.

Ever since she'd read May's letter, she'd thought of nothing else. Her mind was consumed by endless fears and what-ifs.

"Hélène. May I have the honor of a dance?"

For once, she didn't smile at the sound of Eddy's voice behind her. She'd known that he would find her tonight, the way he always did. What she didn't know was what she would say once she saw him.

She put her hand carefully atop his, but instead of leading her to the dance floor, Eddy started toward the terrace.

This palace was small by royal standards, but damn if it didn't have the best view Hélène had ever seen. She took a few involuntary steps toward the limestone railing, which looked like part of the landscape itself, as if it had sprouted from the ground like a flower. The city of Athens spilled out before her, colored roofs and dusty streets giving way to the gleaming white Acropolis and, beyond, the blue haze of the ocean.

"It's beautiful, isn't it?" Eddy braced his hands on the railing next to hers. "None of our palaces have much of a view, unless you count Balmoral. And even that is mostly a view of fog."

Normally Hélène would have said something teasing in reply, like *What good is an island nation without a seaside palace,* but she didn't have the heart. Instead she just nodded. "I've never been to Greece until now. It's lovely."

May was somewhere inside that ballroom. Hélène could go find her, could drag that lying, scheming snake out here and confront her. How satisfying it would feel to tell May precisely what she thought.

But she couldn't afford to do that, not as long as May had that letter from Laurent. If it were only her own future on the line, Hélène might not have cared; she didn't have any particular attachment to her reputation, didn't notice what was said about her.

But she wasn't alone in this anymore. If she lost her reputation, she would unleash a torrent of shame and suffering upon her family—and, worst of all, she would lose Eddy.

As painful as it was to admit, Hélène knew that what May had written was true. A future queen was supposed to be a wholly unsexual being; even after she wed, she shouldn't *enjoy* the marriage bed, but should lie back and think of England. The British people would never accept a queen with a sexual past. Just look at what had happened to Catherine Howard. Once the truth about Hélène came out, she would be beheaded, too—at least, figuratively speaking.

If this were America, or even France, the sordid details of the scandal would be all over the newspapers. Not so in England, where the press still maintained a reverential silence about the monarchy. No, Hélène had been in England long enough to know that its social warfare was more underhanded and backstabbing.

It would start with the women, of course. The society wives were harpies, attacking with sly, oblique insults and veiled remarks. They would discuss Hélène before their servants so that the gossip spread through the city in a malicious drip, until playwrights mocked her onstage and the taverns were rowdy with drinking songs about her. Eventually her family would become a laughingstock, leaving Hélène's parents no choice but to ship her away—to an obscure relative in Switzerland, perhaps, or to a nunnery.

It was exactly what had happened to the girl May had mentioned in her letter: Marie of Mecklenburg-Strelitz. The poor thing had gotten pregnant as an unmarried teenager, and the family completely washed their hands of her. The last Hélène had heard, Marie had married an elderly count who made her life a living hell.

Even if Hélène managed to avoid such a fate, even if she convinced her parents to stand by her side, what good would it do? She would never be able to marry Eddy.

Their engagement would break down slowly. As the rumors gained momentum, Queen Victoria would keep finding excuses to delay, until eventually Eddy had no choice but to end things. And then Hélène's family would be disgraced, her father's chances of returning to France more remote than ever.

She could talk about all of this with Eddy—yet as much as she loved him, Hélène knew that he would make the situation even worse. He would try to confront May or involve his grandmother, and then it would all implode. Eddy might escape such a firestorm unscathed, but not Hélène.

Things weren't the same for women and men. It wasn't right or fair, but it was the truth.

No matter what she did, she would lose Eddy. Or, more accurately . . . he was already lost.

The only thing Hélène still had the power to do was protect her family.

She felt some great axis turning within herself, as if her very bones were remolding to create space for her broken heart. She needed to let go of Eddy—to refocus on the one thing that remained to her, the tie that had bound her since the moment of her birth. The Orléans cause.

Eddy turned to her, smiling. "My father says that he's heard from Lord Posonby," he began, but Hélène cut him off.

"Eddy."

God, this was harder than she'd expected. She looked out into the distance, letting the breeze cool her feverish skin as she fumbled for her next words.

"You shouldn't announce the engagement."

"Of course," Eddy said easily. "Your parents can make the announcement; it's their right, as parents of the bride."

"They will not be making the announcement." Every word was like a knife stabbing into her chest, yet Hélène forced herself to continue. "I can't marry you, Eddy. I'm sorry that I led you to believe otherwise."

The silence that fell between them was sudden and absolute. Hélène kept her eyes fixed on the horizon to avoid looking at Eddy's face. Through the blurriness in her vision, she saw the glow of the sun, amber and crimson and a rich honeyed gold.

"I have consulted my conscience, and I realize that it was wrong of me to agree to convert. I cannot give up my Catholic faith. I am sorry for misleading you," she concluded, in nearly a whisper.

"No." Eddy pressed his palms into the stone railing, his voice gaining momentum. "No, there must be another way. We will petition the pope!"

"That won't work."

He didn't seem to have heard. "We'll get you a dispensation granting you permission to remain Catholic in private but practice the Church of England publicly, in your role as queen."

"He'll never grant it," Hélène said softly.

"All right, then. We'll change the Act of Settlement." Eddy spoke as if it were a simple matter, revising a law that had been in place for nearly two centuries.

"How? You think Parliament will really change the law to accommodate the daughter of an exiled French king, a pseudo-princess whose religion they don't even approve of?" Her voice came out admirably steady despite the wild thrum of her pulse. "No, we need to just accept that things are impossible. This is precisely why our families would have never allowed you to court me. We both knew from the start that we shouldn't have gotten involved: we said as much last year, that night at Marlborough House!"

Eddy turned and seized Hélène's hands roughly in his. "But we *did* get involved, and we're here now. I love you."

"I love you, too."

Hélène hadn't meant to let herself say that; the words were a reflex, torn from her lips without a conscious thought.

"That settles it, then. We'll find a way through this," he said fiercely.

Hélène's throat burned. "Eddy . . . there *is* no way through this, short of me giving up my religion. Which I cannot do. I'm sorry, but I cannot love you more than I love my God."

"I would never expect you to."

If only he were angry. He had every right to be: she had promised his grandmother to convert, only to claim that she had changed her mind. Yet instead of looking at her with disgust or disappointment, Eddy seemed consumed by a grim regret.

She hated herself for the lie, but what choice did she have? She didn't dare tell him the truth.

"Very well, then," Eddy said heavily.

Something in Hélène shattered at those words. He was about to agree with her, to tell her goodbye. And even though it was what she'd wanted, she couldn't bear to hear him say it.

As long as they were talking, they were still together. As long as they were talking, they still had a chance. But once Eddy walked away from her, they would be over for good. To think that after a year of secrets, of passion and infatuation and illicit meetings, after getting approval from the queen herself, they would still end up here.

Walking away from each other, just as they should have done a year ago.

"I'm going to abdicate."

For a moment Hélène thought she hadn't heard correctly. She looked up at Eddy, who was staring at her with clear-eyed purpose.

"You . . . what?"

"I'll abdicate. Or, more accurately, I'll renounce my place in the line of succession." He shrugged. "Technically, you can only abdicate if you're a reigning king."

"No," she breathed. "There's no way."

"Of course there's a way. I just sign a paper and give it to Parliament," Eddy said steadily. "Hélène, you say that you don't love me more than you love your God, and that is as it should be. But I have to admit that I love you more than anything. More than the Church of England, that is for certain. And more than I love being a future king."

There was no trace of his usual irreverence in his expression; Eddy looked more serious than Hélène had ever seen him.

For the first time that she could remember, he looked nothing like a boy, but like a grown man.

Finally she found her voice. "You can't do that, Eddy. They'll never let you—"

"Of course they will. Kings have signed away their rights plenty of times."

"When they're defeated in battle! Not because they want to marry someone they shouldn't!"

"Well then, I suppose I will be the first."

As she became more visibly distraught, Eddy seemed to grow calmer, his certainty increasing with every moment. Hélène's heart seized at the realization of just how much he loved her.

If Eddy really was willing to give up the throne for her sake, then May's threat no longer mattered. Hélène and Eddy could still marry. They could run away from it all, far from the scandal—because they would both be ruined if they did this, Eddy for renouncing his duties and Hélène for the gossip May would spread. But it wouldn't matter, not where they were going. They could escape somewhere impossibly distant, like Venice or Jaipur or maybe even America. There were places out west they could go, to live as she'd always wanted to live, with horses and wild spaces and—

And then what?

Could she live with herself, knowing that she and Eddy had dumped all their responsibilities and scandals onto their families? Were they really going to run away, leaving everyone else to pick up the pieces? Hélène's thoughts drifted to George, who would be forced to take the throne in his brother's place . . . and to her parents. Forget getting their throne back—Marie Isabelle and Philippe wouldn't be able to show their faces in society at all. No one would want anything to do with the former king whose daughter had nearly broken the British monarchy. Her name would be synonymous with betrayal, her family despised to the end of their days.

Eddy might be willing to leave everything for her, but he'd spent his whole life destined for the throne. She knew he would make a good king, despite his family's complaints about his lack of academic motivation. A ruler didn't need to be a scholar; Eddy was smart in other ways, observant and thoughtful and warm. And unlike his father and grandmother, who were both painfully aristocratic, Eddy actually had some grasp of what it meant to be an ordinary person. His time in the military—and his own irreverent, joyful nature—had exposed him to real life, even if he'd never lived it himself. He could speak with his future subjects in a way the rest of his family could not.

Hélène couldn't let him give up on being king. Not when

Eddy might reshape the way the monarchy interacted with the public, with the entire *world*.

No, she would never forgive herself if she let Eddy renounce his future for her sake. And if he couldn't be king while they were together . . . then they would have to part ways.

"I'm sorry," she told him, the words catching in her throat. "But no."

"What do you mean, 'but no'?"

"I mean that I cannot marry you! My decision is final; please just let me be. I am going inside now." Hélène's entire body thrummed with grief and anger, her throat closing in a chokehold of helpless rage. "Don't follow me."

He fell silent at the finality of her words. That was the Frenchwoman in her, too, Hélène thought sadly: not just the passion and impulsivity but the brutal stubbornness. The ability to face hard truths that a demure Englishwoman would have ignored.

She hurried away before she could see the look of utter heartbreak on Eddy's face.

CHAPTER THIRTY-TWO

May

THE MORNING OF SOPHIE AND TINO'S WEDDING DAWNED bleary and cold. What else did one expect from a November wedding in Athens, May thought, as she tugged aside the damask curtains to stare out the window.

She and her parents were staying at the home of the Kallergis family: wealthy and influential Athenians who were only too happy to host a few stray guests, hoping to curry favor with the king and queen. May's father had been grumbling all week about the perceived insult. If they weren't going to be housed in the palace, he complained, they should at least be with a noble family and not a bunch of upstart politicians. In his mind, a politician was about as important as a butler, and far less useful.

But they were here for the wedding, and that was what mattered. May still couldn't believe she'd convinced her father that they should come—though of course he was unaware that she'd had any role in his decision. She had made a point of discussing the wedding in front of their driver, emphasizing that *everyone* would be there—trusting that Charles would let the gossip find its way to his master, as a good servant always did. Then, risky as it was, she'd asked Maud if her father might be willing to check in. She knew that status-obsessed Francis of Teck wouldn't ignore a note from the Prince of Wales.

Sure enough, when Uncle Bertie sent a note asking if the Tecks were coming to Athens, Francis had decided that, yes, they would attend. He announced this fact to May and her mother as if it had been his own idea. As if he hadn't been nudged there by May's careful planning.

At a knock on the door, May looked up in surprise. It had been so long since they'd had a house full of staff, she'd forgotten the cadence of it. "Yes?"

"Miss?" The lady's maid bobbed a quick curtsy. Her English was piecemeal, but it was still better than May's non-existent Greek. "There is a young woman here, she says to see you?"

"Really?" Curiosity piqued, May gestured for the maid to help her into her gown, a gorgeous one of midnight blue trimmed with sable. It was a castoff from Agnes, but still far more beautiful than anything her parents would have purchased.

When she hurried down the stairs, May was oddly unsurprised to see Agnes standing there, looking resplendent in a gown of orange and gold. With her glittering jewelry and rust-colored cape, she looked like a sunrise come to life.

May ran a hand reflexively over her own dress, and Agnes's eyes flickered in recognition.

"That gown looks better on you than it ever did on me. I'm glad you took it off my hands," she said gently.

May hesitated. She'd been ignoring Agnes ever since their conversation about Hélène, when she'd learned about the letter Agnes had tricked Laurent into writing. Her friend had sent a flurry of notes in the weeks leading up to the wedding, notes that May had steadfastly refused to answer.

Now that Agnes was here before her, May found that she still didn't know what to say.

"I can't talk; I need to leave for the wedding soon," she mumbled, but Agnes leapt at her words.

"I know! I wanted to ask if I could give you a ride to the cathedral. Lisette is with me, so there's no need to worry about a chaperone. Please," she insisted. "There are things we need to talk about."

May certainly didn't condone all the digging Agnes had done into Hélène. Yet she found herself wanting to believe that Agnes had, in her own way, meant well. She'd been mis-guided and heavy-handed, but hadn't she been trying to help?

"Just wait a moment," she decided. Upstairs, May col-lected her cloak and gloves before telling the lady's maid that she would meet her parents at the wedding.

Lisette was seated on the back of the Endicotts' carriage, like a postilion, enabling the young women to speak privately inside. May would normally have felt sorry for her, but the maid was bundled against the cold in a heavy coat, her hands tucked into a fur muff that was clearly a hand-me-down from Agnes.

May slid inside, and a moment later they started off, bri-dles jangling as the horses pulled into the street.

"How was your journey?" Agnes said uncertainly, into the silence.

"Fine." Reflexively, May added, "And yours?"

"It was lovely. Have you ever seen Corfu? Apparently the

Waleses were there just before us, on the royal yacht—the *Marine*, I think it's called."

The *Nerine*, May wanted to correct. It was the Greek word for "sea nymph." Not that she'd been on it; she'd never been on a yacht at all, let alone the one belonging to the queen. Whenever her family traveled it was by train or, worse, by carriage.

"And the reception last night?" Agnes prompted, when May said nothing. "How was it? Did you see Prince Eddy?"

May stiffened. "As I told you before, I'm done chasing after Eddy."

"What about Princess Hélène? Did she look unhappy?" Agnes pressed.

May's stomach twisted with a sudden suspicion. Hélène and Eddy had seemed a bit strange last night, hadn't they? At one point May thought she'd caught the French princess staring daggers at her, though she couldn't imagine why.

"Agnes," she said slowly. "What did you do?"

The rubies in Agnes's ears glimmered, looking suddenly grotesque, like droplets of blood. She leaned back with a sigh.

"I'm sorry if you disapprove, but I wrote a letter to Princess Hélène—telling her what we know, urging her to do the right thing."

"Agnes!" May's stomach plummeted. "What did Hélène say? Did she reply?"

"That's what I'm trying to figure out. Has she?" Agnes threw up her hands in an impatient gesture. "Because I wrote the letter as *you!*"

May dug her gloved hands into the cushions. They turned a corner and the carriage swayed, but neither of them moved.

"You *impersonated* me?"

"I did what you were too squeamish and proper to do. Now the way to Eddy is clear, just as you always wanted it to be!"

May should have been livid, yet all she felt was a dull weariness. Why hadn't she seen this coming? After all, Agnes had admitted to forging letters before.

"Maybe *you* should marry Eddy, since you're so fixated on him that you'll resort to blackmail," she snapped.

"Believe me, if I could marry him, I would!" It was perhaps the truest statement Agnes had ever spoken. "Since I can't, it should at the very least be you."

May stared out the window. They had turned onto a street near the harbor; she saw the wind ruffling the white-capped waves, boats hurrying back toward shore. "How dare you. I told you that I didn't want to do anything to Hélène—"

"But we didn't do anything *to* Hélène! She dug her own grave, and will have to live with the consequences of her choices," Agnes exclaimed. "All we did was remind her of what she had already done. You can't let yourself feel guilty about this."

"Of course I feel guilty!" Perhaps it wasn't too late; May could go find Hélène at the reception tonight, explain that this was all a misunderstanding.

"I can tell you're thinking of ways to undo what I've done. Stop," Agnes said brutally. "This is why women are still the weaker sex, because we worry too much about how other people feel. Just look at your mother! She failed to look out for her own interests, and where did it get her? Married to a buffoon who frittered away her inheritance."

"There's no need to speak about my father like that," May shot back, though all Agnes had done was voice May's own secret thoughts.

"I'm sorry!" Agnes held out her hands in a gesture of apology. "All I mean is that men—your father, Prince Eddy, even George—think of themselves first. Men never worry about *hurting* people; they take what they want, when they want it. If women could act like that even a fraction of the time, we wouldn't be at the mercy of men."

May didn't want to listen, but there was a dangerous logic to Agnes's thinking. Her words slipped under May's skin like a whisper, taking root in her brain.

The carriage pulled onto the street that led to the Cathedral of Athens. The flags that lined the road whipped about in the blustery wind. The sidewalks teemed with people, crowds thronging in the hope of glimpsing their future queen.

"You seem angry," Agnes said tentatively.

May didn't know if she wanted to laugh or scream. "Of course I'm angry! I told you I didn't want to go down this road and you did it anyway. You pretended to *be* me!"

Agnes stared at her for a moment. "I see," she said at last, with maddening calm. "You haven't given up, just changed course. You're going after Prince Eddy's brother instead."

When May said nothing, Agnes nodded, vindicated. "Well, May, I have to admit that I'm shocked. I never thought you would settle for a lesser prince."

Even though it was how everyone thought, no one ever spoke such things aloud. It was jarring, hearing Agnes actually refer to George as *lesser*.

But she was right, wasn't she? That was how the laws

of succession worked, not just in the royal family but for everyone. The oldest son inherited while other sons were left to scramble for themselves, to settle for army positions or minor estates while their older brothers took everything: the family castle, the name, the title, the power.

As for daughters? No one spared them a thought except as bargaining chips in the marriage game.

May fumbled for the right words. "I realize that George might not make sense to you. He's very . . ."

"Dull? Stolid? Tedious?"

May bristled. "I think I have a real chance with him."

"A chance at what? Being the inconsequential wife of a second son who will be forgotten by history?"

"A chance at being happy!"

"Happy?" Agnes laughed sharply. "You said it yourself; there's no such thing as happiness for a woman, just security and position. And you could have had the greatest position of all, that of a future queen. You could *still* have it," she added caustically, "if you can set aside your misgivings and see this thing through!"

That was when May heard the note of cruel avarice in Agnes's voice.

"This isn't about me at all, is it," May said slowly. "You want me to be queen because it suits your own purposes."

Agnes crossed her arms over her chest. "May, you're too smart to be the wife of a man who doesn't actually matter. *You* should be the one meeting diplomats and presidents, bestowing knighthoods, having your picture printed on stamps. You should wear the Crown Jewels and ride in parades and be famous throughout the world. Not some French slut who threw away her reputation, sleeping with a commoner on hay bales!"

May flinched at her crudeness, and Agnes let out a breath.

"I just want what's best for my friend," she said heavily. "Is that so wrong? I was trying to help!"

My *friend*, she'd said. Except that May was starting to doubt that they were friends at all.

She thought back to the night they had met. Agnes had appeared out of nowhere, right after Eddy had been so dismissive of May, and had started making conversation with her—*charming* her. Manipulating her, the way she tried to do with everyone else.

How had May failed to see it?

She'd thought their conversation began organically, but she realized now that Agnes had preselected May as the ideal tool for her purposes: highborn enough to be useful, but insecure and lonely enough to be easily played. At first Agnes had probably just wanted someone to introduce her around—a foothold into London society, a rung on the ladder of her social climb. But then, as May shared her hopes about Eddy and made inroads with Maud, Agnes's quest had escalated.

It wasn't enough for Agnes, just being friends with a Serene Highness. She wanted the access that came with knowing a future queen.

"*Am* I your friend?" May asked quietly. "Or am I just another stepping stone, someone you can use?"

Genuine hurt seemed to flash across Agnes's features. "Of course you're my friend. A *real* friend, not like those society women who claim to adore each other, but all they ever talk about is babies and hairstyles! You and I shared the ugly truth of our experiences. We both faced our own kind of adversity, and were frank enough to admit it—and ask for each other's help. That's why I wrote that letter to Princess Hélène for you," Agnes insisted. "I'm a good enough friend to do what you aren't brave enough to do yourself!"

May wanted so desperately to believe that Agnes had meant well, to fall back under the spell cast by Agnes's wealth and determination and bold American conviction. She ran a hand over the fabric of her skirts and felt ill with a sudden realization.

All the beautiful things that Agnes had given her this past year? They weren't gifts at all. They were *bribes*, each of them binding May tighter into Agnes's debt. Their friendship was really just a transaction. Agnes had made a significant investment in May, and now she wanted a return on that investment.

May felt her spine straighten, almost of its own accord. She wasn't as lonely as she'd been a year ago; she didn't need Agnes, was better off without her.

She rapped on the carriage ceiling, prompting the driver to halt. "I'll walk from here. And, Agnes? You and I are done."

"Please, wait—" her former friend began, but May slammed the door on her words.

IT REALLY WAS A SPECTACULAR WEDDING. MAY WAS ACCUStomed to the Anglican service, with its predictable readings and bouquets of generic white lilies; she had never seen a ceremony like this one before, in all its Byzantine splendor. The

Orthodox priest's vestment was even more ornate than Sophie's wedding gown, woven with cloth of gold, and an enormous jeweled crucifix hung over his chest. Incense spilled out
of censers, and a choir chanted from behind a gilded screen.

Not that May could really enjoy any of it, with her father's anger looming over her like a thunderstorm.

She sensed that something was wrong the moment he entered the church. It was clear from Francis's tense jaw, the
flush stealing along his neck. He was probably livid that May
had ridden to the cathedral without asking his permission: he
hated when anything fell outside his control. Or perhaps he
was upset with May's mother. Mary Adelaide would normally
have been effusive at a royal wedding, whispering about her
various distant cousins and the convoluted way they were all
related. Yet today she was subdued, her gaze fixed on the toes
of her slippers rather than the bride.

When they reached the reception, Francis's hand tightened over his daughter's forearm. "May. I need a word with
you," he growled.

May cast one pleading glance around the palace ballroom.
It was filled with white roses—they framed doorways, cas-
caded from golden epergnes set upon tables, their scent min-
gling with perfumes and tight-packed bodies as all the royal
guests swanned about in their glittering finest. She wasn't
sure who she was looking for, because of course no one could
really save her.

She had to face her father alone.

Somehow May pasted on a smile as she stumbled along
in her father's wake, letting him drag her toward the terrace.
When they were far enough from the other guests, he let go

of her arm. May resisted the urge to rub at the place where his fingers had dug into her skin.

"You idiot girl." Her father's voice was low but venomous. "Have you really been cavorting with some American trash?"

Oh, so this was about Agnes. May realized that some part of her had worried her father knew about her plans for Eddy— or her secret hopes for George. He would have thought she was making a fool of herself.

"I am sorry that I came to the wedding without telling you," she said hastily. "Miss Endicott's maid was with us, so there was no question of impropriety."

Francis gave a caustic laugh. "You think I care about your reputation? Maybe if you compromised yourself with some young man, I could wash my hands of you. No, I'm angry that you accepted *charity* from that girl."

Before May could say anything, Francis yanked at the fur trim lining her gown. "Is this one of her old dresses? You would really debase our family name by taking things from people like *that*?"

He must have overheard Agnes's remark that the dress had been hers. Or one of the servants had overheard and told him; it didn't matter. May supposed she should count herself lucky that he hadn't caught on sooner.

"Agnes never even wore this gown. The dressmaker cut it wrong and refused to take it back," May babbled, lying. "No one saw her in it!"

"I don't care whether she wore it. I won't have you taking handouts from anyone, especially not some American nobody." Francis's breath smelled of ale; he must have been drinking before the wedding ceremony. "What about the gown that was delivered last month, the one you said had the fringe repaired? Was that hers, too?"

When she said nothing, a vein pulsed along her father's forehead. "You are a Teck, and we don't need anyone else's money."

"Except we do, because you and Mother spent ours long ago."

May hadn't meant to speak that thought aloud.

Her father's face lit up with frenzied rage, and he lifted a hand to strike her.

She winced and closed her eyes, bracing herself. Her father would hit her, and she was powerless to stop him, because in the eyes of the world—of the law—she was not even really a person. She was just a woman, not entitled to vote or hold property or have any rights at all, outside those granted to her by her father. Or eventually, if she could ever find one, her husband.

"You stupid girl," Francis said at last. May dared to open her eyes and saw that his rage had ebbed. He was staring at her with sneering disgust. "Go ahead and wear a charity dress. It's not as if it'll make you pretty enough for any man to want you, though God knows I pray one would. I'm done with you and your failures. Actually," he said slowly, "I have been done with you a long time."

He turned and walked away without another word.

May put a hand on the stone railing. An unfamiliar emotion coursed through her, pounding through her blood in a molten rush. She closed her eyes, trying to regain control over her breaths, but the insides of her eyelids were tinged red.

It took a while before she recognized the feeling as hatred.

She had wanted to escape her father's house for as long as she could remember, yet it no longer seemed like enough just to get out. She wanted to *destroy* him.

May needed to marry someone higher-born and wealthier than Francis of Teck had ever been, someone who would put her in a position where she would be invincible, untouchable. She would climb so far above Francis that she could protect herself, and her mother too.

And someday, when she was staring down at him, she would make him feel as helpless and insignificant as he'd always done to her. He would learn how it felt to live in fear of someone else's whims.

On her way back to the ballroom, May caught sight of her face in a darkened window and gasped. Her features didn't look like her own; they were spiteful and sharp and hateful. She drew in a slow breath, trying to settle her demure court smile on her face like a mask. It didn't fit right.

She needed to see George. Not that she could tell him what had just happened, of course. But he would steady her, would remind her that she wasn't unwanted trash: that she was a person, and deserved to be loved.

Back in the palace's ballroom, May began scanning the crowds. She saw Sophie and Tino swaying at the center of the dance floor; they were now titled the Duke and Duchess of Sparta, which sounded oddly antiquated to May, but that was Greece for you. She kept looking through the guests, past Danish and German and Russian royals . . . and then she found George.

He was with his cousin Missy.

They weren't dancing. Honestly, if they'd been dancing, May could have talked herself into ignoring it, but this was so much worse. They were tucked into a far corner of the room, their heads tipped together in light, conspiratorial laughter.

May's hatred of her father spilled over to hatred of Missy without any effort at all. She resented Missy for being fresh-faced and beautiful and young. May had never in her life looked like that—glowing with the carefree radiance of someone who has faced no obstacles or hardships. Unlike Missy, who'd been indulged and spoiled and *loved* by both her parents, May had grown up starved of affection. She was several years older than Missy, and oh how she looked it, her features stamped with the weariness of always being on the fringes of royalty.

As she watched, George brushed an invisible fleck off the shoulder of Missy's champagne-colored gown. There was something undeniably intimate about the gesture. The dagger of pain in May's heart twisted itself deeper.

"I'm sorry," a voice near her murmured.

May looked up, startled, to see Alix of Hesse. "What did you say?" she asked, a bit defensively.

Alix bit her lip. May couldn't help noting that Alix didn't look quite right—she was still as beautiful as ever, but flushed and oddly tense.

"Forgive me if I'm mistaken; I thought you and George . . . that is, I saw you dancing at the Cadogans' ball, and . . ." Alix followed May's gaze to George and Missy, her blue eyes brimming with concern. "I know how it feels to lose the person you care about."

Somehow, May knew that Alix wasn't talking about Eddy.

Normally she would have homed in on that fact, would have tried to figure out who Alix did have feelings for, but she lacked the energy right now.

"They're only talking," she said, not bothering to deny her feelings for George.

"I thought you knew. I'm sorry, forget I said anything—"

"Knew what?" May hated begging Alix for information, but couldn't help herself.

Alix paused. "From what I heard, he spent the entire trip down here paying court to Missy. Supposedly their parents have already planned the wedding."

May cast her mind back over all her interactions with George. She had hoped that there might be something between them . . . yet if she was being honest with herself, George had never crossed the bounds of friendship into romance, not once.

He'd certainly never looked at her the way he was now looking at Missy, with overt adoration.

She swallowed; her throat felt dry as sand. "Thank you for telling me. I just . . . I need a moment to myself."

May fled, ignoring the glittering guests in their crowns and jewels, and stumbled into a hallway. Staff members glided past with trays of empty wineglasses or platters of food.

Not caring how she looked, she leaned back against the wall, the bodice of Agnes's old gown heaving with her breaths. Her eyes burned with unshed tears.

Her father had always been cruel; she should have been numb to his rage by now. But it still stung.

The revelation about George and Missy hurt far more.

May hated that Agnes had been proven right. What a fool she'd been, thinking that George might care for her as anything more than a friend. Of course he'd chosen Missy. That was the way of the world, brutal and unforgiving: a world where some girls were born with everything and some girls inherited only misery.

At least she hadn't been foolish enough to declare her feelings for George. Thank god she'd spared herself that embarrassment.

As her mind came to terms with her loss, May felt her sense of control returning to her, melting the shards of ice in her chest. So, George didn't care for her. That didn't change the fact that she needed to marry—and marry well.

George might not be an option, but Eddy still was. Thanks to Agnes.

She would have to tread carefully, May thought, with the hardness that was already calcifying around her heart. She needed to confirm that Hélène had ended things with Eddy, and then, assuming the way was clear, May would begin her campaign.

It wouldn't be easy. She would have to draw Queen Victoria's attention to her slowly, remind everyone that she was an appropriate royal consort: that she, too, had been raised with grand destinations in mind, before her parents let their family sink so low.

This would be a long road, but if May's childhood had given her anything, it was endurance—and a stubborn, indefatigable strength. So her friendship with Agnes hadn't been real, and she'd lost her budding relationship with Alix. So what? May didn't mind loneliness. In fact, loneliness had long ago been braided into the very fibers of her being.

She would go it alone, the way she always had.

CHAPTER THIRTY-THREE

Hélène

"WOULD YOU CARE TO DANCE?"

Hélène noted impassively that the young man who'd spoken was handsome, with dark hair and gleaming hazel eyes. A forest-green uniform with epaulettes and a gold sash set off his broad shoulders.

"I'm sorry, I'm not dancing tonight" was her automatic reply. "However, I'm sure there are plenty of young women who would be eager to oblige."

He sighed, a bit performatively. "Ah yes. All the royal cousins, at yet another family reunion."

He was right, of course. All these kings and queens and princesses, in their embroidered gowns and jeweled coronets, had come to Athens to socialize in the same suffocatingly exclusive circles as always. To gossip about each other, then greet the people they'd just been gossiping about with cries of delight.

It was a bit eerie, hearing this young man speak thoughts Hélène had harbored for years.

The music changed, and Hélène glanced around the ballroom. Seeing her look, the stranger added, "Are you sure you don't want to dance?"

"I find that I lack the energy," she said half-heartedly.

The stranger frowned, studying her for a moment. "But I see—it is an affair of the heart! What has your beloved done to anger you?" A mischievous gleam entered his eyes as he added, "Perhaps you should dance with me, just once, so that he will see how wrong he was."

Something about this man broke through Hélène's self-pity. "You're very bold . . ." She trailed off, not sure of his name.

"Emanuele Filiberto, at your service." Before she could protest, he lifted her hand and placed a kiss on her wrist. A chivalrous gesture, except that Hélène was wearing wrist-length gloves instead of elbow-length, so his lips landed on her bare skin.

He hadn't used his titles, a lack of pretension that Hélène always found refreshing, but she knew who he was. Emanuele Filiberto, the nephew of King Umberto of Italy, and second in line for the Italian throne. Emanuele's father, the king's younger brother, had died tragically years ago; Emanuele lived in Piedmont with his mother and siblings.

In other words, he was exactly the sort of good Catholic prince her parents had wanted her to marry, before she got entangled with Eddy.

"Hélène of France," she said, belatedly remembering to introduce herself.

"Yes, I know." He winked and released her hand.

If she weren't so depressed, Hélène might have enjoyed talking to Emanuele. He had a restless energy that crackled just below the surface—it reminded her of Eddy, except that Eddy was never so overtly irreverent. But then, Emanuele was only a spare, not an heir; he was allowed liberties that Eddy could only dream of.

Would she ever stop doing this, comparing every man she met to Eddy?

Probably not. Hélène would always regret the way things had ended with Eddy. She would always hate herself for her own carelessness, for the fact that she hadn't figured out a way to protect them both.

"I'm sorry," she told Emanuele, before grabbing her skirts with both hands and fleeing the ballroom.

Hélène blinked back angry tears as she ran, hardly looking where she was going. Her heeled slippers left scuff marks on the polished wood floors, but she didn't slow down; her heart beat wildly against her chest. The faces of various Greek ancestors stared disapprovingly down at her from portraits on the walls, matching the very real, shocked faces of staff members who stepped aside as she whirled past.

It wasn't until she burst out the front doors that Hélène realized where she'd been headed. Apparently her feet had carried her here, to where the carriages were—where the horses were.

As always, the sound of their shuffling hooves was calming. Hélène took a step forward, studying the eclectic mix of carriages that lined the great paving stones of the palace's circle drive. While there were still a few people gathered outside the gates, most of the crowds from earlier had dispersed, heading toward the waterfront to watch the upcoming pyrotechnics. The sky overhead was turning a deep purple, fireflies winking in the dusk. Except that they weren't fireflies at all, she realized: the orange glow came from several dozen cigarettes.

That was the nice thing about coachmen. No matter what country you were in, you could always count on them to smoke.

"Excuse me," Hélène called out, starting toward the nearest cluster of drivers. "Could I have a cigarette?"

One of them turned to her with a lopsided grin. He said something in Greek and lifted his hands in a universal gesture of confusion. Hélène tried French, then gave up and tried to convey her meaning with gestures.

"*Ah! Éna tsigáro!*" He laughed, seemingly delighted by the incongruity of the situation—of Hélène, in her lavish cranberry-colored gown, asking him for a cigarette.

He handed one over and leaned forward to light it. Hélène inhaled deeply, relishing the small act of rebellion, though the smoke was sharper than she'd expected. This was a cheap, factory-produced paper cigarette, nothing like the cigars she'd stolen from her father's office.

"Hélène?"

She turned around slowly, shocked beyond belief that Alix of Hesse was out here.

Behind Alix, the windows of the palace were ablaze with the light of countless gas lamps. The honeycombed light gilded Alix from behind, casting her face in shadow.

"What are you doing here, Alix?"

"I saw you in the ballroom. You seemed distraught." Alix's hair was falling loose from its twist; she tucked a strand nervously behind one ear. "Forgive me if I overstepped, following you. I was just worried."

Hélène knew she should say something to make the other girl go away. Yet she felt dangerously like she might shatter into a million pieces.

Holding out the cigarette, she heard herself ask, "Want to smoke?"

Alix's eyes widened, and Hélène stifled a bizarre urge to laugh. "Sorry. I didn't mean to shock you."

"Actually, I find that I am quite unshockable right now."

To Hélène's surprise, Alix accepted the proffered cigarette and drew in a breath—only to immediately burst into a fit of coughing.

"Here, let's sit." Hélène wrapped an arm around Alix and pulled her down to sit on the uppermost stone step. At least now they were out of sight of the front door, should anyone open it.

"Sorry," Alix rasped, when the coughing had subsided. "I've never smoked before."

"I gathered as much," Hélène said drily.

Silence fell between them, but it was a relaxed, almost friendly silence. Hélène took the cigarette back and inhaled again, staring out at the scattered lights of the city.

"Did the Duke of Aosta do something to offend you?" Alix ventured.

Oh, right; that was Emanuele's title. Hélène shook her head. "I wasn't upset with him; it was about—"

She broke off, but Alix finished the sentence for her. "About Eddy."

"I'm sorry. This must be strange for you, talking about him. With me, I mean."

"Not really. Or at least, not any stranger than the rest of this mess." Alix pulled her legs toward her, wrapping her arms around her knees. Her gown—a beautiful silver-blue, the color of glaciers or winter stars—was probably getting dirt stains along the rear. "Things with me and Eddy have been over for a very long time. If they ever even began in the first place."

Hélène said nothing. After a beat, Alix added mournfully, "I've actually had a proposal from someone else."

"Someone awful?" It sounded that way, from the bleakness of Alix's tone.

"Oh no! I love him! But it doesn't matter." Alix tipped her head onto her knees. "His parents won't let us marry. They hate me."

"*Hate* you?" Hélène repeated incredulously. "That's impossible."

"They flat-out denied us permission to marry."

"On what grounds? You're every parent's dream daughter-in-law—you're perfect!"

Alix went rigid, and Hélène knew at once that she'd said the wrong thing. "I assure you, I'm far from perfect," Alix finally answered, in a very small voice.

Hélène stole another glance at her. There was something different about Alix tonight: an angular swiftness to her movements, spots of color in her cheeks. Her normally pale blue eyes seemed mercurial, and darker than normal, as if the evening light had turned them almost violet.

"Did the same thing happen between you and Eddy?" Alix ventured. "You weren't able to get permission to marry him?"

"Not exactly. It's complicated."

"If you want to talk about it, I'm happy to listen. After everything we've been through, I would hope that we can trust each other." Alix smiled sadly. "I spoke with Eddy, and I know you didn't spread those rumors about me fainting."

"I would never do that!" Hélène exclaimed. "When you accused me of being indiscreet, I assumed you meant that I—well—"

"That you loved the man I was supposed to marry?"

"Yes, that." Again Hélène felt an incongruous urge to laugh. Never in a lifetime would she have expected to find herself here: sharing a cigarette with Alix of Hesse, talking about the man they had both been linked to, each in her own way.

We can trust each other, Alix had claimed. Maybe she was right. Hélène had already seen Alix's shameful secret, the way Alix had dissolved into a helpless fit that night at the opera. Maybe she could afford to let Alix in on her own problems.

"You were right, though, when you said I've been indiscreet," she began, which was quite the understatement.

Haltingly, Hélène told Alix about Laurent, and then about Eddy. She tried to sketch over the logistics of their encounters, since Alix, unlike her, was as sheltered and proper as a princess *should* be. Still, there was no judgment in Alix's expression. She just nodded and listened, letting Hélène talk until the cigarette had wound down to an orange stub in her hand.

When she got to the part about May, and the blackmail letter, Alix gasped in indignation.

"May of Teck? But she's so sweet!"

"I used to think so, too. Clearly I was mistaken."

Alix shook her head incredulously. "And here I thought she was in love with George."

"Maybe she's just in love with the idea of marrying a prince."

Alix started to rise to her feet. "I'm going to talk to her. Or better yet, I'll talk to Grandmama—"

Hélène reached up to yank the other princess back down. "Don't, please! That's exactly why I haven't mentioned this to Eddy."

"He doesn't know?"

"I broke things off with him. I had no choice!" Hélène burst out, helpless. "Eddy would have fought for us, but no matter what he did, it would end in my losing him. Even if he revealed the blackmail, May could still show everyone that letter. And we both know that I could never marry him once it got out."

Alix didn't argue with that. She stared out at the horizon, tapping her fingers absent-mindedly against her leg.

"You know, I never figured out who *did* spread gossip about my fainting spell. Now I wonder . . ."

Hélène caught on at once. "You think May did it?"

"She's already proven that she'll resort to blackmail. If she wanted to get you out of the way, hoping she might win Eddy for herself, it stands to reason she would have tried to get rid of me, too."

"She was at the opera that night! She could easily have seen you and not said anything," Hélène agreed. It struck her as unbearably cruel, to find a young woman in the grips of utter panic and do nothing but walk away. To hoard the secret like currency that you would spend for your own gain.

"You're right; we shouldn't tell Eddy. He would want to solve this problem head-on, the way I did at first. No, if you're going to beat May, you'll have to fight dirty," Alix insisted. Her perfect veneer seemed to have cracked, revealing an Alix that surprised Hélène—a passionate Alix, with a rough edge to her voice.

Hélène found that she preferred Alix this way.

"What do you mean, 'fight dirty'?" she asked.

"Didn't you play games as a child where someone cheated?

That's what May is doing," Alix said vehemently, "so it's what you'll need to do in return."

Something sparked, then, in the pool of grief at Hélène's core. It was as if a light had flicked on and let in hope.

"I don't understand."

"You told Eddy the engagement was off, which will keep May satisfied while you figure out your counterattack. To beat her, you're going to have to find her weakness, or secret: a way to escape her control. You won't be safe until you've got a hold over her, like the one she has over you."

"How will I do that?"

"I don't know," Alix admitted. "But you have to try. If you love Eddy the way you say you do, then you must fight for him."

Hélène sat with that for a long moment. May had certainly fought dirty—digging through her past, getting hold of Laurent's letter. Even her threats had been veiled and carefully drawn. Hélène much preferred an open attack, but she wouldn't beat May on a clear field of battle.

She would have to be cunning, the way May was. To listen at keyholes and bribe servants and hide her intentions behind a demure smile.

Hélène turned to Alix. "Promise me you will take your own advice. The man you love, the one whose parents forbade you to marry? Don't give up on him."

"My situation is different."

"Not that different! If you love him the way you say you do, then you must fight for him," Hélène exclaimed, echoing Alix's words.

To her surprise, Alix put an arm around her shoulders

and hugged her, tipping her head onto Hélène's shoulder the way Amélie would.

"All right, then," Alix agreed. "We'll fight for them."

As if on cue, a whistle cut through the darkening night. Both young women looked up to see the opening burst of pyrotechnics exploding in the sky.

They stood, still leaning on each other, and walked around to the side of the palace that looked over ocean. Fireworks shot up into the stars, a vivid tapestry of red and green and blue that dissolved into sparks. Moonlight glittered on the water, reflecting the burning wheels and fiery stars on the ocean's surface.

It was magnificent but deadly. The way Hélène felt. A new determination roared up in her as she thought of everything she would have to do to get Eddy back.

But that was tomorrow's problem. For now she was content to stand here with Alix, watching as the sky burst into flames, both of them wondering what would come next—and how it would all end.

AUTHOR'S NOTE

If you're an avid reader of history, you probably recognize the characters in *A Queen's Game*, as almost all of them are real historical figures. Some—like Bertie, Prince of Wales, and the swoon-worthy tsarevitch Nicholas, and of course Queen Victoria—have been depicted so many times in fiction and film that they've assumed an almost mythic status. Others, like Alix and May, gained prominence later in life; history knows far less about their teenage years. Of course, a few characters are made up, like Agnes—though she was inspired by the American "dollar princesses" who came to London at the end of the Victorian era, hoping to trade their American fortunes for a British title.

I have always wanted to write a historical novel, and the lightbulb moment for *A Queen's Game* came in March 2020, when I was pregnant with my first child and under lockdown during the Covid-19 pandemic. I was reading about Queen Victoria: not her early life and her love for Prince Albert, which most biographies dwell on, but her later years. In particular, this book focused on her relationships with her forty-two grandchildren, explaining how Victoria arranged their marriages so that they were scattered across the thrones of Europe.

I was immediately fascinated by several grandchildren in particular. There was Prince Eddy, the devilishly handsome heir to the British throne; his younger brother, Prince George; and their cousin Nicholas, future tsar of Russia. All three princes were linked at various points to the same three young women: Alix of Hesse, Queen Victoria's favorite granddaughter; the headstrong and vivacious Princess Hélène of France, whose family lived in exile in England; and May of Teck, who would, unexpectedly, become crucial to the future of the British monarchy.

The stories of these three princesses and three princes were hopelessly entangled, with marriages proposed and arranged, only to be broken off when political alliances shifted or scandals emerged. I couldn't believe how juicy and dramatic the real-life history was! I knew at once that it would be my next project, as soon as I was done with the American Royals books.

I have done my best to stay true to the broader points of the real history; each engagement and marriage in these pages really did happen. You may be surprised to learn how many details are also true, documented in letters and diaries. Alix's panic attacks, Hélène and Eddy's passionate affair (their letters are worth a read, rivaled only by Victoria's love letters to Albert!), the Tecks' financial straits and the resulting distress of May's father, who suffered from what the Queen of Hanover referred to as "frightful paroxysms of rage"—all are an accepted part of the historical record. Still, like any writer of historical fiction, I took some liberties with the history. I shifted dates to get my characters in the same place at the same time, imagining their conversations . . . and their secrets.

After all, the fun of historical fiction is where the history ends and the fiction begins.

Thank you for reading *A Queen's Game*—and stay tuned for part two!

Katharine McGee

ACKNOWLEDGMENTS

This book has been a true passion project from the beginning. I am so honored and humbled that it's a reality, and so lucky to work with the incredible team that made it possible!

Caroline Abbey: I knew from the moment we first talked about this project (and geeked out looking at photos of Nicholas and George) that we would have so much fun bringing it to life. Thank you for always being my thought partner, plot guru, and fellow royal enthusiast!

Joelle Hobeika: I'm so glad you took a chance on a historical fiction novel! As always, thank you for the countless hours you have spent making this manuscript the very best version of itself.

I'm grateful to continue working with the fantastic team at Random House Children's Books, especially Michelle Nagler, Mallory Loehr, Kelly McGauley, Elizabeth Ward, Adrienne Waintraub, Tricia Lin, Jasmine Hodge, Katie Halata, Lauren Stewart, Barbara Bakowski, and Karen Sherman. A special thank-you is due to Noreen Herits and Cynthia Lliguichuzhca for helping to publicize another royal series, and to Carolina Melis for this phenomenal cover!

Thanks also to everyone at Alloy Entertainment: Josh Bank, Sara Shandler, Les Morgenstein, Gina Girolamo, Romy

Golan, Matt Bloomgarden, Josephine McKenna, Elysa Dutton, Chelsea Kardos, Sarah Campbell, Kyle Stivers, Malini Narayan, and Kat Jagai.

I am fortunate to work with the talented foreign sales team at Rights People: Charlotte Bodman, Alexandra Devlin, Harim Yim, Claudia Galluzzi, Hannah Whitaker, Amy Threadgold, and Annie Blombach. Thank you for helping share *A Queen's Game* with readers around the world.

Thank you also to the Penguin Random House audio team: Orli Moscowitz and Joseph Ward. Once again, you have created an audiobook that truly brings these characters to life!

I can't imagine doing this job without my family, who have supported me in more ways than I can count. Mom, Dad, Lizzy, John Ed, and MK: Thank you for the infinite free childcare, for putting up with my discussions of Victorian England, and for being my first and fiercest cheerleaders.

Alex: As you can attest, writing a book while pregnant proved harder than I expected. Thank you for keeping me (somewhat) on schedule, for carrying the load when I needed it, and for always making me laugh. I love you, William, and Edward so much.

Most of all, a huge thank-you is due to the readers! It means so much that you were willing to follow me to this project—thank you for taking the leap.